From the award ~~Mystery Series co~~ SECOND book in the Dig Site Mystery series.

"Lively and entertaining, *Make No Bones About It* is full of action and imaginative plot twists. A rousing good read!"
~**Gerri Russell**, Amazon Top 100 Bestselling Author of *Flirting with Felicity*

"Fun, sexy, and filled with paranormal twists … I loved it!"
~**Kristy McCaffrey**, Author of *Blue Sage* and the Wings of the West Series

"*Make No Bones About It* delivers all the page-turning adventure, mystery, and romance I was hoping for. I couldn't put the book down as I raced to the action-packed conclusion. A must read!"
~**Joleen James**, Award-winning Author of the Hometown Alaska Men Series

"Another hit! Jam-packed full of Indiana Jones-style action, sizzling romance and even some Mayan history to boot. Charles not only has crafted an intricate mystery, but as the master of witty repartee, she had this reader laughing out loud. *Make No Bones About It* is the perfect mix of sexy fun and dangerous adventure."
~**Kim Hornsby**, Amazon Top 100 Bestselling Author

"*Make No Bones About It* will not only educate you a little on the Maya culture, but also keep you hoping the story never ends. Ann Charles' stories keep getting better and better!"
~**John Grandinetti**, Avid Reader

Praise for Ann's FIRST book in the Dig Site Mystery series, *Look What the Wind Blew In*:

"Non-stop action … steamy and entertaining mystery with ancient curses, deadly secrets, and heated passion."
~**Chanticleer Book Reviews**

For more on Ann and her books, check out her website, as well as the reader reviews for her books on Amazon, Barnes & Noble, and Goodreads.

Also by Ann Charles

Deadwood Mystery Series
Nearly Departed in Deadwood (Book 1)
Optical Delusions in Deadwood (Book 2)
Dead Case in Deadwood (Book 3)
Better Off Dead in Deadwood (Book 4)
An Ex to Grind in Deadwood (Book 5)
Meanwhile, Back in Deadwood (Book 6)
A Wild Fright in Deadwood (Book 7)

Short Stories from the Deadwood Mystery Series
Deadwood Shorts: Seeing Trouble
Deadwood Shorts: Boot Points
Deadwood Shorts: Cold Flame
Deadwood Shorts: Tequila and Time

Jackrabbit Junction Mystery Series
Dance of the Winnebagos (Book 1)
Jackrabbit Junction Jitters (Book 2)
The Great Jackalope Stampede (Book 3)
The Rowdy Coyote Rumble (Book 4)
The Wild Turkey Tango (Novella 4.5)

Dig Site Mystery Series
Look What the Wind Blew In (Book 1)
Make No Bones About It (Book 2)

Goldwash Mystery Series (a future series)
The Old Man's Back in Town (Short Story)

Coming Next from Ann Charles

Deadwood Mystery Series
Rattling the Heat in Deadwood (Book 8)

Jackrabbit Junction Mystery Series
Title TBA (Book 5)

Dear Reader,

If I were to sum up this book—heck, this series—in one word from my point of view, it'd be: RESEARCH. With every chapter, I had my nose buried in books about the Maya, their language, their religion, their hieroglyphs, their food and drink, etc. The more I learned about this amazing civilization, the more enthralled I was. Ideas filled my head for future possibilities with this series, curiosity kept me seeking out more to read and soak up about their gods, practices, daily life, and superstitions.

When I wasn't learning more about the Maya, I was digging through books and articles about the Yucatán Peninsula's flora and fauna, geology, physical geography, and history. Several times I priced the cost of flying my family down there to immerse myself even more. I'd like to say this appealed for research alone, but to be honest, the idea of cold Coronas and warm Mexican beaches were a big part of the draw. I also spent a fair amount of time learning more about the Olmec and Toltec civilizations, as well as the Aztec. The differences and similarities between all of these great civilizations from our past, along with their achievements in science and cosmology, were humbling.

I immersed myself in the world of archaeology as much as possible, reading articles and books on the behind-the-scenes lives of archaeologists. For motivation, the Indiana Jones and The Mummy movies played in the background.

When I finished the first draft of this book, I was exhausted. All three of my current series challenge me as an author in different ways, but the Dig Site series really forces me to stretch my writing wings. Not only is my goal to entertain you, but I also want to enlighten you about the Maya people (both the ancient and current Maya). I want to share with you an understanding of this civilization's amazing accomplishments and incredible feats in a time before electricity, computers, and all of the other technology that makes our daily modern lives so much easier.

I hope you enjoy another steamy trip to the jungle with Quint, Angélica, Juan, Pedro, Rover, and the rest of the Dig Site series crew! ... Now where did I put that six-pack of Corona?

Ann Charles

For Susy Munk.

You were an amazing, kickass heroine through it all!

Acknowledgments

I owe thanks to many people for this book, but let's see if I can keep it to one page.

For starters, many MANY thanks to my husband for always listening to my what-ifs and for telling me I could do it when I worried that I couldn't

I want to thank my kids for putting up with me having my face buried in my computer or in a Maya research book. One of these days, I'll take you to see the setting for these Dig Site books in person.

I'd also like to thank the following wonderful people:

My First Draft team: my husband, Margo Taylor, Mary Ida Kunkle, Kristy McCaffrey, Jacquie Rogers, Marcia Britton, Paul Franklin, Diane Garland, Vicki Huskey, Lucinda Nelson, Marguerite Phipps, Stephanie Kunkle, and Wendy Gildersleeve. Each of these readers has a unique skillset that I lean on to help me be accurate on various aspects of each story. They are part of what makes your reading experience go so smoothly and on this book they really shined.

My editor, Eilis Flynn, for her great job of not just fixing my grammar and spelling, but also making sure that my word choice was consistent with the first book in this series.

My Beta Team and Sue Stone-Douglas for once again stepping up to the task and giving me excellent feedback. You guys really kicked ass!

My brother, C.S. Kunkle, for his awesome illustrations and great original cover art.

My graphic artist, Sharon Benton, for making the cover rock!

My fans for cheering me on the whole way via email and social media. You all keep me motivated to continue plugging away at this writing gig.

Finally, my brother, Clint, for sending me funny Snapchats of himself that made me laugh in the middle of the night.

Make No Bones About It

Copyright © 2017 by Ann Charles

Cover Art by C.S. Kunkle
Cover Design by Sharon Benton (www.q42designs.com)
Editing by Eilis Flynn

Print ISBN-13: 978-1-940364-47-6
E-book ISBN-13: 978-1-940364-51-3
LCCN: 2017903499

MAKE NO BONES ABOUT IT

ANN CHARLES

ILLUSTRATED BY
C.S. KUNKLE

Author's Note and Glossary

The adjective "Mayan" is used in reference to the language (or languages) and words; "Maya" is used as a noun or adjective when referring to people, places, culture, etc., whether singular or plural.

(http://archaeology.about.com/od/mameterms/a/Maya-or-Mayan.htm)

To learn more about the Maya civilization and their language, I recommend browsing the internet. There are many wonderful Maya-related resources out there to explore.

GLOSSARY

Following are some words used often throughout this book:

Baatz': (*baahtz'*) A monkey (howler).

Cenote: (*suh-noh-tee*) A natural pit, or sinkhole, resulting from the collapse of limestone bedrock that exposes groundwater underneath. Especially associated with the Yucatán Peninsula of Mexico, cenotes were sometimes used by the ancient Maya for sacrificial offerings.

Chakmo'ol: (*chahk-MOH'-OHL*) A jaguar.

Glottal Stops: A glottal stop is represented by the ' in Mayan words, such as in *Chakmo'ol*. The ' signifies the use of a "pop" sound, which is made by stopping the breath. It's similar to when English speakers say words like *uh-oh* or *button* (when said quickly).

Glyph: (*glif*) Maya glyphs (or Maya hieroglyphs), are the writing system of the Maya civilization of Mesoamerica, currently the only Mesoamerican writing system that has been substantially deciphered.

INAH: (The acronym for *Instituto Nacional de Antropología e Historia*, which translated means the *National Institute of Anthropology and History*) A Mexican federal government bureau established in 1939 to guarantee the research, preservation, protection, and promotion of the prehistoric, archaeological, anthropological, historical, and paleontological heritage of Mexico.

Pik: (*peek*) A bedbug.

Sacbe/Sacbeob (singular/plural): A sacbe (*sakbej, sakbejo'ob*), is a raised paved road built by the Maya civilization of pre-Columbian Mesoamerica. Most connect temples, plazas, and groups of structures within ceremonial centers or cities, but some longer roads between cities are also known. The term "sacbe" is Yucatec Maya for "white road"; white because they were originally coated with limestone stucco, which was over stone and rubble fill.

Stela/Stelae (singular/plural): (*stee-luh, stee-lee*) Maya stelae are monuments that were fashioned by the Maya civilization of ancient Mesoamerica. They consist of tall, sculpted stone shafts and are often associated with low circular stones referred to as altars, although their actual function is uncertain.

* * *

A Final Note: There are many different branches of the Mayan language depending on the location within the Maya empire. For the most part, I tried to use Yucatec Mayan in this book.

(Source for Glossary definitions: www.Wikipedia.org and *Maya (Yucatec) Dictionary & Phrasebook*)

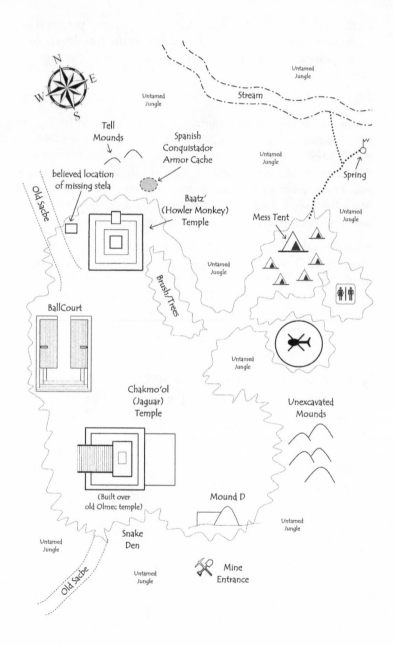

Chapter One

Machete: A broad-bladed, long, heavy knife used for cutting through underbrush by the Maya.

The Mexican jungle had devoured the remains of the dead, bones and all.

Through the thick shroud of vines, bushes, and trees, Angélica García could see only traces of evidence left over from those who'd lived here long, long ago. But in her mind's eye, fueled by her imagination and decades of study, the dig site before her teemed with mounds hiding Maya secrets waiting to be uncovered, explored, and shared.

A twig snapped behind her, followed by the rustling of branches and leaves. She was no longer alone.

"*Gatita*," her father wheezed her childhood nickname in between heavy breaths. Juan García hobbled up beside her, leaning on his crutches when he paused at her side. The citrusy scent of bug spray hovered in the soupy humidity, mixing with the damp musty smell wafting up from the forest floor. "This is a bad idea."

"I agree. If you'll remember, I strongly suggested that you wait for me back at the helicopter."

A howler monkey let out a loud, guttural growl from high above them in the trees, probably annoyed with them for talking during its naptime.

"That's not what I meant and you know it." Her father frowned at the untamed tangle of trees, branches, and bushes surrounding them. "*Ay chihuahua.* This dig site hasn't been worked in a long time."

"Five years and two months, to be exact." The length of human absence explained why the jungle had regained the upper hand on hiding some of the ruins in the satellite images Angélica had spent the last week studying back in her home office in Cancun.

"Look," he said, pointing at a stand of trees. "Those sapodilla trees have no scars from chicle harvesting."

She'd noticed the lack of diagonal cuts marking the tree trunks as well. For centuries, the Maya had been slicing into the bark of the sapodilla trees, tapping them like maple trees for sap. The chicle resin that drained from the trunks was strained and boiled into chicle bricks that were shipped all over the world to make chewing gum. Apparently, not even the local Maya population had bothered this site for decades, if not centuries.

"I was checking out that temple up ahead through my binoculars." She aimed her machete at the structure she'd come here to see specifically. "Strangler fig roots cover the northeast corner. There will likely be some structural damage we'll need to address."

Juan shook his head. "It's going to take too much."

"Too much what?"

"Time and work." He squeezed her shoulder. "Not to mention the heartache. You are biting off more than you can chew—than *we* can chew."

She frowned up at him. "Heartache?"

"Being here won't bring her back, *gatita.*"

"I know that." She swung her machete at some of the spindly branches blocking what she guessed to be a deer trail, plowing forward again. "This isn't about resurrecting the dead."

"Are you sure about that?" His crutches creaked behind her as he limped along the uneven ground.

"Positive." She swung again and again, making slow but steady progress.

"Because," he continued, speaking to her back, "I'm having trouble understanding why you feel so strongly about spending time at the site that killed your mother."

She lowered the machete and turned around, her breath coming in huffs. Taking off her straw sun hat, she wiped the sweat running down her cheek with her damp camp shirt. "I could swear we've gone over this before, Dad." In fact, they'd discussed it many, many groan-filled times since she'd made the decision to come here. "This place didn't kill her. The crash did."

Juan swatted at a fly buzzing around his head. "A crash that was caused by a curse she found here on this site."

Concrete dams gave way more easily than her father when it came to superstitious shit. "It's not a curse this time. It's a warning."

"I know what Marianne's notes say." He smacked her in the middle of her forehead.

"Ouch!" She drew back. "What was that for?"

"The fly." Pulling a handkerchief from his back pocket, he grimaced and held it out. "You might want to wipe that off. It was a juicy one."

She snatched the handkerchief from him, cleaning off the bug remains before jamming her hat back on. "If you know what Mom wrote, why do you insist on arguing with me about those damned glyphs she found?"

"Your mother was one of the brightest, smartest, most amazing women I've ever met in my almost forty years in the archaeology field. But I'm telling you here and now." He pounded the leaf-littered ground with one crutch for emphasis. "She was wrong on this particular theory." He pointed toward the three-story-high structure visible between the breaks in the trees. "What she found at that temple was more than a warning. This place has a history of death."

Angélica's guffaw incited another deep howl from overhead, followed by a bark from a nearby spider monkey.

"Dad, every single Maya dig site on the list sent to me by INAH has a history of death." Mexico's federally funded National Institute of Anthropology and History, known as INAH for short, had hired Angélica to clean up and prepare derelict dig sites, hoping to reel in more archaeotourism income to help support their programs. "You and I are in the business of archaeology, remember? We study the relics of the dead, not those who are still living happily ever after."

"Of course I remember that, *gatita*. I'm not senile."

"Not yet, anyway," she teased.

He poked her calf with a crutch, making her yip. His brown eyes sparkled as she dodged additional jabs.

"Okay," she said, laughing. "I take it back. Stop. Stop!"

He lowered his weapon. His focus shifted to the temple in the distance. "Of all the sites on your list, this one stole my beautiful wife from me." He looked down at her, his face lined with pain. "If we stay, I fear it will rob me of my hard-headed daughter, too."

Her eyes watered. She turned away before he could see any tears. She sniffed, checking her emotions before she told him, "You're too superstitious, Dad."

"And you're too logical, Marianne Jr."

"I take that as a compliment." Returning to the narrow trail and the task at hand, Angélica chopped at a tangle of vines and palm fronds blocking their way. One of the vines thudded harder than the others when it hit the ground, coming to life with a rattle and hiss.

"*¡Dios mío!*" Juan's voice was a notch higher than normal. "What's the Mayan word for 'rattlesnake'?"

She inched backward, not taking her eyes off the snake. "I fail to see why that matters at this moment."

"Oh, I remember. A *tzabcan*."

The rattling grew louder.

"Would you please shush," she whispered. Raising her machete slowly in case it lunged, she held steady as the snake stuck its forked tongue out several more times. Finally, it stopped rattling and slithered into the undergrowth.

Juan blew out a breath. "That was close. The curse almost bit you."

"A warning, Dad." She wiped a drip of sweat from her chin. "The snake wasn't interested in biting me; only *warning* me that he was there and wanted to be left alone."

"A warning of the curse then."

Angélica wasn't going to have this argument with him today. It was too damned hot and humid. "I should have chopped off its head and taken the body back to Teodoro."

Her favorite Maya shaman was always on the lookout for dead rattlesnakes.

"Please don't tell me María uses them in her *panuchos*."

Teodoro's wife, María, was the site's cook. Her tortillas, stuffed with black beans, chicken, and a spicy, delicious orange-colored sauce, always inspired much drooling from Juan and the rest of Angélica's field crew. "No, Teodoro likes to dry rattlesnakes and then roast them."

"Why?"

"He grinds them into some kind of medicinal powder."

"Medicine for what?"

"Probably toothaches," she said, holding back a grin. Her father had suffered from a toothache at the last dig site. Not even Teodoro's homemade numbing ointment could stop the pain that ended up requiring an emergency trip to a dentist in Cancun.

Her father wrinkled his nose. "That cruel sense of humor comes from your mother's side of the family."

A loud *plee* from a crested guan hanging out high up in a nearby ceiba tree urged Angélica back to swinging her machete.

Thirty minutes later, they stood at the base of the gray-stoned, crumbling Maya version of a pyramid. According to the paperwork she'd read on the location, one of the first archaeologists who'd worked the site had named it the *Baatz'* Temple, incorporating the Yucatec Mayan word for "howler monkey." On paper it was just another Mayan name for a large structure, but this particular temple had haunted her dreams and nightmares since she'd read her mother's notebook after the crash.

Angélica uncapped her water bottle and took a swig, staring up at the stone exterior.

The forest hadn't completed its camouflage work on this temple yet, unlike several of the other structures that were painted various shades of green with lichens and wrapped in vines, or those hidden under mounds of dead leaves, verdant shrubs, and palm fronds. The *Baatz'* Temple poked up through the surrounding canopy, reaching for the sky gods. In contrast to the more elegant temples of Chichen Itza and Tikal, the handful of exposed structures at this site were unpolished, ravaged by time's destructive weathering picks and hammers.

A purple butterfly as big as her hand fluttered past, landing high out of reach on the side of the temple wall.

"Your boyfriend is going to hate this place," her dad told her, taking the bottle of water she held out to him.

"Quint Parker's opinion of where I choose to work doesn't matter." She plucked a tick from her father's shirt and flicked it into the weeds, checking the rest of his shirt and hat brim for more. "He'll probably be here only a short time before he has to fly out again anyway." She tried to keep frustration with their whole long-distance relationship folly out of her voice, aiming for a light and carefree tone.

"Uh-oh." Juan handed back her water bottle, his face lined with dirt, sweat, and a frown. "That sounds like a rumble of thunder in paradise."

She should have known better than to say anything at all about Quint. There was no fooling her father, especially as they spent pretty much every day working together since his leave of absence from his tenured professor position at the University of Arizona.

"How can the honeymoon be over already? You two have barely started. What happened?"

"Nothing happened." Nothing besides one static-filled message from him on her voicemail the day after he left. Otherwise, since Quint had kissed her good-bye and climbed onto that plane, she hadn't heard a peep from him. No additional phone calls, no texts, no emails, *nada*. Hell, even a postcard would have been something. "I just don't like the idea that a temporary visitor has a say in where I work day after day."

"A temporary visitor?" Juan sucked air through his teeth. "Is it that bad already?" Leaning against the side of the temple, he fanned himself with his hat.

"I don't want to talk about it, Dad." She turned away from him, hacking at some of the morning-glory vines climbing the side of the temple.

"Come on. Tell dear ol' dad what's got you huffing and puffing."

"I'm not huffing." She swung the machete too wide. It hit the old stone structure with a clang that scared several chattering green parrots out of the tree canopy. The blade left a fresh silver scar on the structure.

"Your nostrils are flaring, *gatita*."

"You can't see my nose from there."

"Your neck is bristling."

"I'm too sweaty to bristle." Angélica swung her machete at a small *Jabin* tree half-strangled with more vines, releasing her frustrations about Quint's lack of contact since he'd left.

After receiving his short, static-filled message, she'd attempted to get through to Quint many times a day for a week. Unfortunately, she received a message that his voicemail box was full every damned time.

It appeared they were on a star-crossed lovers' kick at the moment, which she'd decided late last night was for the best. Quint messed with her head too much, not to mention the ache of doubts and insecurities he and his traveling inspired in her gut.

After recently learning that her ex-husband was not the man she'd thought he was, Angélica suffered from trust issues—as in having no faith in her own ability to judge character. When she piled the stupid choices from her past into one heap, it was clear that she was a bad candidate for a long-distance relationship and its inherent confidence requirements.

She kicked a hacked branch out of the pathway, scowling after it. Besides, much more of this loneliness business and she'd probably take up drinking.

Make that take up drinking *more*.

Her attempts to numb her relationship angst since Quint's departure had those Coronas and *Dos Equis* disappearing from her refrigerator way too quickly. Work had become an escape that settled her qualms, which was one of the reasons this was the perfect site for her to sink her teeth into as well as her trowel.

The other reason had to do with the secrets hidden at this site her mother had learned about on that last visit. Secrets Marianne had not shared with the lead archaeologist at the time. Instead, she'd noted them along with her hesitations and thoughts in her notebook.

Apparently, her mom had planned to return home and study her notes more before conferring with him, and for good reason. Experience had taught Marianne how vindictive other scientists in her field could be when it came to controversial topics and acceptable proof. This professional slander her mother had endured still made Angélica grind her molars. With time and research, she would avenge her mother's jealous foes.

Marianne's helicopter had crashed upon takeoff from this place, and her knowledge about the site's secrets had almost died with her … until Angélica had found her notebook. Unfortunately, there was only one page of notes, albeit a very full page.

"*Gatita.*" Her father's voice interrupted her train of worries and memories. "Tell me."

It took her a moment to snap back to the topic at hand. *Oh, right, Quint.* She shook her head. "I cannot emphasize how much I really don't want to talk about him."

"You shouldn't bottle up your emotions. It's not good for you."

"Neither is Quint Parker," she muttered.

"I disagree. When he's around, you return to your old self."

That was why Quint was bad news. Her old self made some serious screwups. It had taken her "new" self a lot of work to rebuild after the last disaster. She didn't need to return to her old ways.

"Let's get back to the business at hand, Dad. We need to find that block of glyphs with the warning on them so we can fly back to Cancun before dark." She didn't wait for him to agree, swinging the machete at a swarm of gnats as she headed around the side of the *Baatz'* Temple.

"You mean the curse."

"Keep it up and I'll let the mosquitoes have you for lunch."

He followed her along the path that was clearer here with fewer loose stones, exposed roots, and deep ruts. "When is Quint going to return, anyway?"

She shrugged. "Well, *if* he actually follows through on what he said before he flew out, he'll be back in a little over a week."

Ten days to be exact, which she planned to fill with hard labor from sunup until well after sundown. Thankfully, there was a lot of work to do before and after her crew arrived.

"He'll follow through," Juan said, keeping up with her. "He's not the type to make false promises."

Usually, when the sun was shining and logic ruled her world, she knew her dad was right. It was the middle-of-the-night doubts that made her toss and turn, imagining the worst about who Quint really was and if he were truly working up there in Greenland like he'd told her, or if that was just an excuse to escape from her and this corner of the world that he hated so much. Of course, the worry that he wasn't alone every night chewed on her as well, eating at her self-confidence until she was curled into a tight ball while cursing at the jealous ninny she'd become.

She slashed at a bobbing branch that stuck out into the path. "Let's talk about something not so ..."

"Emotional?"

"Annoying." She peered up at the dilapidated temple. The roots of a strangler fig and lichen were hard at work hiding this side of the structure. "This is it, you know," she said, stopping in front of a traditional Maya corbel-vaulted entryway that had partially collapsed under the weight of another fig tree's roots.

"We're not going inside that thing, *gatita*." Juan's fatherly tone left no room for argument. "It's not structurally sound by far."

His specialty was architecture of ancient Mesoamerican structures. During his long and lauded career, he'd worked at various sites analyzing and fortifying Maya temples. In addition to figuring out how to reassemble a temple from a pile of stones, he often drafted structure-filled drawings of what once was to help others gain a clearer picture of the amazing architectural achievements of those who'd lived long ago.

"You may not believe this, Dad, but I have no desire to risk being crushed to death today."

She moved along the deer trail, searching the surrounding jungle as she walked toward the location diagrammed in her mom's notebook of the stone stela covered with chiseled glyphs. The Maya people often posted one or more stelae outside a temple, using them as ancient billboards for messages from the king or his religious leaders to all—locals and strangers.

Angélica kept her eyes open for other chunks of stone with descriptive glyphs carved into them as well. The ancient Maya empires had been full of prolific writers, etching their stories and achievements onto surfaces that long outlasted their great cities.

Looters periodically went through dig sites looking for something that would bring big bucks on the black market.

Unfortunately, in their quest for riches, they tended to throw out important pieces of history, such as chunks of rock with important drawings and glyphs carved into them.

"According to Mom's notes," Angélica said over her shoulder, "she found the warning glyphs on a stela positioned several feet from the west side of the building."

She led the way with much less chopping to the western face of the *Baatz'* Temple. "Be careful where you step—there are a lot of roots poking up here." She made herself slow down, even though her legs were itching to race to the prize.

"Quit treating me like an old man." Her father's crutches creaked as he followed her.

"Your cast may be one of those fiberglass walking ones, but you need to rebuild your strength in that leg again before doing too much hiking around here."

"My leg is healing fine."

The compound fracture from the "accident" that happened well over a month ago appeared to be mending nicely thanks to an excellent surgeon and lots of rest, but Angélica doubted his doctor would condone this trek around a dig site as acceptable physical therapy. That was another reason why she'd wanted her dad to wait for her at the helicopter.

"One misstep could leave you in bad shape for the rest of your golden years, you know."

"You must have taken mother-hen lessons from Pedro. That boy has been driving me nuts with his Florence Nightingale routine. Trust me, I'm being careful and watching every step."

"Where is our third musketeer, anyway?"

Pedro Montañero had been part of her and her parents' life since she was a child. Her parents pretty much adopted the young boy, who volunteered at a very young age to work at their dig site in order to help his mother with the financial responsibility of raising his four sisters. Angélica wasn't sure what had happened to Pedro's father, and neither was he. Fast forward almost thirty years and Pedro was still by their side.

"Pedro stayed back at the helicopter with the other machete. He wanted to cut back the forest for a safer liftoff and landing."

She skirted a pile of loose rubble spilling across the path, pausing to help her dad make it past in spite of his determination to do it on his own. When she rounded the western side of the temple, she shifted her pack off her shoulders and pulled out her mother's dog-eared notebook.

Several thin-trunked guarombo trees crowded the base of the structure. She studied the area, scanning over the *chaya* shrubs with their large leaves while her heart thudded in her ears.

Shit. The stela wasn't where it was supposed to be.

She flipped the pages to her mother's drawing, taking in the small, rough sketch of the temple and the stela's supposed location her mom had noted on the paper.

"Damn it." She lowered the notebook, still searching. "Where is it?"

Juan wiped the back of his neck with his handkerchief, the bug guts she'd left behind on it not a bother apparently. "You mean the stela with the curse?"

"The warning glyphs, wiseacre." Maybe the previous archaeologist and his crew relocated the piece of stone to another area on the site to keep it safe from the elements and looters. Or they figured out the danger of which it told and hid it. "Do you think someone moved it after the helicopter accident?"

"For your sake, I hope so."

She frowned at her father. "You know I won't give up that easily on this site."

"Why not? What is so important about proving a curse exists?"

"It's a *warning*."

He waved off her correction. "It will not bring back your mother."

Of course not, but it was more than just a warning to Angélica. She needed that stela. She needed to see the glyphs for herself. It was the starting line for the hunt. Then she could begin searching for the other glyphs that told the rest of the story. Her mother had laid out the task, planning a return that would never happen thanks to the crash. Without the first puzzle piece, Angélica couldn't fulfill her mother's unfinished objective.

She stabbed the forest floor with the machete. "You don't get it, Dad."

"You're right, I don't." He leaned on his crutches, sweat rolling down from his salt-and-pepper sideburns. "Explain it to me so I can understand, because for the life of me, Angélica, I can't see why you'd want to court death at this site to prove someone else's theory—even if that someone else is your mother. Marianne would certainly never have wanted you to do this."

She paced in front of him. "I will never be as good as Mom."

"You don't know that. You're still young."

"At my age, she was already well known for her epigraphy skills."

Reading Maya glyphs was no easy feat. Each block of carvings could change meaning with the slightest variation. Angélica had worked on deciphering glyphs since she was a child, and she still was not as adept at it as her mother had been. For Marianne, it had seemed to come naturally. It was almost as if she had lived among the Maya during the golden age of their civilization. That she'd been reincarnated to help her people, solving their mysteries in a future they'd tried so hard to predict.

"You're well known as a talented, multi-skilled archaeologist," her father said, "who now has a dream job with the Mexican government. Do you know how smart you have to be to have landed this position? How many archaeologists would love to wear your boots? You weren't even born on Mexican soil and yet here you stand, trowel and plenty of funds from INAH in hand, with your pick of many incredible Maya sites."

Angélica nodded at his words, but ... "If only Mom were still here. I had so much to learn from her about decoding Maya glyphs." She held up the notepad. "But through this, I can work with her again."

"You do realize that what you're holding there is merely bound paper, right? It's not an original Maya codex or a diary belonging to Indiana Jones' dad."

Shaking the notebook at him, she asked, "Do you realize what is written in here?"

"Which part? The pages where she wrote, *Marianne loves Juan*, with little hearts drawn all around my name over and over?" His grin teased, easing the growing tension between them.

"Besides those pages," she said, smiling back.

"I know there are a bunch of chicken scratches about Maya glyphs that you seem to be all worked up about." He shook his head. "I always had trouble reading Marianne's writing when she scribbled."

"This is full of Mom's theories and ideas about all of the different dig sites she visited and worked." Angélica hugged the notebook to her chest. "Through this, she can teach me how to be a better archaeologist. She can show me a different way of seeing the Maya sites she visited over time, to view them through her eyes."

"To what end, though? So you go to each site and prove your mother right. Then what?"

"I'll publish her theories, listing the proof I collect, and add to or change the current thoughts and beliefs in the archaeology world about ancient Maya civilizations."

"And finish Marianne's work in the process?"

"Exactly."

"But what about your work?"

"This notebook becomes partly my work. I'm not going to stop digging until I've proven every theory she wrote down, unearthed every secret."

"What about your life?"

"What do you mean?" She shook the notebook again. "This is my life."

"No, your life should involve far more than what's written on pieces of paper in an old notebook, *gatita*. It should include love, friendship, even children before you're old and gray. And I'm not talking about that pig of yours."

"Rover is a javelina, Dad, and you know it. Respect the javelina. He saved my life."

"I thought Quint saved your life."

Well, him too.

Something panged in her chest. Damn it, she missed Quint. That frustrating man had better return to her as promised, or she'd … she'd what? Chase after him and beg him to come back?

She growled. "Never mind him." Or the way his smile made her feel like the sun had come out after a long dark night. "We have work to do." She pulled the machete out of the ground. "Daylight is burning."

"You need to fix things with Quint." Juan pocketed his handkerchief.

"Why?"

"I want to have grandbabies before I'm too old to bounce them on my knee."

She scoffed, resting the machete on her shoulder. "You want me to have Quint's children?"

"What's wrong with that? You certainly don't seem to have a problem with kissing him. Making grandbabies shouldn't be too arduous a task."

Her cheeks warmed, inspiring another layer of sweat. This was not a discussion she wanted to have with her father in the middle of the Maya jungle. Hell, it was not a conversation she'd like to have with him anywhere. "No more talk about Quint today, Dad." Or tomorrow. Or for the next ten days.

Besides, had he forgotten that Quint traveled all the time?

Instead of furthering the discussion on the pros and cons of acting as a babymaking oven for Quint's little buns of love, she took a few slashes at nearby branches. That stela had to be here somewhere. If she didn't find it today, she'd be back in two more days with part of her crew to begin setting up the site for the field workers the Mexican government had secured in addition to her own men.

The lack of control over choosing the crew made her jaw tighten. One of the drawbacks about her new position was that there were some parts of the golden deal where she had little say. For example, money could be made from students or anyone else who wanted to throw a few thousand dollars INAH's way to gain the experience of working at a real-life dig site—Angélica's dig site. Her insistence at having input on who was allowed to work under her fell on mostly deaf ears.

Another howler monkey let out a series of loud growls, probably trying to shoo her and her father back to the big bird they'd flown in on.

"*Gatita*," her father called from behind her. "Come here and look at this." He stood at the edge of a thick tangle of slender *Piñuela Yucateca* shrubs several feet from the pathway.

"What? Did you find the stela?"

"No." He pointed his crutch at something on the ground. "Do you see that?"

She stared at the dark dirt mostly covered with leaf clutter. "What is it? A scorpion?" Her father had an overblown fear of the pointy-tailed suckers.

"Those little nasties usually don't come out until dusk." He poked the dirt with the crutch. "It's a paw print. Apparently, this is someone's hunting ground."

She squatted, inspecting. Sure enough, it was a feline track, and a large cat from the looks of it. She pulled a leaf aside to get a better look. "What do you think it is? Jaguar?"

"Or puma. Either way, it's an adult. That's too big to be a juvenile."

Criminy. This day just kept sliding downhill. "Well, isn't this just fan-fucking-tastic. A fresh paw print from one of southern Mexico's largest predators but not a single damned warning glyph to be found."

He grimaced down at her. "You swear like your mother."

She glared at the tangled jungle surrounding them. "Ticks, flies, mosquitoes, monkeys, snakes, birds, and big cats, but no stela. Son of a biscuit."

"Don't forget the big spiders."

"What big spiders?"

"Never mind." He messed up the paw print with his crutch. "It's a sign, *gatita*."

She snorted. "Of course you'd say that."

"I'm merely speaking the truth. Don't kill the messenger."

"And what's this so-called sign say, Mr. Resident Wildlife Expert?" She stood, hands on her hips. *"Beware of the jungle?"* she asked in a rotten imitation of Vincent Price's deep, spine-chilling voice.

Scanning the forest, her father wrinkled his forehead. "I was thinking more along the lines of a phrase I once saw on an old geographical map that referred to the dangerous territories yet to be fully explored at the time."

"What phrase is that?"

His brown eyes lowered to hers, not a single twinkle to be found in them. " 'Here be dragons.' "

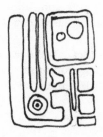

Chapter Two

Muan: A screech owl. In Maya iconography, the muan is often linked with rain, maize, and the Underworld.

Ten days PLUS one additional week later …

"How deep in shit am I?" Quint asked as he secured himself into the helicopter's passenger seat.

His old friend Pedro Montañero held out an aviation headset for him. "When I left the dig site the day before yesterday, *mi angel* was sharpening her machete. That was before she knew I was going to be delayed an extra day, along with her supplies. I didn't dare let her know I was waiting for you to fly in."

Damn it. Angélica was probably breathing flames by now.

Settling the headset over his ears, he stared out the windshield with a frown while Pedro performed a pre-flight check. The Mexican jungle was lying in wait for him at the edge of the tarmac. Somewhere, amidst the trees and bugs and critters, the woman he'd obsessed about for the last several weeks was waiting to tear him a new asshole.

Razor-sharp machete or not, Quint couldn't wait to see her again.

Pedro spoke a few words into his mic to the traffic controllers, and then they were lifting off. They rose above the trees, flying over the thick green sea of canopy broken only by a spider web of roads. Pockets of small towns popped up here and there, as well as clusters of gray stone structures left behind by the ancient Maya.

Since his last visit to this hellish version of paradise, Quint had spent his spare time during his photojournalist travels practicing his Spanish and learning about the Maya people and their leave-behinds. After his crash course, his head still spun when it came to all of their gods and beliefs, but if he were going to try and win Angélica's affection for the long haul, he'd need to start with that big brain of hers. As soon as he'd gained a foothold on her logical side, he'd work his way down to her heart.

"We have visitors." Pedro's static-laced voice came through the headset, interrupting Quint's thoughts about the flame-haired Dr. García, who was undoubtedly waiting to breathe fire all over him for his tardiness. Not to mention his lack of communication.

Visitors? "At the dig site?" he asked Pedro.

Quint hadn't been able to get through to Angélica or Juan since he'd left Cancun, thanks to his own clumsiness while floating along in the north Atlantic. He'd pulled out his phone to check his messages during the boat ride to the remote village where he was to spend a couple of weeks photographing polar bears. The trip up north had been his third and final for an article in a well-known nature magazine that he'd been working on for almost a year. Unfortunately, thanks to his frozen fingers, the phone had slipped from his hand, bounced off the railing, and splashed into the icy water.

With the sinking of his phone went the only number he had for Angélica or anyone else south of the border, which made for many long, dark, lonely nights of shivering in his sleeping bag.

He grimaced and wiped at the sweat coating his forehead. Acclimation was a bitch when traveling from steamy temperatures to freezing … and back to steamy. Luckily, he'd had a few days in between to defrost at home in South Dakota, where he'd been able to dig up Pedro's work phone number and arrange a trip to Angélica's current dig site.

"You know what INAH is?" Pedro asked.

"Yeah." It was the branch of the Mexican government in charge of archaeological sites. It was also the people in charge of Angélica's career at the moment.

Pedro glanced his way. "They have brought in five crew

members to pay for the … what's the word Juan used to make it sound nice … the *pleasure* of working with us."

"Pay? You mean INAH advertised the open field crew positions?"

Quint had heard of this practice before for grad students in anthropology and archaeology programs. If memory served him right, they applied to be "hired" at a particular dig site. After being accepted, they paid a chunk of money, traveled on their own dime to the site, and worked their asses off in exchange for college credits, lousy food, and uncomfortable beds. Finding a dig site with modern plumbing was an even more expensive proposition, of course.

At Pedro's nod, Quint asked, "Did Angélica have a say in any of this?"

"No. She was allowed six of her own crew. INAH picked the others."

He grimaced. The boss lady must be gnashing her teeth about that. "Are these five new crew members already on site with her?"

"*Sí.* She and Fernando have been training them."

Babysitting, in other words. Something she'd had to do with Quint at her last site. He could imagine the range of curse words flying from her sweet lips as of late.

So Fernando was back. Juan had explained to Quint when they'd worked together before that Fernando had been acting as Angélica's foreman since she'd taken over as lead archaeologist after her mother had died. Quint enjoyed working with Fernando, who shared a love for María's *panuchos* along with a mutual loathing of Angélica's ex-husband.

He stared down through the window at a tour bus traveling along one of the roads that wound through the Maya lowland forest. "Who else from the old crew has returned?"

"Teodoro and María, of course. INAH counted them as one instead of two, since they don't actually do field work."

They were more like support crew. Just thinking about Teodoro's homemade *balche*, a sacred, honey-based Maya drink, made Quint's mouth water. The inebriating effects might come in handy when it came to softening up Angélica after his longer-than-promised absence. Of course, María's cooking would keep them fat and happy while they sweated buckets and battled the flies and mosquitoes all the livelong day.

"Esteban agreed to come back."

Good ol' Esteban. Quint chuckled under his breath, remembering some of the snags the boy had gotten himself into at the last site. Angélica's choice to include Esteban made sense. While he might be scared of his shadow and often tripped over his own feet, she had mentioned once that the clumsy Maya youth was extremely smart and very trustworthy. On top of that, his father was disabled, so Esteban was the sole moneymaker for his family. Angélica might be rigid when it came to her rules on her dig site, but for her crew, she'd bend over backward to help them. "Who else?"

"Lorenzo, her *padre*, and me."

"So you're not volunteering your services this time?"

"No. Angélica pulled some ropes and managed to get me paid for flying in her crew and supplies, as well as working on site."

Ropes? He must mean she'd pulled some strings. Pedro was fluent in English, but that didn't stop him from screwing up his metaphors and idioms.

"That's why I waited for you, although you're not officially on the payroll as one of the crew. All INAH needs to know is that I was delayed picking up supplies."

Quint didn't want to be on Angélica's official crew, taking valuable monies out of her budget. He'd aligned a paying job again through another archaeology magazine, a follow-up article about Angélica and her father's progress after his last piece covering their work.

Having been in the business for almost twenty years, he had a contact list that was long. Landing a quick gig filling magazine pages in between contract jobs usually took only one or two calls, especially when the main focus of the piece involved two current stars in the Mesoamerican archaeology arena.

"So, who are these five new crew members?" he asked Pedro. "All college students?" Who else would want to pay to work among snakes, spiders, and man-eating mosquitoes?

"Three of them are students. One is an older lady, very pretty, probably in her fifties. The other is a writer, like you, only he has no camera."

Quint's brow tightened, suspicion bubbling in his gut. Another journalist? Who'd sent him and why? Someone out to get the dirt on Angélica now that her ex-husband had made the news? Someone hired by a rival archaeologist to knock her off the pedestal on which the Mexican government had her placed at the moment?

Juan had once told him that Angélica not being born in Mexico was a black mark on her record as far as the government was concerned, so she had to work extra hard to keep her job with INAH. Being female wasn't doing her any favors either in what had been a male-dominated profession until recently.

"Is this writer working for a magazine or newspaper?"

"Neither. He writes books about monsters."

"A fiction author?"

Pedro nodded. "A cowboy from Nevada."

A cowboy who wrote about monsters? "What's his pseudonym?"

" 'Maverick' is all he has said so far. I can't remember his last name. You know how Anglo names go in and out of my ears."

Maverick, huh? Quint speculated if this so-called author was hiding a devious truth behind his reason for visiting a bug-infested Mexican jungle. "What's a fiction author doing on a Maya dig site?"

"Research. He wants to write a story about us."

That must have gone over with Angélica like a cement blimp. She hated letting anyone handy with a pen on her site. Not having a say regarding what was written about her and her father's work made her hair practically crackle with sparks.

Quint knew that from first-hand experience. She'd tried to throw him off her last dig site multiple times. Unfortunately for her, he was as stubborn as she was when he had his mind set on something he wanted. And he'd really wanted answers to a twenty-year-old mystery, along with some more alone time with a certain brainy, curvy archaeologist.

They flew along in silence for several minutes, Quint trying to think of all the fiction authors he'd read or heard about online or at airport bookstores. No "Maverick" came to mind. That had to be part of a pseudonym, didn't it? He'd never met anyone actually named Maverick.

He glanced at his watch. They were fifteen minutes from the site. He'd find out first-hand about this fiction author soon enough.

Below them, the tree canopy seemed to be growing denser with fewer roads and villages to break up the greenery.

"Tell me about this new dig site," he said to Pedro. "From what I could see on the map, it's practically nonexistent."

The internet hadn't been much help, either. There had been several articles on the neighboring biosphere reserve that had been set aside years ago by the Mexican government, but nothing with the site name Pedro had mentioned when Quint had finally gotten hold of him two nights ago.

"It's in the middle of nowhere and full of insects and animals."

"What kind of bugs are we talking about?"

"Really big hairy bugs." Pedro chuckled at Quint's curses. "Monkeys, too," he added, "and birds, snakes, rats, cats, deer, tapir. You name it, this place has it."

"Did you say cats? I don't suppose you're talking about cute little kittens."

"Ocelots, puma, margays, and jaguars. They mostly come out at night."

"Nocturnal hunters."

"Exactly. The sound of their growl in the dark is enough to make you piss yourself, and when they roar, your *cojones* shrivel up into teeny tiny raisins."

"Holy shit. We're like a buffet line." Quint grimaced at the jungle below. Why in the hell had Angélica chosen this damned site?

"When you go to the bathroom in the night," Pedro continued his tale of horrors, "hundreds of spider eyes shine back at you."

"Christ." All of this for a woman? What was wrong with him?

"I have a light I use to find the scorpions. I'll let you borrow it. They like to hang out around the latrine."

He must mean a black light. Quint shuddered. Truth be told, he didn't think he wanted to know what was out there waiting for him. Ignorance might be bliss on this trip. Then again, with venomous snakes on the loose and hungry cats, this adventure could be the death of him.

"Did you bring earplugs?"

He'd learned long ago in his travels to always keep a pair in his shaving kit. "Sure. Why?"

"The noises in the night make it hard to sleep at first."

"What noises?"

"You'll see. I sleep with a pillow over my head most of the time."

"I can hardly wait to experience this Mexican paradise."

"It's good that you cut your hair."

Quint had purposely asked the barber to trim it shorter than usual to help him keep cooler.

Pedro gave him a toothy smile. "It will be easier to remove the ticks each night."

"*Each* night?" He scratched his head, suddenly feeling little phantom bodies crawling all over his skull. "Jesus, Pedro. Is there anything good about this damned site?"

"Besides your *novia* waiting for you there?"

"And her sharp machete."

"María is probably cooking as we speak."

"Food is definitely good."

"There are lots of butterflies and bats."

Butterflies were great. Maybe he could put together an article on butterflies for one of the popular nature periodicals. Bats were bug eaters, and if there were as many mosquitoes as there had been at the last site, they'd need all of the bats they could round up.

"We have cleared a spot for our tents and the showers."

"Where are you getting water?" Were there *cenotes* this far south?

"There is a stream nearby and several springs. We also brought in a few smaller cisterns."

"How many tents are we talking?" At the last site, there had been enough for most of the crew to have their own quarters.

"*Cinco.*"

"Only five?"

"Plus the mess tent. We are sharing tents."

"Couldn't INAH spring any extra money for more tents?"

"It's not about money, it's about safety."

Safety? "Is Angélica worried about the wildlife attacking?"

"It's not *mi angel* who's scared."

"What do you mean?"

"Juan is not happy about being at this site."

"Because of the snakes, rats, and scorpions?" Angélica's father had a severe dislike for vermin, especially those with sharp teeth, stingers, or venom.

"This is the site that killed his wife, Angélica's *madre*."

Quint did a double take. "Marianne died here?"

"The helicopter taking her away from the site crashed during takeoff. She died in the hospital from her injuries."

Quint knew the story. He'd heard bits of it from Juan and Angélica both. "Why would she want to come back here?" he said to himself as much as to Pedro.

"Marianne left something in her notes about a certain stela with some important glyphs."

"Not another curse," Quint said jokingly.

"Yes, a curse."

His jaw gaped. "You're kidding me."

"No joke. Juan says it's a curse. Angélica says it's a warning, not a curse." Pedro shrugged. "Until they find the stela Marianne wrote about, nobody knows for sure."

"Another curse." Quint scoffed. "What are the chances?"

"Very good. The Maya were very superstitious."

Silence followed, broken only by the thump-thump-thump of the helicopter blades and the high-pitched whine of the engine. Quint pondered Angélica's choice in sites. What good was being here where her mother had met her end? She couldn't bring Marianne back.

Was this so-called curse the appeal? No, Angélica didn't believe in curses. She was too down-to-earth for that. It had to be something her mother had written. Some theory she needed to prove to put her mother's ghost to rest? That was what had made her hell-bent for leather at the last site.

"I agree with Juan." Pedro broke the silence.

"You think it's a curse?"

He nodded. "But not a supernatural curse, more like bad juju."

"Why? Because Marianne died?" What about the other archaeologist? The previous crew? Had anything happened to them?

"Not because she died. Because of *the way* she died."

"You mean the crash?"

"Exactly. It shouldn't have happened. I have an old friend who works for the government. He is part of a team that investigates aircraft crashes, like Marianne's."

Pedro had mentioned this friend previously when talking about Dr. Hughes' plane crash years ago. "Was it pilot error?"

Pedro shook his head. "The official ruling was that a pitch control rod in the main rotor failed. Mechanical failure was listed as the cause of the crash."

"You think the curse had something to do with that?" Quint had trouble believing "bad juju" could cause a mechanical failure.

"According to my friend, a rod failing like it did is highly unlikely. However, his supervisor and the government wanted to be done with the crash investigation, so they swept it under the floor."

Rug, Quint corrected mentally.

"So, either there was a curse at work," Pedro continued, "or someone wanted Marianne dead."

Who would have wanted her dead?

Pedro added, "You must promise not to talk about this around Angélica and Juan."

"Of course not." What good would come of that, especially since Pedro had no real proof to go on besides the unlikelihood of a control rod failing? It would only open old wounds better left scarred over.

"You are an ace detective, right?" Pedro asked.

Quint grimaced. "Not really an ace." His style was more bumbling gumshoe with a shitload of luck mixed into the deal.

"You and I will work together in secret and find out the truth." It wasn't a request, more of a statement.

"You mean if Marianne was murdered or it really was some ancient bad luck?"

"Yes. If it was murder, we have to figure out the killer, because whoever was responsible might decide to remove her daughter from this world, too." He frowned over at Quint. "We don't want to see that happen, do we?"

"Hell, no."

Pedro pointed down at the trees. "That's the site."

A small clearing amid the trees sat below them. Located only a short distance from several crumbling gray stone structures was a group of army-green tents.

Quint mulled over Pedro's words as they began their descent. They'd almost reached canopy level when something slammed into the helicopter's windshield and then ricocheted up into the blades.

Feathers flew.

Pedro cursed in rapid-fire Spanish.

"What was that?" Quint asked, peering up through the windshield.

"Very bad news."

"What do you mean?" The helicopter seemed to be unharmed.

"It was a screech owl." Pedro shot him a quick frown. "A *muan*."

"What's a *muan*?"

"The evil bird of bad tidings."

"Seriously?"

"It's a sign."

"Of what?"

"*Yum Cimil*, or as some call him, *Ah Puch*. The lord of death, ruler of the ninth level of the Maya Underworld."

According to the book Quint had read on Maya gods and religion, the Underworld was the Maya version of Hades. "And a *muan* is his pet bird?"

"Not a pet, a messenger." Pedro craned his neck, checking the landing area as the ground loomed beneath. "When you see or hear a screech owl, someone will die," he said as he set the helicopter onto the grass with a soft bounce.

"And what about when you chop it up in the blades of your helicopter?"

As the engine wound down, Pedro turned to Quint, his brow wrinkled. "I'm afraid to find out."

* * *

At the sound of the helicopter landing, Angélica sent their "researching" author, Maverick, after her father to help Pedro unload the supplies he'd picked up in Cancun.

Her father needed to take it easy on his damned leg. His doctor had given the green light to switch from crutches to a cane, but Juan still needed to rest his leg every afternoon as ordered. Angélica worried that the strain of cleaning up this dig site was going to cause further damage.

After a glance at her watch and then a frown in the direction of the helicopter landing site, she grabbed her machete and headed southwest toward the *Chakmo'ol* Temple. She'd check in with Pedro later to find out what had delayed him an extra day on his return. Her fingers were crossed it wasn't something to do with his mother or his many sisters.

In the meantime, she had more clearing to do around the second-largest temple at the site, which was another potential location for the stela her mother had written about in her notes. She paused on the way past the partially excavated ballcourt to check on one of her INAH-appointed female field workers, Daisy Walker.

Daisy had more spunk in her mid-fifties than most twenty-year-olds. Her steely determination had struck a chord in Angélica, who'd recognized a fellow lonely soul in the silver-haired sprite. Their first night here, Angélica had brought her crew together into a circle, old and new, and had them tell a bit about who they were and why they had signed up for a remote dig site in the middle of the Mexican jungle.

Semi-recently widowed, Daisy had returned to college a couple of years back to find a purpose, something to keep her from focusing on her very empty nest. Archaeology had been her passion in her younger years, but she'd chosen to devote thirty years to a husband and three children instead of digging in the dirt. Now, with nobody waiting for her at home, she'd decided to follow through on the other love of her life—Mesoamerican history, which was something else Angélica had in common with Daisy.

Angélica paused at the northeast corner of the ballcourt near the end wall, looking around the masonry structure with sloping stone-block walls. It was a modest court, unlike the Grand Ballcourt at Chichen Itza with its tall vertical walls covered with elaborate reliefs. This court's design was T-shaped with one enclosed end zone at the bottom of the T. The narrow playing alley was filled with grass and weeds that had long ago worked up through the packed dirt and taken residence. The sloping lichen-coated walls, or *aprons* as her father had corrected her earlier, were only about eight feet tall and topped with a crumbling flat cornice. A two-foot-high bench bracketed the base of the aprons, with one corner of the far bench wall partially demolished under the weight of a strangler fig tree.

With a lot of work, including structural repair, the ballcourt had the potential to be one of the highlights of the site. Tourists would be able to step down into the T-shaped playing alley and imagine how it felt to be a Maya ball player. These players, whose job was to hit a six- to eight-pound ball made of chicle through a small stone ring high up on the aprons without using hands, feet, or head, were an elite group. Unfortunately, the price of losing was sometimes death.

At breakfast, she'd instructed Esteban to focus on the far end of the narrow playing alley beyond the aprons. He was to begin by training Daisy how to measure off and string test areas. Just beyond the strangler fig she could see Daisy down on her hands and knees, but Esteban was walking along the bench wall, searching the weeds.

"Did you lose your keys again?" Angélica asked. Most ballcourts were designed acoustically so that there was no need to yell to be heard from one end to the other.

He squawked at the sound of her voice. "*Hola*, Dr. García." A smile filled his round face as he approached her. *"Señora Walker encontró esto."*

"Inglés, Esteban, ¿recuerdas?" She'd spoken to her Spanish and Maya crew about trying to use English in front of the new field workers in order to make them feel more at ease. If the team was going to meet the objectives she'd submitted to INAH for their month here, she needed everyone to enjoy working together in spite of the heat, humidity, insects, and lack of running water. In her experience, she'd found that a common tongue facilitated cooperation tenfold.

"What did Daisy find?" she asked.

He dropped a dirt-covered jade piece into the palm of her hand. "There *es más*," he said in a blend of languages.

Esteban spoke both Maya and Spanish fluently in a smooth tenor, but he stumbled with English. However, next to Fernando and Teodoro, Esteban had worked the longest with Angélica and her father, starting from when his arms didn't look strong enough to swing a rope, let alone a machete for hours on end.

"You mean there are more jade pieces like this?" she asked. She blew some of the dirt off the cut stone and then held it up in the sunlight. It looked like a carving of a head—a mixture of a skeleton with monkey-looking cheeks and ears.

"No, Dr. García. *Un yugo.*" His forehead furrowed as he glanced at Daisy, who'd joined them with her trowel in hand and a sunny smile on her face. "A ... *que es* word ..." His brown eyes widened. "Ah, *sí*, a yoke."

"A yoke?" Angélica's jaw dropped. "You're kidding me. Where?"

Esteban led the way to the other end of the narrow playing alley to where Daisy had been stringing one-meter squares in the weeds and dirt off to the side of the ballcourt. Angélica dropped her machete and took the paintbrush he held out for her, kneeling next to the prize they'd found. Sure enough, the U-shaped ballgame costume piece was visible next to the tree root that had apparently upended the buried treasure.

"Damn," she whispered in awe. She'd seen plenty of stone yokes on display in various museums, but this was the first time she'd ever come across one on a site.

"Esteban says the ball players used to wear these around their waist to block blows." Daisy knelt next to Angélica. She smelled like lemon eucalyptus oil and olive oil thanks to the natural bug repellent Daisy had made and used in place of the store-bought versions, which she claimed gave her a rash. "Is it a rare find?"

Angélica brushed off more dirt. "No and yes. Over a thousand yokes have been found throughout Mesoamerican sites, but usually they're found in tombs, not out in the open like this."

"How could they wear something so big and heavy while playing the ballgame? This must weigh twenty pounds."

"Probably closer to thirty," she told Daisy. "Most archaeologists agree that these stone yokes were more for ceremonial purposes. The yokes that were actually worn by the ball players were most likely made of wood and disintegrated long ago."

"Oh." Daisy sounded a tad deflated.

Angélica squeezed her shoulder. "But you finding this here on the ground rather than in a tomb is a rare treat. We need to be careful clearing it. Some stone yokes have iconography to decipher that will tell a story about a famous ball player or an important game."

"Like a trophy?"

"Exactly. How did you find this?" Angélica had traversed this end of the ballcourt several times since they'd arrived on site and begun beating back the trees and brush.

Daisy shrugged. "I saw the jade piece first. It was sticking up out of the dirt here." She touched the ground where a rainstorm runoff had cut a rut through the earth. "As soon as we started digging it out, my trowel hit stone and *voilà*, there was the yoke."

Angélica shook her head in amazement. "Do you know how unusual it is to stumble onto finds like these?"

The older woman's cheeks rounded even more. "Well, I've always had a knack for finding 'lost' items around my house—car keys, toys, socks, my husband's wallet. My family used to call me Radar O'Reilly." Daisy's grin took on a sad slant. "You know, from that old television show—"

"*M.A.S.H.*" Angélica nodded. "It's one of my dad's favorite shows." She held up the jade piece for a closer look. The late morning sun shone from behind her, lighting up the jade piece, showing all of its wear and tear as well as its artistic beauty. This one was more turquoise than green. She'd have to research the sources of this particular color of jade back at her lab in Cancun.

"My husband loved it, too," Daisy said. "I always had a crush on Alan Alda. He was such a flirt."

"*Gatita*," Juan called out from the other end of the ballcourt where she'd stood moments before. "You have company."

The jade piece seemed to be slightly jagged at the neck, as if it had been broken off at some …

Company?

Daisy looked across the court, shielding her eyes. "Broad shoulders and long legs." She whistled in appreciation. "My, oh my, this one is tall. He looks like trouble."

Tall? Angélica lowered the jade piece and turned to see for herself, squinting across the length of the ballcourt into the sunlight.

Her breath hitched.

Her heart stumbled.

Her thoughts about Maya jade pieces, ballgames, and yokes crashed down around her.

Quint Parker strode toward her.

Son of a bitch. The dark-haired heartbreaker had finally arrived.

"Oh, he's trouble all right," she told Daisy, rising to her feet. "Trouble with a damned capital T."

Chapter Three

The Snake or Serpent Dance: For the ancient Maya, public dances acted as mechanisms for social, political, and religious endeavors. Many glyphs have been found showing nobility dancing with snakes.

He's handsome trouble at least," Daisy said for Angélica's ears only.

"The worst kind." Angélica grabbed her machete and leveled her shoulders, readying for battle.

"Good morning, Dr. García." Quint's tone was cool and respectful, very professional. His heated stare, on the other hand, blazed a trail from her head to her boots, getting hung up along the way on a couple of bumpy parts.

He'd cut his hair shorter, ditching the wavy, tousled look he'd sported at the last dig site. Other than that, he was the same as she remembered—chiseled jaw and cheekbones, long eyelashes, and great lips. Did he still smell like sunshine and citrus?

Damn, she'd missed him. "You're late, Parker."

Her father chuckled as he limped toward them with his cane and walking cast. "See what I mean, boy?"

Quint's hazel eyes returned north, searching her face. "Your father said you'd give me the lay of the land." His lips twitched at the corners.

She snorted at his pun. Oh, she'd lay him, all right. She'd start with a sucker punch in his breadbasket and then deliver a haymaker, laying him out flat for not sending even a single postcard and then showing up a week late with no notice.

"Dad," she said, skirting Quint without touching him. She couldn't yet, not in front of her crew. "Take this jade piece and help Esteban and Daisy with that yoke over there, please."

She placed the broken figurine in her father's hand and aimed a frown at him. If he knew about Quint coming today and hadn't said anything in order to surprise her, she was going to hide the Zane Grey book he was in the middle of reading, maybe even throw it in the pit toilet with a loud war cry as it hit bottom.

Juan caught her hand and squeezed it, shooting a warning glare in return, his gaze darting to Quint and back. She knew better than to think the warning was for her heart's safety. He knew her temper too well.

She pulled free. Fine, she wouldn't fillet Quint with her machete, but she might tie him up and give him a close shave around his tender spots.

After a good-bye nod to Esteban and Daisy, she strode toward the tents. "Follow me, Parker," she called without looking back to see if he obeyed her order.

Quint swished behind her through the dry grass across the open plaza. She shoved through the flap of the tent she was sharing with her father. Quint joined her inside, zipping the insect mesh flap closed behind them.

The sunlight shining through the tent canvas lit them in a green hue.

They were alone.

A howler monkey barked in a nearby tree.

Well, sort of alone.

She stared at Quint, suddenly speechless now that the exasperating man stood in front of her, live and in his all-too-attractive flesh. The many rants she'd practiced in the small mirror hanging in the camp's makeshift shower faded to a whisper in her mind.

He fanned his white camp shirt. "Would it help if I told you that I've been miserable since I left?"

That made two of them.

"Not one word from you in almost four weeks, Parker. Not a letter, a text, or even a fucking postcard." She'd left an embarrassing amount of voicemails the first week he'd been gone. Voicemails she wished she could erase.

"I lost my phone in the Atlantic my first day in Greenland. With it went the number for your satellite phone."

That was a good excuse, but it wasn't going to cut it with her, not when there were other ways of communicating across vast distances in this day and age.

"And on top of that," she continued, crossing her arms, "you arrive a week late. Hell, I'd just about given up on ever seeing you again."

"I had a small job come in after Greenland that I needed to take so that I could stay down here longer." When she growled in response, he added, "Hey, it's not like there was an easy way of getting a message to you at this remote site. Word on the street is that the carrier pigeons have gone on strike."

The logical side of her understood how his job worked, but right now she wanted to tackle him and pummel the crap out of him. She took a deep breath, needing to handle this like a grownup. "I don't think this long-distance relationship business is going to work, Quint."

He didn't argue.

His silence made her wring her hands.

"While I think there's an interesting spark between us, I'm not sure it's worth pursuing any further."

His face was frozen, unreadable.

She pressed on with her rehearsed breakup speech. "If you'd like to volunteer to stay here at the dig site, we can certainly use your help, but if you'd rather skip out on the bugs and sweating, I understand."

His chest rose and fell, the only indication that he hadn't hardened into a statue.

"I can pay you for your time from my private resources, of course, if the lack of funds is an issue. It's probably not anything close to what you usually make for a photojournalist job, but it includes food, a cot, and a nighttime jungle serenade." Her joke sank as fast as his cell phone probably had. She hesitated with the wrap-up, waiting for him to give some indication he was actually participating in this conversation.

One of his dark eyebrows lifted. "Anything else, boss lady?"

His use of the nickname he'd often called her made her heart pang. It was one thing to practice this speech to a mirror, but saying it to Quint's face made her lips feel like wood.

"Yes." Her gaze traveled downward, stopping at his khakis. "How are your leg and shoulder doing?"

He'd taken bullets in both for her at the last dig site, and one of her nail-biters during his complete and utter silence for weeks on end was that infection had set in while he was on the frozen tundra. That he'd died a painful death because of her.

"I'm fine. I've always been a fast healer."

She'd like to see both wounds for herself, but inspecting his naked flesh probably wasn't a smart idea. "Good."

"I'm not leaving, Angélica." His tone was matter-of-fact.

"Okay, then. Dad and I will appreciate your help. There's a lot of work to do here to open the site to archaeologists and their crews again. It's going to take even more work and time before it's ready for the public." She was rambling and she knew it, but she couldn't seem to stop. "There's no way we can have tourists crawling all over the temples in their current crumbling state, not to mention the dangers that come with the wildlife patrolling the grounds each night."

"My staying has nothing to do with helping your father, although I do enjoy his company when he's not trying to scare the hell out of me." The hard set of his jaw gave her a clue about why he was staying.

She lifted her chin. "Let me guess, you're here to rescue another damsel in distress."

Quint had a bad hero-like habit of diving in front of firing guns for the opposite sex. She didn't need him sticking around to try to save her. This site might be in bad shape, but she could handle what the jungle threw at her and then some.

"Nope. I'm here to spend time with a woman I haven't been able to stop thinking about since I left her bed."

"That woman was naïve."

Angélica had thought she'd be able to handle his absence with only minor twinges, but she'd been a fool. After weeks of feeling the sting of rejection, followed by gut-wrenching stabs of hurt and anger, then resorting to middle-of-the-night bargains with the devil for a single word from Quint, and finally wallowing in depression, she'd accepted the truth: Their careers made a relationship nearly impossible.

"Besides that," she continued, "she's no longer running the show when it comes to you and me. I've taken over."

"I call bullshit. You're being a big chicken, hiding behind this hard-core boss act that allows you to exist without having to invest emotionally in anything that might cause you heartache."

Her internal temperature rocketed as a blast of rage lit her up like a firecracker. She closed the distance between them and lowered her voice to a harsh whisper in case anyone else was within earshot. "I let you inside here," she tapped her temple, "and you made a fucking mess of my world. I'd have to be insane to let you trespass any further."

"Your world needed messing up," he shot back. "You have everything in here," he pointed at her heart, "locked down tight. That's no way to live."

"Me and my heart were doing fine and dandy before you showed up with your camera and secrets."

"You call working yourself to the bone every day and burying your head in books and notes each night 'fine and dandy'?"

"There's nothing wrong with being career-driven."

"There is when you're missing out on the sweet stuff in life."

"Sweet stuff? If you mean sex, you need to open your eyes wider. There's more to a relationship than good sex." Her parents had given her a solid example of what a long-term love affair looked like.

"Sex was better than just 'good' between us and you know it."

She shrugged. "It was sort of memorable, I guess." The snub rolled off her tongue before she could rein it in. Weeks of sleepless nights made her aim low.

His eyes narrowed. "I'm going to bookmark that insult, sweetheart, and we'll revisit it later."

"There isn't going to be a 'later,' Parker." That would involve more traveling for him, which meant more bouts of temporary insanity for her. As far as she was concerned, this falling in love baloney was for the birds, not an archaeologist with a shitload of work on her plate that required concentration and diligence.

His laugh was short and hard. "Proving you wrong this time is going to feel so damned good."

Taking a step back from him, she blew out a breath. This was not going well. While Quint's long, silent break from her life made her want to lash out and wound him, she didn't really want to fight with him. For one thing, it was too damned hot in her tent to think straight; for another, she liked him way too much to keep taking cheap shots.

"Listen, Quint," she said in a level voice, rubbing her forehead. "I went through a twisted version of hell while you were gone."

"Tell me about it," he shot back. When she threatened to clock him in the chin, he held up his hands. "I'm serious. Tell me about how you felt over the last few weeks."

"Four longggg weeks." Well, not quite four, but it had felt like four months, damn it.

"That's a start. Let 'er rip."

"I'd like to rip you a new one, that's how I feel. How do I know you don't have a woman in every country? That all I am is the current 'Ms. Mexico' mark on your bedpost?"

"Jealousy? I didn't expect *that* from you."

"You think I'm some kind of robot?"

"No. I know full well you're flesh and blood from head to toe, but you usually maintain an incredibly tight grip on your emotions."

"Which is the exact reason I can't do this." She threw up her hands. "The head archaeologist of a dig site cannot be caught sniffling in her tent at night like a silly schoolgirl because she misses her damned boyfriend."

His forehead creased. "I'm sorry."

She growled in self-disgust and paced to the other side of the tent, keeping her back to him. "I can't handle your job. I thought I could, but after my ex, I've lost faith in my ability to trust."

"There are no other women, Angélica. Only you."

She turned. "Honestly, it's not really you who I don't trust. It's me. I've made amazingly stupid decisions in my past."

His jaw tightened. "And you see me as one of them?"

"No." She leaned against the tent's center support pole, trying to find the words for how she felt about her situation. "This is going to sound silly, melodramatic, and probably downright absurd, and I can't believe that I am going to say the words aloud, but here goes— I think I'm broken inside."

"You're not broken," he teased, "more like scratched and dented."

That made her smile in spite of her uncertainties. "I can't see how a relationship beyond friendship is ever going to work between us."

"It will work if you want it to."

"What about what you want?"

"I'm easy. I want you." There was no hesitation in his voice.

She frowned. "How can you be so certain?"

"Because every night I was gone I was thinking about little else besides clearing a path back to you and this lovely corner of hell you call home sweet home."

"But what about—"

"Angélica." His hand snaked out and captured her by the wrist. "You're overthinking this."

"I'm using logic, Parker. Your career and mine don't gel."

"We'll find common ground." He pulled her toward him.

"I don't like the emotional roller coaster I go through while you're gone."

"I'll find a way to leave less often."

"That's not fair to you." She rested her palms on his chest, the steady beat of his heart comforting, quelling her worries for the moment. "You hate Mexico."

"That's not true." His fingers combed back a loose strand of her hair. "I dislike only the hot and humid parts. The rest isn't so bad."

"But I can't ask you to—"

"Would you shut up, woman, and kiss me already. It's been a long twenty-four nights without you."

Kissing him was a mistake, but she was going to do it anyway. She was done thinking for now and wanted to focus on feeling for a while. Wrapping her arms around his neck, she went up on her toes and angled her head slightly. His lids lowered as he bent down, his focus on her mouth.

"Quint," she whispered, their breath mingling.

"What?"

"I missed your sorry ass."

His chuckle reverberated in his chest. "What else did you miss?"

"This." She pressed her lips to his, taking her sweet time, using her tongue and teeth as part of the display. When she leaned fully against him, pressing into his rigid form, he groaned under her onslaught. His arms drew her even closer, his hands exploring her curves, stroking, until they were both sweaty from more than the tent's stifling heat.

When she leaned back he smiled down at her. "That's more like it."

"I'm glad you're here." She really was, in spite of the last few weeks of heartache and the cursing sure to come.

"Let me guess, you need my big muscles to help you move some more old stones around?"

"Something like that." Resting her cheek on his chest, she breathed in his scent—yep, sunshine and citrus. Her heart swelled dangerously, wanting something she didn't believe was going to pan out. "How long can you stay this time?" she asked, not sure she wanted to hear his answer.

"That depends."

"On what?"

"The queries I sent out when I stopped back home for a couple of days to repack for my trip down here." He toyed with her braid. "Pedro will check my email for me when he flies to Cancun for supplies and let me know if any of my lures have caught a fish."

At least he was honest and not promising the moon on a silver platter. "I guess Dad and I had better get you moving those old stones as soon as possible."

"Angélica." When she met his hazel eyes, he told her, "We're going to make this work between us."

Doubts shadowed her thoughts, but she hid them behind a bright smile. "How about we start with you avoiding bullet holes this time?"

"But you're so good at kissing them better."

She heard footfalls in the weeds on the other side of the tent flap.

"Dr. García?" Gertrude, one of INAH's assigned grad students from a university in southern Germany, called for her.

"I'm in my tent." She placed her finger over Quint's lips, her gaze warning him to keep silent.

"Pedro sent me to get you," Gertrude said, sounding like she was right outside. "We need you over at the *Chakmo'ol* Temple immediately."

She frowned, stepping clear of Quint's embrace. "Did someone get hurt?"

"No. There's another snake. This one's even longer than the last one."

"Where's Teodoro?"

"He's helping María find herbs in the jungle."

"I'll be there in a moment. Tell everyone to stay away from the snake."

After the footfalls in the weeds had moved away, she returned her focus to Quint. "I have to go."

"*Another* snake?" His forehead had several deep Vs centered on it.

"We seem to have a rattlesnake highway running past the south side of the temple." She grabbed her machete from where it leaned against her cot, along with the burlap bag on the floor next to it. "But don't worry. Teodoro and I have gotten very adept at relocating them."

"What if they don't want to be relocated?"

She shrugged. "María makes a delicious cold snake soup." The horrified expression on his face made her chuckle under her breath. "I'm kidding about the soup."

"Good."

"María uses the snake meat in her *panuchos*."

This time, his full-body cringe made her laugh out loud. God, she'd missed messing with him. She let her gaze wash over him, soaking him up. She'd missed the lightness he always added to her step, too. His grins and charm were infectious, dangerously so.

"Christ, woman. You're as warped as your father."

"He taught me well." She unzipped the tent and stepped out. "We're limited on sleeping arrangements at this site. Nobody has a tent to themselves. How do you feel about sleeping in the same tent as Pedro and Fernando?"

He followed her out. "If you'll remember, Dr. García, the original deal we made on the beach that night was that you would let me share *your* tent at each dig site."

She nodded, remembering that moment clearly, as well as what had happened later in her bed. Unfortunately, there was a slight snag she hadn't planned on at that time. "Okay, you can move your gear into my tent. We'll set up another cot later this afternoon."

"What about the extra cot already in there?"

"It's taken."

"By whom?"

"My father. You'll be bunking with the two of us."

He cocked his head to the side. "Are you screwing with me again, woman?"

"Nope." She rested the machete on her shoulder. "Not now and probably not later either. Dad is a light sleeper most nights."

Quint swore under his breath. "This just keeps getting better."

"Don't worry. It'll get worse again soon." She patted him on the chest. "I'm off to dance with a snake."

"Be careful, boss lady."

She glanced down toward his belt buckle, her gaze flirting when it returned to his. "The snake sharing my tent is more dangerous than any hiding in the jungle."

"Funny. You're a real Joan Rivers today."

"*It's been so long since I've had sex I've forgotten who ties up whom,*" Angélica said in her best imitation of the late, great comedienne.

He reached out and trailed his finger down her arm, his gaze smoldering. "I'll be sure to remind you later."

A zing of longing made her knees feel rubbery. She gripped the machete handle extra hard. "I hope you brought some earplugs."

"Pedro already told me about the nightly jungle serenade."

She scoffed. "The creatures outside of our tent are nothing compared to the old beast on the inside. He snores loud enough to wake the dead."

* * *

Sweat rolled down Quint's back as he chewed on another bite of María's handmade *panucho*. This one was stuffed with wild greens and chicken and coated in her spicy orange sauce. In spite of the nirvana going on inside of his mouth, he was 99.9 percent certain that this remote dig site in the Mexican jungle was really one of the nine levels of the Maya Underworld.

He swallowed, chasing the chicken with a swig of warm beer. He stretched his neck from side to side, trying to ease the tension that had built up after traveling thousands of miles and then performing backbreaking manual labor in an oppressive sauna. He was getting too old for this globe-trotting shit. Settling down appealed more and more every day, but preferably somewhere less stifling than this place. Somewhere like Angélica's comfy beach house outside of Cancun.

Headache and sore muscles aside, Quint could barely keep his eyes open. Tomorrow, Angélica and he could begin figuring out how to work out this long-distance relationship hitch. Tonight, he just wanted to fall asleep with her sharing the same square mile with him. If she felt like getting naked at some point in the night and taking advantage of him while he was half-asleep, he had no problem with that either.

He checked his watch. It was ten past seven. How much longer was Angélica going to hang around after supper? As much as he wanted to catch up on current events at the site, he was going to have to call it a night soon.

Across the table, Pedro sat between Juan and Fernando, telling them about the screech owl that had flown into the helicopter's blades while they were landing. Angélica shifted on the bench seat next to him, horizontal lines forming along her forehead as Pedro threw out the words *"Yum Cimil"* and *"muan* owl." She let Pedro finish his tale without interruption, though, probably because the INAH crew, as well as Esteban and Lorenzo, had already eaten and left the tent. There was no risk of spreading fear or causing heart palpitations from the more superstitious of the bunch with most everyone out of earshot.

By the time Quint had made it to the mess tent after wrapping up the day's work and unpacking his shower supplies from his backpack, there was only one of the INAH crew left behind. He'd had the pleasure of officially meeting Daisy Walker before she'd headed off to her tent for the night. The petite woman's blue eyes had twinkled as she shared a knowing look with Angélica after shaking his hand. Unfortunately, the fiction author hadn't been there. Quint would have to seek out Maverick tomorrow and try to figure out if the guy was legit or not.

Tuning out Pedro and Angélica arguing about the dead owl, Quint scanned the small, crowded mess tent. Pots and pans hung from rope laced between tent poles, and bowls were stacked up knee high like Russian nesting dolls. How did María manage to make delicious food in such a rudimentary setting? Her kitchen was nothing more than a barbecue grill set out behind the tent and two makeshift, wooden worktables inside. There was no running water, only gallon jugs and a couple of buckets.

Not that the rest of the site was any more sophisticated. This time around they were basically camping in the rough. The two pit toilets and three solar camp showers were one step above what Quint had experienced during that backpacking trip along the Continental Divide he'd taken in his mid-twenties.

María's cooking, however, raised the bar when compared to the freeze-dried cardboard he'd eaten every night on that hiking trip. Quint stabbed the last bite of *panucho* on his plate and stuck it in his mouth, savoring the complex spices in the sauce. He washed the last forkful of food down with another swallow of beer.

Earlier, after Angélica had left to deal with the snake, her father had stopped by the tent, taking Quint on a tour of the grounds. Juan's lightweight walking cast and cane slowed them down, but Quint enjoyed the more leisurely pace while trying to adjust to the heat and humidity.

While sharing the known history of the site, Juan added details on what work needed to be accomplished over the next few weeks. By the time he finished and put Quint to work helping to clear the entryway into a temple named after a monkey, Quint understood why Angélica had been willing to pay him from her own reserves to stay and help. There was too much work for too few people.

According to Juan, this new INAH crew had several well-intentioned helpers, but training and monitoring their progress was slowing down the workflow. If Angélica could have had five more of her own experienced crew instead of the newbies, meeting her objectives wouldn't have been insurmountable. But the extra time it took to guide the INAH crew had Angélica working late into the night. Juan's brow had been pinched as he told Quint how many times he'd awoken in the morning and found his daughter sleeping with her pencil in hand and her notebook acting as a pillow.

Quint didn't ask Juan about Marianne's history at the site or why Angélica chose to revisit the place of her mother's death. The timing didn't feel right, nor did Quint want to add to the worry lines on Juan's face.

Instead, he told Juan about the two polar bear cubs in Greenland that had stolen his expensive tripod and bent it all to hell before they'd finished playing with it and dumped it into the icy Atlantic. Juan's laughter smoothed out those lines and lightened his mood for the rest of the afternoon. Keeping Juan talking about his plans for shoring up the site's two main temples made the afternoon fly by as they dripped sweat and swatted away flies and mosquitoes.

Now here Quint sat, still sweating and itching. He needed a shower and then his cot. A yawn escaped before he could stifle it, drawing Juan's gaze from across the table.

"What do you think, sleeping beauty?" Juan asked, his eyebrows raised in question.

"What do I think about what?" Quint's brain was already starting to count sheep, his body more than ready to follow it into dreamland. "This steamy version of Mexico's paradise or that huge rat that chased us out of the monkey temple earlier?"

"Suck it up, Parker," Angélica said, a grin rounding her cheeks. "It's your first day here. You can't start complaining about how miserable you are until tomorrow."

"What do you think about the screech owl?" Juan clarified. "Was it flying into the helicopter an omen like Pedro and I suspect, or was it a ..." he looked at his daughter. "What did you call it?"

"A fluke." She tossed her wadded-up napkin at her dad. "You and Wonder Boy there need to get a grip on your superstitions."

Pedro pointed his beer at Quint. "He's the wanderer, not me."

"Wonder," she corrected. "Not wander."

"Wonder Boy is a video game hero," Quint explained. "Sort of like Superman."

"That owl made a bad decision," Angélica told her father. "It chose to flee in the wrong direction when the helicopter scared it out of its tree." Under the table, Angélica's hand moved to Quint's thigh, squeezing it. "That's all there is to it."

Glancing down at her hand, he wondered what she was up to. He stared at her profile as she continued to argue with her father on the subject of Maya curses, admiring her smooth forehead, strong cheekbones, and upturned nose dotted with tiny freckles. Throughout supper, she had kept several inches of space between them, only brushing his arm by accident once or twice. What was with this sudden change? Was it her attempt to sway him to her court? If so, he was going to require more bribery in the form of nakedness or kisses. Preferably both at the same time.

For now, Quint opted to straddle the fence. "I need more sleep before I can answer that," he told Juan. Downing the last of his beer, he grabbed his plate and stood. "I'll see you in the morning, gentlemen." He nodded good-bye to the three men. To Juan, he added, "I hope you're easier to share a tent with than Rover was."

Juan grinned. "I've been told I snore less than that pig."

"Javelina," Angélica corrected her father with a mock glare. "And I believe I told you that while you do snore less, your snoring is twice as loud as Rover's."

"Where is your javelina?" Quint asked. Last he'd heard, Teodoro and María were taking care of him.

"He's staying with María's sister until we decide if it's safe to bring him here."

"I told you, *gatita*, there's no room at the inn. It's either me or your pig at this site."

"Don't tempt me, Dad. Rover eats less than you most days."

That earned laughter all around.

Quint strolled over and dropped his dirty dishes in a bucket filled with soapy water. On his way out of the mess tent, he flagged Angélica, gaining her attention. "I'd like a minute of your time after I shower, Dr. García."

"Only a minute?" Pedro guffawed. "You must have *really* missed her if that's all it's going to take." Pedro's bark of laughter at his own joke ended with howls of pain as Angélica leaned across the table and doled out physical punishment for his comment.

Without waiting for Angélica to wrap up her beating, Quint left the tent. First a shower to wash off the travel dust and sweat and then sleep. Somewhere in between, he wanted to ask Angélica a question.

Back at the tent, he grabbed a fresh T-shirt and boxer briefs, along with the towel Juan had brought him before supper. The walk to the showers was filled with glowing eyeballs and loud hoots and howls from the surrounding jungle. Lucky for him, he was too damned tired to care.

According to Juan, each crew member was allotted a gallon of water each day for a shower. With the sweltering heat still warming the night air, a rinse-soap-rinse shower was no problem, especially since Quint's hair was so short.

As he rinsed and then soaped, he thought about his rotten track record when it came to keeping a woman in his life for longer than a couple of weeks. Being a photojournalist was harder on relationships than if he'd chosen to be a long-haul trucker. At least truckers could call home each night. Disappearing for weeks at a time grew old fast for most women, and after a time or two of his coming and going, the relationship soured. Love 'em and leave 'em had been his motto for years, but not due to a desire to remain single. Mostly, it was because when it came to choosing a woman or the career he'd worked so hard to build, the job won.

He'd thought things might be different this time, though. Angélica was much stronger emotionally than anyone else he'd been involved with over the last two decades. She didn't *need* a man in her life, a fact he'd figured would mean she had an independent spirit that his absences wouldn't buckle. What he hadn't planned on was that strong independence convincing her to write him off so damned quickly.

He'd expected her to be pissed, but her attempt to cast him aside in her boss-style way without even letting him try to plead his case had lit a fire in his gut, making him determined to dig in his heels and hold on tighter.

Her revelation about her trust issues had been an eye-opener. While she'd said it was her she didn't trust, not him, he'd seen the wariness in her gaze after she'd kissed him. She wasn't broken, like she'd said, but he hadn't been kidding when he'd told her that she was scratched and dented. Her ex had really pulled the wool over her eyes for years, and now Quint was going to pay the price for the shithead's deceptions if he wanted this relationship between them to grow beyond sharing laughs and rolls in the sand.

And he did.

Being away from her for weeks had burned into him how much he wanted to try to make this relationship work. One way or another, before he had to leave again, he was going to convince her that she needed to keep trying, too. But it was going to take time, hard work, and a lot of sweat and frustration—like toiling away at this damned dig site she'd chosen as their home for the next however many weeks.

Quint brushed his teeth before collecting his dirty clothes and leaving the camp shower. He'd have to shave tomorrow morning in the daylight.

Angélica was waiting for him inside the tent when he returned. Her eyes widened as he shed his pants and T-shirt in front of her without pause.

"Quint," she whispered, glancing toward the closed mesh flap. "Dad is going to be here soon."

"Trust me, sweetheart. I don't have anything he hasn't seen before, and I'll be damned if I'm going to wear more than skivvies in this sauna." He stretched, pressing his hands into his lower back, trying to ease a kink he'd acquired while moving rocks earlier with Juan. The tents from INAH were short, with his head nearly brushing the top when he stood up straight, but they made up for their height deficiency with the amount of horizontal space. A third cot was an easy fit opposite the door flap, yet still allowed room for the three of them to move around without stepping on each other's toes.

He clasped his hands together behind his back, shoving out his chest as he loosened his shoulders. He had a feeling sleeping on a cot wasn't going to help relax his muscles, but he was tired enough not to give a rat's ass tonight. He doubted he'd even need earplugs. He unclasped his hands, letting them hang at his side, and rolled his shoulders.

A glance in Angélica's direction made him chuckle. He had a rapt audience.

"Angélica," he said, waving one hand in front of her gaze. When she blinked out of her trance, he smiled. "You're staring."

Her cheeks turned pink. "I wasn't st-staring, I was just … uh … thinking about something I saw today."

"That's funny," he said as he stretched his neck from side to side. "I was just thinking about something I'd like to see tonight. How about you strip down and stretch with me? I hear yoga has a couple of poses that offer remarkable relaxation benefits."

Her lips pursed. "You're all bare chest and charm tonight, Parker."

"You betcha, boss lady. Why don't you come over here and I'll give you a hands-on tour of my chest while I woo you into my cot with my lucky charm."

A smile lit up her face. She shook her head. "That's asking for trouble. It's safer over here."

"Safer, but less fun."

He lowered himself onto the cot, lying back on a soft pillow that had magically appeared while he showered. He turned his head and sniffed the fabric, breathing in Angélica's sweet scent mixed with a hint of coconut sunscreen lotion.

She crossed her arms. "What's your question?"

"Do I at least get a kiss good night?"

"Nobody else does at this site."

"Yeah, but nobody else has seen you naked." He let his eyes travel south over her T-shirt and khakis, remembering every inch of her smooth, soft flesh.

"My father did when I was a baby."

"Naked baby butts don't count." He summoned her with his index finger. "Come here before your dad joins the party."

After zipping the tent's canvas flap closed, she obliged, kneeling next to his cot. "I'll kiss you, Parker, but don't be taking liberties."

"Why not?"

"Because I'm already fighting the urge to strip down and climb on top of you."

He stroked her cheek. "We could hang a 'Closed' sign on the tent flap."

Her fingernails scratched over his bare chest. "These canvas walls don't block sound."

"Maybe not, but the ruckus going on out there in the jungle will." He tugged the neckline of her shirt down, peeking inside. "No pink bra tonight?"

"I gave it to Rover."

"That javelina won't appreciate it as much as I would." He pulled her closer by her neckline until she was leaning over him. "I missed you like crazy, Angélica. I pined for you every night."

"Pined?" She chuckled, low and sexy. "You're such a writer."

"I could fill a book with limericks about your beauty."

This time, she laughed outright. "Wooing me with limericks? I'd drink to that."

. Her eyes lowered to his mouth and she sobered. "Good night, Quint," she whispered and brushed her lips over his, making his blood pressure rise. He slid his palms along her cheeks and pulled her closer, exploring her mouth slowly, teasing her tongue into tangling with his. When she sat back on her heels, his lips still tingled.

"There. Is that better?" she asked, her gaze steaming up the tent even more.

"I think it's worse." He glanced at where her fingers were inching over his briefs. "Much worse." He reached down and caught her hand before she started something he wouldn't be able to stop.

"Spoilsport," she teased, lifting his hand to her lips. "Ask me your real question." She kissed his knuckles.

He was too distracted by her glistening lips to mess around with searching for the safest route to his point and got right to it. "Why did you choose to return to the site where your mother was killed?"

Chapter Four

***Chakmo'ol*: Jaguar.**
The jaguar played a key religious role in Maya life. They were
considered shamanic creatures. Humans often changed
themselves into jaguars during religious rituals.

Angélica stared at Quint. His question seemed to have knocked her brain off the rails. She'd expected him to ask about the possibility of having sex somewhere soon, or what she had planned for tomorrow's workload, maybe even the state of her father's health, but not something to do with her mother.

Before she could come up with a reply, Juan made a point of clearing his throat on the other side of the tent flap.

She froze.

"Is everyone decent?" her father asked loud enough for the whole damned camp to hear.

Growling in her throat at his lack of discretion, she handed Quint the pants he'd taken off upon entering their tent. "Yes, Dad."

She motioned for Quint to hide the results of their fooling around and returned to her side of the tent. There was nothing she could do about her warm cheeks, which her father would undoubtedly notice, dang it. As Juan stepped inside with his cast leading the way, she busied herself shaking out and folding the clothes piled next to her cot.

Out of the corner of her eye, she saw her father look from Quint, who was stretched out on his cot with his pants draped over his nether regions, to her.

"What are you doing, *gatita*?" Juan asked, his voice edged with amusement.

She glanced his way. "What's it look like I'm doing?" She placed the shirt she'd folded onto the stack with the others.

"Normally, I'd say folding clothes, but I'm talking to little Miss Pigpen."

"We have company," she explained. "I'm cleaning up."

Juan turned to Quint. "Now you're official company? It appears you've made it out of the doghouse."

Quint crossed his arms behind his head. "I'm on the rise."

"That's obvious."

"Dad!" Angélica gasped, her cheeks burned even hotter.

He grinned. "If you two need some extra time alone to work out the last of your differences, I could head over to the showers for another rinse."

Her gaze narrowed to a squint. "You already showered tonight," she reminded him.

Her father was part of the pre-supper shower crew. Breaking into pre- and post-supper groups allowed Teodoro the time needed to refill the showers' water bladders.

"I can go pester Pedro and Fernando in their tent for an hour."

"I'm going to need more than an hour with her, Juan," Quint said. "You know how hard it is to get her mind off work while she's on a dig."

Juan stroked his chin. "If memory serves, son, you were pretty adept at distracting her from work last time."

Spitting and sputtering, Angélica whipped her pillow at Quint for laughing and encouraging her father. Grabbing her towel and clean clothes, she grumbled all the way to the showers about her dad's lack of a filter.

By the time she returned to the tent, much calmer after a warm rinsing, both her father and Quint were asleep in their cots, saving her from another round of pink cheeks.

She sat on her cot and stared at Quint. His bare chest rose and fell rhythmically, his cheeks dark with beard stubble. Having him back in her tent felt right, damn it. She sighed. Why couldn't she be drawn to someone who stayed in the same country for more than a month at a time? Someone who didn't hate the humidity and life in the Mexican jungle?

Running her fingers through her damp hair, she reined in her emotions. It was time to think about something less troubling. She pulled her makeshift desk/crate closer. Opening her mother's notebook next to her own, she dug in, studying her mom's scrawls yet again while adding scribbles into her own book.

An hour later, her father rolled onto his back and started sawing logs. His favorite red "sleeping" socks stuck out the end of the thin sheet he liked to use in spite of the heat. She grabbed the earplugs she kept handy next to her bed and squeezed them into her ears. A glance in Quint's direction found him still sleeping away. He must be really exhausted from traveling yesterday if her dad's snores weren't waking him.

Why did you choose to return to the site where your mother was killed? His question replayed in her head.

Who had told him this was the site where her mom had crashed? Her father? Fernando? Pedro? They were the only three who knew. Wait, Teodoro and María knew, but neither of those two were the type to gossip. She'd kept her secret from Esteban and Lorenzo, along with the INAH crew. It was nobody's business but her father's and hers. Well, Pedro's too, since he'd claimed Marianne as his second mother.

She frowned across at Quint. It certainly wasn't *his* business. Nor was it his place to question her choices of dig sites. She didn't demand a say in where he flew off to next.

A voice of reason spoke up in her head, reminding her that being in a relationship with someone meant openness and honesty. If she was going to allow Quint to stay in her life, she needed to let him know her thoughts behind her decisions and more.

She rubbed her hands over her face. But allowing him a visa into her world meant risking so much on a man she barely knew. She'd spent years getting to know her ex-husband before taking her vows, and look how that risk had panned out for her in the end—disastrous, to say the least.

Turning her attention back to her work, she shook the tension out of her hands and held pencil to paper.

Instead of summarizing her thoughts on the block of glyphs Esteban had charted that were carved into the ballcourt's end wall, a memory of her mom a few weeks before she'd died replayed like an old flickering film ...

... *"Pik,* come here, please," Marianne called out as Angélica walked past her office doorway.

Pik? Angélica smiled. Her mother hadn't called her the Mayan word for "bedbug" in years. It warmed her heart in a way much needed after the beatings it had taken over the last six months.

According to her father, *pik* came from *"peek*-a-boo," which was where her mother had gotten the idea for Angélica's nickname. However, Marianne claimed her husband's memory was as holey as his favorite boxer shorts, explaining that she called Angélica "bedbug" because when she was a little girl she would crawl into her parents' bed in the middle of the night and wiggle-wiggle-wiggle until dawn.

Backing up, Angélica stepped into her mom's home office. The scarred wooden floor in the old ranch house they'd renovated creaked as she crossed to where her mom sat staring at several papers strewn across her desk. With her silver-streaked auburn hair piled on top of her head in a thick bun and horn-rimmed reading glasses balanced on the end of her nose, she looked more like a librarian than the adventurous archaeologist that she was.

Angélica had been spending the weekend with her parents at their Tucson ranch, enjoying the scenery, taking a break from her search for a job. As soon as her divorce was final, she'd handed in her resignation at the university where her ex-husband and parents taught.

"I'm thinking about Mexico," she told her mom, perching on the corner of her desk. Angélica had recently received a reply to an application she'd sent to INAH for an assistant archaeologist–historian position they had open in their Mexico City office. The powers that be there were interested in meeting her in person.

"So am I."

"Yeah, but I'm talking about the living inhabitants, not the dead."

"The living are not as much fun. They're too easy to figure out." Marianne looked at Angélica with a smile that made her green eyes sparkle. "For example, why does your father wear socks to bed even when we're in the hot, humid Mexican jungle?"

"I always figured it's because his feet get cold."

Marianne shook her head. "He thinks it will deter any

wandering scorpions."

"You're kidding."

"I'm not. When he was young, he and your uncle Guillermo woke up to find several scorpions in their bed. One stung him on his bare toe and another got him on the heel before he could escape. Uncle Guillermo was wearing socks."

"Let me guess. He didn't get stung."

"Bingo. Ever since then, your father wears socks to bed. Always. He believes it's bad luck to go to sleep barefoot." She stood and went around to the front of her desk. "So you see what I mean when I say the living are easy to figure out. The dead, on the other hand, leave only a few clues. They like to keep you guessing."

"I know what I'm getting Dad for Christmas this year."

Marianne chuckled and leaned back against the desk next to Angélica. She picked up one of the papers on her desktop and handed it to Angélica, pointing at it. "What do you make of those glyphs?"

Angélica looked at the black and white photo on the paper. Centered in the picture was a stela with several glyph blocks on it. "Where did you get this?"

"An old friend of mine has a crew down in Mexico working on a site near Calakmul."

"Calakmul? Isn't that the big biosphere reserve down south?"

Her mother nodded. "It's an extremely remote site with all kinds of wildlife running around day and night, including jaguars."

Angélica smiled. "Your favorite big cat. You'll have to take that fancy new camera lens you bought to capture wildlife."

"They're such gorgeous creatures with those black rosettes. A sleek mix of flowers and beast."

"I know, Mom." She pointed at one of the three jaguar paintings that had been hanging on her mom's office walls since Angélica was a kid.

Marianne looked at the painting. "And the way their eyes light up like gold disks at night makes my heart race."

"Yes, the eyes certainly did make my heart race that night we came across one down by the *cenote*."

"Not to mention they roar and grunt like your father."

"That's bordering on too much information, Mother."

Marianne chuckled. "Anyway, the archaeologist has to have everything flown in, including the crew. He sent me this picture a couple of days ago, asking me to help decipher it."

"It's hard to see the details."

"It's even worse in color. I changed it to grayscale, which helped a little."

"You tried enlarging it?"

"Yes. The image's resolution is very low."

Angélica turned the paper sideways, and then upright again. "Without better resolution, I can't even guess. Glyphs are tricky to read in person, let alone from a fuzzy copy."

"I think I need to go down there and see it in person."

"With Dad?"

"No. He has several lectures scheduled over the next few weeks." She picked up a gold locket she always kept hanging from a framed portrait of Angélica and herself, popping open the latch and smiling down at the picture of Angélica. "Do you want to join me? I'd love to have your help with this, *pik*. We haven't had a chance to spend time together for a long time."

It was tempting. A trip with her mother to decipher glyphs would be a wonderful distraction from the mess she'd made of her life. Spending weeks on end with her parents on dig sites had filled her childhood with heartwarming memories. She'd love the opportunity to spend hours by her mom's side in Maya tombs again, soaking up her theories about the past. Then she remembered the phone call she'd received earlier.

"I don't think I can. I have an interview at UC San Diego lined up next week, and INAH is talking about flying me down a couple of days after that. I probably need to stay close to civilization in case either offers me a position."

"I understand." Marianne's smile dimmed. She closed the locket and hung it back on the picture frame. "Maybe next time."

"Definitely." Angélica bumped shoulders with her mom. "A girls-only trip."

They both focused on the image again, studying it. Angélica held it up, squinting. "There's something different about these glyphs, Mom. Look how big the eyes are on this one."

"That's what I was thinking. Notice the style of this one here." Marianne pointed at one in the upper right corner. "It's not typical for the Classic Maya period."

"Is that when the site was last occupied?"

"I believe so." Marianne rubbed her jaw. "You think it could be from the Post-Classic period? Maybe influenced by a visitor from the north?"

"Aztecs?"

She shrugged. "Or Toltecs."

"Or maybe," Angélica suggested, "it's from a much earlier civilization, like from the Formative Maya time frame."

Marianne took the paper, peering closer. "Hmm, maybe."

"I'd need to see it for myself and touch it. You know how shadows can play tricks with your eyes, especially in photos. Rice paper and charcoal work a lot better for me."

"You always were more tactile. Even as a kid, you had to run your fingers over the surface of glyphs." Her mom leaned over and dropped a kiss on her temple, and then returned to her chair. "Tomorrow, I'm going to book a ticket to Cancun and see if Pedro has time to fly me over to the dig site."

Angélica frowned. "I don't think he's available. I talked to him last night on the phone about meeting me in Mexico City if INAH has me down for an interview, but he said he couldn't. Some rich German CEO and his family hired him and his helicopter for the next two weeks."

"That's too bad. I haven't seen Pedro in a while. I was looking forward to catching up on how his mother and sisters are doing." She leaned back in her chair. "Oh well, I'll contact my old friend then and see who he's been using for transportation to and from the site."

"How long do you think you'll stay down there?"

"A week should be long enough."

"Who's going to take care of Dad while you're gone?"

Marianne grinned. "Why do you think I had a brilliant, loving daughter like you?"

"To make sure Dad wears his socks to bed every night?"

The soft sound of her mother's laughter filled the room. "Listen, if you have these interviews, don't worry. Your father will be just fine on his own. Underneath that big soft teddy bear exterior is a core of solid steel." Marianne sobered. "Trust me, *pik*, he makes one hell of a leaning post."

Angélica could still hear the sound of her mom's laughter, still smell her soft, comforting scent. Her mom was right. Her dad had held her up for years after Marianne's death.

She took a deep breath and blinked away a rush of tears, focusing on some of the last notes her mother had written about the missing stela. Even after visiting the site and seeing the stela in person, Marianne had struggled to decipher several of the glyphs, noting the odd shapes in the carvings that she wrote would require more research back home in Arizona.

But she never made it home, damn it.

And her notes were too few for Angélica to figure out the meanings without that stela. She needed to find it, run her fingers over it, figure out the meaning, and put this mystery to bed. The push to deliver the answers her mother failed to find drove her forward, fueling her to hack away at the jungle with her machete until she'd searched every last nook and cranny at this dig site.

A pair of pants flew across her field of vision. She gasped, pulling out her earplugs.

"Boss lady?" a sleepy voice whispered in between her father's snores.

"What are you doing awake, Parker? Do you need something?" She reached for her canteen of water in case he was thirsty.

"That's a loaded question." He yawned. "How late is it?"

A glance at her watch made her blink in surprise. "Almost midnight." She'd gotten lost in the past.

"You need to get some sleep."

"I need to find answers," she countered.

"You're not going to be sharp enough to figure them out if you don't get some sleep."

Her father snore-coughed, making them both look his way. He rolled onto his side, his back toward them, and resumed his chainsawing, only more muffled.

"Why does your father wear socks to bed when it's like one hundred and ten degrees in here?"

"They're magic socks. They keep the scorpions away."

"No shit." Quint yawned again. "Shut your light off, sweetheart, and close your eyes."

"Are you going to tell me a bedtime story?"

"Sure, if you let me be the boss for once and do as I say."

Why not? Her eyelids were growing heavy. She killed the lamplight, fluffed her pillow, and lay back. She'd given her extra one to Quint. The T-shirt she'd found wadded up at the head of his cot that he'd obviously planned to use would have left him with a sore neck.

"Did anyone check you for ticks tonight?" she asked in the darkness.

"Your father did."

"Good." She snuggled into her pillow, a smile on her lips. Quint was there with her. He'd help her find the stela. He might argue with her about it at first, but he'd understand why she had to come to this site once she told him about her mom's notes. "Tell me that story, Parker."

His cot creaked. "Once upon a time, there was a beautiful, auburn-haired maiden who liked to drink Mexican beer on a beach in the moonlight."

She knew this story already. "Alone?"

"Yes, until she met an amazingly strong, virile, incredibly smart and handsome hero and realized she couldn't live without him."

"That's a lot of adjectives for one hero."

"I'm just getting started." He yawned again. "Wait until I get to the part about how impressive his pectoral and abdominal muscles are. We're talking Incredible Hulk, minus the excess chlorophyll, with six-pack abs stacked on top of a twelve-pack. You'll be drooling all over your pillow before I'm done."

She giggled. "Go to sleep, Quint. You've tempted me enough for one day."

"Your wish is my command, boss lady." Silence followed from his side of the tent.

A short time later, Angélica sank into dreamland where her mother waited for her. Unfortunately, the helicopter crashed there, too, leaving her alone once again.

* * *

Quint awoke sweating in an empty tent. With a groan he sat up and looked around. Juan's cot had a folded sheet placed neatly on top of his pillow, the magic scorpion-repelling socks laid out on the footlocker at the end. Angélica's cot was buried under a pile of clothes, papers, and a couple of empty canteens. It was like camping with the Odd Couple.

He stood and stretched, then walked over to the stack of three books on the crate Angélica had been using as a desk last night. The top two were about deciphering Maya glyphs, while the one on the bottom was a dog-eared reference guide to Mesoamerican gods.

She hadn't answered his question last night about her mother. Was she in the same frame of mind as Pedro, suspecting Marianne had been murdered? If so, was she here to figure out why? Or was there something else going on that Pedro didn't know? Was something compelling Angélica to drag her crew out to this remote site in Mexico to scour the jungle?

He heard the sound of muffled voices passing by outside and checked his watch. Breakfast should be in full swing and he still needed to shave. His stomach growled at the fond memory of María's breakfast burritos. Pulling on his pants and a shirt, he grabbed his shaving kit and headed for the showers.

Fifteen minutes later, Quint pushed aside the mosquito netting and stepped into the mess tent. The smell of barbecued meat and fresh coffee was thick in the warm air. His stomach growled, his mouth starting to water at the sight of María moving about behind one of the worktables.

He glanced around the tent. There were a lot of bodies in too small a space, several of whom he didn't recognize. A fair-skinned light blonde with blue streaks in her hair sat next to a raven-haired girl who looked like she might be of Asian descent. Across from them, Esteban and Lorenzo sat on each side of a guy with wire-rimmed glasses, sunburned shoulders, and a shock of brown hair sticking up like shark fins. The three strangers must be part of the new crew INAH brought in. The new guy definitely had a Woody Allen, writerly look going with his pale skin, glasses, and delicate features.

Sweat rolled down Quint's temple. He pulled at the neckline of his shirt, resisting the urge to step outside and come back later when there were fewer bodies adding to the heat. This was his life for now. He needed to suck it up and get used to the high temperatures, close quarters, and voracious bugs and beasts.

A quick inspection of the other table found Angélica absent. Her father was there, though, nursing a cup of coffee. Quint dished up a burrito, wishing María a good morning in Mayan. He'd been practicing the basics of the language while in Greenland. Her face lit up in response and she rattled off something that left him scratching his head. He nodded with a polite smile and carried his burrito across the room, taking the seat opposite Juan.

"So, is that true?" Juan asked as Quint picked up the burrito, trying to decide where to bite first.

"Is what true?" He sank his teeth into the thick, handmade tortilla, groaning in appreciation. Damn, he'd missed María.

"What María asked. You nodded, so I'm assuming it's true."

He swallowed the food in his mouth. "I couldn't understand her. What did she say?" He tore another piece off the burrito, his taste buds on cloud nine.

"She asked if you were going to make a baby today."

Quint swallowed wrong, coughing.

Someone pounded him on the back.

"¿Estás bien, Señor Parker?" Esteban asked, sitting down beside Quint.

After a couple more coughs, Quint nodded. He took a drink of warm coffee, tasting a hint of rich Maya chocolate in it. He'd missed María's coffee, too.

Setting the mug back down, he pointed at Juan, whose brown eyes gleamed. "You did that on purpose."

"Not me." The old man hid behind his coffee cup. "I could swear that was what I heard her ask."

"¿Quién?" Esteban asked. "Who?" he repeated in English.

"María," Quint said.

"She ask if you was going to work hard today." Esteban's broken English was improving. He must be practicing, too.

Juan raised his hands when Quint nailed him with a glare. "My mistake. My old ears don't hear so well anymore."

"That's hogwash."

"May I join you?" an unfamiliar voice said from behind Quint.

"Of course, Maverick. Have a seat."

Maverick the writer? Quint tried not to stare at the black-haired stranger settling onto the bench next to Juan, doing his best to keep his curiosity hidden. He'd been wrong about the kid at the other table. Maverick the writer looked to be around Quint's age and not even remotely similar to Woody Allen.

"Quint," Juan said, "have you met our resident fiction author?"

"No." But he hoped to have a chance to grill him at some point in the near future. Breakfast probably wasn't the place for that conversation, though. Wiping his fingers on a napkin, Quint offered his hand to shake. "Quint Parker. Nice to meet you."

"Maverick Winters," said the other man, giving Quint's hand a firm shake before digging into his own burrito.

Maverick's palm was well calloused. His shoulders were wide, crowding Juan's when he settled back into his seat. He looked more like a western or action-adventure writer than horror, someone who had crawled down from one of those old Marlboro cigarettes billboards. What had Pedro said the guy did back in Nevada besides writing? Ranching? Stringing barbed-wire fence? Sledgehammering railroad spikes? Bench-pressing stray steers?

"So, you're a writer," Quint said, broaching the subject.

Maverick nodded and then took another bite of burrito.

"Fiction only?"

Juan's brow wrinkled as he stared at Quint over his coffee cup.

After swallowing, Maverick nodded again. "I prefer the land of fiction."

"Why's that?"

"Reality usually sucks."

"Quint!" Pedro called from the doorway. When Quint looked around, Pedro waved him over and then stepped back outside.

"Be right back," he said, rising from the bench.

"I'll keep the flies off your breakfast," Esteban offered, pulling Quint's plate closer to his own.

"The flies are part of the garnish," Juan said. "Besides, Quint needs the added protein to give him strength for all I have in store for him today."

Hell's bells! Angélica's father was going to be the death of him. "No flies, Esteban. My protein levels are fine as they are for Dr. García's diabolical plans." Quint walked away, chased by Juan's evil-sounding laughter.

Outside, the sunshine baked the top of his head. Pedro held his cell phone out.

Quint reached for the phone, asking, "Is the President on the line?"

Pedro laughed. "I turned on my phone to send a quick message to *mi madre* and there was an email waiting for me."

"You have cell service here?" He hadn't noticed any cell towers on their flight to the site, but then again he'd been a little distracted after takeoff.

"It's a satellite phone. I fly to some very remote places." He pointed toward the center of the plaza. "If I stand over there, I can usually get a decent signal in the morning."

Quint looked down at the phone's screen and tried to read the words. He frowned and handed it back. "My Spanish isn't that fluent yet. What's it say?"

Pedro translated for him. " 'It was no accident. The pitch control rod break was smooth. It appeared to have been cut. I told my supervisor it was sabotaged, but for some reason my findings were never mentioned in the official report.' "

"Is that from your friend?"

"Yes. I'd written to him yesterday while waiting for your plane to land. He must have emailed back after I'd finished charging the phone and shut it off for the night."

A generator had been one of the higher-end commodities INAH had granted Angélica, which Pedro had flown in with some of their other supplies. According to Juan, they fired it up each evening for a couple of hours to light the mess tent for supper and charge batteries—cell phones, laptops, and whatever else was needed.

"Is everything okay?" Juan's voice from behind Quint made him cringe. He didn't want Juan to know about the message, but they were too late to hide the phone. Juan didn't miss much. Behind those mirth-filled eyes of his was a sharp and crafty brain. He'd been too observant for Quint's own good at the last dig site.

"Sure," Quint answered, turning to face Angélica's dad with an easy grin. When Juan lowered his gaze to the cell phone in Pedro's hand, Quint added, "We were just checking our email on Pedro's satellite phone." That was no lie, they were looking at an email.

Juan didn't look convinced. "Did you receive any news on your next job?"

"No, just the usual spam. You're stuck with me for a while."

"Excellent. I need your help, and my daughter could use the diversion. She's obsessed again. Finding that stela is all she's thought about until you arrived."

"And pissed her off," Quint finished.

"Better you than me," Pedro said. "Last time she got mad at me she tore me a new leg."

"Not to mention what she did to his hind end," Juan added, his eyes gleaming again. He patted Quint on the shoulder. "Go finish your breakfast. We have a lot of work to do yet clearing that cave-in and it's only going to get hotter. I came up with an idea this morning of how we can shore up that inner chamber enough for one other crew member to work inside with us, making the job go faster."

"You think that's safe?" Yesterday, the whole entrance looked wobbly, the stones seemingly ready to cave in at any moment.

Juan scrunched up one side of his face. "*Safe* is a word I like to use loosely."

"I remember."

"I'm not going in there with you," Pedro told Juan, his phone safely tucked away.

"I didn't ask you to, you big baby." Juan softened his insult with a wink. "That's why I'm taking Quint. He whimpers less."

"I do?"

Juan held up his index finger and thumb close together. "A pinch or so when we're in the tight spots." He turned back to Pedro. "Angélica needs you to help Gertrude and Jane this morning with excavating Mound D. She said your expertise with the shovel cannot be matched by mere mortals."

Pedro puffed out his chest. "She's right. I am incredible."

Quint chuckled. "Where is the boss lady this morning?" he asked Juan.

"She and Teodoro are over at the *Chakmo'ol* Temple trying to figure out why there are so many snakes giving us problems at that end of the site."

"What kind of snakes?"

"Rattlers." Juan shuddered. "My least favorite."

"I have no favorites," Pedro said. "I hate them all."

Quint could handle a snake if necessary, but venom-filled fangs tended to make his shoes want to burn rubber in the opposite direction.

"That's why she didn't ask you to go with her, buttercup," Juan told Pedro.

Quint wondered why she hadn't asked him to go along at least to carry her machete. Two-finger saluting the two men, he returned to the mess tent. Not wasting time with more questions, he gulped down his coffee and grabbed the last half of his burrito to take with him, saying his good-byes to Esteban and Maverick. He met Juan at their tent and followed him over to the temple they'd worked at yesterday.

"Another day of backbreaking labor in stifling heat and humidity," he said, eyeing the rubble-filled entrance. "Come to paradise, the guidebook said. Play in the sunshine. Explore the ruins."

Juan handed him a pry bar and a pair of leather gloves. "On the bright side, there don't seem to be as many ticks around this temple. Over by the *Chakmo'ol* Temple, it's like a buffet of vermin. Angélica is working almost as hard at keeping the pests away as she is at cleaning up the temple."

"What does *chakmo'ol* mean?"

"Jaguar."

"Why do you call it the Jaguar Temple?"

"That was the name given by the previous archaeologist. There are several glyphs and carvings of various jaguar gods along the outside, which I'm guessing contributed to its name." Juan pointed at the wheelbarrow they'd left next to the temple. "Will you grab that?"

Quint wheeled it over.

"They should have named it the Snake Temple," Juan continued.

"It's that bad, huh?"

"I haven't seen so many rattlesnakes in one area at a dig site before. It makes me wonder."

"Wonder what?"

Juan stepped inside the newly shored-up temple entrance and stared at the debris still blocking their path. "If someone has been feeding them."

"To what end?"

"I don't know." Juan frowned. "But one notion is to keep visitors away."

"It doesn't seem to be working with your daughter."

"For some reason that is totally unfathomable to me, my daughter has very little fear of snakes. When she was a child, she'd go out searching for snakes amongst the *cholla* and *ocotillo* cacti, coming back with pink cheeks and heart-stopping tales of how many she'd found. Her mother always encouraged Angélica to get comfortable with her environment. I just worried she'd get hurt."

Quint took a couple of sips of water from his canteen before sliding on gloves. "Is there anything Angélica is afraid of?"

Last month, he'd watched her leap blindly without a moment's hesitation into a *cenote* in the middle of the night to help one of her crew members.

"Besides failure?" Juan shrugged. "You seem to make her

nervous."

Yet a rattlesnake didn't cause her even a hiccup of heartburn. "That's because she's intimidated by my big brain," he joked.

"Undoubtedly." Juan tapped the pry bar with his cane and then pointed at the rocks blocking the inner chamber. "She gets that reckless courage from her mother. Marianne would charge into danger, her focus so bent on finding answers that she ignored warning signs."

"Like a curse?"

Juan's gaze narrowed. "Someone has loose lips along with a pilot's license."

"He's worried about your daughter."

"He's not alone."

Quint jammed the pry bar into the pile of rocks and wiggled it. The two rocks above it shifted slightly. "What happened to the archaeologist who was here before? The group that was working the site when Marianne visited?"

He wasn't sure what was out of bounds with Juan when it came to his wife, so he decided to start slow and off the mark.

"INAH decided that his work didn't show tangible progress, so they refused to renew his contract to work the site."

"So, then what? The site just sat here empty for years?"

Juan nodded. "One thing we've learned in this field of science over the last several decades is that with time, technology evolves and improves. Often it's better to let a site go fallow, if you will, for years rather than have an inexperienced or unqualified archaeologist come and damage the historical footprint left behind by a civilization." He looked at Quint with a raised brow. "Have you ever wondered how many of Egypt's treasures were destroyed by those who believed they were studying the past, when in actuality their more primitive methods of retrieval and rushed excitement to find mummies and museum trinkets actually did more harm than good for the history books?"

Quint had read about looters, but little about archaeologists inadvertently causing destruction. "No, but along those lines, I've read that LiDAR is being used these days, especially in heavily forested areas like down here. I imagine it's much less intrusive when it comes to excavating a site."

The article had been one of many Quint had read lately while trying to bone up on his knowledge about Angélica's career. LiDAR had always interested him. The use of light to measure characteristics of the Earth's surface from a set point above the ground could be used in many areas of science, which had given Quint ideas for articles to research and write.

"It's a wonderful tool," Juan confirmed, "helping us to uncover Maya roads and buildings, along with other features of civilization that we can't see from the ground or the sky, since the trees block visibility from up there." He took out his handkerchief and wiped his brow. "There was a site in Belize where it was used extensively."

"That was the one featured in the article." Quint debated on digging deeper with Juan. He decided to give it a try. "So, has Angélica mentioned why she chose this site?"

Juan stared at him, his gaze measuring. "Why don't you just come out with the real question you want to ask, son?"

"Am I that obvious?"

"Only to the trained eye."

"Okay." Here went nothing. "Is Angélica here because of her mother?"

"Yes."

That was easy. "Is she looking for some kind of closure?"

"No." Juan smirked. "She says she's looking for a stela listed in her mother's notes containing a block of glyphs with some kind of warning on them."

Juan's words jibed with what Pedro had told Quint on the flight to the site.

"However," Juan continued, "I think she's here looking for ghosts."

"Ghosts? You mean Marianne's ghost?"

"Yes, and those of the people who lived here, of course. Unfortunately, I have a gut feeling she's going to get more than she's bargaining for."

"What do you mean?" Was he referring to this new curse Pedro had talked about?

"I suspect this site has been purposely neglected."

"Why would you think that?"

"You see these marks here on the bridge stone that was at the apex of the entrance's corbel vault?"

Quint looked at the scarring on the flat rock where Juan was indicating. "Yeah?"

"These are relatively fresh, as in the last few years, I'd guess."

"How can you tell?"

"Lichens grow slowly. These scars are fresh, the lichen hasn't recoated the rock." He pulled out his tape measure and the notepad he used to keep track of his measurements as they worked. "Someone took a crowbar or a lever of some sort and removed the bridge stone that filled the final gap at the apex of the corbel vault. Without that stone, the effects of gravity made it easy to collapse each side of the entry's archway inward."

"Why would someone purposely cave in the entryway?" He had his own suspicions, but was curious to hear Juan's.

"My guess is to keep someone out or trap someone in."

Quint cringed. Getting trapped inside a temple was one of his worst claustrophobic nightmares. "Trap who?"

"Maybe it's not a *who*. Maybe it's a *what*." Juan shrugged. "I suspect we'll find out the answer soon enough."

Chapter Five

Tzabcan: A Mayan word that translates as rattle ("tzab") and snake ("can")—aka rattlesnake.

Snakes alive! Angélica wiped the sweat from her face. "What the hell did we stumble into, Teodoro?"

"A big problem," he replied in Mayan.

Since it was just the two of them, they kept bouncing back and forth between Teodoro's native tongue and Spanish, in which they were both fluent. Angélica's knowledge of Mayan had its limits.

"How many does that make?" she asked the shaman as he secured the top of the bag.

"Nine."

"*¡Dios mio!*" Nine damned snakes they'd caught and bagged, and the suckers kept coming out of the underbrush. Worse, they were almost out of burlap bags.

"They must have a den somewhere nearby," Teodoro said.

"I hope we don't fall into it."

She chopped away more of the laurel tree limbs blocking their path. Stepping carefully between the dwarf saw palmettos' fan palms, she tested for soft terrain that might mean an underground den.

Upon arriving at the *Chakmo'ol* Temple, they'd caught one rattlesnake on the western side, making its way up the crumbling stone steps that led all of the way to the top. Using her four-foot-long makeshift hook, Angélica had lifted the snake while Teodoro bagged it so fast it barely had time to rattle, let alone strike.

They had walked the southern perimeter of the temple, not even making it twenty feet when they'd heard more rattling. This time, Teodoro worked his magic with his hook, snagging and bagging with a finesse that comes only with many years of experience. Two snakes had turned into four, which then turned into nine. That was nine too many, considering the temple was still in sight through the trees.

Shit. This was a more serious situation than she'd anticipated. It was a wonder nobody had been bitten yet. She hadn't read anything in the previous archaeologist's notes about snakes. Maybe the rattlers had moved in after the last crew left.

As Angélica stood searching the jungle floor for a hole or some other sign of a burrow, she saw movement in the leaves next to her right boot. With a flock of Yucatán jays chatting loudly in the trees above, she couldn't hear the crackling of dry leaves as the snake slithered along in front of her. She kept frozen as the rattler paused with its forked tongue out, checking for danger. Then it started off again, gliding over the leaves and forest clutter toward the temple.

Before it could disappear among the undergrowth, she reached out with her hook and snagged it several inches below the head. Teodoro appeared from nowhere and slid their last bag over it, cinching it tight with hemp string.

"Make that ten," he said, his round Maya face lined with a frown.

She blew out a tense breath. That was close. Too damned close. "This is crazy, Teodoro."

"We'll have to get rid of the snakes and come back."

"Ten snakes? Where are you going to take them?"

He shrugged, pointing to the south. "Further away. Two kilometers should be good for now."

"You could use the wheelbarrow, maybe make it in one trip."

He nodded, scratching his neck. "I saw something a little ways over there you should see. You have time?"

"Of course." If Teodoro saw something worth mentioning, she definitely needed to see it. The shaman was not one to cry wolf.

He led the way, heading southwest. They passed one snake along the way, his rattle barely audible above the cacophony of howler monkey barking going on in the treetops above them. The jungle seemed extra loud today, or maybe it was because she was trying so hard to hear danger before it struck and bit.

Up ahead, Teodoro halted, waiting for her. When she joined him, he scraped away a thin deposit of decaying leaves and grass with his snake hook, uncovering a layer of stone still partially whitewashed with limestone stucco.

"A *sacbe*?" She squatted, pushing debris aside to find the edge. Sure enough, under a camouflage of jungle litter was an old Maya road. She stood, looking back toward the temple. She could see it now, the straight flat line, although the trees and underbrush had done a great job of camouflaging it.

"Of course," she said, wiping away more sweat. "That makes sense. This would have been the main road in from this direction."

"Do you hear that?" he asked.

"All I can hear are those big-mouthed monkeys." She searched in the opposite direction, seeing the underlying signs of the *sacbe* as it disappeared into the forest.

Where did the road go? Most of the old Maya roads were short, connecting groups of structures within ceremonial cities, like temples and ballcourts. However, a few roads were longer, stretching between cities. Some of them had been reused over the last century or two to transport raw chicle blocks for distribution worldwide.

Maybe there was another Maya site out there hidden by the jungle. She needed to check her map of the ancient civilization sites. Had she left that one back home?

"Dr. García," Teodoro whispered loudly from her left. He'd moved several feet away. When she looked his way, he waved her over, warning her to keep quiet.

She tiptoed closer to where he stood at the base of a large sapodilla tree next to a small mound. He pointed at a hole in the ground big enough for her to squeeze into, not that she planned to. She pulled out her flashlight and directed the beam into the darkness. Inside, the floor and walls were alive and slithering.

She cursed in Spanish. "There must be at least thirty rattlesnakes in there," she told Teodoro.

His grimace mirrored hers.

"This explains why we keep coming across snakes. They're practically following the road into the site." Bending again, she lit up the snake den. The writhing mass of snakes shifted. In the midst of their long, muscular bodies her light flickered past a gray stone resting near the back of the den.

Hold up! She moved the beam back to the stone. No, make that a stela, or at least a piece of one, judging from the jagged edges.

"There's something in there with them. I need to take a closer look."

"That is not a good idea," Teodoro enunciated in Spanish.

"I'll be careful."

He shook his head, but waved her forward with his hook.

She stepped closer, shining the light inside again. It took a moment for one of the snakes to slither his way over the stela. Finally, it was clear again. It rose at an angle from the dark earth like a crooked gravestone. She guessed it to be about two feet wide, but the length was difficult to estimate due to it being buried in the dirt.

"Do you see that?" she asked Teodoro, who flanked her.

"I see snakes," he said. "Too many for our good health."

"Look beyond the snakes. Do you see that piece of stone behind them?"

He leaned in, squinting. "What's on it?"

"Glyphs. I can't read them from this distance."

"Maybe they are not meant to be read." He searched the ground around them, hook at the ready.

"I need to read them, Teodoro."

He sighed. "Would you like me to ask the snake gods for permission to take a closer look?" he joked.

"Maybe I would," she shot back, rising. She stuffed her flashlight into her back pocket. A rattlesnake slithered closer.

Teodoro grabbed her by the elbow, pulling her back slowly as it veered toward the *sacbe*, disappearing under the palm fronds.

"Follow me," Teodoro said, leading her around the snake den, keeping a safe distance. They both watched for more of their slithering friends as they explored the surrounding area.

From the opposite viewpoint, she couldn't even see the slight mound, nor any evidence of the danger waiting directly ahead. It looked like a small mound covered with saw palm fronds and agave plants under a sapodilla tree.

"We need to mark that tree somehow so nobody else stumbles into that den," she told Teodoro.

He nodded. "Good idea."

"And then I need to figure out how I can get to that piece of stela."

Teodoro shook his head. "Bad idea."

She headed back toward the temple with him trailing, both keeping an eye out for more rattlers. "What do you have that might put those snakes to sleep for a bit?"

"You joke."

"Not really. I need to see the glyphs on that stela up close."

"It's too dangerous, Dr. García."

She shot him a frown over her shoulder. "And clearing snakes like we have been all morning is child's play?"

"One snake at a time is easy."

They reached the temple's perimeter clearing they'd carved out of the jungle over the last week. "You know we can't leave that den," she told him. "Someone is going to get bit before long, and then we'll have a bigger problem than a snake den."

"We have antivenin."

"Not enough for that many rattlesnakes."

He grunted. "If you go in, you will get bit."

"Not if you work your magic, shaman."

"Your father is not going to be happy."

"Can you think of another solution?"

"Yes, don't go in the snake den."

"You're a funny man."

They walked in silence across the plaza.

What did that piece of stela say? Where was the rest of it? Was it in the *Chakmo'ol* Temple? Was this part of the missing stela she'd come here to find? Had it been broken into pieces by looters and tossed aside? Or had it been purposely thrown in there for the snakes to shield?

She shivered in excitement. This could be something new. Something overlooked by the previous archaeologist. INAH would be happy to have some new information after all of the cleanup work she and her crew had been doing while trying to get the site back into the shape it had been in when her mother had visited.

"There might be something we can do." Teodoro broke the silence. "We'll need help. More hands."

"I'll ask Maverick. He can wear those cowboy boots he brought along." The writer had told her at breakfast yesterday that he'd come across plenty of rattlers on his ranch over the years and would be happy to help her snag and bag them, if needed. She'd rather not put any of her crew at risk, but there were too many snakes for two people.

"What about Quint?" Teodoro asked.

"No." She didn't want to risk him getting bit. Not after what happened to him at the last site.

And not after losing her mother at this site.

"I need to think about this some more," Teodoro said. "Gather supplies."

"We can discuss it further at supper." She needed to check on everyone else anyway and tell her dad what she'd found, including the news about the *sacbe*. Since he was mapping the site, he'd want to take some measurements. But first, she'd have to get rid of more snakes. It was too dangerous for anyone to be near that den, especially someone slowed down by a cast and cane.

She paused at the junction to the *Baatz'* Temple and looked toward it. "How many crew members do you need to help relocate the rattlesnakes we caught this morning?"

He held up one finger.

"Grab Lorenzo. I believe Fernando has him helping Esteban and Daisy at the ballcourt."

At his nod, she turned and headed toward her father and Quint.

A minute or two later, she found them in the narrow shadow of the temple, taking a break. Both men were soaked with sweat, swatting at mosquitoes and flies. "Where are the Coronas?" she asked, joining them.

"*Gatita*, you're smiling. Did you conquer the evil snake god?"

"Not yet." She moved next to Quint and leaned against the shaded wall beside him. He'd shaved. She wasn't sure if she liked him better with or without stubble. "But I did find something."

"What?" Quint asked, taking a glug from his water.

"A piece of a stela."

Juan's eyes widened. "How big?"

"Big enough to have several glyphs on it." She held out her hand for Quint's canteen, which he handed over without hesitation.

"Where did you find it?" Juan pulled out his handkerchief and wiped the back of his neck. "Inside the *Chakmo'ol* Temple?"

"In a rattlesnake den." She tipped the canteen back, swallowing the warm water.

Quint did a double take. "You went inside a snake den?"

"Not yet." She handed back his canteen, purposely making contact with his fingers.

"Why is there a 'yet' in that answer?" her father asked.

She recognized her father's stern glare from the times she'd landed in trouble in the past. "Because I need to see those glyphs."

"How many snakes are we talking about?" Quint capped the canteen, leaning against the side of the temple. He watched her with an intensity that added a fresh layer of sweat down her back.

"Around thirty."

"Holy shit."

"No, *gatita*. I will not allow you to go inside that den."

"Don't worry, Dad. I'm not going to go racing in there swinging my machete around. Teodoro is going to come up with a way to clear out the den. Then I'll get the stela."

Her father looked unconvinced. "This is too dangerous."

"I also found evidence of a *sacbe* leading away from the temple, heading southwest."

Juan's frown eased. "Where? I need to see that."

"It runs right past the snake den."

"Or maybe you could describe it to me in detail."

She chuckled. "Teodoro and Maverick and I are going to deal with the den. When we finish, you and I can check it out and measure the *sacbe* together."

"I don't like the sound of this." Quint crossed his arms.

"Which part?"

"The rattlesnakes. How about you count me in on your snake removal crew?"

"No."

He frowned. "Is there a reason behind that or are you just making a bossy decision on a whim?"

"There's a reason." When he and her father stared at her, she shuffled her feet. "I don't want you to get hurt again."

"I'm a big boy, Angélica."

"You don't like snakes."

"Not as much as bossy archaeologists, but I'm not squeamish around them."

She faced off with him, her hands on her hips. "Have you ever handled a snake?"

The corners of his eyes creased. "Not as much as you have."

She smacked his shoulder. "I'm serious."

"Yes, I have. I've even dealt with rattlers out on the prairie back home. Did I like it? No, but if it means helping you, I'm willing to risk their fangs again."

"I don't like you taking risks for me."

"I'd prefer neither of you two messed with these snakes," Juan said. "Can't we just blow them up with dynamite?"

She gaped at her father. "They're just doing their thing, Dad. We're moving into their space. Besides, did you add dynamite to the supply list without telling me, Mr. Wile E. Coyote? Because if not, we're running a bit short on TNT."

"It's a bad idea. Mark my words." He grabbed his cane. "Quint, when you're done fraternizing with the boss, I'll be waiting." He walked away with a slight limp, disappearing around the corner of the temple.

"I don't like you playing snake charmer, boss lady."

"Well, I don't exactly love it, but somebody has to get rid of those snakes, and that's me."

"And me."

"Listen, Parker," she started.

His eyes narrowed. "What's really going on here?"

"What do you mean?"

"You're out there slaying dragons, but when I take up my sword to help, you try to lock me away in the castle."

"Are you the prince or princess in this fairytale?"

"I'm always the king. Princes are pretty boys," he said with a smirk. "Now tell me, why don't you think I can handle those snakes?"

"It's not that I don't think you can handle them."

"What then?"

"If something happens to you …" She bit her lip, unsure how deep she wanted to dive into her emotions and uncertainties at the moment. "There's no insurance to cover you since you're not a crew member."

"Oh, I see, so you're going to tell me this is about legalities at the dig, not anything to do with losing your mother at this very site."

Crud. He'd seen right through her smokescreen. "It's not just that. I almost lost you and my dad at the last dig, Quint. I don't want a repeat performance."

He caught her hand and pulled her closer. "You can't control that, sweetheart."

"Keeping you two out of the line of fire would be a step in the right direction, though."

"I won't be mollycoddled, especially when you're putting your own life at risk."

"But—"

"I'm serious, Angélica. Where you go in this jungle, I go." His voice lowered as he tipped her chin up. "Now you may be the boss lady in front of your crew, but you and I know that when it comes to us, it's only an act we play in public."

Her gaze dropped to his lips. "That sounds like some sadomasochistic game, Parker."

"Well, I do like it when you run rampant all over me, taking me to task. Maybe we should look into finding you a whip to go with your machete."

"Fine," she gave in with a small smile. "You can help, but if you get bit …"

He leaned over and whispered in her ear. "You'll suck the venom out?"

Chills ran up her arms at the images his words conjured. "That doesn't actually work, you know."

"Are you positive about that?" His lips brushed the shell of her ear. "Maybe we should practice a few times in our tent. You know, to make sure you're up to the task in case it does work a little bit." He pulled back, his smile teasing.

She chuckled at his cheekiness. "If you get bit, Quint, I'm going to kick your ass."

"And *then* you'll kiss the bite better?"

"And then I'll kiss you better." She went up on her toes and showed him exactly how that would go, pressing against him for a few seconds of heavy breathing.

"Wow," he said when she stepped back. "That would probably get me started on the road back to good health."

"If you want more of that, you need to get back to work and keep an eye on my dad. I'm worried about him overstressing his leg."

Quint's eyebrows lifted. "Manipulating me with kisses? What's next? Bribing me with sex?"

"Parker," she warned, pointing after her father.

"All right, boss lady." He grabbed his canteen from the ground. "But to be clear, if you want to use sex to sway me one way or another, I'm easily corrupted."

"I'll keep that in mind."

"Save me a seat at lunch." He winked at her and followed after her father.

She stood there for a moment, enjoying the sight of his broad shoulders and everything below them. Her mind flashed back to Quint, her beach house, and the feel of his mouth trailing over her …

A howler monkey let out a loud growl in the canopy overhead, snapping her back to the present. Fanning her shirt, she headed toward the ballcourt where Esteban and Daisy should still be working.

One way or another, she was going to find some answers at this damned site. There was no way in hell she was going to let a few snakes get in her way.

Chapter Six

Uay: **Form changers; animal spirits of evil sorcerers.**

Quint waited outside the mess tent in the dark. The sound of forks clinking on tin plates and the din of conversation coming through the mesh-covered opening were almost drowned out by the party raging all around him in the trees and thick undergrowth.

He tried to imagine what it must have been like centuries ago with nothing but some scraps of clothing and a spear to fend off bugs and beasts. The buzzing of mosquitoes alone must have driven the Maya people nuts. It was no wonder they had thought ritual bloodletting sounded logical. It would take only a few months of picking off ticks every night and fending off snakes by day for the poke of a stingray spine on a regular basis to seem tolerable. After a few years of living under the trees, sacrificing a goat every now and then to some unseen gods in exchange for relief from the heat and humidity might sound downright reasonable.

"What are you doing out here, Parker?" Angélica's soft voice cut through his thoughts. She approached from the shadowed pathway that led to the tents, joining him at the edge of the light seeping from the mess tent. The humming of the generator was barely audible above the drone of crickets.

"I'm contemplating bloodletting in exchange for a relief from the heat and humidity."

She chuckled, moving closer, playing with one of the buttons on his shirt. "Can I hold the stingray spine?" she asked in a husky voice.

A zing shot through him. "That depends on what you're planning to poke with it."

"Well, the Maya believed that the ritual had a more powerful effect if the blood was drawn from the tongue ... or the penis." She ran her fingertips down his shirt. "Now I know you're going to need your tongue to work your charm on me, but since my father is sharing our tent I doubt you'll have much use for the latter." Her hand hesitated at the top of his fly, her teeth and eyes gleaming in the moonlight. "So, what do you say, Parker? Shall I sterilize a spine tonight?"

"You know," he said, snagging her hand and lifting it to his lips. "On second thought, this heat isn't so bad." He kissed her bold fingers.

Her smile widened. "Damn. And here I was hoping to sting you a little bit for disappearing for weeks on end without a word."

"Don't tell me you're still sore about that silly business," he jested, tugging her around the side of the tent and deeper into the shadows.

"Let me consult my ego and pride," she said, allowing him to draw her into his arms. "Yep, they're still cursing your hide."

"What can I do to make it up to them?"

"The stingray spine is a start."

He grimaced. "How about something that doesn't involve pointy ends."

"There's always my machete."

"*Or* sharp edges." His hands found the hem of her shirt, slipping up inside. The feel of her soft skin under his fingers made his pulse rev. "Something more ..." his fingers grazed her ribs, finding spots he'd memorized last month. "Ticklish."

She squirmed, a giggle escaping into the darkness. "Parker, don't."

"Don't what?" He strummed her ribs again, making her laugh louder this time. When she pressed fully against him, he felt lightheaded. "Don't touch you with my blunt objects?"

"Quint," she whispered, trying to chastise him only to ruin it by laughing into his shirt when he tickled her again. "I'm going to pay you back when you're sleeping," she threatened.

She tried to wriggle free, but he pulled her closer instead, his hands sliding around to her smooth back and then lower. Sweet Jesus, he'd missed her curves.

Her laughter ebbed as he moved against her, her breathing picking up speed to match his.

"Forgive me, Angélica." He leaned down and kissed the side of her neck, trailing his lips down to her collarbone. Her skin tasted sweet and salty at the same time, making him want to strip her naked and nibble further. "I don't like it when you're thinking violent thoughts that involve your machete and me."

Her chuckle was throatier this time. She wrapped her arms around his neck, staring up at him in the moonlight. "I'll think about it."

"Boy, you're a tough nut to crack."

"Maybe I like it when you work extra hard trying to find a weak spot."

"Is that a challenge?" he asked, angling toward her mouth.

She went up on her toes, closing the distance. Her breath was warm against his lips. "More like a tip, heartbreaker."

"*Gatita*?" Juan's voice reached them before Quint's lips made contact. "Where are you?"

She sighed, lowering back onto her heels. "I'm over here, Dad."

Quint dropped a kiss on her forehead, and then pulled his hands free of her shirt. He stepped back as Juan came around the side of the tent.

"What are you doing back here?" A flashlight beam lit up Angélica as she leaned back against Quint.

There was no hiding the truth from her dad. "She's being molested," Quint said. He adjusted his pants, glad for Juan's daughter shielding him at the moment.

Juan chuckled, lowering the light to the ground between them. "I should've known you two were up to no good since you were both playing hooky."

"Is everything okay in there?" she asked, snagging Quint's hand and following her father to the front of the tent.

"We're ready to report in for the evening." Juan led the way into the lighted tent. "And then I'm going to hit the hay." He yawned. "Quint wore this old man out today."

"I think it was the other way around, old man." His shoulders and lower back ached like hell. Sleeping on that cot was going to be a bitch tonight.

Angélica let go of Quint's hand and stepped inside, holding the mesh netting aside for him.

The brightness made him squint for a few blinks. The smell of María's cooking almost had him drooling. He put his hand on Angélica's lower back, propelling her toward the table where Pedro, Daisy, and Fernando were sitting. "Go get things started. I'll grab some food."

María was waiting for him. She handed Quint two plates loaded with tacos, chopped tomatoes, lime slices, and salad. Teodoro sat on a chair behind the table, drinking from a gourd cup. He nodded at Quint, his smile filling his round face. Quint smiled back at the shaman and then took the plates from María, thanking her. He grabbed two bottles of warm beer on his way to where Angélica sat next to Fernando.

He greeted the three university students along with Lorenzo and Esteban as he skirted their table. Juan had formally introduced him to Gertrude, Jane, and Bernard earlier at lunch—a lunch at which Angélica had not joined him and her dad. According to Esteban, she'd been too busy digging in the dirt at the ballcourt with Daisy Walker to take a lunch break. The young Maya had scarfed down his lunch and left with a basket of food María had made up for the two women.

As Quint approached, Angélica scooted closer to Fernando, making room for him on the end of the bench across the table from Pedro. Maverick was missing, but Daisy sat sandwiched between Pedro and Juan.

"Thanks, Parker," Angélica said as he placed a bottle of beer and her plate in front of her.

A glance around the table found everyone else's plates empty. No wonder Juan had come looking for them.

He took a bite of the taco and swooned, nearly falling off the end of the bench. Great horny toads! What in the hell had María put inside of the tacos tonight? He set it down and opened the tortilla. Chunks of brown meat, tomato, onion, and something green were mixed together. What was giving it that delicious tangy flavor?

"María makes the best *poc chuc*," Angélica said, squeezing the lime slices over her taco and salad.

"What's *poc chuc*?" He wrapped up the gastronomical gold and took another bite.

"An ancient Maya recipe for rattlesnake."

He stopped chewing. "What?!" he asked with his mouth full.

She laughed. "I'm kidding. It's wood-fire grilled pork. She salts the meat first and then rinses it with sour-orange juice. It's an old dish made centuries ago when the Maya didn't have refrigeration, one that's been passed down through her family. Sometimes she uses chicken or fish, but Pedro brought her some fresh cuts of meat from Cancun, so tonight we're being treated with pork."

"It tastes incredible."

Angélica picked up her taco. "You should see what she throws together when she's not camping in the middle of the jungle."

"How can you be sure it's a cave?" Daisy's question caught his attention.

"Because I tossed a couple of pebbles into it," Pedro said, "and they bounced several times before quieting."

Quint swallowed. "What did I miss?"

"Pedro found a cave over by Mound D," Angélica explained in between bites.

"He was too chicken to do more than throw pebbles in it, though," Juan said, lifting his coffee cup to his lips. He chuckled when Pedro threatened him with a fork.

"Don't throw stones at chicken houses," Pedro said.

"Don't you mean glass houses?" Daisy asked.

"No, I mean chicken houses. Mr. Scorpion King with his red socks has no right to poke fun." Pedro turned to Quint, leaning across the table. "Guess how I found the cave?"

"You saw a bat fly inside?"

"No. I went to see a man about a dog."

"Mule," Juan corrected.

"You're the mule, old man," Pedro said, clucking a few times at Juan. "Anyway, I tripped over a tree root on the way back and almost fell into it."

"So, it's a hole in the ground?" Daisy asked, her brow drawn.

"More like a hole in a mound that's partially covered by strangler fig roots," he told her. He looked back at Quint. "It took a couple of hours with my shovel and machete to clear enough space to squeeze inside. Some of those fig roots are as thick as a man's leg."

Angélica paused, her fork lowering. "That means the previous archaeological crew probably didn't know about the cave. Did you see any iconography or glyphs on the walls?"

He shook his head. "But the cave looked deep. I didn't go in too far. My flashlight was in my tool pouch back with the girls at Mound D."

Angélica pushed her salad around on her plate. "We'll check it out in the morning." She glanced in Quint's direction, her eyebrows raised.

He gave her a thumbs-up. There was no way in hell she was going inside that cave without him. He could only imagine what might be waiting for them in the dark.

He'd have to borrow Pedro's machete.

And Teodoro's hunting knife.

And Fernando's bow and arrow.

And maybe Juan's red socks.

"So," Angélica said between bites, "Fernando and his crew are still dealing with the big mess the looters left behind in the *Chakmo'ol* Temple." At Fernando's grunt and nod, she continued. "Pedro found what might be an undocumented cave outside of the sites' previously marked boundary *and* uncovered what appears to be the head of a statue at Mound D." She paused to take a swig of beer. "And over at the ballcourt, Daisy found another jade piece to add to her growing collection."

"Don't forget the partial skull she also found this afternoon," Juan said.

She found what? Quint wiped his mouth with his napkin, watching Daisy's cheeks turn pink.

She shrugged, fidgeting with her spoon. "I was lucky."

"You seem to have Lady Luck living in your pocket lately," Angélica said. "I'm amazed at the way you stumble upon these rare finds. You remind me of my mom. She always had a knack for discovering extraordinary things others overlooked."

"Like me." Juan grinned.

While a rumble of laughter flowed around the table, Quint tried to picture what Daisy had found. "What do you mean a partial skull?"

"A piece of jawbone and part of the cranium," Daisy said.

"Esteban thinks it might be from a monkey," Angélica added.

Leaning across the table toward Quint, Daisy added, "But they seem rather large, and the cranium piece has some interesting marks on it."

"Interesting how?"

Juan answered for her. "Like teeth scrapes from one of the big cats around here."

"How is the *Baatz'* Temple entrance clearing coming along, Dad?" Angélica returned the focus to work.

"We nearly broke our backs today," he said, toasting Quint with his coffee cup. "But by tomorrow afternoon, I think we'll have it stable enough for us to go inside and check for looter damage."

After raising his beer to Juan and their hard work today, Quint took a long draw from the bottle. Angélica's father had labored like a man half his age today. Juan might call himself an old man and act soft on the outside, but the guy had a titanium core. Not to mention his seemingly endless supply of energy, and all while wearing a walking cast in sweltering heat. What was María putting in Juan's morning burrito? Spinach? Cocaine?

"Stable enough," Pedro repeated Juan's words with a snort. "Those words don't make me feel good about going inside that temple with you."

Juan chuckled. "Come on, Pedro. When have I ever led you into harm's way?"

"Last week."

"Now, if you'll remember, I warned you that thing was still alive."

"You said it looked dead."

"Well, it did." Juan took a drink of coffee, his smile twitching at the corner of his lips. "Imagine my surprise when it came back to life."

"After I picked it up." Pedro shook his head, grinning across at Quint. "You're brave to sleep in the same tent as *Señor Loco* down there. Make sure you keep one eye open all night."

"10-4." Quint finished off his taco and dug into the salad. María had drizzled some kind of citrus-based, spicy dressing over it that made him eat even faster.

"Dad," Angélica said, still in boss lady mode. "Did the notes and files INAH sent from the last archaeologist include any maps detailing the temple's interior?"

Juan shook his head. "I don't understand why not, either. Mapping is usually one of the first things done at a site. How else are you going to keep track of where you've dug and where you need to go next?"

"No map, huh?" Pedro's gaze narrowed. "That's odd."

Fernando grunted in agreement.

Not odd, more like suspicious. At least that described the look Pedro was sending him. If Pedro had heard the conversation between Juan and Quint about the fresh scars visible on the corbel vault's bridge stone, he would be even more skittish about hanging out inside of that temple.

"Is there anything else I need to know about today's results?" Angélica looked around the table. When they all shook their heads, she called Teodoro over.

The shaman stood next to Quint.

"Did you come up with a plan for clearing the snake den?" she asked.

Teodoro nodded. "Pedro and I fly to Coba in morning," he said in broken English. "Need supplies."

Coba was where Teodoro and María lived in the off season. Quint had stopped by their modest thatched-roof, mud and limestone home with Angélica last month before he'd flown out for Greenland.

"Does that mean we should plan to spend tomorrow afternoon playing fetch with the snakes?" Angélica finished the last bite of her taco.

"Maybe." Teodoro glanced over at his wife, who was trying to lift a bucket full of water. He called out in Mayan and then turned back to Angélica, his expression pained. She tilted her head toward María and he went to help his wife.

Without further ado, Angélica wrapped things up and thanked everyone for their help. She rose from her seat. "I need to go through some notes back in my tent. Are you about done, Parker?" She picked up her plate and held her hand out for his.

Quint did a double take. "Uh, sure." He swallowed the last of the salad and gave up his plate.

"Why do you need Quint to study your notes?" Juan asked with feigned innocence. "Inquiring fathers are curious."

"I don't need him to study, Dad." She glanced over at the other table, which was now empty, the younger crowd having dispersed for the night. "I need him to come with me to the showers."

Pedro wolf whistled and clapped, dodging the napkin she threw at him. Without further explanation, she walked over and set their dirty plates in the wash bucket.

Quint was still trying to process her words. Had she really

publicly voiced an invitation to join her in a shower? He watched as she paused next to the tent flap and wiggled her index finger at him.

Well, if she needed him in the shower, he'd better not make the boss lady wait. Shaking off his temporary stupor, he said his good-nights to the peanut gallery and dropped his empty beer bottle in the trash on the way out.

He caught up with Angélica near their tent. "So are you going to scrub my back first," he asked quietly, "or do I get to start with rubbing your front?"

She held open the tent flap. "I'll lay out a strategy on the way to the showers."

A strategy for sharing a shower? "Wow. You sure know how to romance a guy." He slipped inside.

She joined him, grabbing her towel, clean clothes, and toiletry bag, all of which she handed to him. "Carry these for me, will you?"

He collected his things, bundling them along with hers, and joined her out under the moon where she waited for him. That was when he noticed what she had strapped onto her belt. "Are you planning on shaving your legs with your machete tonight?"

"Nope."

"Then what's the special occasion? You realize that the bloodletting idea we were talking about before supper was a joke, right?"

"While you were getting our food, Fernando told me that he saw something earlier this evening when he was down here cleaning up." She tucked her machete-wielding hand in his elbow and started toward the showers.

"Please tell me it was a big cockroach."

"It was definitely big, but not a cockroach. Dad thought it might be a *uay*."

"What's a *uay*?"

"An evil sorcerer that takes on an animal form."

He shoulder bumped her. "You're a bucket of laughs tonight, boss lady."

"I'm just getting rolling, Parker."

As they drew closer to the showers, she aimed her flashlight into the trees and lit up the canopies. "What Fernando saw had sharp teeth and left behind big paw prints." She pulled her hand free and extracted her machete from its sheath.

"Splendid." Quint squinted into the trees, watching for

movement. "There's nothing more relaxing than stripping down to my birthday suit around a meat-eating predator."

"Don't worry. It probably just likes to watch."

"A voyeur with pointy canines and sharp claws. Sounds like the makings for an exciting new Olympic sport—nude jungle sprinting."

Her laughter was quiet, or maybe it was that the jungle suddenly seemed extra loud with howls, barks, and screeches. There was no way they could hear the approach of a large predator over this cacophony.

"You go first, Parker."

"What? That's not very gentlemanly of me. I think you should hand over the machete and let me guard your nakedness."

She nudged him toward the makeshift shower stalls. "Don't worry. I'll give the critter a close shave if it tries to get anywhere near your sexy buns."

Grumbling, he pulled off his shirt and unbuttoned his pants, pausing when he noticed where she had the flashlight pointed. "My sexy buns and I would appreciate it if you'd turn around and stay focused on the task at hand, oh great huntress."

"I *was* focusing. I have eyes in the back of my head."

"Liar." He spun her around to face the dark jungle. Then he stripped down and grabbed the bar of soap. Warm water sluiced over him for a few seconds. He shut off the water and began soaping up.

"You know," he said, squinting into the darkness, "when I fantasized about getting some tail in the shower for the last few weeks, the only tail involved was yours." At the edge of the flashlight's beam, he thought he saw movement in the brush.

"That's good to hear." She moved the flashlight to the left.

A low-hanging tree limb bobbed.

The others around it didn't.

He heard her curse as she raised the machete. "Scrub faster, Parker," she said over her shoulder. "I think we have company."

* * *

Two hours later back in her tent, Angélica was still cursing, only this time it wasn't at what had turned out to be a pair of rowdy coatis fighting in the bushes next to the showers. Now her curses were for the cryptic notes left behind by her mother about the mysterious stela that seemed to have disappeared into thin air.

"Do you realize you're swearing out loud?" Quint asked, looking over from the magazine he was reading by flashlight.

Her father's chainsaw snoring hadn't roared to life yet. Ironically, before settling onto his pillow he'd inserted earplugs and turned his back on them, telling them to keep the partying to a dull roar so he could get his beauty rest.

"Sorry." She stood and stretched her lower back. "I forgot you were awake." He'd been quiet since he had stripped down to his boxer briefs and settled into his cot after returning from the showers.

Sitting upright, he dropped the magazine onto the floor. "Come here."

"Why?" She glanced in her father's direction, making sure he still had his back to them. "What're you going to do?"

"Tear your clothes off, of course, and then ravish you right here while your father sleeps." He waved her over. "Just come here."

Intrigued, she went. He spun her around so her back was to him. "Now sit."

She hesitated, lowering cautiously to her knees.

"All the way," he ordered and tugged her down.

She obeyed, sitting cross-legged on the floor with her back to him. "Now what?"

He brushed her damp hair aside. "To start with, close your eyes and relax."

"Quint," she said, starting to rise to her feet again, "I don't have time for—"

A solid push downward and she was back on her butt. "Sit and relax," he said, his hands locking onto her shoulders. "And lean your head forward while you're at it."

This time, she succumbed to his demands, letting her hair tumble around her face as his hands began to squeeze and massage her shoulders. Several seconds passed, filled with her grunts of pain in between moans of pleasure.

Damn. Just damn.

"Where have you been all my life, Parker?"

"Stuck in a bottle. The genie hat kept making my head itch, though, so I escaped." He pushed the strap down on her tank top, baring her shoulder.

She tensed, shooting another look toward her father.

"Loosen up. I'm just trying to get better access to these muscles here," Quint told her. His thumbs dug in, making her flinch as he strummed a knotted bunch of banjo strings under her skin.

Closing her eyes, she let him work his magic on her shoulders for several minutes. Her mind stopped spinning and her focus returned to something in her mother's notes that had made her grind her teeth earlier.

"Quint?" she asked, tipping her head to the side to give him more access to the tight chords running up her neck.

"Hmm?"

"I have a feeling there's something going on here that's not as it seems."

"Well, if you must know, I am thinking about you naked right now and where I'd like to massage next. But otherwise, I'm just enjoying the feel of your skin under my fingers and trying to relax you enough so you can get some sleep tonight."

She smiled, scooting back further between his shins so she could rest her temple on his knee. He smelled soapy clean. "I was talking about this dig site, smartass."

He switched sides, tipping her head the other way and tugging down her tank-top strap on the other side. "What makes you think there is something else going on here besides cleaning up after looters and fending off creatures with sharp claws and venom-filled stingers?"

"I don't know. It's just a gut feeling, really, but I keep wondering if this place has been left alone for reasons other than the previous archaeologist not meeting his objectives."

"Do you think that the helicopter crash had something to do with INAH shutting down operations?"

"Maybe." She wrapped her arm around his leg, clinging to his calf as he worked loose another tight bunch of her muscles. "But there are too many flags here for me to ignore or write off as happenstance."

"Like what?" His thumbs moved to the base of her skull.

"For starters, why is the stela my mom wrote about missing?"

"Maybe it's inside the *Baatz'* Temple."

"I guess we'll find out if it is tomorrow."

He tipped her head back into his lap, his fingers moving to her temples. "What else?"

"Why is Daisy finding so many items in the ballcourt?"

"Is that unusual?"

"Sort of. But what's more odd is her ability to home in on an object. It's like she has LiDAR in her head."

"What about Maverick?"

She opened her eyes, looking at his upside-down face. "What about him?"

"Has he been acting suspiciously at all?"

"No. Mainly he's been quiet, keeping to himself."

"You don't find that odd for a writer?"

She snorted. "Maybe. You were a much louder pain in the ass right out of the gate at the last site, that's for sure."

His laughter was low and quiet. "Yeah, but I was that sweet and achy kind of pain, right? The sort that makes you want more of it."

"If you say so."

"You're so sassy on the inside." He leaned in and gave her an upside-down kiss, the breath-stealing kind, then began to feather his fingers over her cheeks, tracing the bones of her face. "Yet so soft on the outside."

She closed her eyes. Her thoughts flitted over the possible dangers they might face over the next few days as they continued to peel away the jungle and years of neglect at the site. She needed to talk to Pedro and make sure he had the helicopter at the ready for an emergency flight at any time.

"What are you going to do if you can't find the stela your mom wrote about before your time here is up?"

"I don't know." She yawned, scooting closer, resting her cheek on his bare thigh. The hairs on his leg tickled her cheek. "Come back here again instead of handing it over to another crew."

His hands stopped. "You mean to tell me that if you find the stela, we may not have to come back to this particular site again in the future?"

She peeked up at him through one eye. "You don't have to come to any of the sites I choose, Parker."

"Don't play games with me, Angélica. We're beyond that and you know it."

"Sorry, but I don't want you to feel stuck."

"I don't, and I'll accept your apology on one condition."

"What?"

"You come up here with me." He patted the cot.

She pointed at her father's sleeping form. "Have you forgotten about someone?"

"I'm not going to try to seduce you." He pulled her up and onto his cot, spooning her body into his on the narrow strip of canvas. "I'm going to stretch out my aching body and I want you next to me."

The frame creaked under their combined weight as she settled back against him. The feel of his warmth against her made her feel like purring even though the night was humid and the air in the tent still. She sighed, settling into the pillow. It smelled like Quint, spicy with an undercurrent of lust.

He toyed with her hair, his breath tickling her ear. "We're going to find that stela, sweetheart."

"How can you be sure? I've been here for weeks and haven't had any luck." If the stela wasn't in the *Baatz'* Temple, she was out of places to look.

"Because I've seen you locked onto a scent before. You're like a bloodhound on the hunt. You'll practically kill yourself trying to find it before you give up."

That wasn't the most flattering of descriptions. She entwined her fingers in his, wrapping his arm around her. "Aren't you going to try to talk sense into me?"

He was silent for a moment, his breathing the only sound. "Tell me something, Angélica. And I want you to be honest."

"What?"

"Have you thought that maybe there could be something on that stela that brought about your mother's death?"

"Don't tell me you're going to start down the curse path, too, Quint."

"I wasn't thinking it was a curse."

She rolled enough to look over her shoulder at him. "Then what?"

He leaned on his elbow, his forehead lined as he looked down at her. "You've said your mom believed there was a warning on the stela."

"Yes." She flipped all of the way over onto her back so she could stare up at him without getting a crook in her neck. "She has something written along those lines in her notes as a possible theory of the stela's overall meaning."

"What if the warning has something to do with a danger at this site? Some kind of ancient danger."

She gave that some thought. "A danger that has lasted for centuries, waiting for my mom to arrive and read the glyphs?"

"It sounds crazy, I know, but just play along for a moment."

"Okay." She waited, trying to open her mind to whatever he was going to throw at her.

His palm slid across her lower stomach, cupping her hipbone through the old boxer shorts she was using for pajama bottoms since her father was sharing her tent. "Do you know what happened to the last group of Maya who lived here?"

She shrugged. "There's not been anything definitive found, but I'd guess they relocated to another site due to famine, disease, or the Spanish invasion."

His gaze held hers, the vertical lines between his brows deepening. "What if something bad happened here? I mean really bad, not a food or sickness issue. Something so bad that whoever was the last to exit the place left that stela behind as a warning to keep others away."

"And my mom's reading it put her life in danger?"

"No. Reading it put others' lives in danger."

She frowned. "You've been hanging around with my father too much the last couple of days."

He didn't even crack a smile at that or argue about it. "Did Marianne ever actually decipher the stela?"

"No. She took notes and made several drawings of what was on it, but she was heading home to decipher it fully."

"But she never made it home."

"Of course not. You know that story."

"And her notes were on the helicopter with her?"

She nodded. "But I have them now."

"All of them?"

"She only had one notebook with her, Quint." She pushed up on her elbows, looking at him eye to eye. "What are you getting at? That someone killed my mom in order to get to her notes?"

"More along the lines of killing her to bury the secrets she'd discovered along with her and her notes."

Angélica's gut tightened. She shot a worried glance toward her father, watching to make sure his breathing was still rhythmic. "But the crash was ruled an accident," she whispered.

There was something unsettling in the way Quint was looking at her. She sat upright. "What is it?"

He opened his mouth, and then hesitated, shaking his head. "Nothing."

"Quint, what?"

He continued to shake his head. "I was playing out what-ifs in my head, that's all. I got carried away." She squinted at him in disbelief. "I've read too many supernatural thrillers and mysteries in my travels, sweetheart. I swear. Now come back down here."

She let him pull her back down, staring up at him from his pillow. Did he know something about her mother's crash that she didn't? How could he? She and her father had been there with her mother as she'd died. They'd collected her belongings that were left after the accident and visited the crash site. The government reports had been copied and sent to them upon request in their search to find closure. Copies of all articles and news reports from the internet, and those from local Mexican papers, were filed away in a drawer in her mom's old desk back in Tucson.

"Angélica." Quint's fingers trailed up her arm and along her shoulder, lightly tickling her as they feathered their way across the upper swell of her breasts. "We'll find the stela and then all of your questions will be answered."

She caught his fingers before they traveled further and landed the two of them into trouble. "I should move to my own cot."

"Not yet." He leaned down and kissed her temple. "Close your eyes and let me help you silence that big brain for a few hours." He clicked off his flashlight, leaving them in darkness.

She turned onto her side, returning to their spooning position. "Are you going to tell me another comic book tale about your impressive biceps?"

"No." He locked onto her hips and pulled her closer. "Tonight, I want to tell you about my time in Greenland and how sad and lonely I was."

"Oh dear, is this going to be a drama? I tend to lean more toward action-adventure stories."

"Criminy, everyone's a critic." He nuzzled her neck below her ear, whispering, "Now shush up and listen."

She closed her eyes and let her mind meander along with him as he told her about a troublemaking pair of polar bear cubs. Then the sandman came dancing through and buried her under a mountain of sleep.

Chapter Seven

Sascabera: Ancient mines (open and capped) where granular limestone was extracted to be used as lime plaster.

"This isn't a cave," Quint told Angélica the next morning. "It's a death trap."

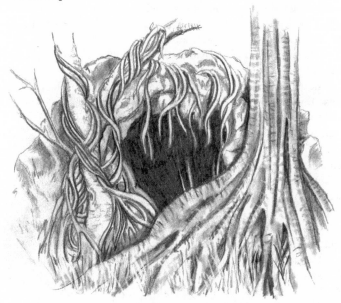

He shone his flashlight into the partially concealed entrance that Pedro had stumbled onto yesterday. He hadn't been kidding about the thickness of the strangler fig roots covering the opening. It looked like a tree from a Dr. Seuss story—one that was planted crookedly on top of a shoulder-high mound and then melted down over the cave's entrance with wax turned to roots.

How long had it taken for the tree to grow to this size? More important, what were the chances of Pedro's root hacking causing the tree's weight to shift and triggering a cave-in while someone was inside? More specifically, while Quint and Angélica were inside?

The scarred-up ground and deep ragged cross-cuts on several of the strangler fig tree's large roots were proof of Pedro's shovel and machete work the day before. As Quint leaned closer to the narrow opening Pedro had made, a breath of air seeped out and swept over his sweaty skin. It felt slightly cooler than the sauna surrounding him. He sniffed, expecting something rank like bat urine or guano, but all he could smell was the cave—dirt and rocks.

"What do you see, Parker?" Twigs and dry leaves crunched under her boots as Angélica moved up next to him. Her hair was pulled back in a ponytail today instead of a braid. Auburn tendrils stuck to her glistening skin along her hairline. Her yellow T-shirt had damp spots across her shoulders and down the front. Beads of perspiration dotted her forehead.

The stifling humidity had her sweating like him for once. It also seemed to have spiked her temper, or maybe waking up in his bed had done the trick. One way or another, something had her more tense this morning, her smile harder to lure to the surface.

"You mean besides a hot woman who likes to hog the bed?" He tried to joke, wiping away a drip of sweat sliding down his temple.

"You should've let me leave your cot when I mentioned it." She nailed him with a frown. "When did you move to mine anyway?"

Was that what was bothering her? That he'd left her alone in his bed?

"Shortly after you turned in your sleep and drove your knee in my upper thigh. An inch or two to the left and I'd be singing soprano this morning."

Her frown deepened. "I didn't knee you where the bullet went in, did I?"

"No. You took aim at my good leg."

"Sorry about that."

"You were sleeping, sweetheart." Rather than risk another kneeing, he'd extracted himself from her side and moved to her cot. Unfortunately, her father had woken before Quint and Angélica this morning and noticed the switcheroo.

"Looks like you have a bedbug problem," Juan had whispered while Quint stretched awake. A melancholy expression replaced her dad's grin as he watched Angélica sleep for a moment before he left the tent. The old buzzard was having way too much fun with their nightly slumber parties.

"So, did I turn you into a nervous nelly after kneeing you?" The corner of Angélica's mouth twitched, her smile almost emerging. "Send you scurrying to safety?"

"Poke fun, boss lady, but I prefer my boys to remain south of my throat, especially while I'm asleep and unable to defend them from knockout blows. I'm going to need to wear a cup for protection the next time we share my bed."

"I should have gone back to my cot." Something in her tone made him wish he'd stayed put last night and risked a second kneeing.

"Angélica, it was an accident."

"I don't know about that. It might have been my subconscious trying to pay you back for losing my phone number in the North Atlantic and almost breaking my heart."

He couldn't tell if she was joking or not. "Thank God it was only 'almost.' I'd hate to see what you'd do to me if I actually broke it."

Her jaw hardened. "Let's not find out." She pointed at the cave, her expression rigid, her boss lady shield back in place. "Tell me what you see inside there or move aside so I can take a look myself."

"Keep your pants on, ramrod." He leaned closer to the entrance, shining his light between the roots. "I see ... a cave."

"Funny man. Don't give up your photojournalist gig."

"And here I was thinking about signing up to be your number one cook, comedian, and bottle washer."

She snorted. "And give up María? No chance. Stick to doing what you do best."

"Which is what?"

Her narrowed gaze met his. "Charming the ladies." She reached out and turned his chin back toward the cave's entrance. "Now, do you see bat guano mounds on the floor?"

He shone his beam around inside the cave. "No."

"What about bat urine stalactites hanging from the ceiling?" When he didn't answer right away, she continued, "The stalactites look like melted brownish-yellow plastic dripping from the ceiling, and can be—"

"I know what bat urine stalactites look like, sweetheart," he said, interrupting her science lesson. "I wrote an article once about spelunking in the Great Smoky Mountains. The crew I traveled with came across several bat colonies along the way." He'd been happy as hell to reach the end of that gig. His time under the earth had given him a whole new respect for miners. "I don't see stalactites or stalagmites or any other sign of bats. Nor do I smell them."

"Neither do I. That seems odd, don't you think?" She nudged him over so she could peer inside with her flashlight. "I'd expect there to be bats in there."

"Maybe the cave has been inaccessible thanks to these roots and vines and … would you look at the size of the thorns on this little tree. What's it called?"

"A ceiba tree. When it's young, the trunks and branches are armed with thick conical spines. Eventually, if left to grow to its full potential, it will be the tallest tree in the forest. Like that giant over there."

"Holy shit, that's huge." The big tree had what looked like buttresses at its base, making it almost ten feet in diameter. Up through the other trees, its umbrella-shaped crown hogged the sunlight, which he was grateful for on this sizzling day.

"They're amazing specimens. Ceiba trees are considered the 'first tree' or 'world tree' in the Maya world, believed to stand at the center of the Earth. Even the modern Maya tend to leave the tree alone out of respect." She carefully pushed aside the ceiba sapling and sliced off a braid of vines that had wrapped around the young trunk with her machete.

"Ceiba wood is soft and light, not really useful for furniture, but down south in Costa Rica they are using it for pallets." She reached out and knocked on a fig root that bisected the opening. It was as thick as Quint's leg and didn't budge. "We're going to need a hatchet for this puppy."

"You ask, my queen, and I deliver." He pulled out a hatchet from the leather bag Juan had given him after finding out at breakfast that Angélica was taking Quint to check out the cave.

Her smile had a brittle edge. "Well-equipped and decent in the sack." She held her hand out for the hatchet. "You're one helluva package deal, Quint Parker."

"*Decent* in the sack?" He pushed her hand away. "We're back to that again, are we?"

One auburn eyebrow lifted. "Back to what again?"

"Sexual slights." He bumped her back from the cave and then took a swing at the thick root blocking the opening. It was harder than he'd expected. "So far," he said, putting more oomph behind his second swing, "you've rated my sexual aptitude as 'good,' 'sort of memorable,' and now 'decent.' "

"Would you rather I use superlatives like 'most' and words ending in 'est' to stroke your ego?"

Pausing to wipe his face with his shirt, he frowned at her. "No, Angélica. I'd rather you be honest with me. If there's something more you need or want from me to redline the pleasure meter while we're doing the wild thing, then I'd like to know."

Her focus lowered to his lips. She swallowed visibly. "Okay."

He waited for her to say something else, to tell him he was reading her all wrong, but she held her cards close to her vest.

Grumbling about the hard-headed woman, he went back to chopping and tried to push aside the doubts she'd raised. She'd certainly seemed to enjoy sex right along with him, but maybe he'd been too caught up in his own pleasure while touching her to see things clearly.

With the removal of one of the large fig roots covering the opening, the hole widened enough for them to slip inside.

He stepped back. "You ready, boss lady?"

"Let's go." She started forward, pulling out a flashlight from her back pocket.

"Christ, Angélica." Quint caught her arm before she could slip inside. "Hold up. I'll go first, thank you very much."

Her eyes sparked. She tugged her arm free. "You don't have to play macho man, Parker. It's just you and me here."

"Exactly." He jammed the hatchet back into its leather pouch. "Listen, we can have a pissing match later, but right now you're going to let me lead the way because I earned the right with my remarkable chopping skills."

His attempt at levity fell flat. "You've only been here a couple of days," she said. "I don't want you getting hurt already. Dad needs you too much."

Juan needed him, huh? Right. What in the hell was going on here? Was she ticked because he'd been gone when she'd woken up in his cot? He'd returned from shaving to an empty tent, finding her at breakfast nursing a cup of coffee with a hard glint in her eyes.

"I won't get hurt, boss lady. And if I do, I'll grit my teeth and work through it, don't you worry."

She sighed, her expression softening. "Quint—"

"Don't make me arm wrestle you for first dibs on this stupid cave. You may have bigger *cojones* than most of us here when it comes to things that hiss and growl in the night, but I'm stronger than you and I'm not going to budge on this."

Her gaze challenged him for a moment. When he didn't back down, she shoved her hard hat on her head and gestured for him to go first. "Fine. You and your beefy muscles lead the way."

"Damned right we will." Grabbing Juan's bag of tricks, Quint pulled out two carbon filter masks and handed her one. "Put this on."

"Why? It's just a cave. There's not even any bat guano in it from what we can tell."

"Your dad insisted that we take extra precautions. With the other problems you two have run into at this site, he's worried there could be gases trapped in there."

Muttering under her breath about overprotective males, she slipped on the mask, securing it over her mouth and nose. "Now can we go?" she asked, her voice muffled.

He put on his mask and his hard hat, then squeezed sideways through the opening. The low ceiling made him bend partway over.

Angélica followed behind him, sliding through with less scraping but more cursing. Once inside, she crowded in behind him in the hall-like entryway. When she tried to step around him, Quint caught her shoulder and stopped her. "Wait a second, Speedy Gonzales."

"What now?"

He pulled out the gas detector Juan had shown him how to use earlier. Quint clicked on the device and pushed several buttons per Juan's instructions, checking the air for poisonous gases and adequate oxygen.

"What's it say?" she peered down at the LCD screen along with him.

"From what I can tell, the oxygen levels look good, and there are no signs of harmful gases." He wrapped the meter's strap around his neck and then added his flashlight beam to look at the scene in front of them.

Stones, splintered with cracks, lined the four-foot-wide throat of the cave. Fingers of roots poked through in spots, hanging down like fish hooks waiting to snag a catch. Angélica looked up and tugged on one of the roots near their hats. Dirt crumbled onto the floor around their hiking boots.

Jeez, she was as fearless as her dad when it came to these underground coffins. Quint grabbed her hand. "How about you don't do that anymore?"

"You feeling antsy, Parker?"

"Being buried alive is *not* on my bucket list."

"Sorry." Her eyes locked with his for several seconds over her mask. "It's mind-blowing."

Quint hadn't seen anything mind-blowing about the dirt walls and low ceiling. A fresh coat of sweat coated his skin from just thinking about how much weight hovered over their heads, thanks to that big fig tree.

"There's nothing mind-blowing about it." He glanced back toward the sunlit opening. It beckoned him with promises of fresh air, blue sky, and the opportunity to see another day. "It looks like a typical cave to me."

She patted him on the chest, drawing his attention back to her. "I wasn't talking about the cave."

As he stood there replaying their conversation, trying to figure out what she was talking about, she headed deeper into the darkness.

A sprinkle of dirt pattered onto the top of his hard hat.

Fuck.

Grimacing, he followed after her, ducking even lower to avoid the dangling roots. "What's mind-blowing?" he asked, trying to keep his mind off the cracks in the ceiling.

"Later, Parker," she said over her shoulder.

About ten feet inside the cave, the width of the tunnel's throat widened even more, making room for three to walk side by side. The ceiling raised, too, enough for Quint to stand upright. Around a bend, a semi-circular chamber spread before them.

Back here, the dirt was packed down and sprinkled with white grains of something. Chunks of salt? Quartz crystals? He squatted to take a closer look. No, they weren't sparkling enough. Was it falling through the cracks overhead? Quint directed his light upward. The ceiling was still bat-free and much less fractured here.

Angélica walked deeper into the chamber, shining her light around. "Any harmful gases registering yet?"

Rising, he checked again, pushing the buttons Juan had showed him. "Oxygen is a little lower, but still well in the green." He pressed more buttons. "Nothing dangerous is registering."

She pulled off her mask, scrubbing her face with her shirt.

"What are you doing?" He lowered Juan's fancy gadget.

"We're in the clear."

"That's not a sure thing yet."

"Trust me on this one." She bent over and scooped up a handful of dirt mixed with white grains, shining her light onto her palm. She gasped. "It's a *sascabera!*"

He tugged off his mask. "What?"

"This place. It's an ancient mine dug out by the Maya."

"How can you tell?" He walked over to her, shining his light around. It looked like a cave to him and nothing more.

She held her palm full of dirt toward him, tipping the dirt into his hand. "Look. They extracted the granular limestone and used it as lime plaster to coat the buildings and the roads."

"I didn't realize they had limestone mines here." Quint lit up his palm, nudging several granules around with his flashlight.

"It's unusual. More often you'll find them farther up on the peninsula. Come on."

He dumped the dirt and looked up while brushing his hand off on his pants. Angélica stood at the edge of another tunnel that appeared to lead farther back into the mine. This one was a tighter squeeze, barely wider than his shoulders.

"Oh, no. I'm not going in there, boss lady."

She nailed him with her beam. "You've been in worse spots."

He shielded his eyes. "And I nearly keeled over from a heart attack each time."

"Would it do any good to bribe you?"

"With what?"

Her beam lowered. "More mind-blowing sex."

His eyes narrowed. Is that what she'd meant earlier when she said *mind-blowing?* She was just feeling sorry for his ego now. "Let's move on from that sticky wicket."

"Whatever you say, Parker. Get your ass over here."

He joined her, peering into the dark tunnel. The ceiling and walls looked solid with no roots hanging down or fractured map lines. "I'm not sure that even the promise of super amazing acrobatic circus sex with fire rings and hungry lions would get me to risk going in there."

"Okay, ringmaster. Wait here for me."

He caught her arm. "You're not going in there without me."

"But you just said—"

"I know what I said." He crammed into the passageway, cursing her obstinacy as he slid along bumping his shoulders periodically on small outcroppings of rock. He'd rounded the second bend when he saw something up ahead that made him stop. "Apparently neither of us is going much further."

"What do you mean?" She came up behind him in the tunnel, peeking around him. "Is that a wall?" As she struggled to slide past him, her knee caught him in the lower thigh.

He grunted.

She grimaced, eye to eye with him in the tunnel. "Sorry. My knees seem to have a thing for your legs."

"Yeah, well, my legs would like your knees to turn around and lead us back out into the sunshine."

"Will do. Just give me a minute here." She took the lead and approached the wall, touching the rocks used to build it. The stones looked similar to the ones the Maya used for the temples at the site. Someone must have hauled them in here when they decided to seal off the mine.

"Is there a way around it?" Quint hoped to hell not.

"Not that I can see."

"Thank Uranus for that," he muttered.

"You should be happy, there's more room back here by the wall."

"I'll be happy when I'm sitting in the sand outside your beach house under the big blue sky." An ice-cold beer would make the fantasy even better.

She ran her fingers along the seams between the rocks. "They used a limestone-based grout." She sounded surprised.

"Makes sense, considering this was a limestone mine."

"Yeah, but why would they block the ..." she stopped, her head cocked. "Do you hear that?"

He listened, trying not to breathe, but heard only his heart pounding. After the loudness of the jungle, the mine was a sanctuary. "Hear what?"

She held up her finger, still silent. Then she shook her head. "Never mind. I'm probably hearing things."

"How about we go back outside and listen from there?"

"It's a lot louder."

"It's also a lot more oxygen-rich with a higher roof."

She led the way back toward the larger chamber. "You're not a fan of this *sascabera*, huh?"

"They didn't make this hole in the ground big enough for someone my size." Standing upright again for a length of time would be a treat.

Quint breathed easier after they'd both squeezed out through the fig tree roots and stood under the tree canopy in the muggy air. "Now what?"

"I'm going to talk to my dad about the mine. I want to hear his take on whether it was normal for Maya to wall up a *sascabera* after it served its purpose."

"Has he been in one before?"

"Several times."

Quint pocketed the flashlight. "At least there were no snakes in there."

"Yeah." She took off her hat and frowned back at the mine entrance. "That sort of bothers me."

"Why?"

"It's not normal down here. Usually, there are rat nests or critter droppings inside unused caves and temples. An old abandoned mine shouldn't be so empty."

She had a point. Even if bigger critters couldn't make it into the opening, rats would've been able to go in and out without a problem.

"Could it have something to do with the limestone granules? Are they a natural pest control?"

"Not that I know of, but I'll have to ask Dad to be sure."

"And you're sure there's been no mention of this mine on any of the documents you've checked out from the last archaeologist."

"Positive."

He looked over at the grand old ceiba tree she'd pointed out earlier. "Do you think that wall inside the tunnel is as old as the last

Maya civilization?"

"It's hard to tell without having data to analyze, but it could be. It's certainly been protected from the elements. Although the grout was crumbly, which leads me to believe it's aged for quite some time."

"How did they move the limestone granules in and out?" He looked at the size of the hole, scratching his head where the hard hat had rubbed. "The entrance is so narrow."

"They had no beasts of burden, so they probably used pots or hemp baskets. The entrance was probably wider back then, too, without all of this overgrowth."

"It sounds backbreaking. Have you ever seen carvings or paintings of this process?"

She nodded. "There are several Post-Classic Maya pots in the museum in Cancun that show examples of mining."

"I'd like to see them someday." He looked inside Juan's leather bag, making sure he had all of Juan's toys and tools. After sparing one last look at the dark mine entrance, he turned to Angélica. "Where to, boss lady?"

"We'll stop by the tent and drop that bag off, then you can head over to help Dad until lunch. I'm afraid he's going to push his leg too hard today in his excitement to explore inside the *Baatz'* Temple."

"Sounds like a plan." Quint wanted to wash his hands and face, too. The mine had left him with a coat of gritty sweat.

He trailed Angélica all of the way to their tent, imagining the Maya digging and hauling one basket of limestone granules and earth at a time up from the mine.

Minutes later, outside their tent, he dropped his hard hat on the ground next to Angélica's. He stepped through the flap, setting down the bag of spelunking tools near Juan's footlocker. When he turned to go back outside, Angélica blocked the way.

She clasped her hands together. "I've been thinking, Quint."

The use of his first name gave him pause. "About what?"

"Something you said."

When? At the mine? He crossed his arms, bracing for whatever it was that had ruffled her feathers this morning. "And?"

"Two things." She held up one finger. "First, my mom didn't list anything in her notes I can think of that would cause someone to want to take her life."

Ah, this was about something he'd said last night. No wonder she was so touchy. Anything to do with her mom was sacred ground.

He wondered if she'd let him take a look at Marianne's notes. Maybe there was something she wasn't seeing due to being too close to all of this. He'd save that request for another time when she was less growly.

A second finger joined the first. She licked her lips, hesitating for a fraction of a second. "Just so you and I are clear, I was upset when you first showed up at the site. My comment about sex with you being sort of memorable that day was intended to sting you for being gone so long."

"It was a well-aimed jab." A solid wallop below the belt.

"I didn't mean it."

"So sex with me isn't memorable?" he joked. Or not.

She sputtered, her gaze lowering, her hands clasping and unclasping. Then she stilled and squared her shoulders. "Here's the deal. Facing off with rattlesnakes and crawling around in tight spaces is not a problem for me. I've been doing it since I was young. But this thing between us …" she shook her head. "Well, it scares the hell out of me."

Was he making it worse somehow? Pushing her too fast? He could try to slow down, somehow. But he wasn't sure how much control he had over the gas pedal when it came to the two of them.

"I'm afraid that I'm not handling things well." She turned away from him, scratching her fingernail over the tent canvas. "You see, you bring out in me everything I'd like to keep hidden. My insecurities, my self-doubts, my fears for the future, all of them keep fighting to run the show." She blew out a breath like a weight had been lifted with her honesty. "Ever since that day you walked onto my last dig site, feelings that I've worked very hard to control and repress over the years have bubbled to the surface." She pulled her hand away from the tent, clenching her fist. "No matter how hard I try, I can't shove them back down again."

"And that's a bad thing?" In his opinion, it was a step in the right direction—his direction.

Her laugh sounded harsh. "I'd sooner be tortured on the rack and done with it all so I can focus on my job again."

"The rack, huh?" He rubbed his jaw. "I can think of less painful sadomasochistic games for the two of us, if that's what you're into."

"What I'm into, Parker, is regaining control of my emotions."

"What do you want to do about it?" His pulse hammered in his ears. He would like to have a say in the matter, but he let her lead for the time being.

The silence dragged. When her gaze returned to his, pain and vulnerability lined her face. She stood before him stripped of all defenses, and it stole his breath.

"I don't know. I'm afraid of letting anyone else inside here." She tapped above her left breast. "Of losing someone else."

There it was, Quint thought, one of the main roots leading to her struggles. Her mom's death still haunted her.

"I'm not going anywhere, Angélica." Not without her, anyway.

She scowled. "You'll be leaving again in a few weeks, remember?"

"That's temporary."

Temporary. There was that word again. A label she'd given him at the last site that had given him plenty of heartburn.

"But you and I are permanent," he reiterated, wanting to cement that in her head.

"You don't know that." She rubbed her brow. "You could get hurt while you're gone."

"I could get hurt here. We both could. Rattlesnakes aren't exactly teddy bears." Not to mention that if Pedro was right, she was in mortal danger the longer she stayed here.

"Your plane could crash."

He didn't miss the correlations she was making between her mother's death and his traveling. "The odds are against it."

Silence filled the tent again. He wanted to reach out to her and reassure her, to blanket that vulnerability she was letting him see. But this was something she was going to have to come to terms with on her own. All he could do was continue to wait and hold on tight, refusing to let go.

"Angélica, I'm like a tick," he quipped, trying to lure her smile again. "You can try to tear me off, but I'll just dig in deeper."

"A tick?" One side of her mouth lifted. "That's not very sexy, Parker."

"Neither is sweating my ass off next to you day and night in this sauna Mexico calls 'paradise' in its commercials, but I'm playing for keeps here. I'll do whatever it takes for a shot at winning you."

Her eyes darkened as she stared at him. "This isn't going to be easy."

"For you or me?"

"Either of us." She stuck her hands in her back pockets. "I'm hard-headed and you're stubborn as hell. Not to mention your overflowing love for this place and all of its difficulties."

"True, but you and your machete will battle the jungle for me, and I'll make you laugh."

She chuckled. "That you will." Her focus traveled lower. "Not to mention that you're really good in the sack."

He grunted. "There's that damned word again."

"Really super duper?" She bridged the distance between them. Her eyes flirted, lashes batting a couple of times.

"That sounds like something you'd say before sticking a gold star on my cheek." He pulled her closer.

She didn't resist, wrapping her arms around his waist. Her chin rested on his chest. "How's this? Every time you touch me, Quint Parker, you rock my world."

"You're getting warmer."

She went up on her toes. "Actually, I'm getting very hot." She kissed him, her lips soft and searching. "And bothered," she breathed against his mouth.

His hands slid along her jaw, framing her face, holding her close. He deepened the kiss, touching her tongue with his. Lust quickly took over, his mouth growing more demanding, her response more frenzied. It'd been so long since he'd had her that his control was slippery at best.

"Sweet Jesus," he said when she slid her hand over the front of his pants, pressing, teasing.

"Quint?" Her breaths came faster.

He groaned when her touch grew bolder. "What?"

"I want you."

"Oh, yeah?"

"Bad."

His mouth took hers again, rougher now. His hunger freed, running the show. "I'm all yours, sweetheart."

"We don't have long." She unbuttoned his pants.

"I don't think speed is going to be a problem for me." The feel of skin on skin alone might blow his gasket if he wasn't careful. He trailed his mouth down her neck.

Her moan rose from low in her throat. "I want to feel your—"

"Angélica?" Juan called. It sounded like he was at the edge of the tent clearing.

She winced. "Fuck me."

He seconded that emotion. Grabbing her by the shoulders, he pushed her back a step before he lost what little restraint he had left and told Juan to come back after he'd finished ravaging the man's daughter.

"Angélica?" Juan called again, close enough this time that Quint could hear the creak of his cane.

"In our tent," she called out. "I'm changing my clothes. What do you need?"

Quint could hear Juan breathing on the other side of the canvas. "We found something inside the *Baatz'* Temple that you should see."

She looked up at Quint, her eyes widening. He raised his eyebrows in reply while fixing everything south of the border and zipping his pants again.

"Is it the stela?" she asked.

"No, but you still need to come see this."

She cursed under her breath. "I'll be along in a minute."

"When you finish getting dressed?"

"Yes. I'll catch up with you before you make it back to the temple."

"Okay. I need to refill Maverick's and my canteens."

"Sounds good, Dad."

"That should give Quint enough time to help you finish getting dressed. He can join us as well."

She looked at the ceiling, shaking her head.

Quint laughed. "I'll be sure to hurry her along, Juan."

Her father's chuckles faded along with the creak of his cane.

"He has the worst timing," she said.

"No, if he'd shown up ten minutes later, *then* he would've had the worst timing."

"Ten minutes? It's been over a month, heartbreaker. You sure either of us would have lasted that long?"

"You're right. Make that five." He leaned down and gave her a slow kiss, taking his time tasting her since Juan would be a couple of minutes refilling canteens. When he stepped back, he shook his head to clear it of lust.

"Damn, Parker." She blew out a breath.

"Apology accepted, by the way."

"Apology for what?"

"Insulting my virility the day I arrived."

Her smile teased. "Well, I can't let your ego get too big now, can I?"

"Encouraging it a little every now and then certainly wouldn't kill you, would it?"

"I'll see what I can do, big boy." She winked and then led the way outside of the tent. When he joined her, she said, "In the meantime, you need to prepare for a shit storm."

He zipped the tent flap closed behind him. "What do you mean?"

She pointed toward the mess tent. "See for yourself."

Quint did, his gaze landing on Juan, who was limping their way, carrying two canteens. A grin hung from ear to ear on her father's face. "Here we go," he muttered, grabbing his hard hat from the grass.

"So," Juan said, handing Quint one of the canteens to carry when he reached their side. "Was it productive?"

"Our visit to the cave?" Angélica asked.

"No. Making feet for children's stockings in the tent just now."

Cursing, Angélica snagged her hat from the ground. "We've created a monster."

"I have a feeling your old man's just getting rolling."

Juan's laughter filled the camp.

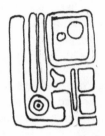

Chapter Eight

The Olmec People: One of the earliest major civilizations in Mesoamerica, thriving from roughly 1200 BC to 400 BC. Among their many great feats: They were prodigious traders, traveling far to the north and south.

What in the hell is that doing here?" Angélica knelt inside the sweltering *Baatz'* Temple, taking a closer look at the mask leaning against the wall. The upper quarter of its round head and one of the hoop earrings were missing, but there was plenty of the mask remaining to recognize its style.

"That was my thought as soon as I saw it." Her father blotted his neck with his handkerchief. "We probably shouldn't stay in here too long. The heat is much worse than it was earlier this morning."

Quint moved up next to her, his shirt mostly soaked but with a few islands of dry spots here and there. "What is that?"

"It's not Maya, that's what it is." Angélica wiped the bead of sweat rolling down her forehead with the back of her hand.

"What do you mean?"

"It's Olmec," Juan explained. "If I had to guess, I'd say it's quite a few centuries older than the Maya people who built this temple."

"You can tell that just by looking at it?"

"The Olmec had a different style from the Maya." Angélica tugged a small paintbrush from her back pocket. She dusted the packed-dirt floor of the temple around the mask. The missing piece might be nearby.

Quint sat down next to her, leaning against the wall, careful to avoid the glyphs. "It seems like I read there are theories about the Olmecs being the ancestors of the Maya but not of the Aztecs. Sort of like it's now thought that the Ancestral Puebloan culture was the predecessor of the Hopi and Zuni Puebloan peoples farther up north."

"Ancestral Puebloan?" Angélica glanced at Quint, her eyebrows raised at his use of the preferred name for those who were formerly called the *Anasazi*. "You know the difference between that term and *Anasazi*?" Not many outside of the Native American tribes of that area and those in the fields of study involving their cultural history knew the distinction.

He shrugged. "I wrote a piece several years ago about the area near the Acoma Pueblo in New Mexico."

"You were at Sky City?" Juan asked.

"Actually, we were right next to it in the *El Malpais* lava fields, but I spent some time nearby at the cultural center and museum. That's where I learned the actual meaning of the term *Anasazi* and why the Puebloan people don't like it being used in relation to their ancestors."

"I can't blame them." Juan moved to the opposite corner of the chamber, checking out the cracks lining the ceiling. "I'm not sure I'd like my ancestors being referred to in the history books as the 'ancient enemies' either."

"Did you do an article at some point on the Olmec and Aztec cultures as well?" Angélica asked, thinking about his response to her back at the cave regarding the Great Smoky Mountains and bat urine stalactites.

Quint shook his head. "But I've been studying up on the Mesoamerican civilizations."

"Studying? You?" She grinned. "And here Dad and I thought you were just another pretty face."

"I didn't call him pretty." Her father used his cane to tap on the ceiling in several spots. "But I did say he had a nice personality."

Quint chuckled at their teasing. He took a swig from his canteen. His brow wrinkled as he watched Juan tap on the bridge stone at the top of the corbel vault leading out of the chamber. "I've seen a thing or two in my thirty-eight years."

Angélica's gaze returned to the mask, but her focus was on Quint's words. Of course, he'd seen a lot in his time, especially with all of the traveling he'd done, but hearing him say it made her realize how little she knew about him. What secrets from his past lay hidden behind those hazel eyes? Maybe she needed to take her paintbrush and trowel to Quint, sweeping away the surface dust, digging deeper into his past. She didn't want a repeat of the mistakes she'd made with her ex-husband.

Wiping her hands off on her pants, she stood. "The Maya people have several of the same gods as the Olmecs. They also shared in the ritual of bloodletting and played a similar style of ballgame. These and other subtle commonalities between the two cultures have led many archaeologists to believe that the Maya are descendants of the Olmecs."

The sound of Juan's tape measure retracting made her glance at her father. He was tugging his notebook from his back pocket. "But there is much debate about this still," he said around the pencil between his teeth.

Angélica grimaced down at the mask, rubbing the back of her neck. Sharing the same gods and practices didn't explain what that piece of Olmec art was doing in here.

Back to Quint, she added, "When it comes to Olmec artwork, most of the pieces are easily distinguishable from other cultures. Notice the thickness of the lips and nose on this mask along with the arch of the eyebrows. You'll see this same style on many Olmec pieces, including those colossal head statues made famous by many of Mexico's tourism ads." She offered her hand to help him stand.

Quint took her up on her offer, careful not to hit his head on the ceiling. He dusted off the back of his pants. "But I thought the Olmec sites were farther north, closer to where the Aztecs settled."

"They were centered near the lowlands of the Gulf coast in southeast Veracruz," Juan said, scribbling something in his notebook. "Sites like La Venta and San Lorenzo are part of the Olmec heartland."

"So why would an Olmec piece be sitting on the floor of a Maya temple this far south?"

"Your guess is as good as mine." She looked at the carvings and glyphs on the temple walls. Her pulse leapt at the stories this temple might tell them about the past. "Maybe there's something in here that might give us a clue."

Juan joined them, spotlighting the wall above the Olmec mask. "I glanced over the glyphs and carvings in here before coming to get you, thinking the same thing, but didn't see anything Olmec based. But then again, I'm not the one who reads Maya glyphs in her sleep."

Angélica stepped toward the wall, keeping her face averted from Quint and her father. Lately, her dreams had been about something much more disturbing than anything she'd read on a Maya glyph.

Since she had arrived at this site, her dreams often included her mother. This was no surprise after all the studying and pondering she'd been doing about Marianne and her notes. But with each passing day that Angélica didn't find that damned stela, her dreams were growing more warped, taking a turn toward something more sinister.

For the last week, she'd spent each night reliving her mother's helicopter crash from both inside of the helicopter and out. Sometimes she was there after the crash watching her mother die all over again, while at other times she was the one who plunged to the ground and lay bleeding while the darkness swallowed her whole. Waking up gasping was becoming normal.

But last night things had taken an all-new frightening turn. Marianne hadn't been the only one in the helicopter this time. She'd had company with her on the flight out—Quint.

Angélica had watched as the two of them buckled up, lifted off, and crashed to their deaths. Screams, both theirs and hers, had echoed through the jungle as they burned alive in the explosion that followed. At the fiery end, she'd jerked upright and found herself with a pounding heart and sweat-soaked camisole in Quint's cot. Her pulse had continued to jackhammer in her ears as she'd pulled on her pants and a dry shirt.

She'd escaped to the mess tent, seeking caffeine to wash away the nightmare, and found it empty other than Maverick and Fernando. After a brief greeting, both men had eaten and slurped their coffee in silence, thankfully.

A cup of coffee had helped with her analysis of the inclusion of Quint in her nightmare. Sleeping on his pillow, surrounded by his scent, must have caused the change. Not to mention her anxiety about his leaving again soon. One thing was for sure, she wasn't going to test that theory again. There'd be no sharing his cot anytime soon, at least not until she found that stela and could return to a less frustration-filled night's sleep.

Slowly, the rest of the crew had filtered into the mess tent, along with her father and Quint, both freshly shaven. She'd debated on skipping the trip to the cave, putting some space between her and Quint, but avoidance was not the solution. Besides, it wasn't his fault that her growing feelings for him were awakening an irrational fear of desertion.

She'd tried to hide from Quint the mess of emotions rippling through her at the mine. Unfortunately, she'd almost messed things up royally between them in the process. Shielding herself with her "boss" role had only increased the tension between them. In the end, total honesty had been her only solution short of hitting her head repeatedly against that wall blocking off the rest of the mine.

Why was there a wall blocking off the mine, anyway? Something wasn't right. Maybe it was just a gut feeling, but there should have been at least a sign of a rat or two, or some other furry vermin inside. Its lack of …

"Angélica?" her father's voice brought her back to the sweltering present. "Did you hear me?"

"Sorry, I was thinking about the past."

Juan chuckled. "You really should try living in the present more often."

"The present is too complicated." From the corner of her eye she saw Quint look her way, but she kept her focus on the wall.

Something down near the ground caught her attention.

She moved closer, squatting in front of the wall, and angled her light for a deeper shadow effect. She ran her fingers over the glyph. Her mother's words echoed in her head: *You always were more tactile.* For Angélica, reading glyphs often required the feel of the stone under her fingers, like reading braille.

"What do you see, *gatita?*" Her father stood over her.

She pointed at the image that someone had so carefully carved into the wall centuries ago.

Juan leaned down, grunting. "What is it? I can't bend that low yet, thanks to my bad leg."

"I believe it's the jester god."

Quint went down on one knee next to her. "Jester god? Like a jester in a king's court?"

"Exactly," Juan said. "The Olmec also had a jester god."

"He's called the jester god because of the circles hanging in front of his head when depicted in glyphs and on artwork. You can see them relatively clearly right here." She pointed at the three small circles in the wall.

Quint leaned closer, and then sat back again, shaking his head. "It all runs together as a bunch of swirling lines for me."

"I'll do a rubbing later and show it to you. These details sometimes appear more clearly on paper."

She stood, glancing around the chamber again, taking in what she hadn't noticed earlier due to her excitement at seeing why her father was limping along so quickly all of the way here. The walls leading into the chamber were still partially coated with red ochre paste, which was used by the Maya in many frescos and hand-painted vessels throughout the Yucatán. After centuries, the floor was littered with stones and dirt along with the usual evidence of animal habitation. The chamber smelled musty, though, as if it had been a long time since even creatures had ventured inside. That was probably due in part to the way the entrance had caved in, temporarily blocking off the outside world.

The *Baatz'* Temple reminded her of the *Ik* Temple at her last dig site, but she doubted this one had as many sub chambers due to its design. The three stories seemed to be more for prestige rather than use. Not to mention this temple appeared to be a couple of centuries older, judging from the architectural style. It wasn't as elaborate as the Post-Classic temples located farther north, nor did it have the elegance of Palenque to the south.

She shone her flashlight around, noticing several more faded paintings up near the ceiling where her father had been inspecting the fractures.

Still, the place might have secrets to share under its plain wrapper. Secrets that her mother had discovered and left behind for Angélica to unearth. If only she could find a single freaking clue where to start digging, she could stop obsessing about what was on that damned stela and maybe even get a solid night's sleep for once.

"What are you contemplating, *gatita*?"

She lowered her flashlight, avoiding her father's eagle eyes. "Where's Maverick?" she asked, changing the subject. "I thought he was working with you in here this morning."

"He was. Right before I came to find you, Bernard came over to get him. Fernando needed his help in the other temple."

"I thought Lorenzo was there helping."

"María needed him to help her gather water this morning since Teodoro flew off with Pedro to get your snake hunting supplies."

Quint crossed his arms, taking a wide stance. "Has Maverick asked either of you any prying questions?"

"What do you mean by 'prying'?" Juan asked.

Angélica chuckled. "Quint means questions like *he* was asking us at the last dig."

"You mean questions like you had about Dr. Hughes and the site's history?" Juan dabbed his neck again with his handkerchief.

Quint nodded once.

"Or the ones about my daughter's availability?"

"Yes. Wait. What?" Quint's gaze narrowed. "Maverick's been asking about Angélica?"

Juan snorted with laughter.

Angélica grabbed Quint's elbow and tugged him toward the temple's exit. "He's messing with you again."

"How do you know? Maverick could very well be interested in you."

"Because I have eyes."

"You think you can read men as easily as you can Mayan glyphs?"

"*Maya* glyphs. *Mayan* refers only to the language. And no, I can't."

"Ha! See."

"Maya glyphs are harder to decipher."

Her father laughed again from behind Quint.

"Oh, really?" Quint said as they stepped back into the sunlight. He shielded his eyes. "What am I thinking right now, Miss Mind-reader?"

She stood for a moment staring up at him, the midday sunshine baking the top of her head. The jungle rippled behind him in the heat. Sweat trickled down his cheek. "You're thinking that it's really freaking hot."

His lips twitched. "No fair. That was too easy."

"Trust me, Quint, not once has Maverick pestered me for answers to anything out of the ordinary." At his continued tight jaw and gunfighter squint, she added with a small smile, "Nor has he tried to put any moves on me. Unlike you, his intentions from the start have been clear. He's here for hands-on research for his next book."

"My intentions were clear, too, especially after I met you."

"And if memory serves me right," Juan chimed in, "Quint did plenty of hands-on research with you as well."

Quint's deep laughter rang out, scaring away several squawking parrots from the trees nearby.

"You're having way too much fun these days, Dad." She planted her hands on her hips, hitting him with a mock glare. "It's time to get back to the business of archaeology."

"Bossy women," Juan scoffed, hitting Quint with a wink. "They muck up all our fun, don't they?"

"Sometimes a good mucking can be quite titillating." Quint gave her a thorough once-over, his gaze warming her more than the ball of fire in the sky. "Wouldn't you agree, boss lady?"

"On that note," Angélica said, holding up both hands in surrender. "I'm outta here. Quint, make sure my dad takes it easy on that leg, please."

"Scaredy-cat," Quint taunted as she walked away.

"Don't forget to check each of these broken stone pieces for glyphs or other important markings," she shouted orders over her shoulder, smiling at the mutterings that followed as she veered off toward the ballcourt.

A short time later, Angélica was kneeling on the ground next to Daisy, checking out the older woman's finds since breakfast. It was like Christmas morning, with excitement filling the air along with the lemony eucalyptus scent of Daisy's homemade bug repellent. This end of the ballcourt was beginning to look like a checkerboard with all of the squares marked off and excavated.

"How in the world are you finding these things so easily?" she asked Daisy. "Do you have some kind of X-ray vision in your fingertips?"

"Esteban has come up with a theory. He thinks I used to live at this site in a past life."

"Where is Esteban?"

"He's in the trees taking care of business."

Angélica held up a two-edged obsidian blade. It was almost as long as her hand. Parts of its sharp edges had been chipped off, but much of the blade remained sharp and deadly. Rarely had she come across tools in such great shape, especially obsidian blades this big. "Maybe Esteban is on to something," Angélica said, placing the blade back into the shallow bin with the other carefully stored and labeled pieces Daisy had found. It would certainly help make sense of how she kept hitting the jackpot.

"Where did you find this flint one?"

Daisy took the curved and sharpened flint knife, fitting her hand around it like she knew how to use it. "Over there, in grid square E4. It was about six inches under the dirt." She twisted her hand, looking at the backside of the weapon. "Its creator must have been a woman. It fits my hand almost perfectly."

Angélica took the flint piece from Daisy, gripping it. "The Maya were a smaller people. Their bones show the males being close to my size on average, like Esteban, only a couple of inches shorter." Quint would have been a giant among them, which was why he often got extra sweaty and ducked his head in the sub chambers inside of their temples.

She placed the flint back into the container. "Do you know what this is?" she asked, lifting another of Daisy's finds.

"A jade bead of some sort? Maybe from one of their necklaces?"

Angélica held the tiny piece of round jade up in the sunlight. "It's a jade tooth inlay." She looked down at the other inlays in the container, counting eight. There must be teeth around there somewhere, too. "The Maya were a fashionable culture. Did you know that they revered anyone who was a little cross-eyed, believing them to be very beautiful? They'd put a headband on their babies with a stone hanging from a string between the child's eyes, hoping the babies' eyes would cross."

Daisy crossed her eyes at Angélica, curling her lips back in a toothy smile. "How do I look now?"

Chuckling, Angélica set the jade piece back in with the others. "Absolutely stunning. You're sure to have all of the warriors at the ballgame worshipping you tonight."

"So long as they don't decide to sacrifice me for some rain from *Chac*."

"The rain god will have to be satisfied with some chickens tonight, since that is what María has planned for supper."

The bushes across the court rustled, sending several jays flying. Esteban came stumbling out seconds later. He waved and headed their way.

"You show it to Dr. García?" he asked Daisy when he joined them.

"Show me what? The blades?"

He shook his head.

Daisy shared a conspiratorial smile with him. "I wanted to wait until you were here, too."

"What is it?" Angélica looked from one to the other.

Daisy lifted her blue and white bag with 'Mexico' written on it that lay next to the container of treasures. Under it was half of a skull. "Ta-da! We found another one."

Angélica pulled out her paintbrush and hooked it through the eyeball socket, lifting what was left of the skull. The back half was gone, but the front looked mostly intact, except a piece from a cheekbone. This one was human, no doubt about it this time. And Maya, too. She could tell by the forehead.

"Esteban told me that Maya parents would press boards against a newborn's forehead to flatten it like this skull."

Angélica nodded. "A sloped forehead and elongated skull was another indication of beauty to the Maya. It had to do with the maize god." She looked at Esteban. "You marked this thoroughly, I'm assuming, noting the location and position and anything else of interest."

"*Sí.* We drew pictures and took many photos, too."

"Were there any other pieces around it?"

He shook his head. "*Solo el cráneo.* Only the skull," he repeated in English for Daisy's sake.

Angélica lowered it into a container with care. She frowned down at the empty eye sockets. Why was there another skull here? In the ballcourt, of all places? Often the losers of the game were sacrificed, sometimes even the winners, but not right here on the field. Depictions she'd seen usually had them either on top of or inside a temple with other Maya around to witness it. A ritual sacrifice, performed for appeasing one god or another.

She stuffed her brush back into her pocket and stood. "Good job, you two." Wait, there were supposed to be three of them here. "Where's Gertrude?"

"Bernard came and got her a while ago." Daisy rose, too. "He said Fernando needed her at the *Chakmo'ol* Temple."

"What's going on in there?" Fernando had started the day with Bernard and Jane, but now he had Maverick and Gertrude, too.

"Maybe they're having a *fiesta*?" Daisy joked.

Angélica scoffed. "Fernando's idea of a fiesta involves everyone working overtime carrying rocks around." She'd have to go check out what he was up to in the *Chakmo'ol* Temple. She glanced down at her watch. "It's almost lunchtime. You two can take a break and get out of this sun for a bit. Today is really cooking."

With a wave, Angélica headed off across the plaza toward the site's largest structure, curious as to what her foreman was up to that required so much help.

She found Gertrude and Jane first. They were outside of the temple working on a pile of what at first glance appeared to be rubble. However, it was actually a three-feet-high, long and narrow platform running parallel to the temple that was in the process of crumbling into the ground in spots. On the remaining pieces of the low wall that wrapped around the base were carvings containing Maya symbolism. Most were still visible through the lichen that had coated much of the stone over the centuries.

What was Gertrude doing out here? Hadn't Fernando needed her help inside the temple?

"How are things going here?" she asked the two college students.

"We've seen four rattlesnakes so far today," Jane said, her mouth downturned as she carefully toed another rock onto its side. "And that's four too many, in my opinion."

"You think there's a burrow under here?" Angélica asked, bending over to dislodge several stones, searching for signs of more snakes.

"No," Gertrude said, sounding certain. She stood on the platform looking down at about twenty to twenty-five stones that were laid out in front of her in three horizontal lines.

Angélica climbed up next to her. "Any luck putting the puzzle together?"

Since Gertrude's field of study was more along the lines of Juan's, ancient architectural styles, she'd been put in charge of reconstructing the broken wall pieces so the carvings all lined up again. It was no easy feat, but according to Juan, the young woman was making progress, albeit slower than Angélica would have liked. At the rate Gertrude was going, she'd have only a small section of the wall pieced together again by the time they had to leave.

Such was archaeology, Angélica thought with a smirk. It moved along at a snail's pace at best much of the time. With all of the cataloging and sketching and recording, it was a wonder they kept ahead of the lichen growth down here in the jungle.

"You two need anything?" Angélica asked.

They both shook their heads.

"It's almost lunchtime, so if you want to take a break and head over to the mess tent, feel free to go."

Angélica hopped down off the platform and trod around the side of the temple, watching for snakes as she walked. The pathway was clear … for now. As she neared the vaulted entryway, she could hear the deep rumble of Fernando's voice. Inside the stone walls, the heat wasn't as bad. There were more large shade trees at this end of the site, like the ceiba tree she'd pointed out to Quint earlier, which seemed to help keep the temperature down a little inside the temple throughout the day.

She made her way through the limestone-whitewashed walls, careful not to touch the paintings made so long ago that were in various states of decay. They had much work to do inside this temple as soon as they finished cleaning out the mess left behind by the looters. After a left turn and a short trek down an uneven slope she found Fernando, Bernard, and Maverick all in one mid-sized chamber. The room smelled like a blend of bug spray, sunblock, dust, and sweat. "What's going on?" she asked her foreman, moving over to where he was studying something in the far corner.

Fernando glanced at her over his shoulder. If he was surprised to see her, his frown didn't show it. He grunted and rose, his knees popping. "We found this."

He held out what looked like an old wrinkled sausage casing. It crackled when she took it from him. It took her a second to make sense of it.

"Snakeskin?" She'd expected to find something Maya under all of the looters' mess, not something more recent from a whole other species.

"There's more," he said, pointing at the floor.

It looked like someone had peeled off the outer layers of a bag full of onions and littered the floor with the flakes of dried skin.

"This was *under* the looters' rubble?"

Maverick and Bernard worked together to lift the last few stones and place them in the wheelbarrow.

"*Sí*," Fernando said, watching Bernard struggle to push the wheelbarrow up and out of the chamber. After he'd cleared the slope and turned toward the exit, Fernando waved Angélica over to another corner of the chamber.

She followed, glancing over at Maverick, who leaned against the far wall, gulping water from his canteen. "You doing okay?" she asked him, Quint's questions about the writer's true purpose flitting through her mind.

"Never better." Maverick capped his canteen, actually smiling for once. It was a rare sight since his arrival. Something usually only her father had been able to spur. "All of this hard work and sweat is good for a bruised spirit."

Quint might beg to differ. But then again, Parker didn't seem to be battling demons like Maverick had been for the last couple of weeks. She too had a feeling the writer was here for more than research purposes, but she'd lay down money that his other reason for coming to this nearly forgotten jungle had nothing to do with his profession. Maybe she was inventing drama for him, but she suspected something back home had sent him running. Whatever it was, he'd arrived here scarred up and pissed off.

She wasn't sure that a Maya dig site was going to heal whatever ailed Maverick, but he was a hard worker and didn't complain about the heat, snakes, or rough quarters. So long as he kept his nose to the grindstone like the rest of her own crew, she had no issues with his profession back in the more-civilized world.

Focusing on Fernando, she shone her flashlight in the direction of where he was pointing. She squatted in front of a square carving and leaned in close, studying the story left behind on the chamber wall. "Is that ..." she tilted the light, deepening shadows, and trailed her fingers over the stone relief.

"*Sí*," Fernando said. "*Yum Cimil.*"

"What's *Yum Cimil?*" Maverick asked, still leaning against the wall.

"It's the Maya lord of death, ruler of the ninth level of the Maya Underworld."

Maverick sniffed. "Sounds like a happy-go-lucky guy."

Scooting back a little, she shone her light around, trying to make sense of the larger picture. The carving was lined with snakes, tail to tail and head to head, the tails intertwined to make a contiguous border around the whole scene.

"It looks like he's down a steep slope, sitting inside a small chamber," she said, taking up her paintbrush and dusting at the carving carefully.

"This chamber, maybe?" Fernando asked.

Footfalls coming closer told her Maverick had joined them for a better look. "Are those snakes he's sitting on?"

"Yes," she said. "It looks like a throne of snakes."

She leaned closer, angling her light again.

A draft of slightly cooler air brushed across her face. She paused, looking at Fernando and then Maverick. Both were too far away for their breath to hit her, and the air from their lungs wouldn't be cooler anyway.

She unhooked her canteen from her belt loop and uncapped it, pouring a small pool of water into her palms, and then rubbed them together.

"What are you doing?" Maverick asked. "Is this some kind of archaeological magic trick?"

"Sure," she said and held her hands up, fingers spread wide, her palms about an inch from the wall. After a few seconds, she moved them around, down, over toward the corner.

There!

She grabbed her flashlight and aimed it in the corner.

"Fernando, do you see that?"

He leaned closer. "A crack."

It was too thin for a pencil to fit through, but twice as long. "Good news, boys. There's more to this temple than meets the eye."

"What do you mean?" Maverick backed up, giving her space as she pushed to her feet.

"I felt cool air coming through that crack."

"You think there's another room like this?"

"I don't know." She looked over at Fernando, who was still frowning down at the crack. "If it were only another chamber sealed within the temple, we probably wouldn't feel cooler air."

"It's breathing." Fernando's tone made it clear that the fact didn't please him.

"If we were farther north on the peninsula," she told Maverick, "I'd guess that we were standing over a *cenote*."

"*Cenote*? That's one of those holes in the limestone shelf filled with water, right?"

"Bingo. *Cenotes* are usually linked via underground tunnels to other *cenotes*."

"So air would be moving through them," he finished.

"But we're not up north. *Cenotes* are few and far between here."

She thought of the limestone mine and the wall someone had built to block it. Maybe there was a connection between it and the temple. The mine's entrance was about fifty yards away. A tunnel could have been dug between the two.

"Maybe there's a ventilation shaft," Fernando suggested.

"That's a possibility." She'd witnessed such airways in other temples around the Yucatán. "The Maya were brilliant architects. Just ask my father."

"He's told me a thing or two." Maverick wiped his forehead. "And then he proceeded to scare the shit out of me by removing what he said was a key bridge stone in an arch back in the *Baatz'* Temple."

Fernando grumbled under his breath in Spanish about her father's practical jokes.

Angélica chuckled. "My dad loves to perform archaeology magic tricks that make the crowd *ooh* and *ahh*."

"More like run screaming in terror out of the temple," Maverick said with a small smile. "He'd make quite a character in one of my books."

"He is *muy loco*," Fernando added.

The sound of Bernard's footfalls coming their way made the three of them turn toward the chamber's entrance. The young Brit ducked and stepped inside the chamber with them, his wide-toothed smile making him look even younger than his twenty-one years. "The helicopter is back."

Great, Pedro and Teodoro had returned. Angélica hoped the shaman had gathered everything they needed to deal with the snakes this afternoon. She didn't think Jane was going to be able to keep working at this end of the site much longer if they didn't try to relocate the den soon. The girl was growing more skittish by the day.

"Now what do we do?" Bernard asked in his English accent, his teeth looking even whiter thanks to his sunburned face. "Shall I bring a dustpan and brush to tidy up? Maybe we could serve tea and biscuits in here later this afternoon."

"In this heat, your biscuits would go stale as soon you took them out of the package," Maverick said.

That reminded her … "It's time for lunch." Angélica pointed at Bernard. "You need to ask Teodoro for some of his sunburn salve before you start to blister. I told you hats are a necessity down here for someone as pale as you and Gertrude."

Although the German girl seemed to have amazingly sunburn-resistant skin. She looked as pale as the day she'd arrived, even though Angélica had seen her walking around without a hat several times. Those bright blue streaks in Gertrude's hair were hard to miss even from across the plaza.

"Are you coming?" Fernando asked. "You know your father likes to make sure you eat enough while working."

She sighed, not understanding why her dad worried so much about food and her. Thanks to María's cooking, she could afford to skip a meal or ten. "How about you bring me back something."

"You sure?"

Glancing around at the freshly cleared room, she rubbed her hands together. Who had time for food when this chamber was finally all hers for the studying? Now she understood why Fernando had been recruiting crew members to come help him. He'd promised her that he'd have the temple cleared by afternoon, and Fernando always delivered on his promises.

"Yes," she said, eyeing his backpack. "I think I'm going to sit a spell in here with the snakeskins and jot down some notes, maybe do some rubbings." This morning, Fernando had filled the backpack with rice paper, charcoal, brushes, and more before leaving the supply tent and heading for the temple with Bernard.

"You sure it's safe to stay in here alone?" Maverick asked.

"She likes to be alone," Fernando told him.

That was true until Quint had come along and messed with her head, damn it.

"We could stay and help you with the rubbings," Bernard offered.

"No, go eat. It's going to take me awhile to survey the walls. You'll be breathing down my neck to hurry up if you stay."

"Survey?" Maverick paused in the room's entryway. "You mean architecturally? I thought that was your father's specialty."

"I'm not talking about architecture. That crack has me wondering about something that the glyphs or carvings in here may explain. With closer examination, I hope to figure out if this chamber is merely another burial tomb of the site's previous nobility, or if it's something else."

Bernard's forehead creased. "Like what?"

She looked at the carving of *Yum Cimil*. "Maybe a gateway to the Maya Underworld."

Chapter Nine

El Perro (the Spanish word for *dog*):
Throughout the Maya world, a dog was considered an
invaluable companion for the dead, guiding their spirits along
on the harrowing journey through the nine levels of the
Underworld.

Quint was one of the first of Angélica's non-INAH crew to arrive
at the mess tent that evening. He debated on waiting for
Angélica, but he wasn't sure she'd even show up after skipping
lunch. His stomach was growling loud enough to scare off the noisy
howler monkeys, so he grabbed a plate and dished up some of
María's usual-but-delicious chicken *panucho* covered with her drool-
inspiring spicy sauce. He nodded at the college crew and Lorenzo,
on his way to the table where Angélica and her father usually sat.

A few bites into Quint's meal, Pedro stormed into the mess
tent. After scanning the place, he marched straight to Quint and slid
onto the bench seat next to him.

His shoulder bumped Quint's as he leaned in close and spoke
quietly. "I need to tell you something."

Quint swallowed a bite. "And here I thought you were sitting so
close to me because you had a crush on me."

When Pedro didn't laugh or joke back, Quint glanced over at
him. The anxious lines on Pedro's face gave him pause. "Is Angélica
okay?"

"She's fine. So is her father." Pedro laced his fingers together, resting his hands on top of the table. "But before either of them arrive, I need to tell you what I learned while hanging out in Coba, waiting for Teodoro to take care of business."

Considering Pedro's willingness to hold off on eating María's *panuchos* in order to tell his tale, Quint suspected Pedro's news wasn't going to make him feel like forming a conga line and snaking his way around the room.

"You better hurry then," he told Pedro, setting his fork down. "Juan's probably not far behind me." Angélica's father had turned toward the showers with his towel in hand when Quint made a beeline for the mess tent.

Pedro continued in a low voice for Quint's ears only. "I had cell phone service in Coba and time on my hands, so I made a few calls, trying to learn more about the pilot who'd been flying the helicopter that crashed with Marianne inside. It took five calls, but I finally got the number of the pilot's old girlfriend." Pedro glanced toward the entrance, which remained empty for the moment. "I called her. She still lives in Cancun, a few blocks from the airport. Still works in the *cantina* where they first met."

"That's kind of sad for her."

"Such is life in Mexico." Pedro scratched at the wooden table. "I asked her if the pilot had mentioned anything odd happening at one of the dig sites where he transported goods and people, anything that might have made the pilot think his life was in danger." Pedro's brown eyes locked onto Quint's. "Her answer gave me a goose rash."

Quint was too interested in what the pilot's girlfriend had said to correct his friend. He leaned in closer. "And?"

"He told her a couple of weeks before his last flight that the archaeologist in charge of a site at the edge of the Calakmul Biosphere Reserve had received several warnings to stop digging there from a few of the locals he'd hired."

"They threatened him?"

"That's what she initially thought, too, but he told her he'd talked to the local boys and they were just repeating stories handed down from their ancestors about the dangers of waking up *Ah Puch* at this site."

"The death god? Same guy as *Yum Cimil*, right?"

Pedro nodded. "Death, disaster, and destruction. He covers all three and then some."

"So why were they working here if they knew about these stories and warnings?"

With a shrug, Pedro said, "They probably needed the money. Riches aren't exactly abundant down here in the jungle, especially during the dry season when crops are struggling."

"So their stories were what? About the death god killing off any who woke him?"

"All the pilot's girlfriend remembered was that he had mentioned hearing the same warning several times from various workers—that continuing their work would end in releasing terror upon themselves."

"But Marianne and the pilot were the only ones who died."

Pedro's black eyebrows lifted. "Are we sure about that?"

"No, we are not. But wouldn't Angélica have found out by now if the other archaeologist and his crew had been snuffed out?"

"Snuffed out? That means killed, yes?" At Quint's nod, Pedro continued, "Maybe. The archaeologist for sure, but not necessarily anyone on his crew. You need to ask her to be certain."

"Why me?"

"You're her lover."

Not lately. He was more like a frisky, frustrated roommate. "But you're like a brother to her."

"A lover is closer than a brother. This is a job for you."

They both sat for a moment, exchanging frowns.

"Has anyone here received warnings of any sort?" he asked Pedro. He figured he would have heard about it if so, but maybe someone was good at keeping secrets.

"Not that I've heard, but remember, Angélica didn't hire locals this time, she brought everyone in from the outside. Maybe we need to take a trip over to the reserve's headquarters, ask the folks in charge if they know of any curses or stories about this site."

Before Quint could reply, Juan stepped into the tent with Angélica on his heels. They both came straight to the table, joining Quint and Pedro, curtailing any further discussion on the subject for the time being.

After a questioning glance in Pedro's direction, Angélica sat down on the bench opposite Quint. "You two look cozy. Did we interrupt your romantic dinner for two?"

With a loud guffaw that sounded fake to Quint's ears, Pedro

clapped him on the back and rose from his seat. "What can I say, Angel, Quint is one hot piece of man flesh."

Juan snickered at Quint from across the table. "Oh, he's hot, all right," he said, playing along. "He's practically melting before our eyes."

Stabbing another piece of his *panucho*, Quint grinned across at Angélica's dad. "I prefer to be referred to as *steamy*." He stuck the bite in his mouth and then scrubbed the gritty mixture of sweat and dirt off his face with his napkin. There was nothing like eating in a sauna.

Angélica's smile lit up her eyes. "It's a good thing I like my men wet."

"How many men are we talking about?" Quint stabbed another piece.

A wink from her was the only answer he received. She stood. "I'll grab you a plate, Dad. You just sit there and ogle Quint for me." She followed Pedro over to María, who was handing out platefuls of happiness by the ladleful.

"I need your help tomorrow," Juan told him, waving Daisy over to join them.

"If you're going to try to lure me inside that other sub chamber, you're going to have to get me wasted off my ass first. I don't like all of the cracks in that damned ceiling."

Inside the *Baatz'* Temple just off the main entrance was what Juan guessed to be a small burial chamber. However, several stones and blocks had fallen from the ceiling, and it needed shoring before it was safe for the crew. Juan had told Quint of his plans to make it "mostly" sound structurally, and Quint had told Juan that being buried alive in a temple named after monkeys was not on his agenda for this trip.

"I'll have to see how much *balche* Teodoro has prepared," Juan said. "A few cups of that potent nectar and you're all mine." He let out a fake evil laugh that quieted when Daisy sat down next to him. After exchanging a quick greeting with her, Juan returned his focus to Quint. "I actually need you to go with me into the critter-free limestone mine Angélica was telling me about on the walk here."

Quint shook his head. "What is it with you and tight spaces under massive amounts of rock or earth?"

"I like to live dangerously."

Snorting, Quint cut the last bit of his *panucho* in half. "I like to live. Period."

After everyone finished eating, each member checked in and shared finds and frustrations with Angélica.

Quint sat across from her, sipping from his drink, distracted by the thoughts racing through his mind.

Did Angélica have any clue what she'd gotten herself into at this site? What she'd possibly gotten them all into? He glanced her way, watching her as she talked to her father, her hands animated.

She'd found something in the *Chakmo'ol* Temple that had her sparkling with excitement. As she talked to her father about needing his guidance on the safest method to break through an interior wall, one that would cause the least amount of damage to the glyphs and overlying structure, Quint felt a tap on his leg.

Under the table, Pedro set a small square of folded paper on his thigh.

What was that? Was Pedro passing notes? When Quint looked up, Pedro mimed zipping his lips.

Quint fingered the paper, trying to decide if it was a good idea to open it now or later. In the end, curiosity got the best of him. He drained his water and stood with the empty cup, heading over to the jug of fresh drinking water. He refilled his cup, keeping his back to Angélica. He pulled the note from his pocket and quickly unwrapped it. The words Pedro had written on the page made no sense.

El perro regresa

What the hell did that mean? He pocketed the paper.

The first part was about a dog, but what did *regresa* mean? He set the cup down and turned around, finding Angélica's attention on him, watchful, studying.

He returned a quick smile. They needed to talk, but not here. He had questions that only she could answer, but he needed to be careful how he asked since they centered on her mom's death.

Her eyes stayed locked on him as he returned to the table.

"You about done?" he asked her.

She nodded, stabbing the last bite of her *panucho*.

"I'm going back to the tent. I'll wait for you there." With a quick glance at Pedro, whose usual good humor had been absent throughout the meal, Quint left the mess tent.

The moon lit the way, the mosquitoes escorting him through the dry grass. The forest seemed louder tonight, or maybe he was more on edge than before. An owl hooted in a nearby tree. He frowned, thinking of *Ah Puch* and his screech owl pal. That was just fucking great. A hoot-a-gram from a harbinger of death was exactly what Quint needed tonight after Pedro's tale about the previous crew's warnings of impending doom.

He unzipped the tent flap and turned on the battery-powered lamp. Pulling out Pedro's note, he frowned at it again, repeating the last word. What did that mean? Was "the dog" some weird reference to the possible dangers at this site? The locals' warnings he'd heard about from the pilot's ex-girlfriend? There were no wild dogs in the Mexican jungle, at least not the sort you'd find in the Australian outback or the African savannah.

Stuffing the note in his duffel bag, he grabbed some fresh clothes and his shower bag. After spending the afternoon sweating his ass off while clearing the brush and trees from along the northern side of the *Baatz'* Temple, he could use a scrub down with a wire brush and a bar of lye soap.

He flexed his right hand, frowning at the soreness he'd acquired from wielding a machete for hours on end. It was a wonder Angélica didn't have Popeye forearms after all of the machete swinging she'd done since arriving here.

The sound of the tent zipper made him look toward the mesh flap.

Angélica stepped inside. She held his gaze. "What's wrong?"

"Why do you ask that?"

"You've been quiet since I arrived at supper."

"I'm tired."

"And you keep watching me when you think I'm not looking."

"What can I say? I'm smitten."

"No games, Parker." She grabbed clothes and shower supplies. "Did something happen with Dad at the temple this afternoon? Something he doesn't want me to know about his leg?"

"Your father is fine. You'd hardly even know his leg was broken months ago."

"Then what is it?"

He tried to come up with a casual way to ask if she'd heard about any death threats delivered to the previous archaeology crew, but he hesitated. With Angélica's level-headedness, she'd probably shrug off any verbal threats that may or may not have actually occurred in the past. She'd figure it was just local agitators trying to keep the Mexican government from invading their lives down here in the jungle. Besides, Pedro's source for this information wasn't the most reliable. For Angélica to take this seriously, they needed something more substantial than a gossip-based story told over the phone by an old girlfriend of a dead pilot.

Quint detoured with, "What's the story about this crack in the wall in the *Chakmo'ol* Temple?"

"You're not telling me something, Parker."

"You caught me." He walked over and tipped up her chin. "I'm embarrassed to say just how much I missed you this afternoon."

Her gaze narrowed. "Hey, everyone, look who's back. It's Prince Charming."

Chuckling, he leaned down and kissed her. "Poke fun," he said when she'd stepped back to hook her machete onto her belt. "But sleeping so close to a beautiful woman all night long and not getting to do more than sneak a kiss now and then is hard on a guy." He took her hand and tugged her along behind him outside under the stars.

They walked in silence for several moments. The jungle's wild beat throbbed around them. Quint could smell the wood smoke from María's cook stove fire in the still air.

"What all did you learn this afternoon in the *Chakmo'ol* Temple?" he asked. "Fernando told us at lunch that there was a carving surrounded by snakes."

"Did he mention the snakeskin left behind on the chamber's floor, too?"

"He left out that particular detail."

"Was Dad there at the time?"

"Yes."

"That's probably why. Fernando knows how much my dad loathes snakes."

"So you think they named that temple wrong?"

"What do you mean?"

"Instead of the Jaguar Temple, it should have been named the Snake Lair?"

"Maybe. We'll see the deeper we dig." She was silent for several steps. As they neared the showers, she pulled him to a stop. "Quint?"

"Yeah?" He looked around at the growing shadows. The waning moonlight was no match for the forest's dark fingers tonight, especially here at the showers where the tall canopy surrounded them. The barks and roars of what sounded like a whole troupe of howler monkeys made him wince. He'd feel a lot less tense if they were packing heat instead of just melting in it.

"I've been thinking about something this afternoon," Angélica continued. "A lot."

"What's that?"

"Sex."

He did a double take. "You were thinking about sex?"

"Yes."

"While you were inside of a tomb-like room amongst snakeskin and death god carvings? That's sort of twisted."

"Sex *and* you."

"I meant twisted in a good way, of course. Were you part of that equation?"

The flirty sound of her laughter eased the anxiety that had been a burr in his gut since Pedro had joined him in the mess tent with his troubling tale. "We both were."

"Were you on the top part of the equation or the bottom during this thought-filled afternoon?"

She trailed her fingernails down his arm. "Both. It was a long afternoon."

"Tell me more."

"I'll have to whisper it in your ear." She pulled the shower curtain back. "You know, I do believe everyone else has taken their shower tonight. I could give you a hands-on demonstration of my day's thoughts in here."

He peeled off his T-shirt. "You're willing to risk someone catching us?"

Unclipping her machete, she hung it next to her towel from one of the nails pounded into the boards outside the stall. "It's been a month. I doubt this is going to take too long for either of us."

He watched as she slowly unbuttoned her shirt. In the feeble silver moonlight, her bra stood out in stark contrast against her skin. A flood of lust made his knees go weak.

She backed into the stall, disappearing in the shadows. "Come here, Parker," she said from the darkness, her voice husky.

Unbuttoning his pants, he took a step closer. "Are you inviting me to the dark side, boss lady?"

"No, I'm ordering you to get your ass in here." She snagged his arm, drawing him deeper in the shadows. She closed the curtain behind him and then wrapped her arms around his neck. "Take off my bra."

He obeyed, hanging it over the side of the stall. After reacquainting himself with her finer points, he asked, "What's next?"

"My pants."

The curve of her hips distracted him from his task, so she finished the job for him and helped remove his pants while she was at it, hanging them from another hook outside.

"If I agree to this shower idea of yours," he said between her rushed kisses, "will you drop the soap for me like you did that night back in Cancun?"

She nibbled along his jawline, tugging on his earlobe with her teeth. "You liked that, did you?"

"I've fantasized about repeating that scene too many times to count, sweetheart." He reached up and turned the handle for the camp shower, letting warm water sluice over them in turn for several seconds each, washing away the dirt and sweat.

As soon as he shut the water off, she was back in his arms, her skin wet, her curves soft. She pressed against him, moaning when he grabbed her by the hips and pulled her even closer, sliding against her. Shit-criminy, he wasn't going to be able to last very long at this rate, at least not the first time. He'd been too long without her.

Angélica took his hand, placing a bar of soap in his palm. "Don't drop it yet," she whispered and turned around.

In the darkness, he felt his way along. The jungle pulsed around them, nearly drowning out the sound of his ragged breath and her sexy gasps as his hand traced her curves with the soap bar. As his touch grew bolder, she pressed back into him, making his head spin. Somewhere along the lines, the soap slipped from his grip and his hand continued without it, slipping and sliding over her slick, supple skin. His other hand joined in, making her moan, the rocking of her hips driving him to the brink.

His hand trailed south, down past her navel, his fingers exploring.

"Quint." She took his hand and guided it lower. "Now."

Her breath caught as he—

Something crashed in the bushes next to the shower stalls,

followed by a rumbling, low growl.

Both of them froze. Quint's pulse rocketed, adrenaline mixing with lust.

A snuffling, snorting sound came from the trees, followed by loud huffing and more crashing.

"Don't move," she whispered, pulling away from him.

"Where are you going?" He reached for her in the darkness, catching only air.

He heard the curtain rustle and then she was back, pushing his clothes against his chest.

As they both scrambled to get dressed in the tight space, elbows and knees bumping, the commotion in the trees grew louder, closer.

"Give me the machete," he said quietly. Those were four words he never once imagined he'd be saying while taking a shower with a woman.

"You stay here. I've got this." She left him, disappearing through the curtain.

The hell she did! He followed her out into the moonlight and took the long knife from her. "Get behind me, woman."

"I don't need a hero, Parker."

"Would you just let me lead this dance for once?" The bushes shook at the forest's edge. Before she could argue further, something dark shot out of the underbrush, running with an odd gait straight for them. It was about the size of a dog, but the dappled shadows made it hard to see clearly.

Quint raised the machete, planting his feet.

It reached a clearing between the shadows, running in the moonlight.

"Quint, no!" Angélica cried, grabbing his forearm to stop him from swinging.

She shoved him aside and the beast was upon her, snorting and wiggling with excitement as it rubbed its snout all over Angélica's knees.

"Rover!" She dropped to the ground, hugging the javelina she'd raised from a wounded baby. "Where did you come from, boy?"

A familiar voice spoke in rapid Spanish from the shadows under the trees. Even as Teodoro came closer, Quint didn't understand what was being said thanks to his sketchy grasp of Spanish and the cacophony going on in the canopy. Rover's rampage through the forest hadn't gone unnoticed by the local wildlife.

"What did he say?" Quint asked Angélica.

"He said he had to remove Rover from María's sister's house in Coba." She stood, still petting the javelina's head. "Apparently, Rover has been getting into trouble. There was talk amongst the villagers of shooting him if Teodoro didn't take him out of there."

Teodoro shook his head. "*Jabali* keeps getting free," he told Quint.

Jabali was another name the Mexicans had given to the javelina, but Juan preferred to call Rover a "pig," shaking his head at the dog name his daughter had given her pet.

Dog name ... "What does *el perro regresa* mean?" he asked Angélica.

Rover came closer to Quint, smelling his knee. The javelina grunted after a few sniffs and rubbed against his jeans, his bristly back making scratchy sounds. Quint scratched the javelina on the neck as Rover had always liked, making sure to reach under the leather dog collar he now wore.

" 'The dog returns,' " she answered. "Why?"

This was what Pedro had meant in his note. Rover was back with Angélica and her crew. But what was with the zipping of the lips?

Teodoro connected a leash to Rover's collar, saying something in Spanish to Angélica about her "*padre*" that Quint didn't quite catch.

"What was that about your dad?" he asked.

She chuckled, taking her machete from him. "He said Dad's going to be mad when he finds out Rover is back, so we should probably try to keep quiet about it for as long as possible."

That explained Pedro's zipped lips.

With a grunt good-bye, Teodoro pulled something wrapped in a napkin from his pocket and tugged on Rover's leash, starting back along the path leading toward the tents. The javelina sniffed the air, and then trotted along after him.

Quint watched them disappear into the canopy shadows. While he was glad to see Rover again, he would have preferred their reunion to have occurred some other time. He had a feeling that hot-as-hell shower moment while Angélica was all wet, slippery, and ready for him was going to haunt him for the rest of the night.

A deep, hair-raising roar came from the direction Rover had burst through the underbrush. Chills ran up his spine at the sound alone. An unspoken threat hung in the suddenly quiet forest.

"That was a cat, wasn't it?" he whispered.

"A big one by the sound of it." Angélica handed him his towel and shower supplies. "Shower time is over. Let's go." She raised the machete, backing away from the growling sound now coming from that part of the brush. "And that's one of the reasons Dad is going to be ticked off. Javelinas make great bait for big cats."

Keeping his light on the trees as they made their way back to the tents, he asked, "What's the other reason?"

"Rover always figures out a way to escape from wherever he's tied and ends up in my tent."

"You mean *our* tent."

"Exactly."

Hot diggity dog. Quint was going to have to start sleeping with a machete under his pillow.

Chapter Ten

Night: A dreaded time of darkness when form-changers, demons, and spooks from the Underworld wreak havoc upon humans.

I must be out of my mind," Quint told Angélica's dad the next morning. They stood outside of the mine entrance in the heavy heat while donning hard hats and masks, checking meters and Juan's camera battery, gearing up to squeeze into the old limestone mine. A rainstorm had blown through last night, soaking the jungle, adding even more swelter to the morning's humidity after the sun had risen.

"Women will do that to you," Juan said, sliding his mask down over his nose and mouth. "I warned you about getting involved with my daughter," he added, his voice muffled.

"Right, next you'll be trying to sell me snake oil to keep those rattlers away." Quint adjusted his mask. "If memory serves me right, old man, you encouraged me to keep trying when I was thinking about giving up and heading home."

"All of that traveling you've done in the last month must have fogged your memory. I distinctly remember telling you that my daughter is hard-headed and extremely bossy, but you were a goner right out of the gate. There were little hearts floating around your head at first sight." He shook his head, feigning disgust, while above his mask laugh lines fanned from the corners of his eyes.

"Please, we both know that if there had been little hearts, Angélica would have pulled out her machete and shredded them into ribbons." The boss lady had wasted no time putting him in his place right from the get-go and intriguing the hell out of him in the process.

"Don't beat yourself up too much, son. Her mother had the same effect on me."

As Quint grabbed the bag full of tools Juan had insisted they bring, Juan slowly angled through the fig roots along with his cane, taking care with his walking cast, and disappeared into the mine.

Keeping in mind Angélica's plea regarding monitoring her father's health before she left for the *Chakmo'ol* Temple with Fernando and Bernard, he shook off the tension that came with entering holes in the earth. "Hold up," he said, easing between the strangler fig roots and following Juan into the mine.

He waited for Quint to catch up.

"How did you meet Marianne?" Quint's question served two purposes—to satisfy his curiosity on that subject and to quell his fears about where they were and what could happen if the earth decided to swallow them whole. "Did you go to college together? Or did you meet on a dig site?"

"She saved my life."

"What do you mean? Were you headed down a bad road?"

"No, I drove off the edge of one." Juan limped deeper into the mine, tapping on the walls and ceiling with his cane as he went.

Quint ducked as he followed, grimacing at the older man's obsession with testing stress fractures. "Is that a metaphor for something?"

"More like a lesson. Don't drive too fast on a twisty gravel road on bald tires."

"I don't get it." When Juan tugged on a low-hanging root that had poked its way down through the rocks, Quint groaned. "Would you quit messing with the ceiling, dammit?"

Juan chuckled and creaked along on his cane. "I had a blowout going around a curve on a gravel mountain road between Mexico City and the Gulf coast. I was in my twenties at the time, single and full of testosterone, driving a little too fast for the road conditions. I hit a patch of loose gravel and my pickup went off the road, tumbling into the valley about thirty feet below. Marianne was coming from the other direction and saw the whole accident. She pulled over and raced down the hill. After extracting me from the mangled mess of my truck, she patched me up enough to haul me up to her Jeep with the help of another passerby who'd stopped. I went in and out of consciousness while she drove me to the hospital. When I woke up two days later, she was still there sleeping in the chair next to my bed."

Juan paused, poking his cane into a hole midway up the wall. Several pebbles clattered onto the floor.

Frowning down at those pebbles, Quint tried not to think about how many pokes it would take for this sucker to crash down on them. "So it was love at first sight then?"

"Not quite. Marianne had waited for me to wake up because she wanted me to pay her back for saving my life."

"You're kidding? Pay her back with money?"

"No." Juan pulled out a handkerchief and wiped his forehead and neck. "While I was unconscious, she'd learned that I was one of the archaeologists working at a dig site a couple of hours from the city. She was visiting the area, immersing herself in the culture and language, freshly graduated with a degree in archaeology. Being female in a male-dominated field at that time made finding a respected job with dig teams tough. She made me hire her for my crew that very day in the hospital room."

"You let her blackmail you?"

Juan's eyes gleamed when he looked back at Quint. "Angélica is almost a mirror image of her mother. All I offered genetically was a stronger jawline, more pronounced cheekbones, and some dark streaks in my *gatita's* version of her mother's red hair." He tucked his handkerchief back into his pocket. "While staring up at the flame-haired angel who'd pulled me from that tangled mess of metal, how long do you think it took me to agree to give her a job on my crew?"

"Ah, I see." Quint fanned his shirt to no avail. Between the heat and his tight surroundings, sweating was his body's way of trying not to spontaneously combust. "I'm sure Marianne was well qualified for the position, though. You probably could tell just by talking to her."

Juan snorted. "She was wearing yellow shorts and this little white tank top that day in the hospital room. At that moment, I can honestly say that her professional qualifications were not at the forefront of my thoughts."

Poor Juan. Quint chuckled. He'd gone off the cliff that day and never fully recovered.

"A year later," Juan continued, "we were married and working at a dig down here in the Yucatán." He extracted his meter that checked for air quality and harmful gases, punching several buttons. "Marianne found out she was pregnant with Angélica a month into the dig." Juan took off his mask, letting it hang around his neck. "I suggested she return to the States to be safe, but she refused to leave me or her work." He shook his head, his gaze far off. His forehead wrinkled. "I was a stressed-out mess for the rest of that dig, constantly fretting about her and the baby being injured. But Marianne had promised me she'd be careful and not take risks, and she stuck to her word. She carried Angélica to full term, delivering a beautiful, red-haired baby girl a month after we made it back to the States."

His own mask now off his face, Quint looked around the mine. He couldn't imagine the daily hell of having his pregnant wife working in a place like this. Every night he'd lie awake in his cot, tossing and turning about a temple caving in on her or a wild animal attacking her. There were too many ways to end up dead in this jungle.

"Don't worry. She's strong," Juan said, a knowing glint in his eyes. "Like her mother."

Quint didn't play dumb with him. They both knew why he'd come back to this hot and miserable jungle for round two. "Physically or mentally?"

"Both. Angélica will keep working as long as she can while pregnant and there's nothing you or I can do about it."

Pregnant? Quint rolled that idea around in his head, wondering what it would be like to have her carrying his child. Was Angélica even interested in taking things that far with him? Her worries about his traveling probably made her want little to do with him when it came to a family.

Not to mention the secret from her past that she hadn't told her father. Only two people knew about the child from her ex-husband that she'd lost early into her pregnancy, and Quint had promised her to keep it that way. Would she want to risk the possibility of losing a child again? Would Quint want to deal with her working at dig sites where she wasn't the top species on the food chain while pregnant with his kid?

Juan creaked onward along the dirt-packed floor, his voice loud in the cottony silence there under the earth. "My daughter is no fool.

She'll be careful if there's a child in the picture, just as her mother was."

"I'm having trouble imagining Angélica letting someone else clear out rattlesnake dens or lead the way through crumbling cracks in the temple walls."

Juan poked at the ceiling again with his cane. "She is a bit daring at times, which was also one of Marianne's traits."

"Right." Quint grabbed Juan's cane, putting an end to his constant poking. "Marianne's trait, you say?" Growling under his breath about Angélica and her father, Quint slipped around Juan and led him into the larger room. He stood aside as the older man inspected the mine's ceiling and walls, keeping silent to give Juan time and space to concentrate on his task.

Juan pulled his digital camera from the side pocket in his cargo pants. He took several pictures, including a closeup of the limestone granules mixed in with a handful of dirt. When he finished, it took Quint's eyes a few seconds to adjust again after all of those flashes.

"Where's this stone and grout wall *gatita* told me about?"

Quint took a deep breath and then squeezed into the cramped tunnel, leading with his light. His pulse pounded in his ears by the time he reached the wall. The urge to claw his way back to the surface tugged at him, but he'd solemnly sworn to the boss lady that he'd make sure Juan made it in and out without damaging his leg, so he stayed put.

Juan tapped on each of the stacked stones in the wall with his cane, stepping back to size it up from floor to ceiling. Then he opened his notebook and jotted down something while holding the flashlight in the side of his mouth. When he finished, he pocketed the notebook. He plucked his flashlight from his jaws and turned to Quint. "I need you to do me a favor."

"What's that?"

"Remove this stone right here." He pointed his flashlight at the top center of the wall.

Remove the stone ... What!? Why? "You want me to pull stones out of a wall that may be supporting the ceiling back here?"

"Only this one." He tapped the stone. "Look, it's already loose. It should come right out with only a little wiggling."

"Why that one?"

"Removing it will not affect the stability of the wall or ceiling back here. Plus, the grout around it is rotten and crumbly."

"You're sure about that?"

"Mostly."

That wasn't very reassuring. "But not one hundred percent?"

"Certainty is overrated."

"You're not making me want to do this favor for you."

Juan shone his light at the bottom of the stone wall, directing the beam along the base. "If you're going to keep hanging around these dig sites with me, son, you're going to have to learn to take risks without squealing so much." He tapped his cane on the floor in several locations in front of the wall, his head cocked to the side. After listening for several seconds, he added, "I'm beginning to think you've been taking diva lessons from Pedro."

The old man's taunting made Quint laugh. "Between your daughter and you, my ego is taking one hell of a beating this trip."

"It's a tough job, but someone has to keep you humble." He stopped tapping and frowned at the wall. "Time has taught me that if I can be one hundred percent sure of two or three things each day, then I'm doing well."

"Name something you're certain of today."

Rubbing the back of his neck, Juan turned to Quint. "The sun will cross the sky and rise again tomorrow."

"That's an easy one."

"Not for the ancient Maya civilization, at least not the rising again part. They had their doubts about the sun making it through the Underworld's nightly obstacles and terrors as it passed through on its way back to the eastern horizon." He focused on the wall again, skimming his fingers along a line of grout at eye-level. "Have you ever seen images of their lord of death, the ruler of the Underworld?"

"*Ah Puch*?"

"That's one moniker for him. God A is another or *Yum Cimil*. The name changes depending on what area of the Maya world you're visiting, but the images and fears are similar."

"I haven't seen any pictures, only read and heard bits about him." Quint didn't explain that Pedro was his teacher, or why the god's doom-and-gloom messenger owl had been a topic of discussion between them. Juan probably wouldn't be thrilled to hear they were trying to figure out if his wife had been murdered or if she was merely the victim of an accident.

"He's not a very handsome devil," he told Quint.

"I imagine living in the lowest level of the Maya version of hell can be rough on a god's appearance. All that nasty death and terror business down there probably clogs the pores and inspires a few wrinkles over time."

Juan shot him a quick grin. "Most images show him with a skeleton head and black patches of rotting flesh on his torso. Sometimes his figure is bloated, like a decaying corpse."

He grimaced. "He sounds a bit sloppy."

Pulling a screwdriver from his pants pocket, Juan pointed it at Quint. "He's not someone you'd want to meet in the dark of night, that's for sure."

"I don't think running into him in the light of day would be much better from the sound of it."

"An owl's head sometimes makes up part of his headdress." Juan's handkerchief appeared, catching some of the grout he was now chiseling free. "Periodically he has a collar made of eyeballs dangling from optic nerves."

"Golly gee, those Maya folks had quite the imagination."

"Oh, and he usually wears bells."

"Bells? Like the jingle-all-the-way kind?" Why would a monster wear bells?

Juan nodded, tying the ends of his handkerchief together, securing the grout inside the cloth. "And then there's his odor."

"I'm guessing he probably doesn't mix lavender oil into his bath water most nights."

Stuffing the handkerchief into his pocket, Juan wrinkled his nose. "Some call him 'the flatulent one' due to the stench that surrounds him."

"He must have been popular at parties."

"I'll have to show you a few pictures of him sometime." Juan turned, holding up a finger. "Wait, I think Marianne might have an image of him sketched in her notebook."

A red flag flapped in Quint's mind. "You mean an image she found here at this site?"

"I believe it's from down in the Chiapas area. Now about this stone …"

Quint wasn't ready to move that stone yet. He'd pulled a stone out of a wall for Angélica at the last site and the damned temple had almost caved in on top of him. He needed a few more minutes to change into his balls of steel for this task, especially with the lack of surety Juan had about the outcome. "What else are you certain of today?"

"That you're going to remove that stone."

"Besides that *possibility*."

Juan grinned, but played along. "Let's see. I'm sure that María's supper tonight will be as delicious as usual."

"Because of her famous sauce?"

"Because Teodoro brought her back some dried mangos from the store in Coba to use in her famous sauce."

Quint licked his chops. "That gives me something to live for today in spite of your attempts to snuff me out in an old mine. What else?"

"You know the layer of white, flakey stuff I pointed out this morning on Angélica's neck?" At Quint's cautious nod, he continued, "That wasn't dried skin. It was dried soap."

Her father had hit the bull's-eye on that one. "You're sure about that?"

"Positive. For some reason, she didn't wash it off last night when she went with you to take a shower."

"That is curious," Quint replied, trying not to fidget under Juan's narrowed gaze.

"I'm guessing that something or someone interrupted her mid-rinse. You wouldn't happen to have an answer for me on that, would you?"

Juan had asked Angélica about the dried soap in front of everyone. Her red cheeks had probably mirrored Quint's, but he was too busy focusing intensely on his plate to see for certain. She'd mumbled a response, claiming she'd been pretty tired and must have forgotten to rinse everywhere.

"We did hear a large cat prowling around in the trees while down at the showers. It was making all sorts of hair-raising noises." He purposefully left out the part about Rover's return. That was Angélica's task. "We didn't hang around long after that. In our rush to leave, she was probably too distracted to rinse."

Several times before falling asleep last night, while lying on his cot listening to the sound of Angélica breathing, Quint had replayed that moment in the shower. The word "distracted" didn't really cut it, especially when it came to his feelings about touching her wet, soft skin that had been so slippery with soap. That fell more along the lines of "utterly bamboozled." Damn that javelina's timing! If Rover could have given them just ten more minutes.

"A large cat, huh? Is that the story you're sticking to for now?"

"Pretty much, yep."

"Fine. I'll let that set, but I'm not done digging yet." He pointed at the wall. "How about you pull out that stone some time before I keel over from old age?"

Quint hesitated still.

Juan crossed his arms. "I'll make a deal with you."

"Name it."

"You pull out that stone and I'll disappear for a while this evening. Let you have some time in our tent all alone with my daughter."

The stone popped right out.

There was no rumbling from the other stones in the wall, no sprinkling of pieces of ceiling falling on Quint's head. No problems at all, thank the Maya wall makers.

He set the stone down on the floor next to the wall and wiped the sweat streaming down his face with his shirt. "Can we go now?"

"Not yet." Juan handed him his light. "You have a few inches on me. Tell me what's on the other side." He handed Quint his camera next. "And take some pictures while you're at it. The flash is on."

Bracing himself for whatever waited on the other side of the wall, Quint raised the light and directed it through the hole. He peeked in after it, wincing in anticipation of something with a skeleton head and black patches of rotting flesh popping up on the other side and making googly-eyed faces at him. Damn Juan for filling his head with ideas.

What he saw left him scratching his head.

"What do you see?" Juan asked, his voice high with excitement. "Any pot shards or jade statues or human remains?"

"I'll show you."

"Are there at least some critter droppings on that side of the wall?" Juan pressed.

"Not that I can see."

"That is just odd."

Quint held the flashlight with one hand and snapped several pictures with the other, tilting the camera up and down and left and right. "Here." He handed it back.

The camera's digital screen lit up Juan's face as he flicked through the pictures, his eyebrows drawing into a series of Vs piled within each other like Russian stacking dolls. "An altar stone? Why would they wall that in? Look at the artifacts spread out on it. What god were they petitioning?"

Quint peered over Juan's shoulder at the screen. "Was there a god of mining?"

"Not specifically."

"What's that white stuff spread on the ground around the altar? It's bigger than the limestone granules out here."

"Hard to tell. Let me see if this helps." Even after Juan enlarged the image, Quint couldn't make heads or tails of it. The white pieces looked blurry and pixilated. "They look like pebbles of limestone spread around." Juan scratched his jaw. "Maybe we should take a few more stones out."

"You mean make the hole bigger so you can see through it yourself?"

"I mean make it wider so you can crawl through it and take a closer look."

Quint stepped back, shaking his head. "That's not happening."

"What if I offered to spend a whole night in Pedro and Fernando's tent instead of an hour?"

"I thought you said you'd leave for a few hours."

"I never gave a time limit."

Quint looked at the hole, still shaking his head. "I'm nuts about your daughter, but I'm not wiggling through a hole in an unstable wall. Especially this crumbling wall in this ancient mine that has no visible support beams. The ceiling will fall and smash me flat."

"Fine, Chicken Little," Juan taunted.

"I'm not a chicken. I'm a rooster who wants to live long enough to get out of here and chase your daughter's tail feathers around the tent."

He valued his life more than sex these days—even hot, soapy shower sex with the woman he'd fantasized about for weeks. What good would Juan's deal be to Quint if he were crushed to death before he got to enjoy the payout? "How about you make a few educated guesses based on that picture and call it good."

Juan sighed, pouring on the drama. "Okay, I'll wait until I can get someone in here without small-space issues."

"There is no amount of manipulation that will sway me on this."

"Angélica would probably—"

"Don't even think about suggesting it to her." She'd climb on her father's shoulders to get through that damned hole in the wall.

Chuckling, Juan clapped him on that back. "Good answer, son."

An idea popped into Quint's mind. "You know," he told Juan, "I might be able to get a clearer shot of the altar stone and that white stuff with my telephoto lens and a stronger flashlight."

"Did you bring your camera with you to the dig site?"

"Yes, it's in my duffel bag with my ... Shit! I brought my camera but I left that lens locked away in Pedro's office back in Cancun." He hadn't figured he'd need that particular lens since they were in the trees. "We could still give it a try with my regular lens."

"You think it will take better pictures than this one?" Juan held up the small digital camera.

"It'd better. It sure cost a hell of a lot more than that one."

"Okay. We'll give it a shot, rooster." Juan pointed at the stone from the wall. "Can you slide that back into place? We should put it back to be safe. This grout is pretty loose in spots, and the ceiling is extremely fractured back here. I don't like how it's flaking off like slabs of slate."

"*Now* you tell me that." Cursing the damned hole in the ground, Quint lifted the rock.

"Hold on," Juan said, shining his light on it. "What's that?"

"What?" Quint flipped the rock over.

"That." Juan pointed at several long parallel gouges in the rock. "This was on the other side of the wall, right?"

"They look like scratches."

He lifted his camera and snapped a shot of the rock. "Okay, you can put it back now."

"Good." Quint carefully slid the stone back into place, sweating out a gallon of water in the process. He blew out a huge breath of relief after taking a step back, his ticker banging in his chest. "Now can we get the hell out of here?"

Juan led the way out to blue sky. The heat of the direct sun was a welcomed relief, the mugginess of the jungle not so much.

"Something wasn't quite right in there," Juan said, frowning back at the cave entrance.

"Are you talking about the lack of critter evidence?"

"Well, yes, but there was something else." After a few more seconds, he shook his head. "I'll figure it out later. We should head for the tent."

"Why's that?" Lunch wasn't for another hour.

Juan patted his shirt pocket where he'd stuffed his handkerchief. "I want to take a look at this grout under my microscope."

"What do you think you'll find?" What could Juan deduce about the Maya from their grout?

"Well, I hope I'm wrong, but I suspect flakes of dried blood."

Quint stopped in his tracks. "Did you say blood?"

"Yep." Juan kept on walking. "From what I could tell, the wall appears to have been coated in it at one time."

Chapter Eleven

Calakmul Biosphere Reserve: The largest tropical forest reserve in Mexico. Slightly larger than the US state of Delaware, the reserve gives refuge to a large mixture of mammals, reptiles, amphibians, and birds (oh, and insects). Crocodiles, snakes, and jaguars are just a few of the predators living there.

Angélica!"

The sound of Pedro's voice cut through the frog-like croaking of a small flock of keel-billed toucans dressed in yellow bibs and black plumage, chatting in the ceiba trees overhead. There was something in his tone that made Angélica's ears perk up.

She wiped her sweaty face with her shirt and turned back toward the *Chakmo'ol* Temple. She detoured off the overgrown trail she'd been exploring with the help of her machete and compass and slashed her way through a patch of *hojo santa* shrubs lining the edge of the site's grassy plaza.

"Angélica!" Pedro shouted again, closer now. She saw him between a poisonous *chechém* tree and a *chaka* tree, its healing counterpart. He was across the plaza, striding hell-bent toward the temple where she'd spent the morning working.

Hours of sitting on the temple floor, recording the glyphs and carvings covering the chamber wall, had made her lower back ache. Her body was starting to protest the long hours on the job and lack of solid sleep night after night. As much as she wanted to find that damned stela, her bed back home was starting to sound like heaven.

Lunchtime had come and gone while she worked. Normally there was no distracting her from her job, but today the need to stretch her muscles and fill her stomach had driven her to pack up her sketches and rubbings. She'd also wanted to talk to her father and Quint to find out how things had gone at the mine. Then she'd found that trail and gotten distracted.

"Angélica!"

She slashed her way into the clearing. "Pedro, over here," she called, sliding her machete into its sheath before heading toward him. She took off her hat as she walked, brushing a tick off the brim. Beating back the jungle always left her with a few battle scratches and usually a blood-sucking pest or two. She'd have to ask her dad to check her for more later. Better yet, Quint could do an up-close inspection after she showered. The thought of what other up-close fun might follow made her steps lighter.

Pedro met her halfway across the plaza. He looked over her shoulder for a couple of seconds, scanning the trees. The lines on his tan forehead deepened. "What were you doing in there?"

"I found an old trail." She shook off her hat once more and then dropped it back onto her head.

"A deer trail?"

She glanced back, unable to tell whence she'd come. The jungle was an ace at playing hide and seek with trails and structures … and people, if they weren't careful enough to leave breadcrumbs. "I don't think so. It was too straight. I'm wondering if it leads to more structures, maybe a living complex."

He sniffed, and then leaned closer and sniffed again. "Why do you smell like licorice?"

"There were *hoja santas* bushes in there." She took a closer look at his shirt and face. "You're drenched in sweat. What's wrong?"

He pulled the neck of his shirt up to wipe off his face. "Jane was bitten by a rattlesnake."

Angélica's gut clenched. "Is she okay?"

He nodded. "I rushed her to Teodoro's tent. She's resting in there right now. He gave her some antivenin and is keeping her cooled off while it works its magic."

"When did this happen?"

"Over an hour ago."

She'd been in the *Chakmo'ol* Temple chamber, which explained why she hadn't heard any shouting or commotion. "Where was Jane when she was bitten? Over by the mound?" Were the snakes spreading farther?

"No. She was at the raised platform over there." He jutted his chin toward the *Chakmo'ol* Temple. "I'd sent her over to help Gertrude for a bit while I worked my magic at the mound with the trowel and brush. According to Jane, she wasn't paying attention and sat down on a rock next to a snake sunning itself."

Damn it. Hadn't Angélica warned the college kids about being careful where they stepped at this end of the site, let alone sat? To keep an eye out for snakes and scorpions always? "So, she scared it."

He nodded. "It woke up with a vicious fang-filled yawn."

"I'll go see her." Angélica started toward the tents.

"Hold on." Pedro caught her arm, playing anchor. "You've got a tick on your back." After he plucked it off, he walked next to her. "What led you to that trail in the trees? Something you saw in the *Chakmo'ol* Temple?"

"No. I was heading to lunch and decided to take a walk around the western side of the temple for a change and search the jungle's edge again for looter leftovers. I ran into a deer on the way and spooked it. The thing headed off into the trees in such a straight line that I decided to follow it. Not more than twenty feet into the brush along the trail, I found a big lump of vines and roots with the corner of an altar stone sticking out. Some of the markings were visible even through the lichen on the stone."

He snagged her arm again, spinning her around. "Are you telling me you went traipsing into the forest alone?"

"Yes." What was with his critical tone? She tugged her arm free, her frown matching his. "What's the big deal? I wasn't very deep into the trees, and I had my machete out and swinging."

He snorted. "That's not a very smart move for a woman with all kinds of capital letters after her name."

"Yeah, well, I know a pain-in-the-ass helicopter pilot who did it the other day and found a limestone mine."

"I also almost fell into that mine."

"You wouldn't have fallen in. There are too many fig roots blocking it."

"Maybe so, but if it had been a *cenote*, I'd have been in trouble."

"But it wasn't a *cenote*, so that's a moot point."

"A girl like you should know better than to go skipping into the jungle on your own."

Girl? Skipping? What the hell had gotten into Pedro? What was with this machismo shit? He hadn't acted like this since they were kids and his testosterone was taking him for a spin.

She crossed her arms. "What's going on here, Pedro? The first time you flew Dad and me to this site, this *girl*," she poked her chest, "went skipping off completely alone and you didn't even think twice about it."

"Your father went with you."

"That's not true. First, he followed me after I explicitly told him not to. Second, I was gone at least twenty minutes before he caught up with me."

"We knew where you were heading, though. You weren't running off alone without checking in with someone like you did today." He grabbed her shoulders, scowling at her. "Angélica, you need to let someone know where you are at all times, especially if you go into the trees. Better yet, take someone with you."

She tilted her head, trying to figure out what had him acting so protective all of a sudden. Was this her father's doing? Quint's? "We are several weeks into this dig, Pedro. Why is my going into the forest alone in broad daylight suddenly such a concern for you? Has someone been whispering stories in your ear about *Xtabay* haunting the area? You know that sexy sorceress only waits under the ceiba tree for wayward men to kill with her embrace, not women."

"Nobody is whispering anything." He let go of her, stepping back, his gaze averted. "You need to be more careful going off alone is all."

"I went off alone plenty at the last site and there were *cenotes* all over there, plus other potential dangers. You never worried about me then."

"This site is different."

"Different how? We're still in a jungle in Mexico."

"There's more potential for danger. Have you forgotten that we're in the middle of a huge biosphere reserve? You could easily be someone's prey."

That was true and it was something she'd been aware of earlier with each step. She'd watched for predator markings while exploring the trail, listening for tell-tale signs of a hunter in the area via other animals in between slashing and …

Wait a second. "*Someone's* prey? Don't you mean *something's* prey?"

"Yes, I meant 'something.' English is my second language, remember?"

Maybe so, but he was very good at that second language. "Pedro, I carry my machete at all times."

His focus returned to her. "That might not be enough."

Something in his eyes gave her pause, a haunted look she hadn't seen since the night he'd joined her at the hospital while her mother lay dying. What did he mean? What did he know?

"Pedro, what's going on?"

"Nothing." His smile came quick, but it didn't ring true with the rest of his face. "Just do me a favor and think twice about going into the trees alone."

"You're hiding something."

"I'm playing big brother, that's all. I worry about you. Let's get going. Your father is waiting." He started toward the tents without looking back to see if she was following.

She frowned after him. There was definitely something going on that Pedro wasn't telling her and he was doing a shitty job of hiding it.

Angélica caught up with him. "Why would you be more worried now than before? Does this have something to do with Mom?"

His steps quickened. "Marianne? No, of course not."

"Pedro!" She had to jog to keep up. "Dammit, what's going on?"

"I told you, Jane got bit."

She growled under her breath. "You're purposely playing dumb now."

As they passed by the first couple of tents she grabbed the back of his shirt, dragging him to a stop. "Pedro Guillermo Montañero, you tell me right now why you are suddenly so worried about my being alone in the forest."

"*Gatita.*" Her father waved her over from where he stood in front of Teodoro's tent.

"Your father is calling." Pedro tried to tug free, dragging her along behind him.

"I know."

He twisted, trying to shake her grip, pushing at her. "Let go of my shirt."

"No." She latched on tighter, wrapping her arms around his waist as he wrestled to be free of her. "Not until you tell me the truth."

Their feet tangled and they both went down, him face first with Angélica landing on top of him. Taking advantage of the moment, she straddled his back and wrenched his arm behind him until he cursed in Spanish.

He turned his head, glaring up at her from the corner of his eye. "No fair using a move on me that I taught you."

"I'll let you up when you tell me what you know."

"*¡Dios mio!* You are heavy, girl. You need to lay off María's *panuchos.*"

She dug her knuckles into the muscles in his lower back, making him squirm. "Now you're going to pay before you tell me your secret."

"What in the daylights is wrong with you two?" Juan limped over to them, frowning down at them.

"Your daughter is being a bully," Pedro said, cursing and writhing under her when she dug her knuckles in again.

"He won't tell me why he's so worried about my being alone in the trees." She tickled his ribs, making him squawk with laughter. "Spit it out or I'll make you squeal like a little girl."

"Why in the world are you two horsing around at a time like this?" Juan scowled at her. "*Gatita*, get off Pedro right now or I'll ..." He sighed in exasperation. "Just get off the poor boy. You're the boss here, remember?"

With warm cheeks from her dad's reprimand, she let go, grabbed her hat, and shoved to her feet. "We're not done with this, Montañero." One way or another, she was going to find out what had Pedro so skittish about the jungle.

Pedro rolled onto his back, wrinkling his nose at her.

"Angélica Mae," her father said to her in a harsh whisper. "How many times have I told you it's not fair to wrestle with Pedro? He's too much of a gentleman to hurt a lady."

"What kind of gentleman keeps secrets from a lady?"

"All sorts." Juan took her hat and placed it on her head. "Now, have you heard about Jane?"

She pointed her thumb at Pedro. "This stubborn mule told me."

"It takes a mule to know a mule," Pedro said, standing and

dusting off his clothes.

"Should we send her home?" her father asked.

"Whether she stays or not is up to her. Is Teodoro inside? I need to talk to him."

"About what?"

"To see if Jane should be flown to the hospital in Chetumal." Angélica glanced away. "And to plan how to move those snakes today." She winced inwardly in anticipation of his reaction to that last part.

"What!" Her father gaped at her as if she was wearing a bunch of said snakes on her head. "You are *not* going into that den. One snake bite a day is enough, thank you very much."

"Dad, I'll be fine."

"We don't have enough antivenin if you get bit."

She turned to Pedro. "Didn't Teodoro bring back more from Coba the other day?"

He nodded, but didn't look happy about his answer.

"See, Dad. Teodoro is ready for the worst. I'm going in."

"I don't like this."

"Well, I don't love it. Snakes aren't exactly puppies. Not that I would know that from experience, mind you, since I never got to have a puppy."

"Oh, dear Lord!" Juan threw up his hands. "Here we go again about how your mother and I ruined your childhood by not letting you have a dog."

Angélica grinned. "Well, it did stunt my mental growth."

"Judging from the way you were wrestling around on the ground with Pedro a moment ago like a couple of foolish kids, I'd have to agree with you on that this time."

Pedro snickered until she poked him in the ribs again.

She turned back to her dad. "One snake-bitten college student is all that's allowed at my dig site. Teodoro has all of the supplies we need to take care of our snake problem. We're relocating them today."

Her father's nostrils flared. "Fine, but you're taking Quint and Maverick with you to help."

"I can help catch them, too," Pedro offered.

"No." Angélica squeezed his shoulder, knowing how much he grumbled and cringed around snakes. "We need our pilot venom-free in case an emergency flight to the nearest hospital becomes a necessity." To her father, she ordered, "Round up Quint and Maverick and have them meet me at the mess tent."

Without waiting for more arguments from her father, she slipped into Teodoro's tent. Jane lay on the spare cot they kept in there amongst the shaman's boxes of medicines and first-aid supplies. Her eyes fluttered open when Angélica approached and kneeled next to her.

"Hi," she said feebly.

"You okay?" Angélica asked, looking down at the bandage wrapped around her leg above her ankle, inspecting Teodoro's work. He was as meticulous as always.

"Teodoro says I can go back to work tomorrow."

Angélica glanced over at Teodoro, who watched from his perch on a hand-hewn stool. He nodded once at her raised brow.

"Do you want to, though?" she asked Jane.

"What do you mean?"

"Would you rather have Pedro fly you back to Cancun?"

"And leave the dig?"

"Yes."

"No!" The fervor in the girl's voice surprised Angélica. "I want to stay here and keep working."

"You're sure? There might be more snakes."

"Now that I've lived through this bite, I'm not as afraid."

Angélica smiled. She'd once come to a similar conclusion. Granted she'd been about eight years old at the time on her dad's ranch in Tucson, but that first bite was a real life lesson. After that, she was more careful, yet less fearful.

"Good." She patted Jane's arm. "You rest today. Tomorrow, I'll put you to work in the *Baatz'* Temple. There are several walls covered with glyphs in there. I'd like you to copy the glyphs on rice paper using the old-fashioned charcoal rubbing process." That would keep the girl resting while still on the clock.

Waving at Teodoro to follow her, Angélica led the way to the mess tent. Quint and Maverick were waiting for her there, along with her father and Pedro.

"Let me just get something to eat and I'll be right over," she told them.

She grabbed a plate of food that María had held back for her, thanking the older woman. Her voice at a whisper, she asked in Mayan how Rover was doing. María's eyes flitted to Juan for a second, but Angélica knew her father's Mayan was rusty even at a normal decibel level.

After being assured that the troublemaking javelina was behaving for the time being, Angélica grabbed a cup of water and sat down at the table across from Quint and her dad. Pedro and Maverick were on either side of her, while Teodoro stood at the end of the table, his arms crossed. She had a feeling he already knew what was coming.

Cutting her *torta* in half, she got right to the point. "Jane was bit this morning by a rattlesnake at the *Chakmo'ol* Temple. While she's on the mend thanks to Pedro's quick thinking and Teodoro's antivenin, we need to clear out that snake den and relocate its occupants this afternoon."

"This is a bad idea," her father said.

She pointed the *torta* she was holding at him. "Opinion duly noted, Dad. While we're clearing out the snakes, I need you to head over to the ballcourt to check on Esteban and Daisy. Tell Fernando to keep Bernard, Lorenzo, and Gertrude in the *Baatz'* Temple and to follow your instructions on the stabilizing work inside. Tomorrow, I'll have Jane get busy recording the glyphs in the inner chamber where we found the Olmec mask."

His lips flatlined. "That's busy work and you know it."

She lowered her sandwich, holding his worried stare. "I don't want you near the snake den with me, Dad."

"*Gatita,*" he started.

"I mean it." She didn't let him finish. "You're not as quick-footed since the accident. I'll be too worried about you getting bit to give the job my full attention, and if I ever needed to stay focused while working, today is that day. I need you to run the dig site for me."

Their stare-off lasted through a couple of bites of her sandwich before he gave in with a single nod.

"Pedro." She plucked up a piece of chicken that had slipped free of the *torta*. "You need to go with us but stay back at the temple. You can transport the bags with the snakes by wheelbarrow to the helicopter as we pile them up." She popped the chicken into her mouth and chewed on the spicy morsel for a few seconds while she tried to think of what else she needed him to do. After she swallowed, she added, "We should probably have the stretcher there in case we have to make a rush to the helicopter. Multiple bites could be deadly even with antivenin on hand."

He finished whatever he had in the cup in front of him and stood. "I'll go check on the helicopter and make sure it's ready for liftoff. I'll meet you at the temple with the stretcher."

After Pedro left, she glanced over at Maverick. "You sure you're game to do this? When you signed up to work at a dig site, handling rattlesnakes wasn't in the job description."

He lifted his leg, pulling up his pant leg to show her his cowboy boot. "I'm dressed for the rodeo."

"Teodoro has some makeshift leather pads we're going to wrap around our shins and ankles to help protect against bites."

"Anti-snake chaps," he said, nodding in approval. "Nice."

That left Quint.

She chewed on another bite, meeting his hazel eyes straight on. What was going on in his head? Was he feeling cornered? Forced to go into battle? If he didn't want to do this, she wasn't going to push him into it. She needed him to be steady and on his game once they started handling the snakes. How could she give him an out without embarrassing him in front of the others?

"Just tell me what I'm supposed to do, boss lady."

He answered her unspoken question for her.

She frowned. While she appreciated having him by her side, she'd rather he wasn't there with all of those snakes. If anything happened to him because of her …

No. She shook off her trepidation. He was going to be fine. She'd make sure of it.

"For starters, you and Maverick need to help Teodoro haul all of the equipment over to the temple while I change into my other boots and grab my gloves. Take the wheelbarrow, since Pedro will be using it to move the snakes." She shot Teodoro a questioning look. "Did you perform the protection ritual you mentioned?"

He'd told her yesterday he needed to make an offering to several of the Maya forest guardian spirits for both the snakes' protection and their own before they started relocating the snakes.

He nodded, telling her in Spanish. "Last night and today after Jane got bit."

"Good."

"*Gatita*, you don't need to do this right now." Her father leaned across the table with his palms spread wide, pleading his case. "We could stay out of that end of the dig site and focus our energy on the

Baatz' Temple, the ballcourt, and those mounds just outside the tree line to the east."

"We've put it off long enough." Too long, actually. She grimaced, wishing she'd done something before Jane had been hurt. "Let's get it done and make that area safe."

His brown eyes narrowed as he stared at her. "You're not doing this because you want to see what was on that piece of stela inside the snake den, are you?"

"No." Well, maybe partly. What if that stela chunk was the missing puzzle piece that she'd been searching for since she'd arrived?

"Because that's not worth risking the lives of four people to see."

"Of course it isn't."

"*Gatita.*"

"Listen, Dad, if things get hairy, I'll pull the damned plug on the operation, okay?"

"Fine. Be like your mother, then." He leaned over the table and kissed her on the forehead. "But be careful. Send someone to let me know when you're done so I can stop worrying and come take a look at that *sacbe* you found, maybe start the mapping process."

He headed out of the tent, followed shortly by Teodoro, who motioned for Maverick to follow him.

That left her alone with Quint.

Before he could chew her out about dealing with the snakes this afternoon, she held up her hand. "I don't want to hear it, Parker."

One eyebrow lifted. "Hear what?"

"How this is a bad idea, and my obsession with finding that missing stela is going to get someone hurt or worse." She picked up the other half of the *torta* and took a big bite, sighing with frustration as she ate. Damn her father for making her feel guilty about something that needed to be done.

"Anything to do with snakes sounds like a bad idea to me, unless we're talking about the snake charmer dance you did for me that night in your bed wearing nothing but ..." he trailed off, flirting with her across the table with his eyes. "You get the picture. And if you don't, I'd be happy to whisper a thousand words about it in your ear."

"Only a thousand, huh?" she smiled both at him and the memory of his enthusiastic reaction to her dance. "Keeping to so few nouns and adjectives would be a major feat for a wordsmith like you."

"If nakedness is involved, I reserve the right to double my word count."

"Nakedness for whom? You or me?"

"Ladies first, of course."

This dig site was just full of gentlemen today. She shook her head. "If either of us is naked, I'm probably not going to be interested in listening to you blather on and on."

"Blather, she says." He mimicked stabbing himself in the chest. "You just killed my Shakespearean heart. I hope you're happy."

She chuckled, feeling herself fall even more head over heels for the damned traveler.

"Seriously," she said, sobering. "I'm sure you have a strong opinion on what I want to do this afternoon."

"Of course I do. We're not going out there to rescue cute baby seals with big black eyes."

"You got a soft spot for baby seals, huh?"

"I have a soft spot for you."

"Soft? That's unfortunate. I was looking forward to exploring your hard parts. Soft isn't going to cut it for the job I have for you."

His eyes creased at the corners. "Such a sassy mouth. I'm going to enjoy taming those lips later."

Her pulse danced in anticipation until she stopped the music. Now was not the time for lust and fantasies. Not with a den filled with snakes awaiting them.

"It's your dig site, Angélica," he said, his tone serious. "I trust that you're doing what's best for your crew."

Was she, though? It was her job to clear a site, but was she jumping the gun on removing the snakes in order to see that stela, or was this really about safety?

Shaking off her doubts, she chewed on a bite of her *torta* while measuring Quint up and down. Did he really trust her or had her father put him up to some kind of trickery? Normally, he'd protest such a decision, at least until she joked with him about being a wuss. "What's your angle, Parker?"

"No angle, boss lady." He leaned his elbows on the table, frowning toward the tent entrance. "Where is Teodoro going to put all of those snakes?"

"He's been scouting around the forest since we found the den.

He located another shallow cave a couple of miles away from here. It's in the middle of the reserve, so they'll still be protected." She finished the rest of her *torta* in a couple of bites, wiping her mouth with a napkin after she'd finished. "He found a spot big enough nearby for Pedro to land the helicopter safely. They'll fly them in and set them free."

"You'd rather move the rattlers than make snake gumbo?"

"We can't kill them. We're the ones encroaching on their territory, not the other way around. Besides, this site sits inside the reserve's boundaries. We can't kill them without getting into a shitload of trouble."

"Fuck." He blew out a breath. "A rattlesnake roundup." He stood, taking her empty plate. "The things I'll do for a pretty girl."

He swung by the wash bucket, leaving her dishes in the sudsy water and then trailed her out of the tent.

"Listen, Quint." She stopped under the hot sunshine, her hat in her hand. "If you don't want to do this, you don't have to." She wanted to give him an out now that nobody else was around. "As a matter of fact, I'd rather you went with my father to make sure nothing happens to him and leave this task to me."

He smirked down at her. "Are you worried I'll drop a snake or two?"

"I'm worried you'll play hero and get yourself killed trying to save me."

His focus lowered to her mouth. "I'm not dying today, boss lady, so stop your frettin'."

"You sound pretty damned certain for a man about to face off with dozens of rattlesnakes."

"No rattlesnake is going to get the best of me. Not after I made a deal with the devil this morning."

"What devil?"

"Your father."

She raised an eyebrow. "And what deal did Dad make that has you so cocky about battling scales and fangs?"

"One stone in exchange for several hours alone with his daughter this evening in our tent."

Alone? With Quint? A string of wicked thoughts flashed through her mind, heating her up even more than the hot sunshine beating down on them.

"Damn it, Parker." She jammed her hands on her hips,

frowning up at him. "How do you expect me to focus on hooking and bagging rattlers all afternoon after sharing that nugget?"

"It's called incentive, sweetheart." He winked at her. "I'll see you at the temple." With a salute, he headed toward the supply tent next to Teodoro's where Maverick was already loading hooks and shin guards into the wheelbarrow.

Her thoughts still on Quint and what she'd like to do with him while they were alone tonight, she headed to her tent and changed into her hiking boots that went partway up her shin, pulling a tick off of her sock in the process. She exchanged her khakis for the thick pair of canvas pants she preferred to use when clearing thorny brush.

A glance at Quint's cot made her face grow warm. A month was a long time to go without doing the bad things she liked to do to him.

Bad things that felt so damned good.

Grabbing her leather gloves, she headed back out into the sunshine, scratching absently at her neck. Between the ticks and Quint, she was feeling way too itchy for her own good.

Chapter Twelve

Xibalba: A "place of fright."
**Another word for the Maya Underworld where all souls went
whether good or evil, rich or poor (only those who died a
violent death escaped the trip through the Underworld).**
Xibalba **and the Maya Underworld could be entered through a
cave or still water, such as a** *cenote.*

Rattlesnakes.

Fuck.

A trickle of sweat ran down Quint's cheek.

What in the hell was he thinking?

Oh yeah … *me Tarzan, you Jane.*

The stupid apeman operating the control panel in his brain had
ignored all *Abort!* orders, refusing to let his woman battle snakes
without him.

His woman.

That thought made Quint grin in spite of the kamikaze mission
he was strapping in for this afternoon. He could imagine the glare
from the boss lady if he said that out loud.

He leaned against the side of the *Chakmo'ol* Temple, tying on his
gear alongside Maverick. Sweat rolled down his back and not only
from the heat. On the ground in front of them, Teodoro had laid
out a line of burlap bags, setting up an assembly line that had Quint

grimacing.

"Shit," he muttered. "That's a lot of snakes."

Maverick looked over at the lineup as he tied the makeshift, heavy-duty leather armor around his cowboy boots. "Reminds me of cadaver bags."

"Said the horror writer." Quint cinched his own leg guard. "Let's hope this is the extent of the research fodder you collect today. I'd rather not give you any inspiration for death by snakebite."

"If you do get bit," Maverick said while securing a second shield, "try to writhe on the ground for a while. I could use a visual of an Oscar-winning demise." He stood, shaking his legs and testing his bindings. Then he walked over to the bags, counting. "How many snakes are we talking here?"

"Maybe thirty," Teodoro answered.

"All in one den?"

"Unfortunately, yes." Angélica appeared from around the side of the temple. She cast a worried glance at the bags and then in Quint's direction.

The urge to puff out his chest and pound on it a few times crossed his mind. Instead, he adjusted his shin guards, tempering his flare of testosterone before he did something even more asinine than insist she let him help catch venomous snakes all afternoon with his bare hands.

"That many rattlesnakes in one den is odd." Maverick stretched his arms, then bent down and reached for his toes.

"What's with the stretching, cowboy?" Quint asked. Were they going to do some Texas two-stepping with the snakes?

Maverick bent to one side and then the other, reaching for the sky. "I was in a car accident last year. I try to loosen up my back and shoulders now before doing strenuous work to save me from pain later."

Quint just hoped to still be breathing later, with or without pain.

"I've never come across that many rattlesnakes together," Maverick told Angélica. "I thought they were mostly solitary, except in the winter when they hibernate."

Frowning as she tugged on her gloves, she told him, "Teodoro thinks someone may have been feeding them before we showed up."

"Why would someone feed them?" Quint stood, testing his own

bindings with a few stomps. And when were they last fed? Were they going to be extra hungry today? Pissy from low blood sugar?

"Teodoro has a theory about that, too." She handed both Quint and Maverick some leather gloves.

"*Alux*." Teodoro made a feeding gesture with his hand. "It give food to snakes."

"What's an *alux*?" Maverick asked, slipping on the gloves.

"A forest spirit in the form of a dwarf trickster," Angélica answered. She glanced at Quint with a teasing grin. "Sort of like Parker here, only shorter and less sweaty in tight spots."

"And missing my gigantic *cojones* of Kryptonite, of course," he told Maverick, whose face split in a wide grin.

Teodoro called Maverick over, pointing toward the wheelbarrow as he doled out instructions.

Quint moved to Angélica's side. "You ready to catch some snakes?"

She nodded. "I want to get this over with. I have a hot date tonight with a slick-tongued charmer whose extra-large balls of Kryptonite are revered by many."

"Even you?"

"Especially me."

They watched as Teodoro showed Maverick how to hold the bag for him, while he pretended to hook a snake.

Keeping his eyes on the tutorial playing out in front of him, Quint told her, "Sweaty in tight spots, huh? I'm going to make you beg tonight, boss lady."

"Promises, promises." She patted him on the butt. "Come on, Parker. It's show time." She grabbed a bunch of bags and rope, handing them to Quint. "You're going to bag while I hook them." She held up a rod three feet long with a hook at the bottom. "Just to be clear, we're going to use the tailing method for catching them."

Maverick frowned over at her. "You're going to tail a rattler?" His tone was a mixture of surprise and admiration. "I've only seen that done on the internet."

"What do you use when you're catching them in Nevada?"

"I prefer a long snake hook and a big plastic tub, herding the hissing devils into the makeshift corral like any good rancher worth his salt. But I'm usually only dealing with one at a time and haven't had someone there to hold a bag for me."

Quint tried to picture grabbing a rattler by the tail while its jaws snapped in his direction and shuddered under his gear. "How are you going to tail it without it reaching around and biting you?"

"Follow me and I'll show you." She led the way into the jungle, slashing with her machete here and there as she walked. Teodoro followed, then Maverick, with Quint bringing up the rear. "Keep an eye out for snakes along the way," she said over her shoulder. "You know the saying."

" 'Always carry a flagon of whiskey in case of snakebite,' " Quint started.

" 'And furthermore, always carry a small snake,' " Maverick finished the quote, adding, "as the late, great W.C. Fields liked to say."

Angélica groaned loudly from the front of the line. "May the Maya gods help us, Teodoro. We've been cursed with two word-happy bards on this snake hunt."

Teodoro grunted.

"Cursed?" Maverick asked, glancing back at Quint. "What did you do at the last site to give writers such a bad rap with the boss?"

"He lied to me," she said, slashing her machete at a low-hanging branch.

"More like told a few small fibs, really." Quint dodged the spines of a thorn-covered branch. "They don't even qualify as white lies."

"And yet she let you return?"

"He wouldn't take no for an answer." Angélica swung her machete again, clearing the path.

"She can't resist me," Quint jested. "I got her number."

Angélica let out a laugh that scared a half-dozen birds from the tree canopy above them. "Which he promptly lost in the North Atlantic shortly after leaving Mexico."

That made Quint chuckle. "Touché."

She smiled back at him before pushing onward through the brush. "Anyway," she said as they skirted a low mound with a young, thorny ceiba tree growing out the top of it. "The quote I was referring to is that for every one snake you see, you probably walked past four."

"Our quote was more entertaining," Maverick said.

Quint agreed. "I should have brought some whiskey along for the hunt."

They fell silent for a short while, crunching over twigs and dead leaves as they slowly made their way deeper into the brush. The jungle whistled, chattered, and screeched around them, vibrating with life. The smell of fresh air was mixed with pockets of musty earth and molding jungle detritus.

The rattle of a tail could be heard here and there as they walked, but Quint couldn't see any snakes. The slithering bastards' ability to camouflage with the dead tree litter and leaves made his mouth dry. More than once a gnarled stick made his pulse redline. If he made it through the day without his ticker popping a spring or two, he would count himself lucky.

Up ahead, Angélica slowed. "Teodoro." She waved him up next to her. She pointed at something on the ground.

Teodoro nodded.

She glanced back. "Okay, you two, watch how we do this. I'm going to hook and tail while Teodoro bags."

Maverick stepped aside to make room for Quint. They both watched as Angélica eased up to the coiled snake. Its tail rattled slowly at first, picking up speed as she inched closer. Quint held his breath as she reached out with the hook and started uncoiling the snake. It lashed out several times, hissing, shaking its tail harder. She toyed with it, sliding the hook under it as it tried to coil again and again. She seemed to dance with it as it twisted and rallied, striking out at her repeatedly.

Using her hook she looped it under the snake about six inches back from its head and lifted it into the air. As the snake squirmed forward to touch back down to earth, Angélica seized its tail.

The snake tango shifted, the dancers now connected by hand and tail as well as hook and head. Angélica lifted the tail, continuing to hook and re-hook the snake up near its hissing mouth.

"It's important that you let the head keep touching down," she told them in a quiet voice, "so that it doesn't try to climb up itself and bite you on the arm or hand."

She waltzed the snake closer to where Teodoro was waiting with the bag. "See how Teodoro has a stick in the mouth of the bag to keep it open? Don't put your hands down near the bag's mouth until we get the snake's head inside, and even then you need to move quickly and with care."

Teodoro demonstrated Quint and Maverick's job, making it look easy. He waited until the rattler's head was completely inside of the bag and then grabbed the upper edge as he yanked out the stick, pulling the bag up the snake like a sheath as Angélica used the hook to lift the reptile further into it. When only the tail end was left sticking out and rattling, Teodoro lifted the bag completely off the ground. He held it far away from his body as the snake writhed inside.

"Snakes can bite through the bag," Angélica told them. "So make sure you keep it at arm's length away from your torso." She took the hook and poked the snake lightly through the bag. "Sometimes they need a little tickling to get them the rest of the way inside."

After a few more gentle pokes, the snake slid the rest of the way inside. Teodoro wasted no time, twisting the bag until the neck was almost a foot-long pretzel stick. Then he set the bag on the ground. Angélica laid her hook across the bottom of the twist and stepped on the hook's end to seal it tight while Teodoro tied the rope around the bag right above her snake hook.

"*Voilà!*" She picked up the bag for them to see, keeping it far from her torso. "One snake ready to relocate." She set it on the ground next to a tree. "After we fill the bags you two brought along, we'll take the snakes back to the temple for Pedro to haul off, grab more bags, and clear out this damned snake den."

Quint gaped at her, awed at how smoothly she'd danced that big rattlesnake into the bag. Hot damn!

"Any questions?"

"Yeah," Maverick spoke up. "How many times have *you* bagged a snake?"

"Enough to know not to get cocky during the process or you'll get bit."

"You were incredible." Maverick's tone was edged with admiration. He turned to Quint. "I can't believe you lied to her and she let you live."

"She tried to bag me once or twice, but she got cocky."

Maverick grinned. "And you bit her?"

"A few times. She's very soft on the fangs."

"Parker!" Angélica shot him a warning glare. "Keep it up and I'll let one of the snakes bite your smart ass."

Maverick looked back at Angélica. "Where'd you learn how to work a hook like that?"

She patted Teodoro on the shoulder. "I was taught by the best. If you ask nicely, maybe he'll let you work the hook once or twice this afternoon, teach you the magic touch, too."

"Watching him work is going to be a treat," Maverick said.

She looked back toward the forest. "Where do you want to start, Teodoro?"

They conversed in Mayan for a few beats and then Teodoro and Maverick traipsed off into the trees, leaving Quint alone with Angélica and her bagged snake.

"Well, Parker? You ready to get busy?"

He raised one eyebrow at her double entendre. "What did you have in mind, boss lady?"

Her eyelashes lowered, her lips curving. "You." She moved closer to him, running her fingernails down his chest. "And me." She went up on her toes, her lips closing the distance between them. "And several bags full of snakes."

He dropped a quick kiss on her upturned lips, unable to resist. "Why can't we go out on dates like a normal couple?"

She stepped back, resting her hook on her shoulder. "Where's the fun in that? I'd probably bore you to pieces in ten minutes going on and on about the history of the Maya. I don't have much else of a life these days, you know, what with my boyfriend always on the road."

"I think you underestimate my ability to sit and stare at you while fantasizing about your naked body for hours on end."

"What happens in these fantasies?" She took a handful of his shirt and tugged him along after her, treading carefully as she searched the ground.

"Before or after you get naked?"

"After *you* get naked." Several steps farther, she stopped short and held up her hand, indicating for him to hold still.

As much as he'd prefer to be thinking about nakedness on both of their parts—particularly her parts—the rattlesnake lying still on the ground in front of Angélica kicked all other thoughts aside.

Batter up, he thought, hoisting a bag.

"Is the den up ahead?" he whispered as he grabbed a stick to prop the bag open.

"No. It's over there." She nudged her head in the direction Teodoro and Maverick had gone.

"Then why are we heading this way?"

"Because the idea is to work the radius of the den first, clearing the incoming and outgoing snakes so that by the time we reach the den we don't have any surprise visitors showing up at the party."

"Gotcha. Are you going to get that hook ready and do your snake dance or what, boss lady?"

She lowered her hook and eased forward. "Stand back until I get it uncoiled."

"Your wish is my command."

He watched in silence, sweat dripping down his back as she maneuvered the hook under the snake. Again, she danced and teased until she had a clear shot at its tail. Then she dragged it across the jungle floor while lifting and lowering the front end with the hook. He had the bag ready for the snake, but his heart was running at a dead sprint when his turn at bat came.

"I'm sliding it in now," she said, sweat rolling down her cheek. "Get ready."

"That's what he said," he joked.

A chirp of laughter escaped her lips as she worked the head into the bag. "Okay, grab the bag but watch out. It could still turn back and bite you."

Quint did as Teodoro had shown, only not as gracefully or quickly. As he pulled the bag along the snake's body, he could feel its muscled length thrashing inside. The tail rattled all of the way into the bag.

"Twist the neck of the bag tight."

Quint followed her instructions, blinking through the sweat that ran into his eyes and blurred his vision. As soon as he'd twisted as far as the bag allowed, he lowered the twist onto the jungle floor. She blocked any escape of the snake with the rod part of her hook. He tied the rope and stood, wiping his damp hands on his pants. His heart pounded. Adrenaline pulsed throughout his body.

"Let's get another one," he said. At that moment, he felt like he could take on a den full of rattlers.

"Hold on, stallion." She reached down and grabbed a broken branch lying close to her heel. "I want to show you something."

She tapped the bag with the stick a couple of times and then slowly pushed the end into the side of the fabric. The bag jerked. A pair of fangs popped through the burlap, scraping over the stick.

"Fuck me!" Quint winced. "That was fast."

"You see how dangerous they are even inside of the bag?" At his nod, she continued. "Many people get bit while the snake is in the bag because of the no-see, no-fear concept. But at all times, it's important that you keep that snake away from your body."

"Lesson learned, boss," he said, serious.

She frowned, rising. "I'm not trying to be bossy, Quint. I just don't want anything to happen to you. I've seen too many snakebites in my time. Having you here catching snakes with me makes me nervous."

"There is no way in hell I'm going to hide back in the tent while you go gallivanting about with your snake hook, like Don Quixote chasing windmills."

Her face softened. "You think I gallivant with the snakes, huh?"

"Actually, it's more of a tango. A scary tango. Sort of sexy, though. But I'll be glad when you're done with this snake dance."

"Me, too. I have some begging I'm looking forward to doing tonight."

"I like the idea of you on your knees."

Her cheeks rounded. "Do you now?"

"It's the keystone of one of my favorite fantasies."

"You'll have to show me how it plays out later." She pointed her hook to the left. "Do you see that big fig tree over there?"

He nodded.

"That's where the den is. You ready to fill another bag?"

"Quint Parker's the name. Bagging snakes is my game."

"Oh, Lord. Not poetry, too. Just let the snakes have at me." She led the way, using her hook to shake the bushes as they moved forward through the thick trees. "Tell me more about your deal with the devil this morning."

"If I pulled a stone out from that wall in the mine, he would leave us alone in our tent for a few hours."

"Sounds like borderline blackmail to me."

"I prefer to call it a 'deal' so I feel less manipulated."

She pointed her hook at a thick, coiled body up ahead next to the trail. "Damn, that's a big one."

"That's what she said," he joked again.

She reached back and poked him in the ribs. "Please tell me this isn't going to go on and on all afternoon."

"She also said that."

Her laughter warmed the cockles of his heart.

The huge rattlesnake lunging out of the bag at his shins a short time later shrank his balls into tiny BBs. Luckily for him, Angélica jerked Quint back in time, the snake's fangs missing their mark. In a flash, she hooked the snake again and slid it into the bag far enough that it couldn't double back as easily. It hissed and rattled as they twisted the bag and tied it off.

"Holy hell." Quint shook the tension out of his hands. "How did you know he was going to do that?"

"I felt it buck and knew he wasn't going in easy. I should have warned you. Sorry."

"You can make up for it later."

"How about I promise to kiss it better?"

"I didn't get bit."

She looked pointedly at him. "And yet I could still kiss it better."

Ohhhhh. He was an idiot. He shrugged, playing it cool. "Actually, I prefer to have my wounds licked."

"I've heard that about you, Parker."

"What else have you heard?"

"You'll have to torture me to get the rest."

"I'll grab my thumbscrews."

"Grab that first." She pointed at the bag. "Let's go get the other two rattlers and take them back to the temple."

The ten-minute trek back through the jungle went without a snake sighting. "What was on the other side of the wall?" she asked as they cleared the tree line.

"An altar."

Pedro waited for them with the wheelbarrow. They placed their snake bags inside, careful to leave the ends draped over the edge to make it easier for Pedro to lift the bags back out.

"Was anything on it?" she asked.

"On what?" Pedro asked.

"The altar Juan and I found behind the wall in the limestone mine." Quint grabbed several more bags and rope. "I took some pictures using your dad's camera, but the flash on those cheap digital rigs can only light so much." He draped the bags over his shoulder and took the canteen she offered him, swigging some water. "Your dad tried to bribe me to take out more stones and crawl through the hole for a better look, but I drew the line on that notion."

"Good." Angélica took back the canteen. "As much as I'd like to know what's inside, I don't want you going through a hole in an unstable wall."

He watched her throat as she tipped her head back and

swallowed, following the graceful lines of her neck. A neck he was going to enjoy kissing in a few hours.

Shaking off his wayward thoughts, he returned to the topic at hand. "You squeezed through a very unstable hole at the last site when I explicitly advised against it."

"Quint has a good point."

She pointed her machete at Pedro. "Leave Quint's points to me, Montañero." Turning back to Quint, she lowered her machete. "That was before you got into my head and screwed me up."

"Oh, sweetheart. You're so romantic."

"I wouldn't do something so crazy nowadays."

Pedro scoffed. "No, you'll just go running off all alone into the jungle without skipping a jump and forget to tell anyone where you're going."

She whirled on him, hands planted on her hips. "It's skipping a *beat*, buster, and what is with you and this skipping nonsense? When was the last time you saw me skip?"

"When did she go into the forest alone?" Quint asked, suddenly sober.

"Earlier today. She said she was following an old trail."

"I was."

"Alone?" Quint frowned at her. After what they'd learned about Marianne possibly being murdered, not to mention the damned predators lurking out there in the trees, what in the hell was she thinking?

"Yes, alone. Why? What's the big deal?" Her eyes narrowed. "What do you know?"

Behind her, Pedro zipped his lips repeatedly, his brown eyes wide.

Son of a bitch. He'd just walked into a trap. "I know a lot of things," he answered, stalling.

Angélica shot a look in Pedro's direction, catching him with his hand near his face.

Pedro pretended to scratch his jaw.

"You two are hiding something from me."

"I don't know what you're talking about." Pedro tugged on his gloves and walked over to the wheelbarrow, exiting the conversation. The big chicken.

"Fine, play dumb, Pedro," she said to his back, focusing back on Quint. "But you're going to tell me the truth, Parker, if you ever want to finish our conversation about soap from last night."

He squirmed under her stare. Shit. She was going to shut the door on sex tonight if he didn't come clean. Damn Pedro for leading him into this corner.

"Let's go," she said to him after aiming a last look at Pedro, who was making a point of adjusting his gloves.

As they headed back into the jungle for more snakes, they passed Teodoro and Maverick coming out with writhing bags of their own.

"Anybody get hurt yet?" Angélica asked.

"One tried to bite me," Maverick said. "But I kicked it mid-lunge."

"You're kidding?" Quint said.

"He no joke." Teodoro grinned. "This one is *loco*."

Maverick shrugged. "My ex-wife had a worse bite than any of these snakes. During the divorce I got used to dealing with forked tongues and poisonous fangs."

They parted and returned to the task at hand. Throughout an afternoon filled with bugs and stifling heat, they caught one snake after another. Some went easily into the bag, while others thrashed and hissed even after the bag was tied off. Twice Quint almost got bit, and once one of them slipped off Angélica's hook and its fangs glanced off her shin pad, but for the most part, the hours passed with only sweat running, not blood.

Angélica didn't bring up Pedro and her earlier suspicions once, but Quint had no doubt that they were festering inside. She was probably just waiting for tonight when they were alone and she had him by the balls. Then she'd put the squeeze on him, and not the squeezing he liked.

By the time they'd cleared the way to the snake den, there were only about ten or so rattlers left to wrangle. Teodoro and Maverick took the lead, with the shaman scooping up a snake with his hook and gently pulling it from the den. He tailed it and worked it into the bag so fast Quint would have missed it if he'd blinked.

"He's something, isn't he?" Angélica said, smiling proudly. "I've never seen anyone else as smooth at snake handling as Teodoro. He told me years ago that one of his jobs as a child was clearing snakes from his village's *milpas*."

"*Milpas* are fields, right?" Maverick asked as he set a burlap bag down a few feet from them.

"*Sí*," Teodoro answered. "Many snakes."

Angélica stepped up next, Quint following with a bag ready as she hooked and gently lifted and dragged a snake out far enough to grab its tail. As she reached for the rattling end, something moved in Quint's peripheral vision. Before he could react, a machete sliced down, whistling through the air next to his ear.

A piece of snake thumped onto the ground next to his boot.

He touched his ear to make sure it was still attached.

Thankfully, it was, but the head of a rattlesnake lay bleeding onto the jungle floor.

"Don't touch!" Teodoro kicked it aside. "Still venom after dead."

Angélica finished her hook and tailing, nudging back several snakes as Quint tied the bag. He moved quickly, lifting the bag and dropping it next to the one Maverick had set down.

"What the hell just happened?" he asked Maverick.

"A snake came down out of the tree and lunged for Angélica. Teodoro sliced its head off before it reached her. It happened so fast that all I could do was watch."

"Quick reflexes."

"The man isn't human, I swear. I've been catching flies with my mouth all day watching him work his magic."

Quint looked over at Angélica. "You okay?"

She nodded, frowning. "I should have looked up before moving in for the tail grab, but that damned snake kept wiggling off my hook."

"*Es muy peligroso ahora.*" Teodoro wiped the blood off his machete on a leaf and then picked up his hook again.

"What did he say?" Maverick asked.

"It's more dangerous now." She pulled out her machete and inched forward along with Teodoro. "We'll have to keep a spotter until we clear the den of the rest."

No other snakes were injured in the removal process, but Quint lost a gallon of sweat … or three.

Finally, they emptied the den. With the last snake bagged, Angélica didn't waste time celebrating. She dropped down onto her hands and knees and started to crawl through the hole into the den.

"Oh no you don't, woman," Quint said, grabbing her by the hips as she started inside. He tailed her and dragged her backward, not even bothering with hooking her first.

"Quint!" She rolled over onto her back, glaring up at him. "What are you doing? I'm the smallest. I'll fit in the hole best."

"You're not going in there. I am."

"Why?"

"Because I'm stronger, that's why. You can't drag that big chunk of stone out on your own, but I can."

"Yeah, but—"

"And you're better with a machete." He pulled her to her feet, dusting off her backside for her. "You and Teodoro watch for snakes coming back to the den. I'll get the damned rock."

Before she could argue further, he was down on his stomach, belly crawling into the den.

The inside reeked with a stench that made him gag. His eyes watered. He didn't even want to think about how much snake shit and animal remains he was crawling through. Where was that damned mask Juan had made him wear in the mine? He grabbed the chunk of stone and tugged on it. The sucker had to weigh sixty to seventy pounds. He dragged it through the dirt, backing out of the den slowly.

Once Quint was back in the hot jungle air, Maverick held out a hand to help him up while Angélica knelt to inspect the stone.

"What's it say?" Quint stood, brushing off his shirt.

"I can't read it yet. It's coated with dirt and mud. I need to clean it off."

"Uh, Dr. García," Maverick said, bending over and shining his flashlight into the den. "I hate to interrupt your Indiana Jones moment, but I think I figured out the reason that piece of stone was in the den."

"What do you mean?" Angélica asked. She pulled out her paintbrush and began to clear off dirt.

"Take a look for yourself."

Quint leaned down, peering in next to Maverick. Teodoro joined them.

"You've got to be fucking kidding me," Quint whispered.

"What?" Angélica said, joining them finally. "Is that ..." she trailed off. "Crap."

Inside of the den, there were now two rattlesnakes writhing around while three more slithered out of a hole in the back wall that Quint had exposed when he removed the rock.

"It was a plug," she said.

"What the hell?" Quint asked as the hole filled with more snakes, like rats fleeing a sinking ship.

Maverick leaned closer, aiming his beam deeper into the exposed hole. "Jesus! Look at all of them back there. Where are they coming from?"

Teodoro said something in Mayan, stepping back, his face pale. He made a quick sign in the air with his fingers and chanted something up at the sky.

"What did he say?" Quint asked Angélica.

"He said the snakes are coming from the Maya Underworld."

"Son of a bitch." Quint lifted the piece of stela with a grunt and stepped back, keeping Angélica behind him as a snake that had been slithering their way coiled up. Its rattle began to shake. "We've stumbled onto a portal to hell."

Chapter Thirteen

Balche Tree: A tree whose bark is used, along with other ingredients such as honey and sugar, to produce wine for traditional ceremonies.

Goddamned rattlesnakes!

It was bad enough that Quint's afternoon had been spent avoiding their fangs one burlap bag after another, but now the assholes were screwing up his plans for an evening alone with the boss lady.

Quint lowered himself onto a log acting as a bench next to the fire Teodoro had built. The rest of the crew lounged around the fire as well, minus Angélica and Daisy, who were helping María prepare large thick tortillas called *nohua*, a ritual bread for the *Lolcatali* ceremony.

After finding that snake hole, Teodoro had insisted on having the ceremony to petition the spirits to protect the camp from evil spirits ASAP—as in tonight, which scratched Quint's opportunity to get Angélica alone off the calendar.

It turned out that a hole into the Maya Underworld was really bad juju in the shaman's eyes. Angélica must have understood the significance of that hole, because she didn't argue at all when Teodoro had announced after wrapping up with the snake den that he was going to start the ceremony when the sun was setting.

And now, here Quint sat along with most of the crew. A few yards away on the other side of the fire, Teodoro played his traditional part at an altar made of arched branches and wood planks. Lit candles stood next to gourd bowls, two filled with cacao and two with wine made from a *balche* tree. Each bowl sat at a corner of the altar, representing four of something in the Maya world that Quint couldn't remember at the moment.

The low rumbling sound of Teodoro's voice filled the evening, lulling Quint, along with the crackle of flames. Incense and wood smoke blended in the heavy humidity to create a sweet, light scent in the still air. If he closed his eyes he might fall asleep …

What are you? A voice whispered in the darkness.

Quint opened his eyes with a start. Who said that? He looked behind him toward the dark forest but found only shadows. He could swear someone had spoken right next to him.

He turned back, frowning into the flames. He must have been dreaming, but damn, that was …

Do you know what you are doing?

What the fuck? He looked around again. Who was talking? Was Angélica messing with him?

His scalp prickled.

Someone was watching him.

Quint looked up from the flames, scanning faces.

The boys were still helping Teodoro.

Juan was busy talking to Jane, pointing down at her injured leg while she nodded.

Gertrude was … Gertrude was staring at him.

He stared back through the fire, trying to figure out if she was dazed from the wine and chanting or if she was actually focused on him. In the flickering light, her skin looked almost luminescent.

"Any trouble at the shower, Quint?" Juan called.

Shaking out of what felt like a trance, Quint answered, "Trouble? You mean with snakes?"

"I mean trouble with rinsing that pesky soap off this time." Juan's face split into a shit-eating grin.

Angélica's father was too damned observant for Quint's good. Thankfully, Pedro joined them before Juan had a chance to further harass him. He sat down next to Quint on the log.

Across the fire, Jane and Gertrude both began to question Juan about the purpose of the *Lolcatali* ceremony and what would happen next.

Quint watched the three of them for a moment, especially

Gertrude. He waited to see if she looked back his way again, but she didn't.

Pedro leaned in close. "I heard from my friend in Cancun," he whispered, his gaze locked on the flames.

Quint glanced his way. "How? Via the monkey hotline? Are you part of the Jungle VIP?"

"I checked my messages on my phone when I was up in the air earlier, moving those snakes."

"You checked your messages while you were operating a helicopter?"

Pedro shrugged. "I just push a few buttons and the helicopter does the rest of the work."

Quint was pretty positive there was a lot more to flying a helicopter than pushing a few buttons. "What did you hear?"

Lines formed on Pedro's forehead. "Not good news." He paused while Lorenzo offered several small gourd bowls full of *balche* wine around the fire. Pedro took one for himself.

Quint followed suit, ready for some of Teodoro's homemade honey-sweetened wine after a day filled with hissing snakes. "*Gracias*," he told Lorenzo. As soon as the boy was out of earshot, he bumped his knee once against Pedro's. "Spit it out."

"No way. I like this wine."

"The news, smartass."

Pedro waited for Juan to continue his tour guide translation of the ceremony before speaking. "The Mexican government has a policy that states in the event of an aircraft-related fatality, pilots must have a forensic toxicology test done in addition to an autopsy. They test for all sorts of chemicals in the blood, including alcohol, drugs, and more."

There was only one reason Pedro would be bringing this up now. "What did they find?"

"Poison. Neurotoxin from snake venom was listed in the report."

"Snake venom?"

He nodded. "After the toxicology report came back, the pictures of the body were re-examined. The multiple puncture wounds on the pilot's legs were then determined to be snake bites."

Quint had a feeling he knew what kind of snake did the damage. "Rattlesnakes. What the fuck?"

"So, he was either bit before liftoff or during the flight."

"Not after the crash?"

"The chances of his being bit after the accident are not good. Snakes aren't going to rush to a crash scene to bite a dead man."

"So, he was dead upon landing?"

Pedro nodded. "At least that's what the coroner's report says based on the time of death determined from the autopsy. We know for certain that the pilot was dead when the rescue team arrived."

"What size helicopter are we talking?

"A Robinson R-44 Raven, 4-seater."

"What's the typical payload on those?"

"Around 750 pounds."

"So if it were a 4-seater, Marianne could have been sitting in front with the pilot or in the back. Was there any evidence of Marianne being bitten?"

Pedro shrugged. "I don't remember anything else being mentioned about bites. Marianne's wounds were pretty extensive, though. The crash threw her from the helicopter. I don't know that the doctors were looking for bites. They were just trying to keep her alive long enough for Juan and Angélica to get to the hospital and say good-bye." Pedro paused, clearing his throat. "I'm beginning to wonder if Marianne was the murder victim, or if the pilot was the objective and Marianne was killed because she was in the wrong place at the wrong time."

They both sat in silence for a moment, drinking *balche*, letting Pedro's announcement settle in the warm air.

Quint listened to the popping and sizzling of the fire as Teodoro's humming rose and fell. Across the flames, Juan continued to answer Jane's and Gertrude's questions in a low voice. The evening light had faded, leaving the night's dark cloak draped over them. The jungle sounds were louder now; the party in the trees was really rocking. Occasionally piercing the racket was a howl or two from a monkey.

Glancing around into the shadows, Quint wondered what was keeping Angélica. How long did it take to make enough ceremonial bread for tonight's event?

Pedro finished his bowl of wine and set it down on the ground next to his boots. "Where do we go from here?"

"Did they do an autopsy on Marianne?"

"I don't think so. I could ask Juan, but I'm not sure how to bring it up without inspiring a lot of questions in return."

"True." Quint blew out a breath of frustration. He was going to have enough of a problem with Angélica. He had a feeling that before anything was going to happen involving nakedness the next time they were alone, she was going to hold out on him until he answered questions about what secret Pedro was keeping from her.

How much to tell her still had Quint scratching his jaw. How would she feel about Pedro and him looking into her mother's death, raising all sorts of questions about the accident?

A second gourd of wine later, Quint was beginning to feel light on his feet, even though he hadn't moved from the log. Pedro went back for more *balche* and refilled Quint's small gourd bowl again as well. The girls across the way had quieted down, their eyes growing glassier with each swallow of wine. Bernard was now helping Teodoro alongside Fernando, Lorenzo, and Esteban. Maverick sat next to Juan, sharing an occasional comment as they watched Teodoro move about behind the altar.

A hand touched his shoulder. He looked up. Angélica smiled at him, her dark auburn hair free for once, cascading over her shoulders. Maybe it was a side effect of the wine, but he couldn't stop staring at her. She was drop-dead gorgeous in the flickering light. Quint cursed those damned snakes and their hole to hell again.

"How are things going?" she asked, lowering herself onto the log next to him. She took his bowl of wine from him and tipped it up to her mouth. "Ummmm, delicious." She licked her lips, flames reflecting in her eyes. "How much wine has Pedro poured down your throat?" She handed the gourd back to him.

"This is my third," he said, his focus locked onto her lips. They glistened in the firelight. He'd like to lean in and taste the sweet wine on them, but he held back. Barely.

"Teodoro has to be exhausted," she said, scooting closer to Quint until their thighs touched. He poured more wine down his throat, trying to deaden his lust. "After all of those snakes he caught and released today, a *Lolcatali* ceremony is going to wear him out."

"How are you doing?" he asked her. She'd caught quite a few snakes herself this afternoon.

"Frustrated. From what I can tell, that stela you pulled out of the snake den only lists information about one of the kings, nothing about the warning Mom wrote about."

"I meant how are you doing physically, sweetheart. You had a snake-filled afternoon, too."

She rested her head on his shoulder, sighing. "Sleepy around the edges."

"Trust me, sweetheart, you have no edges, only curves." He leaned down and breathed in the scent of her hair, the light citrusy smell made his head float more than Teodoro's wine.

"*Gatita*," Juan said, seeming to suddenly realize his daughter had joined them. "Where's Daisy?"

"She was worn out and went back to her tent."

"She needs to be here for this. Teodoro wanted all of us to be here for protection purposes."

"Dad, she was practically asleep on her feet. I didn't want to drag her here and force her to sit on a log for hours. Besides, her tent is right there," she said, pointing to the one closest to them, which was about thirty feet away. "She's near enough to be included in the protection ritual."

Juan stood and dragged his chair closer, planting it at the end of the log Quint was using as a bench.

"Where's Pedro?" Angélica asked.

"He's watering the trees." Quint tilted his head toward the jungle behind them where Pedro had gone to take care of business.

"We need to shut down the *Chakmo'ol* Temple," Juan said, keeping his voice low.

"I don't want to talk about this right now, Dad."

"You didn't want to talk about it earlier, either." Juan leaned forward to speak around Quint. "You can't avoid the reality of the situation. Those snakes are dangerous."

"Quint plugged the hole," she said. "Remember?"

Yes, Quint did, still shuddering from the experience. It had taken the four of them working as a team to get the snakes cleared out enough for Quint to maneuver another large stone into the den. After he'd crawled back out, he and Maverick had used long branches to jam it into the hole that kept leaking snakes. Finally, they were left with the rattling of only those snakes that had made it through before they'd wedged the stone in tight.

"That's only a temporary fix and you know it," Juan whispered. "I'm sure that piece of stela was wedged in there, too, at one point. The snakes will find a way around it like they did before."

"I need to keep working in the *Chakmo'ol* Temple, Dad."

"Fine, you continue working in there, but you need to move the college kids to the other end of the site. Let them focus on the ballcourt and the *Baatz'* Temple."

"Okay, but you'll have to stay down there and help Fernando supervise them in my place."

Juan nodded, looking unhappy about it. "What about Quint?"

"What about me?" he asked.

"Where are you going to work?"

Quint looked at Angélica. "Where am I going to work?"

"He can help me. Maverick, too, since he doesn't mind the snakes so much." She stared over at Teodoro, who was drinking from one of the gourds.

Pedro returned, sitting on the log again between Quint and Juan's chair.

"Has he positioned the *tancazche* wood and obsidian in the four corners to protect us yet?" Angélica asked.

"No." Pedro picked up his wine gourd. "He's been praying to the *alux*."

"Why must you continue to work in the *Chakmo'ol* Temple?" Juan leaned forward to speak around Pedro and Quint this time. "We've cleared it out for now and can seal it up and leave it for a future crew."

Angélica huffed, shaking her head. "Absolutely not, Dad. My job is to clean up sites, make them safe and ready for archaeology crews and the public. Sealing up the temple is not accomplishing any of my objectives. This site currently has three things going for it in the archaeotourism world—the ballcourt, the *Baatz'* Temple, and the *Chakmo'ol* Temple. We have a few more weeks to get all three prepped for the next archaeology crew the Mexican government allows to come here and dig, and I'm going to make sure that happens."

"What do you mean by 'prepped'?" Quint asked, handing her his drink. He should probably stop for the night before Angélica turned into twins before his very eyes. The morning sunshine was not his friend on a normal day, let alone when a hangover was stabbing him between the eyes.

"Relatively snake-free, for starters." She took another drink of the wine.

Juan grunted in disagreement. "You're obsessing about that glyph and using your job as an excuse to keep the temple open."

She leaned across Quint's thighs toward her father, her face lined with tension, her body rigid. The soft weight of her breast rested on his forearm. He closed his eyes, trying to block out the images that suddenly filled his head.

"I'm not obsessing about that glyph," she bit out. "I'm too busy obsessing about that stupid stela that Mom wrote about to have time to fixate on the glyphs in the temple."

"At least we agree you're obsessed, *gatita*." Juan leaned forward and ran his thumb down her cheek. "Your mother would be so proud of how far along your monomania has come," he joked.

Angélica stuck her tongue out at him, settling back onto her part of the log, crossing her ankles. She took another drink of wine while staring into the fire.

After a few minutes of Teodoro's rhythmic chanting, Quint pushed to his feet, stretching. His tailbone ached from the hard seat, his lower back protesting hours of bending over to bag snakes.

"I'll be right back," he told the three of them.

Angélica looked up at him. "Where are you going?"

"I need to grab my canteen and some ibuprofen from the tent. This wine is hitting me fast. I don't need a hangover while I sweat my ass off tomorrow."

He tottered a little on his way to the tent in the dark, the wine making his knees loosey-goosey. His flashlight bobbed as the dry grass crunched under his boots. His mind rang with questions about what in the hell had happened years ago with Marianne and the pilot. Had someone put snakes in the helicopter? Wasn't damaging the rotor enough of a guarantee for the killer?

Unzipping the tent, he turned on his flashlight and set it on the floor next to his bag, spotlighting the canvas wall. The light was dim, but lit the tent enough to help him find what he needed from his backpack. He grabbed his canteen from the floor and tossed back two pills, washing them down and swallowing a few more mouthfuls as a chaser.

The sound of the tent flap rustling made him turn.

Angélica zipped the flap closed behind her. She shut off her flashlight and set it on the floor. "Parker, we need to clear the air about something."

He capped his canteen. He knew what this was about. She'd been patient all afternoon, not badgering him about Pedro's big secret, but her patience must have come to an end. "If this is about Pedro's comment earlier—"

"Shhhhh." She closed the distance between them, taking his

canteen from him and lowering it to the floor.

He lifted one eyebrow. "Did you just shush me?"

"Yes." Her eyes were dark pools in the feeble light. "We need to talk about that, but there's something I need to take care of first, and then I need to get back to the ceremony."

"What?"

Angélica took a step back and in a blink pulled her shirt up over her head. It was a slow blink for Quint, thanks to the wine slowing down reality. She tossed her shirt onto her cot and then stood before him in her khakis and a black bra.

At least it looked black in low light.

And gauzy.

Very gauzy.

Practically transparent.

Hello, siren! He rubbed his hand over his eyes and blinked again. His gaze locked onto the dark tips peeking out through the thin material, his mouth going dry. Was this for real?

"We have a problem," she said, kicking off her tennis shoes and unbuttoning her pants.

"We do?" His focus slid lower as she eased her pants over her hips. A matching pair of black gauzy underwear slung low on her hips gave him a peep show that almost made his wine-wobbly knees give way.

"I want something from you." She stepped out of her pants and tugged off her socks, throwing them onto her cot after her shirt.

She stood in front of him in her gauzy black bits, her auburn hair curling around her shoulders. When she licked her lips, he nearly keeled over.

"What do you say?" She glanced down at her chest, grimaced, and adjusted one of her breasts in the see-through cup.

"Suffering succotash," he whispered.

"Did you just quote Sylvester James Pussycat, Sr.?"

His gaze raced up and down her body, his heart running neck-and-neck with his breath. "Were you wearing those while you were hooking snakes?" He imagined her handling that hook in her black bra and panties and a blast of heat knocked him back a step. Holy smokes, that was hot—minus the lunging rattlesnakes, of course.

She laughed. It sounded extra breathy in Quint's wine-soaked brain, sexy as hell. "Of course not. I put them on after my shower tonight. I packed these in case you actually showed up to the dig site and I decided to forgive you for not contacting me for-fucking-ever."

"Those are for me?" He flexed his hands, not sure where to touch first.

"Are you drunk, Parker?"

"I think so." His gaze met hers. "But trust me, it's not going to be a problem."

She rested her hands on her hips, making her chest jut out at him. "So, are you going to make me beg like you promised earlier or not? Because if you're physically up to the task, we don't have time to discuss my lingerie any longer. I have a ceremony to get back to before anyone notices how long it's taking me to visit the latrine."

That no-nonsense tone of hers was his undoing. He went in fast and hard, yanking her against him. He gripped her hair, tugging her head back, tipping her mouth up to his.

"Take off my pants," he ordered and then lowered his mouth to hers, tasting sweet *balche* wine on her soft lips. With a groan from a month's worth of pent-up frustration, he dipped his tongue into her mouth, teasing hers with quick flicks.

He felt his pants loosen a moment before her hand slid inside his boxer briefs, her fingers wasting no time taking hold. He pulled back, extracting her hand from his briefs. There was no way he'd last another ten seconds if she continued doing that.

"I didn't tell you to touch me yet." If he was going to make her beg, she needed to let him lead this dance.

"Quint." Her voice sounded hoarse, digging up memories from heated nights back in her bed in Cancun. "We don't have time to fool around first."

"I told you I'd make you beg."

"Please." She reached for him again.

He held her hand away. "I mean *really* beg." His grip still on her wrist, he drew her back against him. "You seem to be confused about who's running the show here."

This time when he kissed her, he took total control, not giving her an opportunity to take charge. In no time, she was moaning and moving against him, pushing his limits.

He broke away from her, his breath ragged. "Show me what you want."

She took his hand and ran it down over her bra, circling the center of his palm over the hard tip under the gauzy fabric. He let her guide him, keeping his hand rigid, fighting the urge to palm the softness.

Her breath quickened as she brushed his palm over her again and again. His body throbbed, but he held steady, wanting to hear her really beg.

She looked up at him, her lips swollen from his kisses. He couldn't resist, lowering to her mouth again, sinking his teeth into her lower lip and tugging gently. The sweet taste of Angélica along with the effects of wine made his head spin. He sank his fingers in her hair, pressing his hips into hers as he deepened the kiss.

"Quint," she murmured when he came up for air. "Hurry."

"Not yet."

"Please."

"That's not good enough." He returned his palm to her breast, brushing over the tip. "Show me what else you want."

She captured his hand and moved it lower, over the soft skin of her stomach, inside the waistband of her panties. "Do you think you can take it from here?" she teased, turning slightly to give him a better angle.

"Let's see." His hand slid lower, a growl of lust rumbling up from his chest when he felt how ready she was for him. Christ, this game wasn't going to last much longer. He paused, leaning down to nip her bare shoulder. His free hand itched to explore that gauzy bra and the softness underneath it, but there was no time for that. "Do you want me to keep going?"

"Yes." Her response came out in a rush of breath.

"Beg, sweetheart."

She covered his hand with hers, directing. She looked up at him, her eyelids half-lowered in pleasure. "Please."

"Please what?" He strummed once, remembering exactly how she liked to be caressed.

Her mouth parted in a soft gasp, her hand pressing his harder against her, urging him onward. "Please, make me yours."

At her submission, his control slipped away. His hand moved lower, his touch lighting her up.

She moaned and panted in the semi-darkness. When he moved in close to kiss her, unable to resist her lush mouth, she shook her head, avoiding his kiss. "No."

"No what?" His head was rummy with wine-laced lust, making it hard to think.

"No kisses yet. I want you to watch what you do to me."

Watch? No, he wanted to … *Oh!* "You mean when I do this?" He stroked deeper.

Her eyes widened in response. "Yes."

He did it again. That was all it took. Her body began to tremble. Quint stared down at her in the soft light as a wave of pleasure rocked her. Seeing the raw emotion flow over her face as she clung to him was staggering. He clutched her tighter, his body nearly letting loose from watching her.

As soon as her body stopped trembling, Quint pulled away and struggled with his pants, which got caught up on his damned boots. "Take those off now," he said, pointing at her bra and underwear.

He tried to unlace his boots, the wine and lust making his fingers stupid. Before he could free even one eyelet, she was naked.

"Forget about your boots." She pushed him down onto his cot. "There's no time for them." She straddled him, teasing just out of reach. "Maybe I should make you beg now."

"Bad idea." He locked onto her hips and pulled her down onto him, sliding into heaven. The initial rush was almost his undoing. "Oh, baby. I missed you."

"Show me how much." Her body rocked against him, skin sliding on skin. A wave of pleasure made him lightheaded.

Still palming her hips, he helped her move, speeding up their dance. Now was not the time for a leisurely waltz. The cot creaked under them as his breath grew ragged.

She grasped his upper arms, her fingers digging into his muscles. Her lips burned a trail across his cheek to his ear. "Harder, Parker."

Sweet Jesus, if she didn't stop sucking on his earlobe like that he wasn't going to last much longer.

"Oh my …" She cupped his face, her kisses frenzied, moaning into his mouth. Then her body arched into his, her knees squeezing his hips as she tightened and pulsed around him.

So. Damned. Sexy.

He slid against her, lengthening her quivers.

When her trembling stopped, she whispered, "Your turn, heartbreaker." She bit him lightly on the shoulder, sucking hard on his skin.

A bolt of lust shot through him, taking the last of his control with it. A month of fantasizing about her had him on a short leash. His body bowed, rigid with release, as he gripped her hips and held her still. He shuddered and quaked, stars floating behind his eyes.

When he could think straight again, he leaned forward, resting his head on her sweat-dampened chest. "Holy hell, Angélica. That about killed me."

"Death by sex in the Maya jungle," she said in a news announcer voice. "Tune in at ten for the full story of how an archaeologist-turned-*Xtabay* used her deadly embrace to steal the breath from a charming photojournalist, killing him in the midst of sex."

He chuckled. "On a happier note, he died with his pants around his ankles and a huge smile on his face."

Giggling, she continued, "His mother is beside herself, worrying about whether he had put on clean underwear that morning."

"Dear Lord, sweetheart. Don't bring up my mom so soon after sex. I'll never recover for another round."

She stroked his back, her fingers bumping down his spine. "Next time we get naked, I want to do things to you that make *you* beg."

"What sort of things?" Did it involve more biting? Some sort of Maya-inspired jaguar sex position?

"Bad things that I think you'll enjoy."

"Okay, but if it involves an obsidian blade, my family jewels, and a blood offering to the Maya gods, I'm going to have to take a rain check."

Mock, evil laughter filled the tent. She tipped his chin up. "No bloodletting, I promise." Then she kissed him thoroughly, making him stir inside of her again.

"Hold that thought," she said when she pulled back. Before he could snap out of his lust-inebriated haze, she left him, moving over to her pile of clean clothes. She fished out some underwear and a white bra. "I have to get back to the ceremony."

Quint's fingers fumbled with his pants as he watched her dress, his head definitely rummy. "Crap," he said as he shook his head, trying to clear it, while she wiggled her hips into her khakis. "We're going to have to do this again soon." Next time, he wanted to be stone-cold sober with more time to explore all of her skin.

"Name the time and place, heartbreaker, and I'll be there with or without underwear, your choice." Her smile was soft and inviting. She pulled her shirt on over her head.

He grabbed his own shirt from the floor, pausing with a frown, unable to remember when he'd taken it off. Or had she? Damned wine. "What now?" he asked, pulling it on.

"You need to wait about five or ten minutes before coming back to the fire."

"You really think your father and the others won't know what we've been up to? Both of us disappeared for …" He didn't know how long he'd been gone. "For a long time. Juan will put one and one together and smile at me with that shit-eating grin of his."

Her forehead wrinkled. "He was talking to Fernando when I left. I don't think he saw me go."

"Yeah, well, I was just supposed to be getting some pills for a headache. How do I explain why it took so long?"

"You're a writer. Can't you come up with some good fiction?"

"Maverick writes fiction, not me."

"You'll think of something." She put on her boots and walked over to him, wrapping her arms around his neck. "Have I told you that I'm nuts about you?"

"No." He slid his hands down her sides, rounding her curves. "But you've threatened to slice off my nuts with your machete a couple of times."

She grinned. "That's your fault. You make me crazy."

"I've got news for you, woman. You were crazy when I met you."

"But you like crazy women, right?"

"No, I like *you*, Dr. García. I also like your choice in lingerie."

"I like you, too, Parker, especially when your hands are inside of my lingerie."

"Angélica." Pedro's hushed voice came through the tent canvas. "Are you in there?"

"Shit," she whispered. "Don't say anything. Maybe he'll go away."

The zipper on their tent started to slide open.

She stepped away from Quint. "Pedro, don't come in."

"Why not?"

"I'm not decent."

There was a pause from the other side of the tent, and then Pedro spoke again. "Have you seen Quint?"

Angélica raised her finger to her lips, shaking her head. "He's around here somewhere."

"You need to hurry up and get back to the ceremony."

"Why? Is something wrong?"

"We sort of have a problem."

She growled, lowering her hand. "What now?"

"We had a visitor while you were gone."

"Who?"

"Not a who, more like a bristly haired, pain-in-the-ass *what*."

Angélica's forehead furrowed. "Did something come out of the jungle?"

"No, something came out of María's tent, scared the living daylights out of your half-drunken father, who fell over backward in his chair."

She gasped. "He fell?"

"Juan's leg is fine, don't worry, but your damned javelina ran off into the trees."

Quint shook his head. Rover was at it again.

"Dad's okay?"

"Yes, but he's pissed about that javelina being here and putting us all at risk with predators."

"Crud. I was hoping he wouldn't find out for another day or two. I wanted to break it to him gently."

"You need to get back to the ceremony to help Teodoro while Quint and I go looking for Rover."

What? In the dark with predators on their nightly prowl while he was rummy with wine?

"Right now?" Quint whispered to Angélica.

"If you wait too long, something else might find Rover first. Come on." She took his hand, pulling him toward the flap.

Angélica grabbed her flashlight and unzipped the tent, stepping out with Quint following.

"You're amazing, Angel." Pedro's teeth gleamed in the moonlight. "You've made Quint magically appear out of nowhere."

"Yeah, well, I'm talented that way," she said. "Don't piss me off or I'll make you magically disappear."

"Judging by that big grin on Quint's face, I bet he likes all of the ways you're talented."

"Shush up." She punched Pedro's shoulder. "If you say a thing to Dad, I'll tell him that you were the one who painted his face and hair with red ochre paste when he was passed out at that *Chac* ceremony that time in Coba."

"You wouldn't! You promised."

"*And* that it was you who started the rumor about his being a red devil from the Underworld."

"She always fights dirty," Pedro said to Quint. "Remember that if you value your hide."

"You don't know the half of it," Quint replied, smiling wide about how she'd played dirty, too, in the tent moments ago, taking advantage of his inebriated state. He grunted when Angélica poked him in the ribs.

Snickering, Pedro patted his shoulder. "Grab a machete, Don Juan, and meet me at the fire." He left them, heading back to the ceremony.

Angélica touched Quint's arm. "I don't like you two going out there in the jungle at night."

He didn't either. "It's Rover."

"I know. I just don't want anything to happen to you."

"If I didn't know better, boss lady, I'd say you're sweet on me."

"Don't let it go to your drunken brain, Parker." She patted his butt. "Grab Dad's machete and let's go."

Quint stepped inside the tent long enough to grab Juan's machete and shoot a longing look at his cot. Next time, maybe they'd have more time to enjoy a second round.

Angélica waited for him under the pale half moon. "You ready?" she asked after he'd zipped the tent closed.

Ready to walk through a jungle full of deadly predators in the dark looking for an ornery javelina? Fuck, no. The thought of what waited out there for Pedro and him made him sweaty.

He gripped the machete. "If I don't make it back alive tonight, siren, promise me you'll bury me somewhere cool and snake-free."

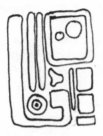

Chapter Fourteen

**Syllabary: A set of written symbols representing the syllables
that make up words.
Due to the hundreds of unique Maya glyphs in the form of
animals, humans, supernatural beings, and objects, the Maya
writing system has an extensive set of phonetic signs that
represent syllables rather than individual sounds like in
alphabetic systems. These signs (or glyphs) are used to write
words, phrases, and sentences.**

The next morning, Angélica stood inside the corbel-vaulted
entrance of the *Chakmo'ol* Temple with Quint and Daisy. Sweat
trailed down her forehead. The relief from the sun's hot rays was
debatable when pitted against the heavy warm blanket of humidity
inside the structure.

Luckily, Rover had returned to camp last night when Angélica
called for him, saving Quint and Pedro a dark trek into the jungle to
look for him. She led the javelina back to the makeshift pen behind
Teodoro's tent while the *Lolcatali* ceremony continued. With Quint's
and Pedro's help, they secured Rover inside again and calmed him
down with a bowlful of vegetable scraps from María's kitchen.

Unlike Rover, her father hadn't been so easy to pacify now that
the cat was out of the bag—or rather the javelina was out of the

tent. Once they were in private, Juan had spent fifteen minutes berating her, spelling out the dangers of having a javelina in the camp while predators were on the hunt. Rather than argue, she let him rant until the *balche* wine had worked its magic and put him to sleep.

Morning light hadn't changed her dad's disposition much. However, in spite of his growling during breakfast about Angélica dragging Daisy along with Quint to the *Chakmo'ol* temple, both were going to be spending the day at this end of the dig site helping her. Maverick would be joining them soon, too, although he and Quint were going to take up where Gertrude and Jane had left off on the platform outside of the temple, rattlesnakes be damned. She'd left them the hooks used on the hunt the day before and a few burlap bags.

She looked around at the temple walls, breathing in the musty air. Her gut told her this structure was hiding a treasure trove of Maya history, which would translate into more money from archaeological tourism. More money equaled more government funding. While she wasn't a big advocate of turning the Maya ruins into a theme park, her mother had died trying to help solve a mystery at this site. For her mom's sake, Angélica was going to make sure it had a place on the map along with the other well-known Central American Maya sites.

Daisy walked up next to her. "Wow."

Angélica couldn't tell if the wide-eyed expression on the woman's face was one of wonderment or awe, or maybe a mixture of the two. "What do you see?"

"I don't think I can describe it with mere words," Daisy answered.

"I can," Quint said, joining them inside the temple's entryway. "It's a big, stone death trap." He wiped his grinning face with the sleeve of his T-shirt. "A rather elaborate one with all of the fancy paintings, carvings, glyphs, and door lintels, but definitely a booby trap waiting to crash down around our heads."

Daisy laughed and moved deeper into the temple, focusing on one of the partially flaked off paintings further along the stone-walled hallway.

Angélica backhanded Quint playfully in the stomach. "I was talking to Daisy, you big chicken."

"As I told … I say as I told your father," he imitated Foghorn

Leghorn's voice from the old *Looney Tunes* show, puffing out his chest as the big rooster always had. "I'm no chicken, sister. I'm a … I say I'm a rooster." He winked at her. "Cock-a-doodle-doo, Miss Prissy."

She laughed. "You watched too much TV as a kid, Parker."

Sitting in front of the television had been a sporadic pleasure for her as a child due to growing up in the jungle on dig sites for part of each year. However, her father had been a big fan of the small screen whenever they were home on the ranch, especially old westerns and *Twilight Zone* episodes.

"Hush those lovely lips, boss lady." His eyes lowered to her mouth, his gaze heated when it returned to hers. "I learned a lot about life from the ol' boob tube."

Angélica glanced in Daisy's direction. Flirting in front of the hired crew was a new experience for her, making her squirm. She could either nix this right now or …

"We'll be right back, Daisy," she said and took Quint's hand, dragging him outside. She stopped in the shade of the temple wall, looking around to make sure they were alone. "Okay, I'll bite. What did you learn?"

He leaned against the wall, still holding her hand. "I can't give away my secrets, but I can show you one or two tricks sometime when you have another ten minutes to waste in our tent."

"Was it actually ten minutes last night?" she joked. "I don't remember it taking very long."

One of his eyebrows lifted. "If memory serves me right, sweetheart, *you* didn't take long at all." He tugged her closer. "Not the first time," he said, kissing her knuckles. "Or the second."

"Touché, heartbreaker."

It was a wonder she'd even lasted that long once he'd started kissing her. Hell, she'd been ready for him ever since he'd stepped foot on the dig site that first day. A month was way too long to go without him in her bed.

How long would he be gone next time?

A cold shadow gripped her at the thought of him leaving again.

Go away, dammit! She shook off the angst and returned to the present. Today, right here and now, Quint was with her. She needed to enjoy him while she could. When he left again, she'd pick up the pieces and go on alone, as she'd done for years.

"Angélica, what's wrong?" His eyes narrowed, searching.

"Nothing." Shit, he'd seen too much. "I was just thinking about Rover's escapades last night and worrying that next time he might not come back at just the sound of my voice."

"Teodoro mentioned something at breakfast about building a better pen today."

"Good, because Rover could give Houdini and his chains a run for his money given enough time." She squeezed Quint's hand, hiding her worries behind a smile. "Come on, Parker." She adopted Foghorn's voice. "Quit drag ... I say quit dragging your tail feathers and help me with these blocks so you can get the hell out of this death trap."

His eyes crinkled in the corners. "You need to work on that impression, boss lady."

"You can kiss my tail feathers."

She led him back inside, releasing his hand as they drew near Daisy, who had moved deeper into the temple.

"Follow me, Daisy. I'll take you to the chamber I was telling you about last night when we were helping María." She clicked on her flashlight and treaded deeper into the temple. Quint motioned for Daisy to walk in front of him while he brought up the rear.

Seconds later, Angélica ducked inside the chamber she'd worked in yesterday morning. Had it been only yesterday? Damn. Between chopping her way through the forest on that old trail and then hunting snakes all afternoon, not to mention her private party with Quint in their tent last night, she felt like a week had passed since she'd been there last.

"Amazing," Daisy said, her voice breathy. She walked to the wall that had blocks of glyphs carved into it mixed with several full-sized images. "Can you read all of this?"

"Not without help from my research books and notes." Angélica joined her, looking up at the ancient work of an incredibly talented artist. Having been protected by the temple all of these centuries, the carvings were still in excellent shape. "My mom could, though, with only a little help from the syllabary she kept in her notebook." She lifted her flashlight and angled the light so that the shadows added contrast, defining the carvings. "She was a natural at reading the Maya glyphs. I doubt I'll ever come close to her talent, but I'll keep fumbling along."

"You're being extra critical of yourself," Quint said from where he stood in the vaulted entryway, stooped over to fit. The Maya hadn't built the chamber for someone of his height.

"Not really." She shrugged off her backpack, extracting her rubbing equipment and a couple of paintbrushes. "I used to beat myself up about not being as knowledgeable as my mom, but since her death I've come to realize that reading glyphs will always be a challenge for me and that's okay. We each have our own areas of expertise in life."

Daisy took the paintbrush Angélica handed her, sticking it into her back pocket. "Like your father and his knowledge of architecture?"

Angélica nodded. "Exactly. He can look at a temple and see in his mind what its purpose was, where the weaknesses are structurally, and what is needed to shore it up."

A chuckle came from Quint. "And which blocks or boards he can pull out without bringing it down while scaring the hell out of Pedro and me."

"He's very good at practical jokes, too." Angélica set down her pack. "Dad's specialty is architecture. Mom's expertise was reading the glyphs. They made a good match since they were both in love with the Maya culture."

"What's your forte?" Daisy asked.

"Bossing people around." Quint's eyes sparkled when she hit him with a mock glare.

She turned back to Daisy and then lowered her gaze to her tools of the trade. She'd asked herself that question many, many times. "I'm more of a jack of all trades in the archaeology world. A master at nothing."

Daisy touched her arm. "That's not true, *pik*."

Quint scoffed. "Are you forgetting what happened at the last site? What you found? Your successes were because of your bulldog tenacity. Once you sink your teeth into something, you won't let go. Not to mention your ability to see and grasp the big picture instead of focusing on the details."

He went on to tell Daisy about the shell and the king's tomb at the last dig site, but Angélica wasn't listening. She was watching Daisy, frozen with the cogs in her brain grinding and spitting sparks.

What did she call me?

Daisy laughed at something Quint said, and Angélica felt the blood drain from her face.

That laugh!

She touched her hand to her chest. Her heart rat-a-tat-tatted under her palm.

She knew that laugh. It wasn't Daisy's normal, light and airy titter. There was something different—different but familiar. The tone, maybe? No, it was the cadence. That was it! It was a throaty pulsing sound that reminded Angélica of …

No, that was silly. Impossible. She must be overheated or tired. Although she'd slept like a log last night.

"Are you okay, boss lady?" Quint asked, bringing her back to the moment.

The damned man was too perceptive for *her* own good. She nodded. "I need some water, that's all." She unscrewed the cap of her canteen, taking a sip.

Yeah, that had to be it. A little too much heat already this morning was the problem.

But it wasn't any hotter than usual.

Was she losing her mind? Had all of the pressure to deliver and the day-after-day routine of hard labor warped her sanity? Or was it merely too many memories clouding her head because of her mother's history at this site?

She decided to test if it was all in her head.

"Daisy," she said, holding out a piece of rice paper and charcoal from her pack. "Will you please make a rubbing of this glyph here and show Quint how it's done?"

Angélica cast Quint a silencing glance, fingers crossed that he'd take the hint to keep quiet about already having plenty of experience making rubbings after the last dig.

His gaze narrowed, but at her slight shake of the head, he shrugged. "Do you have to press hard or do you let the charcoal do the work?" He played along.

"I'd be happy to show you. I don't often get to be a teacher anymore." Daisy took the paper and charcoal. Holding the paper against the wall with her right hand, she rubbed with charcoal over it with her left.

As she rubbed, she explained to Quint how to line up the paper, which direction worked best for rubbing the charcoal, and how to double-check that he'd recorded all of the finer details before removing the paper.

Angélica watched with her pulse pounding in her ears.

No fucking way!

She gaped at Daisy's profile, her brain swirling with a dust devil of memories.

"Did I do it right?" Daisy asked, smiling at Angélica after lowering the paper.

"Uhhh," Angélica coughed, trying to form a smile on her shaky lips. "You did great, thanks. Do you mind continuing with the other glyphs on this carving while I show Quint what I need his help with in another chamber before sending him on his way?"

"Sure." Daisy lifted another piece of rice paper and got to work, humming under her breath.

As she started to walk toward the arched entryway, Angélica's ears perked up. She paused mid-step and glanced back. "What's that song you're humming?"

" 'Poor, Poor Pitiful Me.' "

"Linda Ronstadt. That's what I thought."

Leading the way back out into the hallway, she moved deeper into the temple on trembling legs, slipping into a small, low-ceilinged burial chamber that the looters had cleared of small trinkets but left otherwise intact.

"There's a lot of ceiling on the floor in here," Quint said when he joined her.

Angélica had to stoop to walk inside the chamber, which meant Quint had to bend over almost halfway. "It's stable enough."

"You sound like your father."

How ironic! A high-pitched cackle escaped her lips before she could seal it inside.

Quint did a double take. "That was kind of weird."

He didn't know the half of it.

"What was this altar used for?" he asked, knocking on the stone surface.

"I don't know, probably sacrifices." She pulled him inside a few more steps, glancing behind him to make sure Daisy didn't follow.

"What are we doing in here besides risking our lives?" Quint aimed his flashlight at the ceiling. His brow had wrinkles on top of wrinkles as he inspected the cracks road-mapping the overhead stones.

"I needed a moment of privacy with you."

"You want some *privacy* in here?" He shook his head. "I'll be honest, sweetheart, I'm not going to be on my game right now. This place feels too much like a tomb."

"It *is* a tomb, Quint. And when I say *privacy*, that's not code for having sex in a dead king's burial chamber."

"Just for the record, and for my morbid sense of curiosity, what would be the code word for having sex in a dead guy's tomb?"

She nailed him with a squint. "I'm going to sacrifice you to the Maya gods."

"What? Why?"

"No, that would be the code word."

"That's multiple words. A code sentence to be more accurate."

"Parker," she warned, holding up her fist between them.

He chuckled, "Okay, boss lady. What's going on? You're acting skittish as hell. It's not like you."

She moved closer to him, worried about her voice carrying along the stone walls. "Did you hear what Daisy called me?"

"No," he whispered back.

"She called me *pik*."

"Okay, I did hear that, but I didn't think much about it. What's it mean?"

"It's the Mayan word for 'bedbug.'"

"That's sort of sweet."

"No, it's eerie."

"Well, I've heard more bizarre nicknames. At least she didn't call you 'The Flatulent One.'"

"You've been listening to my dad's stories." That was her father's favorite name for the lord of death.

"I try not to, especially in tombs like this one, but your father has his sights set on me."

"He likes you. You make him laugh."

"He wants me to produce his heirs."

Damn her dad for his heavy-handed attempts at getting grandchildren. "It takes two to make that happen."

"Does it?" Quint's eyes teased. "Maybe you need to give me a hands-on demonstration on how that works."

"You're full of it this morning, Parker." She waved that whole pothole-filled topic of children off for the time being. They had a bigger problem. "*Pik* is a nickname that only one other person in my life has called me—my mom."

"Your mom called you 'bedbug'?"

"She called me *pik*."

"Which means 'bedbug.'"

"Parker, why are we circling this? Aren't you listening to what I'm saying?"

"Between the heat and this low ceiling full of stress fractures, boss lady, I'm having trouble following your rather abstract train of thought. Maybe you could line up the rail cars for me, because the sooner we can go back to standing upright under the big open sky, the happier I'll be."

She slid down the wall, sitting on the floor with bent knees. "What are the chances that Daisy would know my mom's childhood nickname for me?"

"I don't know. I was never very good with statistics. All of those numbers and possibilities make me sleepy."

"Either Daisy learned my nickname from my father or ..." she trailed off, frowning at her kneecaps. Saying the words aloud would make it official—she might be losing her marbles.

Quint's knees popped as he squatted in front of her. "Or what?"

"Or she's channeling my mom's ghost."

Quint cocked his head, rubbing his jaw. "I could swear you just said that the woman in the other room is channeling Dr. Marianne García."

"You heard me right." She started to chew on her thumb but tasted dirt and stopped, wiping her thumb on her pants. How could this be possible? Was she dreaming?

"You know last night when I said you were crazy?" Quint asked, tipping her chin up so she could meet his gaze. "I was just joking. You are actually the most level-headed woman I've ever met. So when you say something as kooky sounding as that, you can understand why I'm concerned about your mental health, considering how hard you've been overworking yourself lately."

"I thought you believed in the supernatural."

"I believe odd things happen. Things that science can't always explain, several of which I've experienced myself, but you're talking about the ghost of your mother inhabiting a stranger in a Maya temple."

"How do you explain Daisy using her left hand when she made that rubbing?"

"She's left-handed."

"I've watched Daisy dig with a trowel out in the ballcourt. She's right-handed."

"Maybe she's ambidextrous."

That could explain her choice of hand to hold the charcoal. "But I've never had her do a rubbing for me before, and yet she trained you the same way my mom trained me when I was young. The same technique."

"Daisy might have learned how to do rubbings at a past site similar to your mom's technique. Think about it, Angélica. How many ways can there be to rub charcoal on paper? We're not creating portraits with oil paints."

"Daisy laughed like Mom, too." When he continued to frown at her, she added, "And she was humming Linda Ronstadt."

"Linda is special because why?"

"She was one of my mom's favorite singers."

"Maybe she's Daisy's favorite, too. Linda used to be a huge star years ago. Daisy would be about your mom's age, right?"

Angélica growled at him. "Dammit, Quint. If you're going to explain away each piece of evidence that shows my mom's ghost is temporarily possessing that woman in the other room, I'm going to punch you."

He held up his hands. "I'm sorry. But come on, Angélica. Think about what you're suggesting. You, of all people, would never for a minute believe me if I told you a story like that. Your father, however, is a different story."

"I'm telling you, Quint, there is something odd about Daisy. From the start, I've felt totally at ease with her, like I've known her all of my life. I keep finding myself opening up to her, sharing thoughts and memories that I usually keep buried."

"You? At ease with someone? Well, that does it. She must be possessed. Or she's an alien from one of Saturn's moons. You probably shouldn't bend over to pick up any soap while she's around. I hear ass-probing is all the rage for those green folks from outer space."

She pinched his forearm. "Next time, I'll aim lower."

Rubbing his arm, he frowned at her. "I thought you didn't believe in the supernatural, sweetheart. You told me so yourself at the last dig."

"But then I kind of changed my mind. Remember, that night on the beach when we talked about the curse and you?"

The corners of his eyes creased. "Yes, but I figured that was just the Coronas, moonlight, and your need for my body talking."

She chuckled in spite of her chaotic thoughts, grateful for Quint's humor keeping her grounded at the moment. "The need for your body inspires a whole different type of insanity, Parker."

"At least we can agree that you're cuckoo for my coconuts."

"Don't you mean your Cocoa Puffs?"

"Leave them out of this. As for your mother's ghost returning to visit you via Daisy, are you sure you hadn't mentioned before that your mom called you *pik*?"

"I'd remember that, I think." She frowned toward the chamber's narrow entrance, remembering their conversation last night while helping María prepare the *nohua* ceremonial tortilla. Her lips had been loose thanks to several sips of *balche* María had shared with them. "Maybe you're right. Maybe I've been working too hard, surrounded by too many things that remind me of my mom."

"Your father could've mentioned that nickname to Daisy when he was working with her yesterday while we were rounding up snakes."

"True." She scrubbed her hands down her face. "Criminy. If only I could find that damned stela Mom drew in her notepad. Or better yet, if we could just dig up a series of glyphs that explains what was going on at this site, and why there are Olmec pieces and references mixed in with the Classic Maya structures."

"Could it be possible that there was a Maya traveler who paid a visit to one of the old Olmec sites and brought back souvenirs for the king?"

She nodded. "Or there could have been Olmecs living at this location long before the Maya civilization settled here."

"I thought your dad said the Olmec heartland was up north."

"A small group could have migrated south. A dispute within one of their civilization groups might have resulted in a situation similar to the pilgrims who traveled to the American continents. A sect could've moved down here to establish their own population center." She blew out a sigh. "Without written records, we can speculate all day long. That's why I want to find that stela. According to Mom's notes, there was a warning on it about something that had happened here in the past."

"But she didn't write down what the warning actually said, or what she thought it might be saying?"

"Unfortunately, she didn't finish what she'd started in her notes. When I got the notebook, a couple of pages were stuck together. It wasn't until I pulled them apart that I found her rough sketch of the stela and the things she wrote about it. After that one page, she doesn't mention it again, which doesn't make sense. That was the whole reason she flew down here."

"This notebook of hers," Quint said, all traces of humor gone from his face. "Was it with her when the helicopter crashed?" At her nod, he continued, "Have you ever wondered if someone removed those pages on purpose, leaving that one page behind because it was stuck and they didn't realize it was there?"

She blinked at him a few times, her cogs sparking and grinding again. "What are you saying, Quint? Why would they want only those pages?"

"I don't know. I'm just throwing out some random thoughts. That's all." He looked away too quickly, making her suspicious.

"No, you're not. You have something on your mind—you and Pedro both—about my mom and this site and that crash, don't you?" Her gaze narrowed, daring him to deny it.

He didn't. Instead, he said, "I can't speak for Pedro."

"Then speak for yourself. What's going on, Quint?"

"We should discuss this somewhere else. I don't like the looks of that ceiling."

"Sit down, and start talking, Parker."

After a frown at the ceiling, he crawled over beside her and leaned back against the wall, his shoulder touching hers. "I don't know where to start."

"We're short on time, so get to the meat of it."

"Okay." He took her hand in his, lacing their fingers together. "Pedro and I have a theory that your mom's helicopter crash was no accident."

"You think someone was trying to kill her?"

"Or kill the pilot."

For the next few minutes, he filled her head with tidbits of information Pedro and he had collected since his arrival about the crash and the pilot. When he finished, Angélica felt as blindsided as she'd been when Daisy called her *pik*.

She stared down at their interlaced fingers, her mind a flurry of doubts interspersed with showers of what-ifs and bolts of rage.

"So, you two think that maybe someone sabotaged the helicopter and unleashed rattlesnakes on the pilot in order to have my mom killed so that she wouldn't share whatever it was she'd found on that stela?"

"I honestly don't know what to think, Angélica."

"And ripping out those notebook pages would help ensure the stela's story would remain lost to history."

"Removing the notebook pages is just one theory that came to mind when you mentioned that her notes seem to be missing information. If there was something about this site that was meant to remain a secret and that stela had something to do with it, then a surefire way to keep things quiet would be to remove the notes, the stela, and your mom from the equation. Crashing the helicopter is a good diversion for anyone investigating her death."

Angélica was going to need some time to chew on this. If he was right, they were treading on dangerous ground here.

"So Pedro is freaked out about me going into the jungle alone because he thinks I could suffer the same fate as my mother?"

"Yes. He and I are both scared shitless that you're next in line, especially with your lovely bulldog tendencies that I praised back there with Daisy." He raised their entwined fingers to his lips, kissing the back of her hand. "We both know you won't stop until you find answers. But at what cost will those answers be found? Your life?"

Had her mom been murdered? Killed over some stupid stela and what was on it? She blinked away a rush of tears. She swiped at her eyes and sniffed. "This is fucked up."

"Which part?"

"Someone purposely taking down that helicopter to kill my mother."

"It's just a theory, Angélica. The pilot could have been the objective and your mom got caught in the line of fire."

"That doesn't make it any better. Honestly, I prefer her being the target."

Quint frowned at her. "Why's that?"

"Because it makes me more determined than ever to find out what was on that damned stela and see what was worth taking the life of someone as beautiful and loving as her."

"Jesus, Angélica. Is some ancient tale carved onto a rock worth risking your life? Do you think your mom would want you to do that? How do you think your dad will feel if something happens to you here? If he loses you in the same place he lost his wife?"

She closed her eyes for a few moments, leaning her head back against the wall while trying to get a grip on her confusion, her grief, her rage. "You're right. I shouldn't make any decisions until I calm down and let this all stew for a while."

Several seconds of silence passed, filled only with the sound of their breathing.

"What are you going to do now?" Quint asked.

"What I do best."

"Work too hard and boss people around?"

She chuckled. "I'm going to go back into that chamber with Daisy and continue recording the stories from the past for further offsite analysis."

"And if Daisy acts like your mom again?"

"It's a bizarre coincidence, that's all." She wasn't one hundred percent sure of it, but for this afternoon she was going to run with that notion.

He squeezed her hand slightly. "If you need a break, feel free to come outside and crack the whip over me. I have this fantasy that includes thigh-high leather boots, a red velvet corset, and a bullwhip that's just waiting to be made into nonfiction."

"How long have you had this fantasy about wearing a corset?" It was all she could do to keep a straight face. "They can be quite painful with the way the boning digs into your ribs, you know. And those laces are real bitches."

He leaned over and kissed her silent. "Don't sass me, woman, or I'll be forced to take you in hand again."

"Sass, sass, sass." She patted his cheek and then stood as far upright as the ceiling allowed. "Get off your ass, Parker. I need you to bring those brawny muscles along and help me move some pieces of a wall that came down further back in this temple. There's a carving with glyphs that's partially buried. It might explain more about the dynasty that built this temple and to which king this burial tomb belongs."

"That sounds like a lot of hot and sweaty work." Quint leaned his head back, one eyebrow raised. "What's in it for me and my big muscles if I help you?"

"I don't know. Probably whips and sex."

"What about the boots?"

"Well, if you insist, I'll let you wear them, but only this once."

He half-stood, staying bent over as he followed her out into the hall where he could stand upright again.

"You're not going to let this rest, are you?" he asked, serious again as he frowned down at her.

She didn't pretend to misunderstand his underlying question. "If there is something hidden at this site—something important enough that it's worth killing for—then I have a new objective. I need to figure out the big secret and do whatever it takes to make this site safe for future research and development. Plus, I owe it to my mom to find her killer."

His gaze narrowed. "Don't make this about revenge, Angélica."

How could she not? "If you want to walk away, I understand. This isn't your fight."

"When are you going to get it through your thick, beautiful skull that if something involves you, then it involves me? We're a team."

"Quint," she started. But then she saw something in his eyes shining back at her that made her breath catch. Something that cracked her heart wide open.

"What, Angélica?"

She took his hand in hers. "I'd rather be a dynamic duo."

A smile crept up his face. "We could wear masks."

"Are we back to the topic of whips and sex again?"

"When did we leave it?"

She let go of his hand and led the way back to the partially collapsed wall, worrying her lip all the way.

If her mom had been murdered, she wanted to know why. But at what cost?

What was she willing to risk to find out the answers that would smother the fire in her stomach and finally lay her mother's memory to rest?

Chapter Fifteen

Olmec Art: Olmec art often includes anthropomorphic creatures (such as "were-jaguars," aka half human/half-jaguar), using iconography with religious meaning. Olmec-style artifacts, designs, figurines, and monuments have been found in sites far outside the Olmec heartland suggesting trade, colonization, imitation by developing cultures, or Olmec military domination.

D id you see any snakes today?" a voice asked from behind Quint as he ladled his second helping of María's avocado soup into his gourd bowl. The first helping had gone down the hatch in one long gulp with a cool and refreshing lime kick at the end.

Glancing behind him, Quint smiled down at Jane. He'd noticed she was up and moving around at lunch, with only a limp and a few winces after her snakebite experience.

"I saw two rattlers. One was busy working on his tan. The other stopped by to bum a cigarette, but I was all out. After throwing a hissy fit, he slithered off to bite someone else when she wasn't looking."

Jane giggled, grabbing a bowl from the clean stack and moving up beside him. "You're funny."

"Yeah, well, looks aren't everything." Quint made room for her at the soup pot. He grabbed a couple of homemade, thick tortillas and set them on top of his bowl of green goodness.

"Gertrude told me that you and Dr. García are dating. Is that true?" she asked, glancing at him out of the corner of her eye as she dished up some soup.

Dating? Uh, was that what was going on with them? They had sort of skipped right past a first date at the last dig and went straight to angry kisses followed by sex in a tent. Not that he was complaining. Dating was overrated these days. He much preferred sex in a tent to dinner and a movie most nights.

"That depends," he answered.

"On what?"

"On which Dr. García you are talking about. Juan flat-out turned me down, but lucky for me his daughter likes my sparkling personality."

Speaking of Juan's daughter, where was she? Angélica and Daisy were both late to supper. If they didn't show up by the time he was finished, Quint planned to head back to the *Chakmo'ol* Temple to determine the holdup.

"What's it like to date someone like her?"

Quint frowned as he grabbed a bottle of beer from the end of the table. Where was this going? He wasn't a fan of talking about his private life, and Angélica would string him up by the nuts if he said anything that could be used against her in print or online.

"Have you ever tried to lasso a tornado?" he asked.

"You mean like Pecos Bill?"

"Exactly." He toasted her with his beer bottle and headed over to the table where Pecos Bill's father—so to speak—waited for him with a cocky smile. "You remind me of the Joker tonight, Juan, sporting manic grins and insane cackles." Quint set his soup and beer down, lowering onto the bench across from Juan. "What's going on? Are you plotting to destroy Gotham City later?"

"He's missing his green hair," Pedro said and held up his bowl of soup. "Maybe I should dump María's *sopa de aguacate* over his head, eh Parker? Then all we need is a purple suit."

"Are you *loco*?" Quint grinned. "That's a waste of good soup."

"You're darn right it is," Juan said, taking Pedro's bowl from him and pretending to dig in with his spoon.

Pedro laughed and grabbed it back. "Stealing María's soup from a man will get you into a fight to the death."

"I've seen you punch." Juan winked at Quint, and with an exaggerated whisper he added, "He learned to fight from his little *seester.*" Juan emphasized that last word with a Spanish accent, throwing fake girly punches in Pedro's direction.

Pedro laughed even harder. "I'm going to unleash my *seester* on you the next time you come over for dinner, old man."

"I wouldn't piss off any of Pedro's sisters, Dad," Angélica said from behind Quint. "Catalina in particular has a wicked uppercut."

"Not to mention her roundhouse kick," Pedro added. "She's a black belt now, you know."

Angélica squeezed Quint's shoulder. "Did you leave me any soup, Parker?"

"Sure." He slid his bowl over and moved his beer next to it. "All for you."

"That's yours. I can get my own."

He grabbed her wrist and pulled her down onto the seat next to him. "Sit and eat, boss lady. I'll go grab some more soup and tortillas." When she hesitated, he pointed at the bowl. "Eat. I'll be right back."

Daisy was up at the soup pot filling a bowl. He waited for her to finish before picking up a clean bowl.

"How was your afternoon?" he asked, grabbing the ladle.

She smiled over at him, her eyes alight. "We found something."

No shit. That seemed to be yesterday's news with Daisy, who seemed to be equipped with some kind of internal treasure radar.

"What did you find?"

"Angélica told me to let her explain." She grabbed a cup and filled it with water from the pitcher sitting next to the bottles of beer. "I'll see you back at the table."

Quint didn't dally getting more soup and tortillas. He returned to Angélica's side, setting his bowl and bottle of beer down and then stacking several tortillas on the table between them.

Pedro reached for a tortilla and Angélica slapped his hand away. "Don't make me take you down again, Montañero."

"You need to teach her to be nicer to men," he told Juan.

"That's not my job anymore." He pointed at Quint. "It's his."

"I don't want her being nice to other men." Quint shot Pedro a smirk. "How am I supposed to keep her pining for me if there are a bunch of other guys around thinking she's nice?"

"True," Juan said. "But nobody takes abuse better than you, Quint." He leaned his elbows on the table. "And while we're on the subject of abuse, how about you and I head back to the mine tomorrow morning after breakfast with your fancy camera? I'd like to get some pictures of that hole in the wall."

Quint groaned. "I'd sooner hunt more rattlesnakes." He took a swig of warm beer.

"Well, if you take some good pictures in the mine for me, I'll let you go hunting alone with Angélica after we're done."

Pausing in the midst of ripping up a tortilla, Quint looked over at Juan with one raised eyebrow. Was that code for Juan agreeing to disappear for a couple of hours, giving him time alone with Angélica inside their tent?

Juan's mouth twitched below his smiling brown eyes, which didn't answer Quint's unspoken question one way or another. His focus moved to his daughter. "You owe me a boot, *gatita*."

Angélica smirked. "Which one? Right or left?"

"Left."

"You're not even wearing a shoe on that foot yet."

Juan's fiberglass-cast boot was taking a beating in place of his hiking boot, requiring nightly cleanings with a toothbrush, which he claimed belonged to Pedro.

"I will be after we finish this dig."

She looked up at him, her brow pinched. "Why do I owe you a left boot, Dad?"

"Because your pig ate mine."

"Rover?"

"Are you the owner of any other pigs you haven't told me about?"

"He's a javelina, not a pig."

"He's a menace, not a javelina."

"What makes you think Rover is the guilty party?" She returned to her soup. "There are plenty of other animals roaming this jungle that might like the taste of your foot sweat."

Juan's upper lip wrinkled. "Because out of all of those animals, your pig is the only one able to open tent zippers and steal boots from under my cot when he's supposed to be locked up in his pen."

"What proof do you have that it's Rover?" she challenged, barely holding back a grin.

"Don't get smart with me, young lady." His tone was more playful than stern.

Her grin slipped free. "I thought I was playing dumb."

"Don't think you're too old to be grounded to your tent."

Quint pointed his beer bottle at Juan. "That's a great idea, Juan. Lock her up. I'll guard the key."

"I wouldn't trust Quint within a mile of her." Pedro's smile was too big for his face.

"He seems like the perfect gentleman," Daisy said from her seat next to Juan. She winked at Quint, joining in the banter.

" 'Gentleman'?" Angélica teased, knocking his knee with hers under the table. "More like the perfect rogue. You know, the kind of guy local villagers hide their daughters from."

"Unless their daughters are well-seasoned and need to settle down and produce a grandchild or four for their dear old dad."

Angélica shot Quint a worried glance before turning back to her dad with a scowl. "You have a one-track mind, Dad."

"That's not true. I have two tracks—grandkids and María's cooking." Juan picked up his coffee cup. "Where were you and Daisy this evening, *gatita*?"

Angélica shrugged. "We found something in the *Chakmo'ol* Temple. Actually, Daisy found it. I just helped with the rubbing and sketching to make sure we got several good replicas of it before we left for the evening."

"What did Daisy the bloodhound find now?" Juan asked, winking at Daisy, who blushed in response.

Angélica sipped another spoonful of soup before answering. "Several glyphs that tell a tale about *Yum Cimil*."

The name alone elicited a frown from Quint. Pedro crossed himself.

"You mean besides what you found that depicted him in a cave?" Juan asked.

She nodded. "It started with a date that I'm almost positive is pre-Classic Maya." Grabbing a tortilla, she dipped it into her soup. "The glyphs read that there was a long battle between the Maya warriors and *Yum Cimil*. Then it tells that he took fifty-seven warriors captive in his Underworld lair and ate them."

Quint looked at Angélica, trying to read if she was serious. "Is this sort of horror-filled tale typical for temple glyphs? I thought they usually focused on accolades for the leader of the time." The leader who was typically buried in said tomb.

"There are a lot of stories of war in the glyphs at Maya sites, often touting the lord or king's conquests. In the post-Classic period, the leaders of two civilization groups would sometimes stage battles for the purpose of collecting captives, who they'd use for sacrifices because they didn't want to kill their own people."

"Does it say anything else about *Yum Cimil* and these warriors?" Pedro asked.

"There's a carving that goes with the block of glyphs that shows *Yum Cimil* in his skeletal glory eating a human leg bone."

Quint grimaced. "Why couldn't they tell stories full of sunshine and lollipops?"

"Or pretty girls in sexy loincloths," Pedro added, wiggling his eyebrows.

"Tell them about the final glyphs," Daisy urged.

Angélica stared down at the bottle of beer in her hand. "The last few glyphs are hard to read. They were scratched up and partly worn away. From what I can tell based on Mom's syllabary, it's a warning."

Shit. Another warning. Quint took a swig of beer to wash that news down.

"It says that *Yum Cimil* would return when the twin scribes arrived. It lists a date near the end of the Classic Maya period for the scribes' arrival."

"Is there anything after that? Something left by the Classic Maya when they lived here?" Juan asked.

"Not that I can tell, but there are so many glyph blocks on that wall that there could be a continuation somewhere, and I just haven't had a chance to decipher it yet."

Silence held the table in its grip for several beats as they each soaked up Angélica's story.

"It's like a curse," Juan said.

Angélica scoffed. "I knew you'd say that, but a curse would say something like, 'If you trespass on this site, a giant feathered serpent will devour you.'"

"Giant feathered serpents were more Olmec style and you know it," her father said. "However, there are lots of serpents near that temple with rattles on their tails."

"They aren't trying to eat us, though."

"That's probably because we haven't kick-started the curse yet."

"There is no curse," Angélica snapped. "Don't start with that crap again, Dad."

Quint had déjà vu from the last dig site. "What is it with the Maya and curses?"

Juan rubbed his chin. "They were huge believers in the supernatural. Every day they would pray to gods, offer tributes and sacrifices, and live within a supernatural world with the goal of continually appeasing the many beings that ruled above, on, and below the earth's surface." He lifted his coffee cup to his lips, pausing to add, "I'm not surprised you found those glyphs, *gatita*. I have yet to find a Maya site that doesn't come with at least one token curse."

"It's not a curse." Angélica ripped off a piece of tortilla with her teeth. "It's an old story, that's all."

"If it's just an old story," Juan challenged, "then why did you spend the time recording it so well before coming to supper?"

She chewed on the tortilla, holding her father's gaze. "Because I haven't seen a tale like it told in glyphs before. I wanted to make sure I have it all down in case something happens."

"Like what?"

"I don't know. The temple wall caves in and ruins the block of glyphs."

"There are a lot of cracks in that room," Quint said.

"I'm glad I wasn't in there with you," Pedro said, standing with his empty plate in hand. He headed off toward the trash.

"Tell me more about the carved image that went with these glyphs," Juan said.

Angélica looked at Daisy. "Why don't you tell him? You're the one who sketched it."

While Daisy was talking to Juan with a lot of fluttering hand movements, excitement making her cheeks pink, Angélica leaned over to Quint and whispered, "It was almost as if she knew right where to find it."

"What do you mean?"

"On that whole wall covered with glyphs, she went right to that section shortly after I returned from moving those stones with you."

"Maybe she saw it while we were working."

"I had her rubbing a different section of glyphs while we were gone. When I returned she'd obviously been busy following my instructions."

"Angélica," Daisy interrupted. "What do you call that bird on *Yum Cimil's* shoulder?"

"A *muan*."

"That's it." Daisy's face was bright with excitement. Juan's full attention was locked on the woman as she continued with her tale of discovery.

"There's something odd about that block of glyphs," Angélica told Quint quietly.

Pedro, who'd returned with a second beer, overheard her. "Besides some pissed-off death god eating his captives?"

"*Yum Cimil* looked different than usual. He was his decomposing self, but his body was shaped differently and larger than usual, with hair on the back of his head and neck along with pointy ears, like some kind of cat-human-skeleton mix. Plus his teeth were extra long and sharp."

Wonderful, Quint thought, taking another drink. What was next down here in paradise? Zombie monkeys?

"What do you think it all means?" Juan asked Angélica after Daisy finished her account.

"I don't think the carvings mean anything beyond an artist showing off his skills and horror-edged imagination." Angélica finished her soup and wiped the corners of her mouth. "For all we know at this point, *Yum Cimil* could represent the king at the time and all of the sacrifices he demanded. The eating of the captives could be a metaphor for something dark that the king liked to do, like eat their flesh for strength or drink their blood for courage."

"Or it could be a visual representation of the curse at this site," Juan threw back at her.

She let out a loud sigh and then stood. "This discussion is over for tonight." She gathered her dirty dishes and half full bottle of beer. "I'm going back to our tent to look at the rubbings some more and continue trying to decipher the glyphs."

"You can deny it until you're blue in the face, *gatita*, but you cannot change what was carved into the stone."

"It's not a curse, dammit."

Quint wasn't sure who she was trying to convince—her father or herself.

* * *

The next morning, Quint stood in front of the mine entrance as Juan pulled gadgets from his duffel bag of tricks in preparation for heading inside the dark throat leading to the belly of the mine.

The sun beat down on them. The damned ball of fire was a relentless bully. In spite of the sizzling heat, the birds were singing, the monkeys were screeching, and the flies were buzzing. Quint, however, wasn't feeling nearly as energetic, and today he couldn't blame it on the heat. A night of tossing and turning in his cot had left him feeling hungover.

When he'd returned to the tent last night after his shower, Angélica had been sitting on her cot staring at the tent wall with a frown etched on her forehead. She'd gone with Daisy to take her shower immediately after supper since she'd kept the other woman longer than usual in the *Chakmo'ol* Temple.

Quint had hung his towel on a peg and joined her on the cot, his hands dangling between his knees as he looked across at the tent wall, too. When he'd offered a penny for her thoughts, she'd told him something that still gave him chills in the light of day.

"Are you going to stand there all morning and let the bugs eat you, son?" Juan asked, watching him with narrowed eyes.

Quint shoved his dark thoughts aside and hid them behind a grin. "You lead the way inside, *diablo*. I'll follow."

"I'm the devil?" Juan laughed, sliding his good leg through the opening, carefully maneuvering his walking cast through after him. "You're the one who blew in like a whirlwind at our last site and spun everyone into a tizzy, especially my daughter."

"Causing chaos is my specialty." Quint eased into the mine, pulling out his flashlight as he joined Juan. "Besides, Angélica needed some mayhem in her life. You weren't getting the job done."

Juan nodded. "She's a hard girl to rattle. But you're off to a good start." His cane creaked with every other step, his flashlight beam bouncing off the walls and ceiling. "Although I got the feeling last night something about those glyphs isn't sitting well with her. Did you notice how quiet she was later in our tent?"

Yes, especially after she'd filled Quint in on what she'd found when she'd applied her charcoal rubbing skills to her mom's notebook. When she rubbed the back of the only page with notes about the stela glyph and a blank area in the same spot on the next page, the impressions didn't line up. Quint had been right. There was at least one page missing, if not more, about that stela and this dig site.

But Juan didn't need to know about that until Angélica was ready to share the idea that Marianne may have indeed been murdered. "I was too wiped to notice much more than my pillow and my cot."

"Hmmm," was Juan's reply.

Quint had the feeling Juan wasn't buying his tall tale. Angélica's father was too shrewd to fool, but he didn't prod Quint for anything else ... not yet, anyway.

A few creaks of the cane later, he said, "Yesterday after lunch when I was resting my leg I read through some of the structural diagrams from the last archaeologist at this site and noticed a side note he made about the *Baatz'* Temple."

Quint glanced at him, but said nothing.

"He had an interesting theory based on some carvings that he found on the walls in there."

"What's that?"

"That this was an Olmec site before the Maya moved in and built over it." Juan paused to shine his light on a crack that ran from the middle of the ceiling to halfway down the wall. "That would explain the mask we found there and a broken jade piece that Daisy found a few days ago in the ballcourt that looks like an Olmec rain baby."

So, rather than the Olmec traveler theory he had discussed with Angélica, there may have been a group of Olmecs living here? Was that a rare occurrence on Maya sites?

"There's something else," Juan continued. "Something I noticed in one of the crappy pictures you took the other day through the hole in the wall."

"I can only work so much magic with your dime-store camera."

"That's why I wanted you to bring yours along today. From what I could see, it looks like there may be petroglyphs on the cave wall above that altar, but until we have a clearer picture, I can't be sure."

"And you think these petroglyphs are Olmec?" Quint connected the dots.

"Yes."

"How can you tell from a shitty picture?"

"Because there appears to be a dragon, which happens to be the Olmecs' principal sky god, in one of the drawings next to an open-mawed, toothless image that usually represents a personified image of an entry into the earth. In other words, a cave, like the one we're standing in right now."

"So a mine is the same as a cave to the Olmecs?"

"Maybe. Or maybe the Maya group that came after the Olmec people found the cave and recognized it as a limestone source. Needing the mineral to make plaster for their temples and roads, they dug deeper and turned it into a mine. I need a clearer picture of those petroglyphs to make sure that the eyes on the toothless image have crossed bands and that the exterior of the maw has foliage sprouting from it. Both of these would align with other images that archaeologists have found of the Olmecs' other personified cave carvings and petroglyphs."

Quint raised his camera. "Let's go see."

As they traversed onward and inward, Quint's thoughts slid back to this morning. He'd woken to an empty tent. The low din of conversation from the mess tent filtered through the canvas walls. His stomach growled at his laziness, rushing him to see what María was cooking for breakfast.

While getting dressed for another day of sweating, he'd made a couple of decisions. First, he was going to do what Pedro had done and switch his cot out for one of María's handmade hammocks. Pedro swore by how much more comfortable they were because they allowed the air to cool him from below and above.

Nights in this hellhole were only marginally cooler than days. Having to be shut up in a tent to keep from being eaten alive by mosquitoes didn't help with the air conditioning. Neither did sharing the space with two other bodies, especially since one of those bodies made him positively steam when she walked around braless in her tank top and faded boxer shorts with her curves peeking out at him. Kissing her good night and then having to lay there only a few feet away night after night was a form of torture.

He followed Juan through the larger chamber into the tunnel that led to the stone wall, suppressing the urge to check the cracks in the ceiling.

The other decision he'd made had to do with Angélica. If they were going to have any kind of future together, they needed to find a compromise on the career front. But before he approached her with his idea, he needed to make sure she made it off of this dig site alive. As melodramatic as that sounded, he was beginning to wonder if Angélica was some kind of magnet for trouble. It was almost as if she sniffed out danger and then charged it with her machete held at the ready.

"That's odd," Juan said. Something in his voice snapped Quint out of his thoughts and back to the moment.

"What's odd?" He drew up next to Juan, following the beam of his flashlight. "How did that happen?"

The stone Quint had pulled out the other day and then put back was gone along with two others, leaving a dark gaping hole.

Juan approached the wall slowly, shining his flashlight around the stone floor. "They must have fallen through to the other side." He moved his beam to Quint's legs. "Hey, you have two perfectly good long legs. How about you peek through that hole and see if I'm right?"

"How long are you going to play that busted-leg card?" Quint approached the wall slowly.

"As long as it keeps coming in handy."

Quint smirked and checked the wall for new cracks. "You sure this wall is stable? What about the ceiling?" He pressed lightly on the wall, wincing as he tested it.

" 'Stable' is a word I like to use—"

"Loosely," Quint finished for him. "I know." He lifted his flashlight and peered through the hole.

"What do you see?"

Pointing the beam at the floor, Quint told Juan, "I see the missing stones."

"Do you see anything that would explain why they fell out of the wall?"

Quint's stomach tightened as he noticed something else in the dust from the crumbled wall grout. "Yes."

"What? Loose limestone granules?"

"No." He stepped back, frowning down at Juan. "A boot print. Somebody went through the hole."

Chapter Sixteen

Conquistador: A person whose goal is to conquer new territory. (Often used to refer to the soldiers from Spain and Portugal who "conquered" Central and Southern America between the 15th and 17th centuries.)

Murdered.

Angélica stared blankly at the floor. The sound of Jane rubbing charcoal over the rice paper from the other side of the sub chamber in the *Baatz'* Temple faded as her thoughts returned yet again this morning to her mother's death.

Why would someone want to kill her mom? What was on those missing notebook pages? What could be worth taking the life from someone so kind and altruistic? Someone so knowledgeable about the Maya people who wanted nothing more than to help the world understand what had happened to the great civilization? To learn from the mistakes of the past?

Was the killer some local who wanted this dig site's secrets to stay buried? Was it a member of the last archaeologist's crew? A budding grad student whose career could have been destroyed by whatever was in her mother's notes?

Maybe her mom had stumbled upon some black market antiquities theft going on here and had written details in her notes— details that required murder in order to keep it all under wraps.

Who? Why?

Where were those missing notes now? Destroyed?

So many questions with no answers, damn it!

"Dr. García?" Jane's voice pulled Angélica back to the present.

"Yes?"

"Could you come over here and take a look at this? I think I'm doing it wrong."

Angélica crossed the stone floor, squatting next to Jane. She smelled something sweet. "Do I smell raspberries?"

Jane nodded. "It's my lotion. Do you like it?"

"It'll attract bugs." She returned her focus to the rice paper in Jane's hand. "Doing what wrong?"

"These rubbings." Her hand trembled slightly as she held up the paper. "You can barely see the relief patterns on this last one."

Angélica inspected the rubbing and then picked up the previous two. "You're circling for one thing. I'd hazard a guess that you're pressing too hard as well." She picked up a piece of paper and held it against the wall. "My mother taught me long ago that if you brush over it in the same direction with a firm, consistent motion, you can catch the relief with more clarity."

She held out her hand for the charcoal. With practiced strokes, she brushed it over the paper a few times to demonstrate. "See what I mean?"

Jane scooted closer to her and held out her right hand. "Show me, please. I'm not sure how hard to press."

Angélica took her hand, wondering what in the hell the girl had been thinking wearing that lotion. Was she trying to get bit again?

"Like this," she said, moving Jane's hand and the charcoal over the wall. "With long strokes." When she looked back at Jane, the girl's dark brown eyes were focused on her instead of the wall. Angélica stilled, sensing an odd tension between them. "What's wrong?"

"Nothing," Jane said, blinking and pulling her hand away. She tittered under her breath, sounding as uncomfortable as she looked. "Thank you for helping me. My ex always said I was too intense. I guess that passion rises to the surface when I'm doing rubbings."

Angélica gave her a pat on the shoulder. "You're not alone. According to my father, I'm in the dictionary next to the word *obsession*. I've learned to redirect my passion and vent that energy into my work and studies." She thought of Quint and the craziness he inspired both in and out of the bedroom. "Mostly."

She brushed her hands off on her khakis and returned to the other side of the chamber. What had she been doing before she'd gotten distracted yet again by her thoughts about her mom's death? Oh yeah, she'd been trying to decipher a group of glyphs next to a carving of what looked like *Chac*, the Maya rain god, only this version was different than many she'd seen in the past.

With a sigh, she settled back onto the floor and picked up her notepad. Nothing in the *Baatz'* Temple was simple to decipher, leading her to theorize with even more conviction that this temple pre-dated the Post-Classic and Classic Maya civilization groups. Her father's suspicions about the Olmecs having a heavy influence on the site rang more true the deeper she dug.

"Dr. García?" Jane's voice cut through her thoughts a few minutes later. "I was wondering something."

Angélica glanced over her shoulder. The girl was seated, leaning back on her hands, looking her way. "What's that?"

"How do you balance a private life with an archaeology career? I mean, with so much time dedicated to working on remote dig sites and building your career, when do you find time to even have a private life?"

That was an odd question, one Angélica hadn't been asked by any crew member previously. Then again, she'd mainly worked with males up until taking on this site. Local males at that, whose families lived close by and whose lifelong dreams didn't involve archaeology careers. "Are you talking about archaeologists in general?"

Jane shrugged. "Or you, since you seem to have it all going for you—the dream job and a steady boyfriend."

Stifling a smirk at Jane's misconception of reality, Angélica returned her attention to her notes. Up until a few years ago, her dream job had involved a prestigious position at a university, not hopping from one dig site to another playing clean-up crew.

As for that boyfriend, Quint was not exactly steady thanks to his traveling. Hell, she'd been afraid he wasn't coming back after his silence for weeks on end. Part of her was still afraid that this was just a brief respite from her years of loneliness and that their time here was a last hurrah for them.

She cleared the dust from her throat. "I'm not going to lie to you, Jane. This is not an ideal career if having a spouse and family is what you want in your future."

"But your dad and mom did it. They were revered as one of the best teams in the Mesoamerican archaeological field years ago."

Angélica squinted at the girl, feeling bristly at the mention of her parents. "How do you know about my parents?"

"I read several articles written by your mother and a bunch written about your father after I was accepted as part of this crew. I wanted to have a solid background about who I was going to be working with down here."

That meant she'd read up on Angélica, too. How far back had she gone?

Jane arched her back, stretching. "Blame it on my intense nature and need to do well. I always overstudy for tests, too. It's partly why I now have an ex in my life."

Her wariness easing, Angélica returned her attention to the *Chac* carving. "My parents worked in the same field of study. It was a little easier for them to pair up and make their marriage work."

The same could have been said for Angélica and her ex-husband since they were both archaeologists working for the same university, but their romance had gone cold before she'd even said her vows. The child in her womb at that time had been her only reason for going through with the wedding.

After losing the baby, there'd been nothing left to keep her in the relationship, so she'd ended it in spite of her ex's objections to how it would affect *his* career. Shortly after that, she'd left the university and moved south after landing a job with the Mexican government. The rest was history, or rather ancient history, since her main focus ever since had been on the great Maya civilization and its mysterious downfall.

"Quint's a photojournalist, right?" Jane asked.

"Yes." Angélica's wariness returned full fledged. As with her parents, she preferred to keep the topic of her relationships off the table.

"And he travels around for the job?"

"Correct." Where was this going?

"That must make it tough sometimes."

So far, it made it tough a lot, not just sometimes, but that wasn't any of Jane's business. "It's a challenge, but we are managing."

Sort of. At least for now.

Angélica returned to her notes, putting an end to Jane's game of Twenty Questions.

A few minutes later, Jane spoke again. "I really admire you." The girl's voice sounded husky, shy maybe. "You're a great role model, you know."

Angélica shifted, uncomfortable with the admiration.

"Have you ever—"

"Dr. García?" Gertrude's voice came from the chamber entrance, interrupting whatever Jane had been about to say. "Fernando needs your help outside."

Thank the Maya gods! Scooping up her notes, Angélica stood. "Are you going to be okay working in here alone for a bit?" she asked Jane.

The girl nodded, her eyes averted. "There are no snakes on this end of the site."

That wasn't necessarily true. There just weren't as many visible near this temple. "I'll send Lorenzo in here to join you shortly. He's very good at doing rubbings."

"Thank you, Dr. García."

She felt Jane's gaze on her as she followed Gertrude out of the chamber. Something in that whole conversation didn't set well. By the time she'd stepped out into the hot sunlight, Angélica had summed it up to being too personal for her comfort level. Letting anyone inside of her guarded bubble usually involved a lot of tension and snarls. Except where Daisy was concerned. There was something about that woman that allowed her to walk right through Angélica's defenses without causing a single bristle.

Fernando, Pedro, and Lorenzo waited for her to join them over near one of the mounds at the edge of the forest clearing. All three held shovels and dripped with sweat.

"What is it?" she asked as she approached.

Fernando pointed at the area he'd been excavating next to the remains of a small single-story structure mostly covered with tree roots and centuries of forest detritus. "You have your trowel and brush?"

She nodded, patted her tool pouch, and knelt next to the shallow hole they'd excavated. "What did you find?" She could see a small mound at the bottom of it.

"Something hard."

Pedro mopped his face with his shirt. "It sounded like metal when my blade hit it. Fernando thought you might want to be here before we go any further."

"Thank you," she told her foreman and leaned into the hole. The scent of fresh dirt greeted her. "Hand me the horsehair brush, please."

Lorenzo held out the bricklayer's brush, handle first.

After several swipes over the dirt-covered lumps, she sat back on her heels.

"Son of a bitch," she said, wiping away a trickle of sweat with the back of her wrist. "Nothing at this damned dig site is making sense anymore."

* * *

Quint lay flat on his back, blinking up at the thick shadows hovering near the mine's ceiling. He coughed in the dust, his elbow throbbing along with his left butt cheek. The two had taken the brunt of his fall after he'd squeezed partway through the hole in the wall, dangled for a few seconds, and then succumbed to gravity with a curse-filled crash.

A beam of light shone through the hole, dancing wildly along the upper walls. "You okay, flyboy?" Juan called through the opening. "It sounded like you flubbed your superhero landing."

Quint coughed again, slowly sitting up. He rolled his shoulder. There'd be kinks to work loose later. He was getting too old for this sort of tough-guy shit. "You're not paying me enough for this job."

"What? I'm letting you sleep with my daughter, aren't I?"

"Not with her, next to her. And by your definition, you're sleeping with me, too."

"Aren't you lucky, getting two Garcías for the price of one?"

With a groan, Quint pushed to his feet. He grabbed his hard hat from the floor and dropped it onto his head. He snagged the flashlight Juan held out for him. "For the record," he said through the hole, "I'm not a fan of your wheeling and dealing."

"I don't remember twisting your arm to get you to agree to climb through there." Juan held out Quint's camera.

"Pedro is right. You're the devil in disguise." He looped the camera strap around his neck, keeping it from tangling with the dust mask that Juan had insisted he wear once he was through the wall.

"*El diablo*, eh? I like that." Juan laughed in a deep, diabolical tone, acting the part as he handed his poisonous gas-reading gadget through the hole. "Don't you forget about me and my pitchfork when it comes to my daughter."

Quint scoffed, dusting off his pants and shirt. "The two of you and these damned dig sites are going to be the death of me yet."

"When you're done fussing, let me know what you see in there."

No mercy, not even a hint of it. Quint chuckled.

"For starters, Dr. *Diablo*, I see dirt and rocks." He shone the flashlight on the mine's floor. "And a few more boot prints."

He squatted for a closer look and raised his camera, grimacing at the pain still throbbing in his elbow. After taking a few pictures of the prints, including a few next to his own boot for a size comparison, he stood again.

Next he moved over to the altar. He took several pictures of the petroglyphs carved into the walls from different angles, remembering Angélica's words about how important it could be to view glyphs and carvings from various perspectives.

Finally, he focused on the little dust-covered figurines on the roughly hewn stone altar. He counted nine. Four appeared to be sitting, two standing, and the remaining three crouching.

"Okay," he told Juan. "I have your closeups."

"What do you see farther back?"

"The deal we made was for pictures of the boot prints, petroglyphs, and figurines."

"True, but now that you're in there, you might as well explore a little further."

Quint aimed the flashlight upward. The ceiling was less fractured here, but small chunks of rock littered the floor. "I can see my gravestone now. 'Here lies Quint Parker. He explored a little too far.' "

"You're assuming we'll be able to dig your body out after the mine collapses."

A chill ran down his spine at the thought of being buried alive in here. "Keep it up, old man, and I'll hide your scorpion socks."

"Okay, okay." Juan's voice brimmed with laughter. "I'll be good."

With the flashlight aimed deeper down the dark throat of the mine again, Quint called out, "How far am I going?"

"That depends on how that ceiling looks."

"Like the sky will be falling any minute now."

"Have any pebbles fallen on your hard hat?"

"Not yet."

"Then it's stable enough, Chicken Little."

Stable enough? Famous last words. Quint swore under his breath while adjusting the lighting settings on his camera. "I'm a photojournalist, remember. Not an obsessed history nut with a bunch of capital letters after my name."

A snickering sound came through the hole. "You'll be fine. Trust me. Now hurry up and take some pictures, Mr. Big-Time Photojournalist, before I shrivel up and turn to dust out here and become another part of Maya history."

"Shouldn't we be concerned about me messing up something important by just being here?" It was a desperate last-ditch effort on Quint's part, but worth a shot because several feet deeper into the tunnel, the walls narrowed. He tugged at the neck of his shirt, gulping as a wave of sweat washed over him.

"You mean in regard to your future with my daughter or with whatever is on the other side of this wall?"

"In here, smartass." He doubted there was much Juan could do to fix any screwups he made with Angélica, both in the past and future.

"You'll most likely be fine when it's all said and done with maybe a lasting twitch for a day or two. Just don't touch anything, be sure to check the meter often, and keep that mask on your face."

"If I come across any Maya ghosts, I'm sending them your way."

"Good, I have a lot of questions for them. If you run into the Lord of Death, get his autograph for me. I've been a big fan of his for decades."

"Got it, Dr. *Diablo*."

Fake evil laughter came through the hole. "Now go take some pictures and then get your superhero buns back out here. If anything were to happen to you, my daughter will kill me, for starters."

Lowering the flashlight, Quint focused on the floor just beyond the altar. The white granules of rock he'd noticed previously were scattered here and there in small groupings, like someone had spread them via a pepper grinder. He squatted to take a closer look, scooping up a handful mixed with dirt. Up close, they didn't look like limestone granules, more like fragments. Some were sharp edged, reminding him of shale flakes. All were a pale gray that looked almost white under the flashlight's beam. He sifted the dirt away through his fingers and dumped the remaining dirt and flakes in a sandwich bag Juan had given him for show-and-tell later.

Securing his mask, he took a deep breath.

Knock-knock, Underworld. Anyone home?

Gearing up mentally for the task before him, he edged deeper into the mine. His breathing sounded loud and harsh through the mask, reminding him of something out of a science fiction horror movie. Rounding a sharp bend, he lost sight of the wall that divided the present from the past.

The boot prints in the thick layer of dust on the rock floor were still visible here and there, heading both ways as he wound deeper into the earth. Quint knelt and lifted his camera, taking a few more closeups of them to make sure they matched the prints back near the wall.

Another bend farther into the mine, the boot prints stopped. Whoever had snuck in must have chickened out and turned around.

Aiming the light up at the ceiling and then down over the walls, Quint saw no reason for the visitor to turn tail. With a shrug, he continued onward and downward. Maybe he'd see the paw prints of a big cat further up, or some other critter that had caused the owner of the boot prints to scurry away.

For a few more turns, there was nothing besides rock and dirt all around him. No paw prints, no petroglyphs, no figurines, nothing.

He was about to head back to Juan when he came across a grouping of petroglyphs on one wall.

Raising his camera, he snapped several shots. As he moved further along the wall, he noticed a dark cavity up ahead on the right. The top of the small opening was at waist level and went clear to the floor. Was it a shallow cave? An animal den? He bent over and directed the flashlight into the dark cavity.

It wasn't a cave or a den, but rather a side tunnel.

He eased down onto his knees, wincing as a small pebble dug into his kneecap.

The side tunnel walls looked the same as those in the main adit of the mine. There were more flakes of larger pieces of limestone, lining the base of the wall like they'd been swept to the side. When he aimed the flashlight deeper into the tunnel, his beam met darkness. Either the tunnel was long, or there was an opening on the other side—maybe a small chamber or another tunnel leading to a separate limestone-laden section of the mine. That would explain the grayish-white flakes lining the tunnel's floor.

After taking a look at Juan's meter to make sure the air was safe, he lowered his mask. He sniffed a few times, checking to see if there was a musky, urine-heavy odor in the air or some other sign of an animal holing up somewhere back in the shadows, but he smelled nothing other than the musty cave scent that had been with him since entering the mine.

He paused for a moment, listening for any sounds coming from the other end of the tunnel. Other than his own breathing, nothing but silence filled his ears. He tossed a pebble along the tunnel floor into the darkness. When it stilled, silence followed.

Shining the light back in the direction he'd come, he cursed. The words were especially loud in the quiet darkness.

He wiped his face with his shirt hem, exchanging sweat for more dust and grit. Jesus, what in the hell was he doing in here? Was a woman really worth crawling through overgrown wormholes into the Maya Underworld?

As much as he wanted to leave, he knew he had to crawl through the damned tunnel and see what was on the other side. There was no doubt in his mind that when Angélica saw his photographs, she'd probably want to come through the wall and see it all for herself—the boot prints, the petroglyphs, the figurines, and whatever was at the other end of this tunnel. Unlike him, she wouldn't think twice about following the path of that pebble.

"Fuck." A tunnel within a tunnel deep in the earth—this was the seed of long-term insanity. Angélica was going to owe him big for this.

He checked the air quality one more time and then donned his mask even though no dangerous gases registered. After tucking his camera inside his shirt to protect it from the rocky floor, he dropped to his hands and knees. He tried not to think about the weight of the world above him as he crawled along, or about how long it would take Juan to go get help and dig out his body if the ceiling crashed down on top of him. Sweat dripped into his eyes.

At what appeared to be the end of the tunnel, he paused, once again listening for any sounds of life. He aimed his light through the dark exit, wincing in anticipation. If a pair of eyes glowed back at him, his poor heart was going to blow a gasket.

All was silent and dark ahead. No signs of a large cat, a small mouse, or a gold-loving dragon to be found.

Slowly, he crawled out of the tunnel. He stood, dusting his hands off on his pants, and shining his flashlight around an oval-shaped cavern not much bigger than his living room back home. The ceiling was higher, though, probably twelve feet at the highest point. All it was missing was his sectional couch, flat-screen television, and coffee table laden with cold beer and María's *panuchos*.

Shit, he was getting delusional.

Forcing himself to move deeper into the cavern, he approached what looked like a small pile of broken sticks—one of many such piles in the room. On the other side of the sticks was another slightly bigger pile consisting of what looked like round rocks.

He started to move his flashlight beam over to the far wall, but then stopped, returning to that last pile.

Those weren't rocks.

His mouth suddenly dry, he took a step toward them, stepping onto one of the sticks.

His beam lowered to his boot.

That wasn't a stick.

The hair rose on the back of his neck.

He lifted his boot, planting it on solid ground. Fumbling, he pulled out the gas meter, making sure he was still in the clear. The air was stable, but his breath was erratic. If he kept this up he'd hyperventilate.

Closing his eyes, he imagined blue sky and sunshine, taking several deep breaths. When he opened his eyes, he extracted his camera from his shirt. He needed to take some pictures so that Angélica and her father could see this. Maybe they could give him a logical reason as to why there was a mound of skulls and several piles of bones inside a cavern deep within a limestone mine, because all of his ideas stemmed from horror movies and childhood boogeymen.

He directed the light around the walls, making sure there were no other entrances or alcoves that could hide some terror lying in wait for him. A large chunk of rock sat against the wall across the way with two other slightly smaller ones in front of it. Someone must have positioned them there, but where had they come from? Had the Maya people left them behind when they dug out the mine? He checked overhead. The ceiling looked jagged above him, but more solid than the rest of the mine had so far. They could have come from there.

Stepping forward carefully, he lifted his camera. As he checked the settings, his pulse pounded in his ears. Sweat slicked his back, running down his spine as he tried to avoid coming down on anything that used to belong inside of a layer of skin.

What in the hell *was* this place? A mass burial chamber? In a mine? Was this where they disposed of any miners killed while on the job? If so, shouldn't there be hair or jewelry or some other evidence of their humanity besides bones? How long would it take for a body to decompose down here?

Shaking all of those morbid thoughts from his head, he blocked out the questions and focused on taking the best pictures he could under the circumstances. This was a job. That was all. Maybe if he took enough photos, Angélica wouldn't feel so strongly about wanting to see this for herself.

He bent down and held his flashlight on what appeared to be a broken human femur bone, snapping a picture. He moved his flashlight to another piece and another, clicking the shutter button again and again.

Why were most of the bones broken? Why so many?

Shaking away the questions, he moved to the next pile, clicking away as his flash lit the room repeatedly.

Maybe this was a mass burial site for one of the losing ball teams. Or had these been warriors from a particular battle whose story was told by the petroglyphs outside?

Click-flash. Click-flash. Click-flash.

Were they sacrificial victims? Was it their blood that had been used to coat the wall where Juan was waiting for him?

Stepping around a scattering of broken bones, he focused on one of the skulls in the "head" mound. It had a chunk missing near the right eye socket. Was that from a blunt instrument during a battle? He'd have to search through Juan and Angélica's books on the Maya to see what sort of weapons they used.

He lowered onto his knees and chose the macro setting on his camera, moving in closer to another skull. The metering light flickered for a moment, then the flash lit up the room. He took several more pictures of the skull along with a couple of others from slightly different angles, and then he returned to the scattering of broken bones and did the same.

When he finished, he stepped back and tried to take a few wider-angled shots of all the rubble, holding the flashlight in his armpit, but the room was so dark that it was hard to get the full macabre scene.

By the time he'd finished, his camera battery indicator showed twenty percent remaining. His own tolerance level was closer to five percent when it came to this creepy catacomb and its bony treasures.

Itching to return to the wall and Juan's easy laughter, he picked his way through the bones back to the tunnel exit. As he reached the dark hole, something glittered at eye-level, catching his attention. He aimed the beam at the wall above the tunnel. A figurine sat inside a pocket chiseled into the rock. Only one this time, not nine, and it was bigger than the others.

He stepped closer, lifting his camera. He snapped several shots, double-checking them to make sure he had a clear picture. This one looked different from the others, the sculpture more detailed … and ugly. The top half looked to be some kind of feral cat, the bottom half human. The other figurines were made of jade, while this one appeared to be obsidian.

He leaned forward, blowing some of the dust off the figure. Yep, black and shiny. He tried to imagine what it would look like if it were real, coming up with a comic book image.

Something clattered behind him.

He whirled, his light bouncing all around the room as stars

swirled back into vision. One of the skulls rolled a short way along the floor, coming to rest against a bone.

Okay, enough of this shit.

He stuffed his camera back inside his shirt and did his best Speedy Gonzales imitation back through the tunnel. After a flashlight check to make sure nothing was lying in wait for him in the adit leading off deeper into the mine, he returned to the hole in the wall in record time.

He could hear Juan whistling and creaking about as he drew near. The sounds of another living being sent a surge of relief through his limbs. As he unwrapped his camera strap from around his neck, he realized how wet his shirt was. It was not the heat that had him hot and bothered this time.

"I'm back." He handed his camera through the hole.

"Hey, you're still alive," Juan joked. "Did you find anything else in there?"

Besides a monster's den? "A few things." He handed the gas meter through and then his hard hat and mask.

After one last glance behind him with his flashlight to make sure nothing had followed him, he gripped the bottom edges of the hole and hoisted himself up the wall. Not giving a shit about scratches or bruises, he pulled himself through the hole. Dangling down the other side of the wall, he reached for the ground.

"Need some help?" Juan asked.

"Nope. Stay back."

He slid farther through the hole, moving quickly, half-afraid something would latch onto his ankle or foot from the other side and try to drag him back into that catacomb. As before, gravity exerted its usual force and Quint tumbled the rest of the way through. This time he managed to roll out of the fall with only a few scrapes in the process.

"Impressive." Juan offered a hand up, which Quint took. "You looked like an Olympic gymnast." He handed Quint the camera and tried to brush the dust off Quint's back. "Wow, you're soaked clear through."

"Why couldn't the Maya people build open-air arenas like the Roman Coliseum instead of these damned temples and underground hellholes?" He thought about all of those skulls piled together and shuddered.

Juan's eyes narrowed as he stared up at him. "What happened in there, Quint?"

"I don't want to talk about it until I'm standing under blue sky and sunshine." He didn't wait for Juan to start for the exit, but rather led the way, jamming his hard hat on his head as he walked.

Juan's boot scuffed over the floor behind him, his cane creaking as he tried to keep up with Quint. When they neared the entrance, Juan pressed him again for answers. "What did you see back there, Quint? Did you find another altar stone?"

"No." With the sunlight visible at the end of the tunnel, he stopped and waited. The older man's worried expression matched Quint's own feelings. "No altar stone, but there were more petroglyphs."

"What else?" Juan searched Quint's face. "What did you see that has you wanting to get the hell out of Dodge, son?"

Quint frowned over Juan's shoulder at the darkness beyond. "I found a cavern. It had several piles of bones on the floor."

"What kind of bones?"

"The human kind."

* * *

"I need your help with something," Angélica said to Pedro.

He was working alongside Fernando and Gertrude, excavating the small cache of morion-style helmets, breastplates, and arm and leg greaves left behind by the Spanish conquistadors. Why there was a collection of centuries-old, rusted body armor but no bones or weapons was a mystery in itself.

Once again, Angélica was left scratching her head. What in the hell had happened at this site? Had her mom stumbled onto something that explained the artifacts left from various groups over the centuries? Was that why she'd been murdered?

Had she been murdered? Or was this all some weird coincidence?

"Where are the swords?" Pedro rubbed the back of his neck, scowling at the excavation site. "Those Spanish bastards usually carried three-foot-long, double-edged steel swords made in Toledo, Spain. I've seen them in museums in Cancun and Mexico City. Between the conquistadors' weapons and full set of armor, the natives never had a chance."

"It was one mercenary bloodbath after another, I know, but I need your help on something else right now." Angélica motioned him to follow her around the side of the temple for a little more privacy. She waited for him in the shade of a mahogany tree.

She spoke to him in Spanish in case one of the INAH crew happened to be out of sight but within earshot. "Quint told me about your theory."

He switched to his native language without a blink. "You mean about Daisy?"

"What about Daisy?"

He grimaced. "Never mind. Which theory do you mean?"

She shelved the Daisy question for later and stayed on her original course. "The one about my mom being murdered."

Pedro's eyes widened for a moment. "When did he tell you?"

"Yesterday when we were in the *Chakmo'ol* Temple. Last night, I looked through Mom's notebook and figured out that someone had removed all the pages of notes she had written about this site except for one, which was stuck to the page before it."

"The one left behind—those are the notes you have spoken about? The words and drawings that don't make a lot of sense?"

"Exactly." She took a steadying breath. Talking to Pedro about her mom caused a welling of emotions she hadn't expected. "Quint and I are thinking that someone killed her to hide whatever she'd found. They stole her notes and left her for dead, trying to keep what she'd discovered here a secret."

He nodded slowly, his face lined with a mixture of anger and sadness. "What would be worth taking her life? Some rare jade piece or a golden treasure, maybe?"

"That's one possibility." Black market treasure hunters could be ruthless. They'd stop at nothing in their hunt for fortune, using people as "mules" to move stolen goods across borders, killing anyone who stood in their way. She'd read about it time and again, listened to firsthand accounts even from archaeologists who'd been victims of gun threats and worse.

"Or did it have something to do with local politics and fighting?" Pedro continued. "Was Marianne involved in anything to do with the guerrilla warfare that has flared up now and then in this area?"

"Mom wanted nothing to do with violence. She always said that enough blood had been spilled on Mexico's soil to stain the ground red for a millennium to come."

"That's true. So how can I help?"

"I need you to find out who was at this site when my mom was here."

One eyebrow lifted. "You work for INAH. You have more access to that information than I do."

"Yes, but if I start asking a lot of questions, it will draw attention to us."

He crossed his arms. "And you."

"And me, Marianne's daughter." She blew out a breath. "I need to appear to be focused on my job—cleaning, cataloging, and prepping for tourists. You, on the other hand, know a lot of people in Cancun."

"I thought you and your father went through the files from the last group and brought copies here. Wasn't there a list of the crew in the files?"

She shook her head. "The notes filed with INAH were about the site. The last archaeologist doesn't appear to have kept any personnel notes."

"Or someone removed them."

"Or they were eliminated along with my mother." She wiped at a drop of sweat trickling down her temple. "I was thinking that maybe there might be notes from the helicopter pilot in his logbook about passengers he transported to and from the site. I've seen your logbooks. You keep notes on each flight, including names and cargo."

Pedro's frown deepened. "That's because when it comes to my log books, I am … what is the word your father uses?"

"Anal?" she supplied, trying not to grin.

He poked her in the ribs, making her screech. "Nitpicky," he said, switching to English.

"Detailed" was a better word for Pedro's need to keep copious records. "Do you think you can get hold of the pilot's logbook?"

"Maybe. Unless it was lost in the crash."

She lowered her voice, speaking Spanish. "You can use our satellite phone after lunch to make any phone calls. Make sure everyone has left the tent area, though, especially my dad. I don't want him to know about this until we have something more definite. It took him years to get over Mom's death. Bringing all of this back up is going to break his heart all over again."

He nodded, his dark gaze holding hers. "What about your heart?"

"It's hurting," she admitted.

"Come here, *hermanita*."

Little sister. He hadn't called her that in years.

She let him pull her into his embrace. He kissed her on the forehead like he used to when they were kids and she'd get hurt. "I miss your mama, too. We'll figure this out together and make sure Marianne's killer is brought to justice."

"She was so young." She blinked back tears.

"I know." Pedro pulled back, frowning at her. "We have company."

"We do?" she asked in English and turned to find Quint striding toward them. Good, she needed to talk to him.

"Hey, Parker," she said as he joined them. "I was hoping—" That was all she got out before he grabbed her by the shoulders and hauled her close. "Quint, what are y—" He planted a kiss on her lips, bending her backward and shutting her up in one fell swoop.

After a couple of surprised blinks, she looped her arms around his neck, closed her eyes, and kissed him back. The thrill he inspired as he held her tightly wrapped in his arms was just what she needed to soothe the ache of sadness in her heart. For that moment, she forgot about the conquistadors' rusted armor, the noisy jungle, and the frustrating mess she'd landed in at this site. Not even Pedro's noisy throat clearing disturbed her.

There was Quint and only Quint.

When he pulled back, his eyes roamed her face as if he'd forgotten what she looked like. "Thanks, boss lady. I earned that this morning."

Earned? She licked her lips as he pulled her back upright, wondering if he needed to be further reimbursed later.

"Where's *my* 'hello' kiss, Don Juan?" Pedro's wide grin rounded his cheeks. "Is this how she's paying you for your hard work and time? Personally, I'd have taken the money." In a stage whisper, he added, "She howls louder than the monkeys around here when she's mad, not to mention that she smells like one, too." He leaned closer, pretending to sniff her neck, and then pinched his nose.

Without taking her eyes off Quint, Angélica socked Pedro in the gut hard enough to make him let out an "Oof" in between his chuckles.

"Did you make another deal with Dad?"

"Yes, but not for you." He massaged his left shoulder, rotating it forward and then backward.

"Guess what Fernando found today?" Pedro asked, still rubbing his gut.

"A catacomb full of human bones?" Quint shot back. He had no humor in his tone; not a hint of a smile lining his face.

Angélica's gaze lowered to his shirt. There was a lot more dirt covering it than usual, along with his pants. He looked like he'd fallen in a *cenote* and then rolled in the dirt.

Something was wrong.

Her gut clenched. "Is Dad okay?"

He nodded. "He went back to the tent to look into a few things."

"Where did you find a catacomb full of bones?" Pedro asked.

Quint glanced around, leaning in closer. "There was a hole in the wall."

"I know about the hole," Angélica reminded him. "You and Dad told me you'd removed a stone so you could peek through to the other side."

"I mean a bigger hole. Someone else went in there."

Her gaze narrowed. A mixture of surprise and disbelief bubbled in her thoughts. "Are you sure a few stones didn't just come loose after you took out that other stone?"

"There are boot prints on the other side of the wall."

She swore. Who in the hell went in there? And when?

"I followed the prints," he added.

"*You* went through the hole?" She caught his forearm. "Quint, that was dangerous. We don't know how stable the mine is on either side. If something had happened, Dad wouldn't have—"

"Your father is the one who convinced me to squeeze through to the other side."

"Did he blackmail you?" Pedro asked. "Because he's very good at blackmail, especially when you are drinking *balche* with him."

"No blackmail. We made a deal." He glanced at Angélica. "Not about you either."

"That's even worse," Pedro said. "The man is a wolf when it comes to deals."

Did he mean *shark*? Angélica shrugged, both worked actually.

"This time it's to my benefit. He has to co-write an article I'm contracted to deliver in a few weeks."

"Wow." Angélica's eyebrows climbed up her forehead. "Dad loathes writing articles. He must have really wanted you to go through that hole."

"He knew as well as I did that if I didn't go through the hole, you would."

She started to open her mouth to deny it and then closed her lips. He was right. She would have been too curious to see what was on the other side.

With a wink, he added, "He and I would both rather put my life at risk than yours."

Not her. It was her dig site. She was the one who should be taking the biggest risks. If something had happened to Quint, she'd … She didn't finish that thought, not wanting to go there right now.

Instead of arguing her point, she asked, "What did you find?"

"Besides more boot prints?"

She nodded.

"Petroglyphs, broken bones, and little carved figurines." He jammed his hand in his front pocket. "Oh, and this." He took her hand and dropped something into it.

She stared down at the plastic sandwich bag with whitish-gray flecks mixed in with the dirt. "Limestone?"

"Looks more like flakes of shale to me. After finding the bones farther back in the mine, I'm starting to suspect those are bone fragments."

"Tell me about the figurines," she said as she tucked the bag in her pouch to inspect later. Were they the ones on the altar her father had mentioned before?

"They were made from jade. One of them was obsidian."

"Obsidian?" she asked. That was rare around here. "You're sure?"

"Not one hundred percent. It was back in the catacomb with the piles of human bones."

Pedro cocked his head to the side. "Was it a burial chamber for Maya warriors?"

Quint shrugged, hitting Pedro with a crooked grin. "When I asked around in there, nobody answered."

"Do you have pictures of the figurines?" Angélica asked.

"Sure, but shouldn't we be more concerned with the bones?"

"The bones don't tell as much of a story as the figurines and petroglyphs, at least not at first. You took plenty of pictures of everything, right?"

He gave a single nod. "I'll show them to you at lunch. I left my camera in the tent with your father."

"Did Dad see the pictures already?"

"He was going through them a second time when I left."

"What did the old devil have to say about them?" Pedro asked.

Quint's eyes locked onto Angélica's, not a single glint of humor in their hazel depths. "He told me to find you to let you know that he has a new theory."

She sighed. "Of course he does. What now?" She winced in anticipation. "Let me guess, it's about that damned curse, right?"

"I believe his exact words were: *This place isn't cursed. It's doomed!*"

Chapter Seventeen

Tell: An artificial mound formed from the accumulated debris of the site's previous inhabitants. Scraped off layer by layer, these mounds can be hundreds to thousands of years old and often "tell" details about previous civilizations, including site purpose and dates of occupation.

Food had never tasted so damned good.

Quint dug into his second helping of María's lunch—egg and green chili tamales topped with a sweet mango salsa that made him want to lick his plate clean.

"You eating for two, son?" Juan asked from across the table. He lifted his coffee cup, watching Quint over the rim with a twinkle in his eyes.

Quint held out his left arm, flexing like a bodybuilder in response. "Must grow stronger," he said, impersonating Arnold Schwarzenegger.

Juan's lips twitched. "Keep going, then. I have big plans for you and your strong muscles."

Uh-oh. That couldn't be good.

He took another bite, groaning in appreciation of the complex Maya spices María used. Apparently, hanging out in that death trap Angélica and her father called a mine while tiptoeing between the skulls and broken bones in an eerie catacomb had roused one hell of an appetite—and not just for food.

Finishing the last bite of tamale, he stared across the table at the flame-haired woman who was sitting next to her father clicking through the digital photos Quint had taken earlier. He picked up his glass of bright red *jamaica*, which Angélica had informed him was a blend of a part of the hibiscus flower along with water and sugar, and took a long draw. Whatever it was, it left him wanting more, same as Angélica had earlier when she'd kissed him back—with gusto—at the *Baatz'* Temple.

His trip into the hole in the ground had given him a solid ass-kicking. He'd returned to the sunlight with a new purpose. No more plodding along at a slow and steady pace, letting the wind blow him along with the other tumbleweeds. No more playing it safe. No more …

"What is this?" Angélica said in a quiet voice, holding out his camera. She pointed at the corner of the camera's digital screen.

"Why are you whispering?" Juan asked, sliding his reading glasses on to take a look. "We're the only ones in here."

Quint glanced around the empty mess tent. Even María had stepped out, taking the food scraps to Rover.

Lunch was almost over when Quint arrived in the mess tent with his camera strapped around his neck. Angélica had planned it that way after he'd told her about the boot prints. He would come in late for lunch, showing up with his camera in hand as if he'd been busy doing his regular job, taking pictures for an article.

Everything needed to appear normal in front of the crew, including with her father, even though he already knew about the prints. Only Quint, Angélica, and Pedro needed to know about Marianne's murder and the possible threat Angélica now faced as they continued to dig for more answers about the recent past.

"I'm whispering because these tent walls are paper-thin when it comes to eavesdropping. We need to be extremely careful now."

Juan lowered his glasses on his nose, looking over the top of them at his daughter. "Just to be clear, you're worried about someone hearing that we saw the boot prints in the mine?"

"Of course!"

Angélica spoke a little too vehemently in Quint's opinion. Big-brained archaeologist and ace machete handler she might be, but any dreams of trying out for roles at the local theater should probably be forgotten.

She focused back on the camera screen. "I'm just concerned

that whoever went into the mine will hide the boots if we let on that we're looking for them."

Judging from Juan's narrowed expression, Quint had a feeling Angélica's father had picked up the scent of her omission. When the brown-eyed archaeologist turned that squint his way, Quint held up his hands. "Don't look at me. I'm just here for some fun in the sun with a pretty girl."

Juan's squint stayed in place until Angélica nudged him with her elbow. "Let's get back to this." She pointed at the camera screen again. "What is this, Parker?"

He leaned forward to see the screen better. "It's a closeup of one of the skulls."

"Why did you take it?"

Taking the camera from her, he enlarged the image. "Because that hole above the eye socket doesn't seem right." He handed the camera back to her. "Look at the edges. They're ragged and scraped up. If it was caused by blunt force through flesh, I don't think it would look like that." Quint glanced at Juan. "Most of the skulls had similar, ragged breaks and chunks of bone missing from the back and sides of the cranium." He grimaced at the memory, wondering if the musty scent in the chamber included dried human remains along with the rock dust.

A frown was Angélica's only response as she peered at the picture. Then she went through them all again while Quint disposed of their dishes and refilled his cup with more *jamaica*.

When she finished, she handed him his camera. "Those crouching figurines on the altar look like Olmec were-jaguars."

"Yep." Juan sloshed his coffee around in his cup. "That black one is different, though, and not just because it's obsidian. A mix of Olmec and something else, maybe."

"Maya and Olmec? Have you ever seen that blending before?" she asked him.

"No, but there is so much history hidden out there under the forest's veil that the archaeological teams here haven't even touched yet. We only have a sliver of knowledge about the Maya, and even less when it comes to the Olmec people."

"You said that black one was above the exit from the chamber?" she asked Quint.

"The chamber of death," he confirmed, in a spooky voice.

"Hey, that's good," Juan said. "We could use that to help sell this site to tourists."

"Next you'll want me to have it renamed the City of the Dead." She shook her head at her father's enthusiastic agreement. "Back to the picture, Dad. Why do you think the black one was only inside of that chamber and not out on the altar with the others?"

"Maybe it was acting as a ward," he answered. "Placed there to keep something inside."

"Come on. I'm serious."

"So am I, *gatita*."

Keep what inside? Quint powered off his camera. Besides the bones, what would be inside that chamber? Ghosts? Some kind of Olmec god equivalent to a Maya Underworld god?

"I need to see it all for myself," she said.

Quint wasn't surprised at her declaration. She seemed to be a hands-on learner, always touching things to get a better understanding.

"I'm going back in with you," he told her.

As much as the idea of returning to that place made his gut feel like he'd swallowed an anvil, there was no way he would wait on the safe side of the wall while she traipsed through the oversized coffin.

"You don't need to do that, Parker. I know how much you loathe being in tight spots."

He raised his eyebrows. "That depends on the tight spot."

Juan chuckled.

"Fine. You can come with me."

Quint and Juan exchanged a surprised glance. That was easy. In the past, she would have bucked more.

Angélica added, "Bring your camera. I can use you in there to take some more pictures."

"And you'd like my strong, manly protection," he joked, flexing both arms for Juan's admiration this time.

A chortle came from her father. "Maybe you should have a fourth tamale. Tell María to include some spinach in this one, Popeye."

The boss lady's smile was fleeting as she looked at each of them. She was obviously too preoccupied with the mine's macabre treasures to play along with them. "We need to figure out who went in the mine and why. I told everyone that place was unstable and off limits. If the trespasser was a member of my crew, then disciplinary actions need to be taken. If a relic was stolen from the mine, then

INAH needs to be notified."

"And if it's someone else? Someone who isn't working here?" Quint asked.

Her eyes flashed a warning after a glance in her father's direction. "Who else could it be?"

Quint shrugged. "An outsider looking to make a quick buck on the black market with some Maya treasures."

"Or a ghost," Juan supplied.

She rolled her eyes at her father. "I thought ghosts floated, Dad. Or are they wearing hiking boots now?"

"Have you ever seen a ghost?"

"Of course not."

"Then you don't know what traces they leave behind, do you, Miss Know-It-All."

"Ectoplasmic goo seems to be a popular theory on the big screen," Quint threw out.

She reached across the table and slapped his forearm. "You're not helping, Parker."

Catching her fingers, he squeezed them lightly before letting go with a wink.

"Why do you think whoever it was turned back?" she asked them. "Was someone waiting for them at the wall, a partner in crime, and called them back? Or was the trespasser working alone?"

"Maybe your hiking boot–wearing ghost chickened out," Quint offered. "It gets a little cramped back in there." At least for his comfort level. A sarcophagus seemed roomier in retrospect.

"That's because your muscles are so big," Juan said.

"You should see how huge and green they become when something pisses me off."

"Angélica's favorite color is green. It's no wonder she scribbles your name in her notebook over and over."

"Boys," she said, a small smile tilting the corners of her lips. "Stay focused, please."

"I can't help it, *gatita*. Quint's muscles fluster me."

"Me, too," she played along, "but we can admire his big guns some other time when someone's life isn't in danger."

Quint hit her with a raised brow. Had she forgotten that they weren't going to discuss Marianne's murder or anything regarding her own potential danger in front of her father?

She winced at her own slip of the lip. Keeping secrets from her father was obviously not a usual practice for her.

"Have you considered, *gatita*, that you are making more out of these boot prints than necessary? Maybe one of the college kids got curious and decided to try a little spelunking on their own. That's all. Nothing malevolent or greed-inspired, just a kid being a kid."

She chewed on her lower lip. "Maybe." Her gaze locked with Quint's. "We'll keep that in mind tonight when we sneak in there after everyone retires to their tents."

"I don't like you two going alone through the wall." Juan's voice was stern all of a sudden.

"Pedro can go with us and wait on the other side," she offered.

Juan's reluctance was apparent from the lines on his face, but he nodded anyway. "You will check in with me as soon as you return."

She nodded.

"And you will take my air quality meter just to be safe."

She nodded again.

"And a pickax and hard hats."

"Of course."

"And—"

"Dad, Quint and I will be extra careful, I promise."

Juan's brown eyes moved to Quint. "Keep her out of trouble."

"I'll carry her out kicking and screaming, if needed."

"Excellent. Pedro says she fights dirty, so you might want to wear a cup."

"Dammit, Dad, quit giving away my secret moves."

Quint laughed at the mock glares they exchanged.

"I have an idea," Quint told Angélica when she turned back to him. "How about I take a stroll around camp this afternoon, check in with everyone and try to get a look at their boots." When she began to object, he held up his hand. "It makes more sense for me to do it than you since I saw the boot prints first hand. Tell her, Juan."

"What the muscle-head said."

"You might raise suspicions."

"Give me a little credit, boss lady. I'll carry that clipboard of yours and explain that you're busy and asked me to make notes on everyone's progress in your place."

"And if you see a print match?"

"I wait for your instructions before making a move."

She nodded, but her lips were pinched.

Juan knocked on the table. "I still don't like the idea of you two going in that mine tonight. How about you wait until tomorrow?"

"Why tomorrow?" Angélica asked.

"Because it's dark at night."

"He has a point." Quint shared Juan's feelings and then some. "Or how about the day after that?"

She crossed her arms, readying for battle. "The outside world doesn't matter if we're in a cave."

"It does to me," her father said. "Have you forgotten that the Maya Underworld gods are active in the dark?"

"Another good reason not to go in there tonight." Quint raised his empty glass, seconding the motion.

"That's all superstition and hoopla," she dismissed.

"Is it, *gatita*? Are you certain?"

She sighed, squeezing the bridge of her nose. "He's been like this all of my life," she told Quint.

"And she's been like this since she stopped wearing diapers." Her father stood with a grunt. "If you're not going to listen to me, darling daughter, I'm going to go find someone who will. If you need me, I'll be with Daisy and Esteban."

"Why them?" Angélica asked. "I thought you wanted to do some more measuring in the temples this afternoon."

"I do, but Esteban told me before lunch that Fernando needs his help this afternoon. That leaves Daisy alone in the ballcourt."

"I could send Jane over to work with her."

"Is there a problem with *me* working with Daisy?"

"I was hoping you'd come with me to the *Chakmo'ol* Temple."

"You mean Snakeville? I'd rather not."

"What if I promise to protect you from the evil, dastardly snakes, princess?" she jested.

"You always were the mouthiest of my offspring." Juan reached down and tweaked her nose.

"I'm your only offspring, remember? Unless you have a skeleton to drag out of some closet."

"There are plenty in that old mine if you need one," Quint said.

"No. Your mother and I decided that one mouthy, obstinate child was all we could handle."

"I thought my lack of siblings had more to do with Mom's career taking off than my charming personality."

"That too." Juan frowned down at his daughter. "Why do you

need to go in that temple again so soon? I thought you wanted to analyze your notes before returning for more snake dancing."

She shrugged. "I was thinking about something Daisy traced on one of her rubbings when we were in there a few days ago. I'm having trouble reading the surrounding glyphs clearly, and I think it's because there is an Olmec reference mixed in with them. I want to see it all again first hand. Since you know more about the Olmec than I do, I need your eyes in there with me."

"Okay, but give me a few hours. I'll meet you over there after Esteban finishes helping Fernando and returns to the ballcourt." After dropping a kiss on the top of her head, he left the tent.

Quint watched him go. When he turned back, Angélica was staring at him with open admiration.

She lowered her elbows onto the table, leaning toward him. Her gaze traveled over his features. "Quint." When she spoke, her voice was husky. "I don't know how I'll possibly be able to sleep tonight without seeing first hand what's in that mine chamber."

He leaned forward, matching her pose. His fingers snagged hers. "I have a surefire fix for your insomnia."

"Me, too." She took his hand in hers and circled her finger around his palm, tickling while teasing. "And I know the perfect place where we could find a little privacy."

"The showers?" he flirted back.

"A little dryer."

He raised one eyebrow. "The helicopter?"

"A little darker."

"One of the temples?"

"A little deeper."

His eyes narrowed. "You have a one-track mind, boss lady."

"We could finish what you started earlier at the *Baatz'* Temple."

"That's not the track I'm talking about."

She lifted his hand to her mouth, grazing her soft, wet lips across his knuckles. Chills snaked up his arm. "If you go with me into the mine tonight and take a few pictures, I'll make it worth your while."

"I won't be manipulated that easily."

"What if I offer to throw in a bonus?"

"Then I'd be curious about what this bonus is."

She wiggled her eyebrows like Groucho Marx.

He grinned. "What's that mean? You're going to stick a cigar in your mouth and crack jokes?"

"Not a cigar. And only one or two jokes."

That sobered him. He stared at her mouth. "Okay, but I draw the line at another rubber chicken. That damned squeaky bird almost made my ticker pop last time."

"Ah, and here I thought you liked Dad's rubber chicken." Her eyes sparkled. "If memory serves me right, you were able to finish the show, rubber chicken included."

"Well, you were naked, and I didn't want to let you down after all of the work you put into that encore performance." He leaned forward, sliding his hand along her jaw and urging her closer. "If we figure out this mess, Dr. García," he whispered against her lips, "do you promise to take me home to Cancun and reward me properly? No cigars, no rubber chickens, no clothes?"

"I'd rather reward you improperly," she whispered in return and stole a kiss. "You taste sweet, heartbreaker."

"Come back here." He cupped her face and zeroed in for more. "I wasn't done yet." He kissed her thoroughly this time.

"Angélica!" Pedro called from the other side of the tent wall.

She broke away from Quint with a string of curses.

"To be continued," he promised, his pulse zooming.

"I'll hold you to that, Mr. Love 'Em and Leave 'Em." She settled back into her seat before hollering, "I'm in the mess tent with Quint."

Pedro joined them seconds later. "I made the call."

"What call?" Quint asked.

Angélica quickly filled him in about her idea to have Pedro look into the last crew at the site via the previous pilot's logbook.

"What do you think the chances are of this logbook actually getting us anywhere?" he asked Pedro.

"A few names may be listed, so it's worth a shot."

Angélica squeezed Quint's arm, her fingers lingering. "Stop over at the *Chakmo'ol* Temple after you've made your rounds."

He nodded. "I'll start at the ballcourt with Daisy."

"While you're there, remind my father to take a few breaks this afternoon. I don't think he's resting that leg enough."

"Will do." He stood to leave.

"And let me know if you notice anything odd about Jane."

"Is she still having reactions to the snakebite?"

She worried her lip. "Not the bite. Maybe it's just me, but she was acting oddly this morning, asking me peculiar questions about my personal life."

Quint rubbed his jaw. "She asked me a few questions about our dating life the other evening at supper."

"Dating?" Her brow rose. "Is that what we're doing?"

No. They'd skipped that phase and moved straight to something much more intense.

He met her stare head-on. "Do you really want to have this conversation right now?"

Nodding with enthusiasm, Pedro grinned. "Yes, we do."

She aimed a squint his way. "No comment from you or you'll be leaving here bruised." Her focus returned to Quint, her expression guarded now. "We'll finish this discussion some other time. Alone," she added, lightly punching Pedro in the shoulder.

Alone in that damned mine.

It was a high price to pay for some one-on-one time with the boss lady.

Quint stopped by their tent to grab her clipboard before heading out to search for Cinderella's boot under the scorching afternoon sunshine. He followed the worn path through the shin-high grass to the ballcourt. Judging from the heat raining down, the Earth was spinning about six inches from the damned sun today.

He looked around, trying to imagine what it must have been like to grow up around the ruins as Angélica had. Childhood would have been full of adventures abundant with treasures, but lonely without siblings.

He'd been fortunate enough to have two sisters to give him hell, although his younger sister was seven years his junior, too far behind in age to have much of an effect on his youth. Susan had come along after his parents had separated and didn't share the same father, but his dad had adopted her later when he'd mended the marriage with their mom. Unfortunately, she'd learned the truth of her parentage and still suffered with a sharp-edged inferiority complex directed mainly at his other sister.

Only three years his junior, Violet had followed him around like a lost puppy for the first ten years of her life. His childhood memories were filled with her crazy blond curls and tomboy tricks. His heart panged a little with homesickness at the thought of her and her two kids. The next time he flew back to South Dakota, he was going to stay up in Deadwood where they were living with his favorite aunt so he could spend more time with them. Those kids were growing up too fast.

Maybe he could convince Angélica to fly home with him after this dig was over and meet his family. Or would that be moving too fast for her? Hell, he'd not only met her dad, but was now sleeping next to him each night.

Speaking of the old devil, Juan waved at Quint as he entered the narrow playing field at the ballcourt. Dr. *Diablo* was sitting on the ground under an umbrella with his bad leg stretched out in front of him, his cane resting parallel to it on the ground. Daisy was on her knees next to him, working in the dirt. All around them were squares cut into the weeds, outlined with twine.

Quint looked for Esteban, but came up empty. Juan must have relieved the boy from his ballcourt duties already.

Stopping just outside of the umbrella's shade, he glanced down at Daisy's footwear. Quint doubted the tiny woman could climb up and through that hole in the wall, but he'd wanted to double-check before marking her off the suspect list.

"Nice high-tops," he said, pretending to admire her dusty red canvas tennis shoes. "How's the support in those?" The tread was nothing even close to what he'd seen in the mine, and her foot was smaller.

"I wear inserts to help with that. Otherwise, they are like slippers, light and comfortable. Hiking boots like what Dr. García wears make my weak ankles ache."

"You should try a boot like this," Juan jested, pointing at his fiberglass cast. "It'll make your whole leg ache."

"I'll stick with my old red tires here."

"Angélica's going to be happy when she hears what Daisy found in the weeds on her way back from lunch." Juan smiled over at his digging partner.

Quint watched Juan, noticing how his gaze lingered on Daisy's profile as she worked. Was that just a casual interest or was something more going on here under the Mexican sunshine? She was close to his age and single, not to mention in great shape and almost always cheery. Her name suited her to a T.

"What did you find now, Daisy?" he asked. "The hood ornament from a 1956 Chevy Bel Air?"

Daisy shielded her eyes, peering up at him from under her hand. "I wish! That's a sweet piece of steel. My uncle had one years ago."

"You like old cars?" Juan asked.

"The old muscle cars are more my flavor, but I wouldn't turn down a ride in a souped-up old '51 Pontiac Streamliner or '48 Chevrolet Fleetline."

Dr. *Diablo's* mouth fell open. "Where did you learn about old cars?"

She hit him with a wide smile, her own brand of sunshine. Quint could feel the warmth from where he stood. "My daddy was a mechanic. We grew up hearing about cars at the dinner table each night."

"You're just full of surprises." Juan dragged his gaze away from her, holding out his open palm toward Quint. "Daisy found Angélica's locket."

Taking the necklace, Quint opened the locket. On one side was a picture of a very young version of Angélica, probably in her young teens. The other side had an older version of Angélica, with redder hair, less-pronounced cheekbones, and a narrower face. *Marianne.* Quint had seen pictures of Angélica's mother at her house in Cancun, displayed on the walls and her desk.

"They had matching lockets," Juan explained. "Angélica must have dropped hers."

Quint looked up. The older man's smile had grown melancholy while he stared off across the ballcourt.

It must have been hell to lose his wife. Quint couldn't imagine the pain, the loneliness, or the constant ache left in her place. He'd watched the wife of another archaeologist go through something similar after her husband disappeared down in this damned jungle without a trace. She'd died decades later still alone, trying to find the missing puzzle pieces that would explain the mystery behind his death.

There was no way in hell Quint was going to let history repeat itself with Angélica.

Closing the locket, he handed it back to Juan. "I'm sure she'll be glad to have it back." He turned toward the temple where Angélica was planning to spend the afternoon. "Your daughter wanted me to remind you to rest your leg plenty this afternoon."

"She's as bossy as her mother was."

"Her mother wasn't bossy," Daisy said, cutting a long piece of twine. "She just had better ideas than you."

Juan started to laugh and then froze, doing a double take. "What did you say?"

Without looking up from where she was marking off the corners of a dig area, Daisy started to repeat her comment and then stopped. "It doesn't matter. I was just playing around. I'm sorry. I didn't mean any disrespect."

"None taken." Juan frowned as he watched Daisy line up her sifting trays and pull a well-used paintbrush from her tool pouch. "You just reminded me of something my wife used to say about being bossy." He seemed to shake off whatever had given him pause, although his smile seemed a bit dimmer than when Quint had first joined them.

Having checked out Daisy's shoes, Quint left the two and headed for the *Baatz'* Temple to look in on Jane. It took one glance at her hiking boots to cross her off the list. Her feet were way too small. Not to mention, getting through that hole would be difficult due to the snakebite that was still giving her some pain judging from the winces she made while switching sitting positions.

Lorenzo was inside with her, guiding her on how to catalog the various glyphs inside of a temple based on the good doctor's practice in the past. While Quint stood pretending to take notes, Jane asked Lorenzo about his family, at which point Quint made his exit. Angélica may have thought Jane was acting funny earlier, but it seemed the girl's only crime might be having a curious personality.

Next, he stopped over by where Fernando, Esteban, and Pedro were digging up a cache of conquistadors' armor. Quint didn't bother checking out their boots. Esteban had a history of running with his feathers flying behind him at the sight of his own shadow. There was no way the kid would have traversed that mine alone. Fernando was too busy working his ass off every day to screw around in an old mine, not to mention he had a wife and kids to think about and support. His loyalty to Angélica ran deeper than any limestone mine and its underground treasures.

"Where are Bernard, Maverick, and Gertrude?" he asked Fernando.

The foreman pointed toward the trees behind him. "There's a small tell over there." His English was not as clear as Pedro's by far, but he was still easy enough to understand.

Through an opening in the trees, Quint could see Bernard and Gertrude. They were working along the edge of what he'd guess was a five-feet-high broad mound of dirt and vines, bordered by a large strangler fig tree.

"They are working on scraping off the top layer," Fernando added.

If Quint remembered right from his reading while up in the frigid land of ice and polar bears, a "tell" was a mound that grew as one generation after another built over whatever was there in the past. Tells caused a lot of excitement in the archaeology world because they often had layer after layer of artifacts, including building materials, pottery shards, tools, and more. To Quint and— he figured—the rest of the world not infatuated with the past, they looked like just another mound or hill.

"Dr. García is having them start on that mound instead of continuing Pedro's work on that small tell down near the *Chakmo'ol* Temple?"

That sounded like busywork to him, especially when there was so much work to be done yet with the two main temples.

"She doesn't want the university kids near the snakes," Fernando explained, taking a draw from his canteen.

Right, the snakes. Quint wondered if her father had had a say in making her decision. "What about Maverick?"

Capping his canteen, Fernando thumbed in the direction of the mess tent. "Teodoro took him to the river. They are hauling water for showers and María. Today she washes our clothes."

That was where his pile of dirty clothes had gone. He'd need to thank María after supper. His pants were beginning to walk on their own, and he was down to his last pair of underwear. Another day and he'd have to start going commando.

"When they are done with water," Fernando continued, "Maverick will help me, and Esteban will return to the ballcourt."

Quint would have to take a look at the fiction author's boots another time. With a "Be right back," Quint trekked through the opening in the trees toward Bernard and Gertrude. Both were on their hands and knees, carefully digging with trowels into the top of the mound.

"How's it going over here?" Quint asked. "Are you two any closer to finding that treasure chest of Maya gold the Spanish conquistadors were determined to dig up somewhere around these parts?"

Bernard laughed and sat back on his knees, swiping away the sweat dripping from his eyebrows. "Nothing but dirt and dead leaves for me, but Gertrude found a broken pottery shard."

"I read somewhere that tells are often garbage heaps." Quint played dumb to try to make conversation.

"Garbage heaps of gold when it comes to information about how people lived," Bernard explained.

"But still garbage," Gertrude added, standing up to stretch with her back to Quint. She pulled out her canteen and took a swig. Then she took off her broad-rimmed sombrero, drew her blond hair into a ponytail and lifted it up, and splashed her face and neck. Water ran down a tattoo that covered the nape of her neck. From where Quint stood, it looked like a sun with a skeleton face in the middle. She lowered her hair and plopped her hat back onto her head.

Quint shook his head. How in the world the girl kept from burning with skin so pale was beyond him. Even with the hat and long sleeves, he would think her chalky-white skin should have some color—tan or red—after spending day in and day out under the hot Mexican sun. If it weren't for her dark eyes, she could have been an albino.

"Damn, it's hot today," Bernard said, leaning back against the mound, kicking his legs out in front of him. "We rarely ever even come close to this kind of heat in England."

Quint peeked down at Bernard's boots. His peek turned into an all-out stare. "Nice boots. They look brand-new."

"They are," Gertrude said.

Quint glanced over to find her watching him with an intensity that gave him pause. She'd been staring across the fire at him with a similar level of attention during the *Lolcatali* ceremony. When he raised his brows in return, she turned back toward Bernard.

Bernard shot her a chagrined look. "My boots up and walked away last night, so I had to borrow Gertrude's extra pair." He lifted his leg and held one boot out for Quint's view.

"Did you file a missing-boots report?" Quint joked, noticing the straight lines on the tread prints at Bernard's feet. The boot prints in the mine had been wavy.

"I thought you have to wait twenty-four hours before filing," Bernard said, playing along.

Quint's focus turned to Gertrude's well-worn hikers. They looked almost identical to Bernard's, only more worn. "You two wear the same size, huh?"

"I come from a family of men with smaller feet and hands." Bernard held up his hands, thin but short fingers splayed.

Gertrude capped her water and set it on the ground. "My feet are big for a woman. My *mutter* always said I should have been a man." Her hands were big, too. She would be able to carry several large steins of German beer without spilling a drop.

"You're too pretty to be a man," Bernard said, flirting. "You're a pale, Amazonian beauty who's come to carry me away to your jungle paradise."

Gertrude laughed. "And you're a skinny Casanova."

Quint left them, joking back and forth under the jungle canopy and made his way back to Fernando and Esteban, who were busy taking notes on the exact location of what looked like a broken piece of armor breastplate.

Pedro waved him over to the side, leading him several steps away, and asked in a lowered voice, "Any luck with the boot prints?"

"No, but Bernard says his boots are missing, which is one hell of a coincidence."

"I thought his boots looked new when he walked past."

"They are, but they're not his, they're Gertrude's spare pair. Apparently, Bernard didn't think to pack extra."

"Gertrude's boots?"

"She has big feet for a woman."

"She is taller than I like my women. You only have an inch or two on her."

"I'd certainly put money on her over you in a leg-wrestling match."

Pedro chuckled. "I would, too. Have you seen her eat? She's twice the man I am at the table." He sobered. "You think Bernard ditched his boots in the jungle so we couldn't match the prints?"

"Maybe."

"What else could it be?"

"Someone wants to throw us off their scent and is setting Bernard up to take the fall."

Several curses rolled off Pedro's tongue.

Quint nodded, smashing a mosquito that landed on his arm. It always sounded so much more melodic when people cursed in Spanish.

"Now what?"

Shrugging, he frowned out across the courtyard toward where the *Chakmo'ol* Temple waited with Angélica inside. "We see if your pilot buddy's logbook is any help."

"That may take a couple of days, though."

"I don't doubt it. Until then, maybe we can figure out how to connect the damned dots to see if someone sneaking into an old mine has anything to do with a murder plot."

Chapter Eighteen

Baak: The Maya glyph for "captive."

"Hold up, boss lady," Quint called.

Angélica cringed. *Shit!* He'd seen her.

She waited for him under the hot afternoon sunshine, preparing mentally for battle while Quint crossed the plaza to join her. She had little doubt how the next ten minutes were going to go after she came clean about her plan.

He'd just have to accept what was going to happen, because short of him throwing her over his shoulder and carrying her away from the *Chakmo'ol* Temple, she wasn't going to let him stop her.

Quint reached her side, a frown wrinkling his forehead as he looked down at her. "Where are you going with your dad's bag of safety equipment?"

"I found something. You can follow or not, up to you." She continued her trek across the plaza toward the temple, glancing over toward the ballcourt to make sure her father wasn't watching.

"What did you find?" He kept her hurried pace with ease thanks to his long legs. "Something inside the temple?"

"I'm not sure it's technically inside of the temple itself."

"That sounds purposely vague." He held out her clipboard. "Here, trade me for the bag."

"It's not that heavy."

"Let me play the hero for a moment. Don't worry, nobody is watching."

She squinted over at him. "You're not going to try to stop me, are you?"

"I don't think I could. You appear to have one hell of a head of steam built up. Besides, I'm sort of curious what has you all in a lather."

She handed off the bag, taking the clipboard. "Did you get anywhere with the boot prints mystery?"

"Sort of, but not."

"That's an ambiguous answer."

"I'm taking lessons from you."

She chuckled, slowing as they rounded the platform where Jane had been bitten by the snake. "I don't want to tell you what I found because I'm afraid you'll try to interfere with my plans."

"Me? Aren't you the boss at this dig site?"

"Technically, yes." She peeked over at him as she stepped inside the *Chakmo'ol* Temple's entrance. "But your opinion counts."

His deep laughter bounced off the interior stone walls of the temple. "Right. Since when?"

She stopped, facing him. "Since you came back for more."

His eyes lowered to her lips. "I couldn't stay away."

"Yes, you could have, but you didn't. For that, you get a say in matters here."

"A say?" His gaze lifted, a smile growing on his lips. "Does that mean I get to play boss once in a while when it comes to you?"

"Don't push your luck, Parker."

"How about when we're alone in our tent?"

She pursed her lips, pretending to consider his words. "Maybe."

She started to turn away, but he caught her arm and pulled her back around, drawing her close. "Kiss me, Dr. García."

"Is that an order, boss man?"

"Yes."

She grabbed his shirt in her fist and pulled him down to her level. "One kiss in exchange for your help this afternoon."

"Two kisses."

"Fine." She kissed him, soft and slow, enjoying the way he made her stomach flutter when he stroked his tongue along hers. When she released his shirt and stepped back, she blew out a shaky breath. "Wow."

"Damn, that just makes me want more." He shook his head as if to clear it. "Now, didn't it feel good to let go of some of that control?"

Not as good as it had the other night when he'd rocked her world in their tent. She was going to need another hit of that drug soon. "Maybe," she said, having fun with him. She turned and headed deeper into the temple.

"Hey, we're not done." He caught up with her. "The deal was for two kisses."

"Exactly. One kiss now and the other when you finish the job I have for you."

"Ha! You've been schooled by your father in the art of deal making."

"The dark lord trained me well and don't you forget it." She led him past the chamber with the snake-outlined *Yum Cimil* carving.

His footfalls paused. "Aren't we going in there?"

She shook her head, continuing toward the small burial room where she'd learned his theory about her mother's murder. "I figured out the mystery."

"Which particular mystery are we talking about? We seem to have several going at the moment."

"The one carved into the wall in the other chamber that shows *Yum Cimil* down in a cave." She stooped and entered the small burial tomb. "I know where the entrance to his cave is."

He lingered outside of the low-ceilinged room. "Great. Shouldn't we bar the door? Put a few really big rocks in front of it? Run the other way?"

Underlying his humor, she could sense his hesitation. She knew from the past dig site that holes inside these temples made him twitchy. "You don't have to stay in here." But she didn't want him to leave. She took the bag from him and set it against the wall. "However, I'll remind you that you did make a deal to help me."

He muttered something.

"What's that, Parker?" She joined him outside of the burial chamber, looking up at him with a raised brow.

"I said that you're my sunshine in these dark, claustrophobic hellholes, sweetheart."

She laughed. "Good answer, lover boy." She patted him on the chest. "Seriously, all I need you to do is help me move this altar stone aside. I can do the rest on my own."

His hand covered hers, holding it against him. "If I promise to be your sex slave for the next month, would you consider *not* moving that altar stone?"

She shook her head. "A month isn't long enough."

"You drive a hard bargain, lady. Let's move that stone before I give in to my inner caveman and drag you out of here by the hair."

She stooped again and moved inside. He followed, lowering himself onto his knees when he reached the altar stone. "How do we move this without breaking something?"

"Both the top stone and base are thick. I doubt they'll break."

"I was talking about me, not the stones."

She stared at him as he inspected the underside of the top altar stone. What was it about him? Sure, he was funny, caring, sexy even when coated in dirt and sweat, and great in the sack, but there was something else that she couldn't put her finger on. Something that had her heart teetering dangerously close to the edge of an abyss. Before it could take a leap into never-never land, she needed to wrangle the damned organ. Quint might leave after all of this and not come back for a third round. She needed to be prepared for that possibility.

"We could take the top stone off and lay it over there," he suggested.

She shook off her dark thoughts. "You read my mind, Parker. Between the two of us, we should be able to push this lower stone aside far enough to see if I'm right."

"Right about what, exactly?"

"That there's a hole behind this altar that leads down into a subterranean room of some sort."

His hazel eyes met hers. "A room where *Yum Cimil* is hanging out in that carving?"

"Yes."

"Shouldn't we be concerned about letting him out?"

"Quint, that's just a tall tale carved into a wall."

"Are you sure?"

"Yes."

"But are you *really* sure?"

"Just lift the damned stone."

On the count of three, they did, tipping it onto its narrow edge, taking care not to damage the carvings. "Watch your fingers," he warned, holding it up long enough for her to get clear before leaning it against the opposite wall.

He brushed his hands on his pants, crawling back over to the larger square bottom stone. "Which way do you want to push this?"

"I was thinking toward the doorway. That would allow us to use that wall to push off. Better leverage that way."

"Okay, but that's going to make for a tight exit."

"You think you'll fit?"

"One way or another." He squeezed past her in the tight quarters, moving into position with his back to the bottom stone and his boots braced against the wall.

"You need to make room for me," she told him.

"Just stay back, boss lady."

He pressed his feet into the wall and pushed with his back. The stone shifted several inches toward the doorway.

Quint leaned forward so she could see past him to the wall behind the stone. Her pulse leapt. She'd been right about the hidden entrance!

A hint of something foul smelling leaked up through the hole along with a breath of air.

"Do you smell that?" she asked, sitting back.

"Yeah. Maybe we should put the stone back."

She wrinkled her nose at him. "Good try, Parker."

Several shoves later, the block cleared the hole. Quint moved out of her way, peering down into the darkness along with her. Her flashlight beam didn't reach far.

What was down there? Was it a tomb belonging to a king from a Maya dynasty? Had this temple been built over another, older one? Was this the doorway into a buried past? Her mind whirled with so many possibilities.

"That smell isn't getting any better," Quint said. "Do you see any boogeymen down there?"

"It's too dark."

"That's comforting."

Cursing her foolishness, she reached in her dad's bag and pulled out his air quality meter, handing it to Quint. "Do me a favor and make sure there's nothing noxious blowing out of there."

"What do you call that underlying stench?"

"The smell of life."

"It reeks more like death, if you ask me." He played with the meter, checking for different types of gases as she collected her flashlight, gas mask, and the rope she'd brought along.

"It's all clear," Quint said, lowering the meter. He directed his light down the hole. "It looks like it's about a forty-five percent grade. What do you think they ..." He turned and saw the rope laying on the floor next to her knees. "What's that for?"

"Me." She slipped the mask over her head, letting it dangle from her neck.

His eyes narrowed. "No, Angélica."

"I'm not asking, Quint." She pulled her tactical rappel harness from the bag, sliding it through the belt hoops on her khakis, cinching it good and tight.

He watched with a growing frown as she connected the leg loops and secured them in place. "Don't do this."

"Don't worry. I've rappelled many times before. This isn't my first rodeo." She threaded and secured the rope as she'd done many times in the past before rappelling down into *cenotes*. "Can you grab my Taser out of Dad's bag?"

He gaped at her. "Do you hear yourself?"

She grabbed the Taser herself, hooking it in the loop on her belt made for a firearm. She didn't figure she'd need it, but it was better to be safe than sorry at this site. "I'll tug twice on the rope when I need you to pull me up."

"This is bat-shit insane."

She took the air quality meter and looped it around her neck along with her mask. "I'll be careful."

"Let me go down there first," he said.

She shook her head. "Your shoulders are too big. It'll be a tight squeeze, and we both know how you feel about small spaces." She secured her rappelling hard hat, tightening the chinstrap.

"Then wait and let someone else go down. Lorenzo's shoulders aren't much bigger than yours."

"I can't send any of my crew down that hole and you know it." She grabbed her backup shatterproof flashlight and stuck it in the cargo pocket on the side of her leg next to her dad's cheap digital camera. After doing a quick mental check that she had everything she'd need to scout out the sub chamber, she tugged on her rappelling rope-gloves.

"God damn it, woman." He blocked the tunnel with his body, leaning back against the wall with his long legs out in front of him. "I can't let you do this. It's too dangerous."

"Quint, listen," she said, crawling over to him, straddling his thighs. She squeezed his shoulders, trying to reassure him. "I promise I'll go slow and not do anything rash."

"We don't know what's down there."

"That's why I need to go see."

"Your father would never let you go down there."

"He might try to talk me out of it, but he wouldn't stand in my way if I insisted on going."

He shook his head, his face lined with worry. "What if you slip?"

"I've closed the system." She held up the end of the rope, showing the triple-barrel knot she'd tied there. "Plus, I have a friction hitch with a blocker knot below it."

"You're speaking Greek to me."

"It means I'll only fall a short distance before the rope stops me."

"What if the ceiling is unstable in there and you bring the whole damned temple down on your head?"

"Then we'll both be dead."

"That's not funny, Angélica."

She took his hand in hers, kissing his knuckles. "I appreciate that you are concerned about me, but trust me, this isn't my first time rappelling down a dark hole."

"That's supposed to comfort me?"

She smiled. "I'll be okay. Admit it, deep down inside you're curious what's down that hole."

He stared at her, his jaw rigid. "I'll make you a deal."

"I'm all ears."

"You can go down that hole if you agree to go somewhere with me, no questions asked."

"Where?"

"No questions asked," he reiterated.

Oh, secretive. Nice. As long as it was with him, she was game. "Okay."

"*And* I want that second kiss now in case you end up liking it down there and decide to stay." When she didn't agree right away, he added, "Deal or no deal, Angélica."

With a shrug, she cupped his face in her gloved hands. "Deal." She kissed him, same as before, except this time he held onto her tighter, drawing out the kiss longer. When he let go, she sat back.

Her lips tingled, among other areas of her body. "Parker, have I ever told you that you're a marvelous kisser?"

"You're not so bad yourself, boss lady." He shifted under her. "Now get off me and get that sweet little ass down into that hole."

She finished prepping for the descent, giving herself about ten feet of rope length to fall if her other safety measures failed. Quint double-checked her lines to his satisfaction and then wrapped his end of the rope around the big bottom altar stone for leverage.

"Okay, sweetheart, you're ready."

She climbed into the hole feet first and then flipped onto her stomach, sliding down so only her head was sticking out. She smiled at Quint, excitement churning in her stomach. "Don't let go of that rope," she ordered.

"I got you, babe," he sang in a falsetto.

She groaned. "I'm going to kick your butt for that earworm when I get back up here."

"Be careful, Angélica," he said, suddenly serious. "Let's not repeat the past here today."

She blew him a kiss, slipped on the mask, and then inched backward down the smooth slope into the darkness. She'd tucked in her shirt to keep from scraping her stomach, but her elbows took a beating as she slid deeper and deeper.

"How you doing?" Quint called down.

"My feet just hit open air." She let the rope hold her weight as her knees and then thighs joined her feet in mid-air. She stopped herself then, turning and shining her flashlight down past her legs. The stench was worse down here, making her wish she'd brought nose plugs.

"Can you see anything?" he asked.

"Hold on." She squinted in the semi-darkness. The floor was about twelve feet below the edge of the hole—far down enough to get stuck if she didn't have the rope to climb back out. Why was the floor blurry looking? Was that water? What was that piled in the far corner?

Pocketing her flashlight, she slid fully out of the chute. The rope creaked as she dangled there in the dark. With a shove, she pushed away from the wall and turned so her back was to it. Before she scouted the chamber, she lifted the gas reader, punching the buttons, making sure she was in the green.

Something bumped the rope hanging below her.

She stilled, lowering the meter, listening in the darkness. What was that sound? It was like a smooth crinkling noise mixed with a soft swooshing.

Plucking her flashlight from her pocket, she spotlighted the floor.

There was no water.

"You've got to be fucking kidding me."

At the sound of her voice, the rattling started.

* * *

"It was an Indiana Jones moment," Angélica said later that evening in their tent. "You should have seen all the snakes."

I'd rather not, Quint thought.

He lay in his new hammock in a clean T-shirt and boxer briefs with his hands behind his head, listening as the crazy woman retold her adventures in that underground chamber to her father and Pedro.

Her eyes sparkled as she paced back and forth in front of them. Her hands were animated as she described the various small piles of broken bones that she'd seen from where she hung at the end of the chute, safely out of reach of the slithering bodies and venomous fangs below.

Juan shuddered, echoing Quint's feelings about all of those damned snakes. "*Dios mio, gatita.*" Her father covered his face, speaking through his fingers. "You should have waited for me to get there as we'd planned. You're going to be the death of your old man."

"That's what I told her when I pulled her out of there," Quint said, crossing his ankles. The hammock rocked gently, cradling him. Pedro was right. This was much better than a cot. Next he'd like to kick everyone out of the tent except a certain snake charmer and spend an hour or two ravishing the hell out of her in his new hammock.

Stuck holding the rope in that sardine can called a tomb for too many sweat-filled minutes as Angélica risked life and limb down in the darkness had pushed his calm to the limit. Her rope tugs to haul her back up hadn't come soon enough for his sanity. He'd dragged her out of that hole and hugged her long and hard, until she'd gasped for breath.

"How many bones are we talking?" Pedro asked.

She shrugged. "I couldn't tell. There were too many snakes moving around, covering the bones. It was hard to get a handle on how many skeletons might be down there."

"We're lucky you didn't add one more today," Juan said dryly.

"Dad, I told you that I made sure I was safe." She pointed at Quint. "Plus, Parker here was at the other end making sure I wasn't going anywhere but up."

Quint had wanted to haul her out of there as soon as she'd hollered up the hole that the floor was covered with rattlesnakes, but she'd insisted he let her scope out the space some more and try to take a few pictures. Pictures that turned out blurry and dark, of course, since all she had was her dad's cheap digital camera.

"Tell them about the wall," Quint said, letting the sway of the hammock soothe him after an afternoon that had probably taken ten years off his life.

The depth of his fear about losing Angélica down that hole had made him realize how far gone he was when it came to her. While he sat there holding that damned rope, he realized there'd be no leaving the Yucatán now, at least not for more than a few weeks at a time. High humidity, bugs, and howling monkeys were going to be a way of life. He was going to have to figure out if he wanted to sell or lease out his place up in South Dakota.

"There was a walled-up hole down there," Angélica told Pedro and her dad. "It reminded me of the wall in the mine. The style was similar with stones and grout."

"You could see the grout from your wall perch?" Juan asked doubtfully. "What are you? Part hawk now?"

"Of course I couldn't see it clearly, Dad, but I could tell there was grout between the stones."

Pedro leaned against the center pole, crossing his arms over his chest. "You think the mine and the *Chakmo'ol* Temple are connected by some underground passage?"

"I don't know, maybe." She grabbed her canteen from the floor. "Maybe not. But the similar building style of that wall could link the underground chamber to the mine on the Maya timeline. I'd have to go down in there again and take a grout sample to be certain."

"No!" Juan beat Quint to the punch. "You are not going in there with all of those snakes again, *gatita*. I forbid it. If something were to happen to you, we'd have no way of getting you out quickly."

Angélica's eyes narrowed, her mouth tightening at her father's heavy hand.

Quint and Juan appeared to be reading from the same playbook, only Quint had known better than to out-and-out say "I forbid it" to the stubborn woman. His solution was to squeeze down in that hole himself next time. He'd let her hold the damned rope for once. No, better yet, Pedro.

Before Angélica started spitting and sputtering at her father, Quint prompted her with, "Tell them about the snakes."

She glanced in his direction as she unscrewed the cap on her canteen, her gaze traveling the length of his bare legs before returning to his face. "What about the snakes?"

"How they were getting into the chamber."

Turning back to her dad and Pedro, she explained, "There was a stone-lined tunnel about a foot in diameter at the base of one of the walls. It was full of snakes."

"Stone-lined?" Juan asked. "So it was meant to be a drainage of some sort."

She nodded. "Either the chamber used to flood or they purposely created an entryway for the snakes."

"Why would they create a way for snakes to get in?" Pedro asked.

Quint had wondered the same thing, imagining how it would feel to be stuck down in that chamber with an open-door policy set up for rattlesnakes.

"I don't know," Angélica said, "but on that carving in the other room, the image of *Yum Cimil* is sitting on a throne of snakes, remember?"

"He's also outlined by snakes," Quint said, repeating what Angélica and he had discussed while she slipped out of her rappelling gear and stowed it all back in her father's bag.

"Two walls," her father repeated, apparently still focused on that part of her tale. "What were they walling inside the room?"

Quint draped one bare leg over the edge of the hammock, swinging it slightly. "Or were they keeping something out? Something they dug up deep in the mine?"

"You've seen too many movies, Parker."

That was true, but he'd also seen a few inexplicable things in his travels. Things that gave him chills when he witnessed them. But those tales were for another time.

"You're sure the bones were broken?" Pedro asked her. "In the same condition Quint described in that catacomb back in the mine?"

She nodded, taking a drink from her canteen. "Those I could clearly see were broken. There was a small pile of them stacked up in the corner, including several skulls, which appeared to be missing chunks or were broken in half."

"Do you think they were holding prisoners captive down there?"

"Yes," she said.

Juan frowned at her. "How can you be so sure?"

"Look." She picked up her notebook and held it out to him, pointing at a part of the carving she'd copied down on the paper. "See that right there? That's the *baak* glyph. It stands for 'captive.'"

Juan took the notebook, grimacing down at it. "You're sure about the meaning of this?"

"Yes, and I'll tell you something else. If you were to slide down that chute, you're not getting back out without a rope or a pair of tall shoulders to stand up on."

"Unless you went out through the tunnel they walled up," Pedro said.

"Well, yes, there was that escape."

"But there were skeletons in the room," Juan said. "So not everyone escaped."

"Maybe those were the snakes' victims," Pedro said.

"Juan." Quint looked over at the older man's lined face. "Have you ever heard of the Maya keeping their sacrificial victims in an underground prison?"

"No. But I suppose it could have happened."

"Broken bones?" Pedro asked again. When she nodded, he looked at Quint. "And you're positive the ones you saw were broken, too?"

"Yep."

"Why? What are you thinking?" Angélica asked him.

Pedro grimaced. "Years ago, I remember reading an article about a tribe of cannibals in the Amazon. Human bone marrow was a delicacy for them. The article said that after they finished with the flesh, they would break the bones and suck out the marrow. The journalist called it their dessert."

"Cannibals?" Quint glanced over at Angélica. "What do you think, boss lady? Could you have picked a site with an even more grisly past than human sacrifices?"

"There certainly are a lot of broken bones at this site." She sat down on her cot. "But what's with all of the snakes, both now and in the past?"

"Maybe the ruler at the time all this was going on had a snake fetish," Pedro suggested.

"What do you think, Dad?"

Juan puffed his cheeks and blew out a breath. "I don't know what to think. Add to this that cache of conquistador armor and all of the artifacts Daisy keeps finding ..." He snapped his fingers. "That reminds me. I have something for you, *gatita*." He opened his footlocker and pulled out the locket he'd shown Quint earlier, dangling it out toward Angélica.

"What's this?" she asked, taking the locket. She opened it, staring down at the pictures. "Where did you get this, Dad?" she whispered, swallowing visibly.

"Daisy found it in the weeds at the edge of the ballcourt. You're lucky she stumbled onto it."

Angélica's face seemed to pale, her eyes widening. She closed her fingers around it, her gaze flitting to Quint's. Something in her expression made him stop rocking. "What's wrong?"

She chewed on her lower lip. "Nothing. I'm fine. It's ... it's nothing. I just miss my mom."

"I told you this place was going to be tough for you, *gatita*." Juan pulled on his red scorpion socks. "Lord knows it's getting under my skin, making me imagine all sorts of crazy stuff."

"I need to use the restroom," Angélica said suddenly, sliding the locket under her pillow. She grabbed her machete and flashlight. "Parker, do you mind walking me down there?"

"I can go with you," Pedro offered.

She patted his shoulder. "Thanks, but I'd sort of like a little alone time with Quint, if you know what I mean."

Her reply made Quint sit up. What was going on? First of all, Angélica had used the latrine when they'd gone down to shower before this little get-together in their tent. Second, she'd normally not be so blatant about wanting to get him alone.

"What do you say, Parker?" she asked. "You feel like putting your pants back on?"

He nodded. "Let me shake out my boots."

The moon was high in the sky as they walked silently through the weeds, coloring the world in shades of silver. The flashlight lit the path down to the latrines.

"Are you okay?" he asked after they were out of earshot of the tents.

"Not really."

"What is it? Something to do with the hidden chamber?" The idea of those poor prisoners suffering such a cruel fate certainly gave him goose bumps.

"That locket Dad gave me isn't mine."

"But it has your picture in it." When she looked over at him, he explained. "He showed it to me earlier when I checked up on Daisy at the ballcourt."

"My locket is hanging on my dresser in Cancun."

"What?"

"The one Daisy found was my mom's. She bought us matching lockets for my thirteenth birthday."

He caught her hand, squeezing it. "I'm sorry, sweetheart."

"I didn't even realize she'd brought her locket here with her on that trip. I figured it was back home in Tucson with the rest of her stuff we boxed up."

No wonder Angélica had paled so much when Juan handed it to her.

They walked in silence for a few steps, his hand still holding hers. The weeds crunched underfoot, seeming louder than usual in the darkness.

Angélica cleared her throat. "Do you find it odd that Daisy just stumbled upon Mom's locket? What are the chances of that?"

"Pretty low, although it is shiny. I'm surprised one of the monkeys around here didn't ..." Quint stopped, pulling her up short. "Listen," he whispered.

Angélica frowned up at him. "What do you hear?"

"Nothing." As in none of the usual jungle cacophony raging around them. The forest was oddly silent. "It's too quiet."

"Shit." She unsheathed her machete. "There must be a big cat prowling nearby."

Quint scanned the tree line with his flashlight.

"We should go back," Angélica whispered.

"I thought you had to go to the bathroom."

"I lied. I just wanted to tell you about the locket without my dad hearing."

A deep, guttural growl came from the thick brush to their left. The cat couldn't be more than twenty feet away from the sound of it.

He pushed Angélica behind him, backing slowly toward the tents.

"Quint," she said, her voice edged with tension. "That doesn't sound like a cat."

"What else could it be?"

"I'm afraid to find out."

A loud hiss made his breath catch. The roar that followed nearly burst his heart.

He spotlighted the trees, catching glimpses of spots as a jaguar raced through the bushes. It dove into the brush on the other side of the latrines and disappeared into the jungle.

Before he could register what he'd just seen, something else crashed through the brush after the cat. Something big ... and fast. He pointed his flashlight in the direction of the hunter, catching sight of its haunches as it chased after the cat.

"What the fuck was that?" he asked as the sound of the two racing through the underbrush faded.

"I don't know. Something really big with black fur on the back of its neck." She grabbed his wrist and tugged on him. "Let's get back to the others."

They started up the path.

A loud roar echoed, followed by a piercing yowl.

The hair on the back of Quint's neck stood up. He stopped, frowning toward the dark tree line. "Holy shit! Was that the jaguar?"

"I think so," she whispered.

After a few seconds, the jungle racketed back to normal life around them.

"Come on." She towed him along, jogging now with her machete at the ready. "We need to get to Teodoro's tent."

"Why Teodoro's tent?" Quint wasn't sure one of the shaman's ceremonies could protect them from whatever took down that jaguar.

"Because that's where we keep Pedro's shotgun."

Chapter Nineteen

Baak: (Also) The Maya glyph for "bone."

The sun rose the next morning without giving light to any answers to the questions that had pestered Angélica throughout most of the long, dark night.

She climbed out of her cot shortly after the ball of fire popped up over the horizon, dressing quietly as her dad slept. She was ready to play detective now that she could see under the forest canopy.

She'd pondered the scene down by the latrines too many times to count since returning to her tent late last night, trying to figure out what she'd seen chasing that jaguar. It was all a blur. A hulking black blur that had been hunting a 150- to 200-pound, sharp-clawed cat. Besides humans, jaguars and the other large Mesoamerican cats were the top predators down here.

Maybe it had been just another cat, only bigger. The jaguar could've been a female, the predator a male. The moon was known to play tricks with shapes, too. But the creature's fur had seemed longer than a regular cat's, and its gait less graceful. The growling sound right before the jaguar had hissed was like nothing she'd heard outside of a movie theater. It reminded her of the pre-rumbles of an angry gorilla's roar when it was about to engage in a fight, only raspier. However, unless someone had recently misplaced their gorilla, great apes didn't frequent the Mexican jungle.

So what in the hell was it?

Maybe Teodoro would have some ideas after his trip into the

jungle today. Paw or footprints might shed light on the beast.

She grabbed her canteen and headed for breakfast, her father stirring as she zipped the mesh flap closed.

Quint was already in the mess tent nursing a cup of coffee when she stepped inside, his eyes edged with fatigue.

She did her best to act normal around the other early birds as she stood in line to load up a plate of food, pretending she hadn't been up most of the night listening for the sound of that creature returning to the dig site for a second helping.

Jane and Daisy weren't there yet, but Bernard and Gertrude were already eating. Lorenzo and Esteban dished up in front of her, while Fernando filed in behind her.

After handing her empty canteen to María to refill while she ate, Angélica grabbed a plate full of eggs and black beans, fried plantains, and yellow corn tortillas. María had made a traditional Maya breakfast for them. In spite of her anxiety, the smell of the delicious food had Angélica's stomach eager to eat. She dug into her steaming breakfast as soon as she sat down next to Quint and his empty plate.

"Tired much?" she asked him in between bites.

Even his smile looked worn out. "With enough coffee, I'll make it to lunch, but then I'll be needing a *siesta*."

Quint had offered to keep guard with Pedro last night while the rest of the camp slept. Part of her tossing and turning throughout the night had been due to the two of them being out in the darkness with only one shotgun and two machetes to defend themselves.

"Did your dad notice I wasn't there last night?"

She shook her head. "After we told him about the cat fight, he rolled over and went to sleep."

They'd decided to keep what they really saw under wraps except for Pedro and Teodoro, claiming the commotion was two big cats fighting, nothing more. Until they could get a better handle of what exactly the hunter was, she didn't want to worry her father. He might insist on helping keep guard and injure his leg further while out and about in the dark.

"He's probably shaving now. You might want to think up some explanation for your beard stubble, since it appears you beat him up and out of the tent this morning."

Quint nodded, frowning at his coffee. "I've thought a lot about what we saw last night."

"Yeah?"

"I can't figure it out. What could run down a jaguar that easily?" he asked, spinning his mug around slowly. "You and I were sitting ducks out there. It could have taken one of us in a heartbeat."

"Maybe it didn't want us."

"Why not?"

"I don't know." She scooped up some eggs with her tortilla. "Where's Pedro?"

"Sleeping. He spelled me for an hour in the middle of the night when I couldn't keep my eyes open anymore. As soon as it started getting light, I told him to crash for a few hours, that I'd cover for him."

"What about Teodoro?"

"He woke Maverick at first light and they went into the forest to gather some water and herbs. They took Rover along on the leash."

"Rover? Why?"

"He believes your javelina might sniff out trouble for them."

Javelinas had bad eyesight, but they had good hearing and a keen sense of smell. Rover should be able to alert them well ahead of danger.

"Teodoro told me he's going to head out in the direction we saw the jaguar run and see what the forest spirits tell him about what happened."

She paused mid-chew, swallowing. "Did he tell you this in front of Maverick?"

"No."

"Good."

The shaman had been worried last night when she'd described what little bit she saw of the creature to him. He'd told her that he'd run into another older Maya man in the forest a couple days ago while collecting water and been warned that this site had a bad history. At the time, Teodoro had figured it had something to do with the deaths of Marianne and the pilot, but now he suspected there was an older evil living under the forest floor. Angélica's find under the *Chakmo'ol* Temple yesterday afternoon had made him even more certain of this.

Thinking about that underground chamber had led her to remember something else in the middle of the night.

"How about you come with me to the *Chakmo'ol* Temple this morning?"

His gaze narrowed. "Please tell me you aren't thinking of going down in that hole again."

"Not the hole, only the upper chamber that has the wall carving of *Yum Cimil* and his snake throne. I want to go over those glyphs again."

"Okay. What do you need me to do?"

"Catch up on your beauty sleep while I work. You can use my backpack as a pillow."

His forehead wrinkled. "I thought we were going down into the mine this morning."

"Not until you get some sleep. Plus, if you're in the temple with me, Dad won't catch you snoozing on the job because he'll be busy supervising everyone at the other end of the site. I'll tell him that Pedro and you are both helping me this morning." Actually, that was true. Since midnight, both Quint and Pedro had been helping her keep an eye on the crew.

"How long do you think we can hide this from him?"

"Not long. Until we see if Teodoro returns with any new details, we need to—"

"He's here," Quint interrupted, smiling and waving at her father.

"Lay low," she finished and returned to her breakfast, wolfing down the second tortilla while it was still warm.

For the next twenty minutes, Angélica pretended last night had been like the others before it. Quint hid a couple of yawns behind his coffee cup, telling Juan that he'd woken up early, been unable to fall back to sleep, and decided to head out to watch the sun rise. He'd given some excuse about being too lazy to shave. As far as she could tell, her dad bought Quint's story.

Daisy joined them ten minutes later, asking Angélica if her father had given her the locket. Angélica's smile felt brittle as she thanked her. She tried not to stare at the other woman, sneaking peeks under her eyelashes. How Daisy had just stumbled onto that locket had Angélica rattling with suspicion. She wanted to return to Cancun and perform a full-fledged background check on the woman. She wouldn't be at all surprised to find out that Daisy had been to this site before and worked alongside Marianne.

When Angélica finished eating, Quint took her plate over to the wash bucket, where Gertrude joined him. She said something to him that made Quint stop and frown for a moment. Then he returned to the table with Angélica's canteen in hand.

"You ready, boss lady?"

Her father lowered his fork, eyeing each in turn. "Where are you two off to so soon this morning?"

"I want his help clearing some of the platform stones around the *Chakmo'ol* Temple." Okay, that was a lie, but a harmless one.

"She's calling in the big muscles," Daisy said, winking at Quint.

Juan's narrowed gaze clearly relayed his concerns. "You're not going to do any more exploring in that temple today, are you?"

"I'm going inside of the temple, but only to do some basic rubbing and charting." She kissed him on the forehead. "Don't worry, Papa," she whispered, using her childhood name for him. "I'll be safe."

He squeezed her hand. "You better, *gatita*." As she followed Quint out into the morning sunshine, her dad called after them, "And play nice with that boy, too."

Quint chuckled, putting his arm around her shoulders as they walked toward their tent. "You hear that? I get to have some playtime with you today."

"Yeah, but not until you take your nap."

They stopped by their tent. While he changed into fresh clothes, she filled her backpack with her notebook, some rice paper and charcoal, and a few shirts to give it some cushion for Quint. Grabbing her tool pouch, her dad's duffel bag of safety supplies, and the refilled canteen on the way out, she led the way across the plaza to the temple.

Insects circled their legs in the early morning heat. Quint followed her more slowly than usual, obviously feeling the effects of the long night. Inside the temple, he wasted no time sliding to the floor in the corner of the chamber, setting her sheathed machete on the floor next to him.

She pulled out her notebook and rubbing tools, taking her pack over to him.

"Move forward, please."

He did as told and then leaned against her backpack after she'd settled it behind him. He caught her hand before she could return to her tools. "Thanks, sweetheart."

"Don't thank me yet. I might get bored and decide to mess with you while you sleep."

He smiled, and kissed the back of her hand before letting it go. Then he leaned his head against the wall and closed his eyes. "If you decide to molest me while I'm out, please be gentle. I'm just an innocent prairie boy."

She stared down at him for a few seconds, admiring his rugged features. That dark beard stubble added an extra layer of sexiness. Maybe he should keep it when they returned to civilization.

One of his eyes opened. "You had better be here with me when I wake up. Sleeping in a creepy chamber covered with carvings about a lord of death while a bunch of rattlesnakes slither around one floor below me is more Maverick's taste in research than mine."

"I'll be right over here, scaredy-cat," she teased, returning to her tools.

Time passed swiftly as she worked and he snoozed. She paused several times to watch him sleep. There was something right about him being there with her, more than just comforting. How did that happen already? The damned man had managed to break through every wall she'd built to stop him. It had to be that hard head of his along with his smooth charm greasing the way.

He awoke awhile later, sitting up and rubbing his head. "How long was I out?"

"A couple of hours."

He took a long swig from his canteen and then splashed his face before standing and stretching as much as he could under the low ceiling. "Did you find what you were looking for?"

She nodded, pointing at several glyphs at the bottom left corner of the carving. "You see these?"

He joined her, squatting next to where she sat cross-legged. "Yeah?"

"They're the glyphs I was talking about last night that mean 'captive.' " She pointed at more in several other places in the carving and the surrounding blocks of glyphs. "I wanted to take a second look at them in relation to the rest of the carving and other glyphs, because in the middle of the night I remembered the other meaning for the *baak* glyph."

"Other meaning? Like a homonym?"

"Exactly. While these here most likely mean 'captive,' these three instances here," she pointed at the glyphs that were part of the throne of snakes, "could very well refer to the other meaning."

"What's the other meaning?"

"Bone."

"Bone as in the broken bones piled underneath us in *Yum*

Cimil's lair?"

She nodded.

"Christ." He rubbed his hand over his stubble-covered jaw. "What was this place?"

She leaned back on her hands, staring up at the twisted story the carving showed. "I don't know. At one end of the site we have artifacts from the Olmec civilization. Then there's this temple and the mine and all of these bones and snakes. I'm relatively certain we are looking at multiple layers of civilizations. Which one is on top depends on where you're standing."

"What are you going to do?"

She looked over at him. "What do you mean?"

"Your job is to clean this place up for other dig teams, right?"

"In a nutshell, yes."

"And then you're supposed to move on to the next site with your broom and dustpan."

"Right."

"But wouldn't you rather stay here and figure out more about these mysteries? Dig in like you did at the last site?"

His questions were the same ones that she had contemplated several times over the last few weeks. She liked to dive deep into a site's history and end a dig season with a feeling of completion. This new role meant she was only allowed to skim along the surface, dipping in a finger or two before moving on to the next site.

"Yes, I would rather come back and keep digging for answers, but I had to make a choice between struggling for funding every year at the same place or jumping site to site while my crew receives a regular paycheck, which includes a bonus for my father's time and expertise."

"And Pedro as a contracted pilot and crew member."

"Exactly. It came down to my family or my career." She shrugged. "When I took a moment to really think about it, the decision was easy." Plus, this job allowed her the opportunity to chase down her mom's theories. She could work on proving them without having to petition each year for a new grant to pay for an old theory.

"Family versus career," Quint said, nodding. "I get it."

"Get what?"

"Nothing." He stood and moved over to another wall. "What's this?" He pointed at the carving Daisy had found that prophesized the return of the lord of death when the twin scribes arrived at the site.

She pushed to her feet and joined him, brushing the dust off her pants. "It's one of your predecessors, sitting at the king's feet, playing secretary." The young scribe's profile was carved in detail, including spools in his ears and a ring in his nose. "The other twin is on a carving over there, recording the king's lineage."

"What's that on his leg?"

Angling her flashlight over the scribe's leg, she studied the carving for a moment. "From what I can tell, it looks like a sun with a skeleton face carved inside of it."

Quint frowned down at her with a sudden intensity that made her take a step back. "Are you sure?"

"Mostly. Why?"

"Gertrude has a tattoo on the back of her neck. It's a sun with a skeleton face inside of it. I saw it yesterday while making rounds, looking at boots."

"That's an odd coincidence," she said slowly, feeling it out. Gertrude usually had her hair down, so Angélica hadn't noticed her tattoo before.

"What's it mean?"

She wiped at a drop of sweat rolling down her cheek. "Only she knows that, since tattoos are personal. But I can tell you that for the Maya the sun is a symbol of awareness and enlightenment. It often represents the creation of life or life itself. The skull is usually a symbol of the lord of death and the Underworld."

Quint crossed his arms. "So mixing the two together could mean she's aware of *Yum Cimil?*"

"Sure. Or she could just like mixing life with death in symbolism to show off her wild side. Unless we ask her what that tattoo means to her, we could speculate all day about it. Trust me, I know. This is the shit I do for a living and often pull my hair out in the process."

"There's something else," he said. "When I was in the mess tent this morning before anyone else had shown up, Gertrude came in. When she saw me, she came over and sat down next to me, asking me all sorts of questions about where I'm from and what sort of adventures my job involves." He squeezed the back of his neck. "I figured she was just making small talk, maybe interested in pursuing a photojournalism career, but then she did something that sort of blew me out of the water."

"What?"

"She leaned in close and sniffed my neck."

"She did what?"

"Smelled me. It reminded me of a dog checking me out. When I asked her what she was doing, she said she liked the scent of my cologne." He shook his head. "I wasn't wearing any cologne. After that, she asked me if I had any ancestors from the Black Forest."

"Do you?"

"I don't know. My dad's family has German ancestry, but what did that matter? The woman had just sniffed me."

"Maybe she has a crush on you."

"Please, sweetheart. I don't think so. I'm almost twice her age."

"She still might be crushing on you. I certainly am, although I'm not so bonkers about you that I'd want to smell your shirt after you pulled an all-nighter worrying about something attacking the camp."

"A crush?" He grinned. "I'd like to see what you're like in the sack when you've really fallen for a guy."

He already had the other night in their tent. She may not have said those three little words, but she'd certainly done her best to show him. "Did she say anything else about your smell or your ancestry?"

"No. Bernard walked in then. She left me to join him."

"That's odd." She looked back at the carving. "And you're certain this sun with the skeleton looks like her tattoo?"

"Well, that's carved on stone, which leaves a lot of room for detail, but mostly, yes. What are the chances of it being similar, though?"

Angélica shrugged. "If Gertrude is really into the Maya, she might have seen a similar symbol in a reference book or textbook on Maya art. She might be obsessed enough to get a tattoo of it. Look up Maya-inspired tattoos on the internet sometime—there are thousands of them." She returned to her tools, gathering the rice paper rubs she'd made. "For the Maya people, tattoos were one of the ways they could please their gods. Body mutilation done for a god's appreciation was common. Filed teeth, body piercing, altering skull shape—those were all done in part to appease the gods."

"I'm surprised you don't have any Maya tattoos."

She chuckled. "I'm afraid if I get started I won't stop. There are too many symbols that mean something to me based on my history in the Yucatán. I couldn't pick just a few." She grabbed her backpack and slid her notebook and rubbings into it. "To be honest, the tattoo doesn't concern me as much as a pretty young grad student sniffing around my boyfriend," she joked ... sort of.

Sniffing was stepping over a line she'd drawn around Quint. He was hers while he was here, dammit.

"There's something else," he said.

Something in his tone made her stop and look over at him. "What?"

"After breakfast was over, she came up to me again."

Angélica remembered. She'd been watching that exchange. "I noticed her talking to you by the soap bucket."

"At the time, I was still kind of weirded out by her sniffing me and didn't put much thought into it, but after seeing these carvings with the twins, I'm sort of wondering if she knows something about Maverick that we don't."

"Why? What did she say?"

"She asked me if I found it curious that two scribes were seduced into returning to this particular dig site."

Angélica frowned, wondering how Gertrude knew of the glyphs prophesizing about the twin scribes. Then a light went on over her head. "Oh, Daisy shares a tent with Jane and Gertrude. She must have told them about the warning in here after she found it that day."

"So you think Gertrude is just spinning webs?"

"Possibly. She might be in need of attention, seeking it out via different physical means and mental games."

"Or she could be slightly delusional?"

"Or that. The heat down here sometimes affects people mentally. It's like the bends that way."

"Decompression sickness?"

She nodded. "The neurological symptoms of it, anyway. I've seen visitors suffer from visual abnormalities, unexplained behavioral changes, confusion and memory loss, and more. Between dehydration and possible sunstroke, this place can knock your knees out from under you. That's why I suggested at the last site and this one that you drink a lot of water and rest up when you first arrived."

"Suggested, you say?" he smirked. "More like ordered."

"Come to think of it," she continued, lightly smacking him for his smartass comment. "Maybe that's what's going on with Jane.

Between the heat and the snakebite, she may be struggling mentally. The Yucatán jungle can crack a brain."

"More like melt it." Quint took her backpack from her. "You ready to go?"

"Yes. I want to stop by the mine on the way back to the tents, though."

He groaned, grabbing her dad's duffel bag on their way out of the chamber.

"You don't have to go through the wall with me, Parker, or even inside of the mine for that matter." She led the way outside. "I can check it out on my own."

"I can let you go inside a hole in the earth full of skulls and bones alone?" His guffaw overflowed with sarcasm. "Not going to happen. Lead the way. The Underworld awaits us."

She bumped shoulders with him as they walked, poking him in the ribs, trying to make him smile. "Come on, Eeyore, cheer up. I'll make this quick. I just want to see the chamber and see if it looks similar to the one below the *Chakmo'ol* Temple."

"And if it does?"

"Then I can theorize that both were built by the same people. After I do some research work back in Cancun, I may be able to come up with a rough date for the pieces and cave art."

Quint let her continue to lead the way into the mine. She helped him fit her backpack and her dad's bag through the strangler fig's roots.

"So where are we going?" she asked.

"Uh, into the Maya Underworld?" he asked back as they stepped into the larger chamber. "Or as Pedro calls it, a Maya hellhole."

She laughed, ducking into the tunnel leading back to the stone wall. "I wasn't talking about where we are going in this mine. I mean where are we going per the deal I made with you yesterday?"

"Ah. No questions asked, remember?"

"Yeah, but I thought you meant at the time of the deal."

"I meant no questions asked, period. I'll let you know where when we're on our way."

"Sounds mysterious," she said, rounding the last bend before the wall.

"Well, you know me. I'm an incredibly enigmatic puzzle without any visible edge pieces."

"You're incredible, all right. Incredibly full of bullsh—" The words froze on her tongue. She stopped so fast Quint bumped into her.

"Oops, sorry about th …" he trailed off.

"Do you see what I see?" she whispered.

"Holy shit."

"What did that?"

He slipped around her, approaching what remained of the wall, stepping over stones that used to be aligned in grout. Now that grout was covering the floor in powdery chunks.

"Whatever did this was a strong son of a bitch." He frowned at all of the wall stones spread out on the floor around them. "And determined to get out of the mine."

"Yeah."

"We should leave," he said.

"No."

"Are you crazy, woman?" He pointed at what remained of the wall, which wasn't much. "Someone or something didn't just sneak into the mine this time. They busted the goddamned wall trying to leave in a hurry. That's a sign to run the other way if I ever saw one."

She pushed past him, stepping over the wall, dodging his grasp when he tried to stop her. "I'm going back there, Quint."

"Why?"

"Because whoever did this—"

"Or whatever did it," he interrupted, following her over the wall.

"*Whoever* did this is either trying to get something out of this mine or scare us away."

"Or maybe it was clearing a path for death and destruction."

She shook her head, shining her light on the altar stone with the figurines and the paintings on the wall above it. "You've been hanging out with my dad and Pedro too much."

"And you're letting your obsession with the past put your life at risk again."

"You don't understand, Quint."

"You're right, I don't. You seem determined as hell to follow in your mother's footsteps."

She whirled, a tender nerve tweaked. "Watch what you say next, Parker. My mother wasn't down here trying to get killed. She came to solve a mystery."

"And how is that different from you, Angélica?" he stared at her, not backing down. His flashlight spotlighted their feet.

She opened her mouth to reply, and then decided that ending this discussion before it went any further and one of them said something they couldn't take back was the best choice. "I'm going to see that catacomb. Wait here for me."

She made it a few steps away when he called, "Angélica, stop!"

The urgency in his voice made her pause. She squared her shoulders and turned back to see what he had to say.

Only he wasn't looking at her. He was squatting, pointing his flashlight at the floor of the mine.

"What?"

"Come here. You need to see this."

She walked back and stood over him. "See what?"

He pointed at the dirt. "That's not a boot print."

No, it wasn't. She lowered to her knees next to him. "What in the hell made that?"

"I don't know." He shone his light along the floor toward the throat of the mine and the catacomb full of bones. The large paw-like prints continued into the darkness. "But whatever it was apparently didn't like being walled in under the earth."

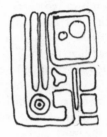

Chapter Twenty

Alux: A forest spirit.
When treated with respect, an *alux* will protect and bring good
luck. When slighted, an *alux* may spread illness and wreak
havoc.

Teodoro wants to perform a sacrifice," Angélica told Quint an hour later, joining him inside the mess tent. She eased onto the bench opposite him, her shoulders hunched as she fidgeted with the saltshaker.

A sacrifice? Quint thought. What did Teodoro want to sacrifice that had her avoiding eye contact? A young virgin in white? This was becoming one hell of a fucked-up situation in record time. Quint took a swig from his canteen, wiping off a couple of drops of water that dribbled down his chin with the back of his wrist. "What are we thinking here? A chicken or two to appease the gods?"

"Well, about that …" she trailed off, looking over his shoulder. "Dad's here."

Upon their return from the mine, they'd found Teodoro and Maverick filling the water bladders at the showers. Angélica told Teodoro she needed to talk to him and asked Maverick to find her father and send him her way. Quint had walked with Maverick as far as the mess tent where he stopped to refill their canteens, leaving

Angélica to tell Teodoro what they'd found in the mine. Along the way, Maverick gave Quint the details on the scene of the crime, including how Teodoro had watched Rover's physical responses to smells as they'd made their way through the trees to help them locate the kill site. Apparently, the javelina was good for more than just making Angélica smile and chewing up Dr. *Diablo's* boot.

Juan's cane creaked as he crossed the mess tent toward the carafe of cold Maya coffee María kept out between meals.

"A big Nevada birdie told me you wanted to talk to me." He poured himself a cup. "Did you find some more snakes in the *Chakmo'ol* Temple? Wait, let me guess." He stirred in a spoonful of sugar. "You found a hidden chamber full of ancient Chinese terracotta statues."

Quint exchanged frowns with Angélica.

"Dad, you should come sit down." She patted the seat next to her.

"I don't want to hear about more snakes." He limped over to them, lowering himself onto the bench next to his daughter. His gaze bounced back and forth between them, his expression sobering. "What happened?"

Angélica clasped her hands together on the table. "We may have a problem."

May? Quint smirked. There was no "may" about it, in his opinion. A rogue predator was on the loose.

Back in the mine, Angélica and he had followed those weird prints around the bend, deeper into the mine. While the wall had been broken out toward the exit, the tracks went the opposite way. Further back, they'd caught a whiff of something foul in the still air. His comment that it was a hint of death left behind as a calling card earned him an eye-roll. After explaining to the headstrong woman that he hadn't smelled anything besides rock and dirt the last time he was in the mine, they argued about how fresh the prints were, what could be causing the stench, and who was more stubborn—her for wanting to keep going or him for refusing to listen to her reasoning. At that point, Quint was ready to throw her over his shoulder and carry her out of that mine if she tried to go any farther. Thankfully, her common sense prevailed over her curiosity and they turned back toward blue sky.

"We already had a problem, *gatita*," Juan told her. "A snake problem. What could be worse than hundreds of cold-blooded slithering bodies full of venom?"

Angélica stared down at her clasped hands. "Something hunted and killed a full-grown jaguar last night down by the latrines."

"Really? Was it another cat?" He lowered his coffee cup.

"That's what I was initially thinking, but based on what Teodoro found in the forest this morning, I'm not sure."

She went on to explain what they had witnessed the previous night and ended with a repeat of what Quint had learned from Maverick on his way to the mess tent. Blood wasn't the only evidence of the kill left on the forest floor. The poor female jaguar had been torn in half and left for scavengers.

Juan's forehead creased. "You should have told me the truth about what you heard last night, Angélica."

"There's more." Taking a deep breath, she spilled the details of what they had found in the mine this morning. By the time she finished, her father had his head in his hands.

"I told you this place was trouble that first day we visited." Juan peeked over his fingers at her. "We need to evacuate."

"Damned straight," Quint said, raising his canteen to Juan in agreement.

"Or not." Angélica straightened her shoulders.

Here we go. Quint crossed his arms over his chest, waiting for the two of them to lock horns and begin a battle of wills.

"Angélica Mae García! How many times do I—"

She played traffic cop, both hands in the air. "Hear me out before you tear me a new asshole."

Juan huffed. "Okay, but I can tell by the way your chin is jutting that I'm not going to like what you have to say."

"First of all, we don't know for sure what we're dealing with here."

"I do," Juan interrupted. "Trouble. That's what we're dealing with here."

"With a capital T," Quint added. She'd given him the same song and dance at the mine. Watching her performance a second time wasn't going to change his mind. Let Mother Nature continue burying this site under the jungle floor.

"Zip it, Parker," she said, still focused on her dad. "Most likely it's a rogue male mountain lion or jaguar, based on its size and strength."

"The key word is *rogue*, child. There is no telling what or who is its next prey. Jane, Daisy, and you are all smaller than a full-grown female jaguar, which it managed to tear in half." He leaned forward. "Did you hear what I just said? *Tear in half.* That's like rogue on PCP."

"I know, but between Pedro's shotgun and the Glock 9mm pistol he keeps stowed away in his helicopter, plus all of our machetes, we have some solid defensive power."

Pedro had a Glock stowed away? Since when? At the last dig site he'd only had a flare gun. Then again, look what had happened at the last site. A 9mm, huh? Why hadn't he gotten it out last night? He must have figured the shotgun was plenty of firepower. Quint wasn't so sure.

"Guns and knives?" Juan smirked at Quint. "She thinks she's a female Rambo."

"Well, she does have an incredible set of guns on her."

"Parker!" Her cheeks turned rosy.

"What?" He chuckled. "I'm talking about your impressive arms from all of that machete swinging. What did you think I was referring to, sweetheart?" He played innocent while picturing her guns and much more sans clothing.

"Anyway," she continued, "I'm going to call a meeting, explain the situation to the crew, and offer to have Pedro fly anybody who wants to leave over to Chetumal. They've earned a couple of days' leave."

"Can you afford that with the budget INAH gave us?"

If not, Quint doubted INAH was going to be interested in footing that additional bill, so she must be planning on covering the crew's room and board out of her own savings.

"I think so." She scraped at something on the table. "I'd like you to go with them, Dad."

"I'm not a babysitter."

"I didn't say you had to monitor them. They're all adults."

"Then why should I go?"

"Because you're easy bait with your leg in that cast."

"So I'm supposed to go enjoy some sunshine on the beach while you stay here and what? Get eaten?"

"Hunt down the rogue cat."

He laughed with disbelief. "You? A hunter? You don't even like to step on tarantulas."

"That's because they're gentle giants. This is different. Besides, I won't be alone." She cast a glance in Quint's direction. "Parker here already informed me that he's going to stick around and keep an eye on me."

"Both eyes," Quint told her with a wink. "And maybe a hand or two."

Juan's mouth twitched at the corners. "What does Teodoro have to say about this?"

"He wants to try something tonight with those of us who stay behind."

Quint waited for her to share the news about the sacrifice with her father. He was still curious to hear exactly what Teodoro planned to offer up to the gods.

"Try what?" Juan's suspicion was clear in his tone.

"He wants to have another protection ceremony."

"Another *Lolcatali* ceremony? We just had one."

"No, a different kind of ritual. He said his grandfather performed it when Teodoro was young to protect their household from a mountain lion that had killed several small children in his village."

"Different how?"

She chewed on her lower lip. "It includes a sacrifice."

"A sacrifice?" Juan's eyebrows climbed high on his forehead. "Please tell me he's thinking about offering up a certain javelina that keeps eating my boot."

"That's not funny, Dad."

"None of this is funny, *gatita*."

"Also, Teodoro is going to make a special drink."

"Oh no, not another one of his secret potions," Juan groaned. "I absolutely refuse to drink it."

"You don't need to refuse it because you're going to be in Chetumal."

"I'm not leaving here without you."

"Damn it, Dad, you—"

"What's in this secret special drink?" Quint asked, running interference.

"I asked him that once about another one of his secret potions," Juan said. "His answer was that if he told me it wouldn't be a secret anymore."

"Anyway," Angélica interrupted, "Teodoro said that those of us who stay behind will need the help of an *alux* to find the rogue animal. Offerings need to be made."

"*Alux*?" Quint scratched his jaw. "That's a forest spirit, right?"

"Of sorts, yes," Angélica answered. "Most down here usually refer to them as spirits of the land. Some Maya believe they are the spirits of their ancestors."

"They are usually invisible," Juan explained, "but when they want to communicate, they take the form of miniature Maya people dressed in traditional clothing."

"Are they good spirits or bad spirits?" Quint asked.

"That depends." Angélica stole his canteen and took a drink. "Farmers will make offerings to an *alux* in exchange for help with their crops. If treated with respect, an *alux* is said to be able to protect you from thieves and bring good luck." She took another sip.

"However," Juan chimed in, "if an *alux* asks for an offering from a farmer—or a traveler—and is refused for whatever reason, the *alux* will often spread illness and wreak havoc."

"Sounds like they can be tricky little bastards." Quint took the canteen Angélica held out to him, capping it.

This all seemed so bizarre, like something out of one of Maverick's books. Weeks ago, Quint was freezing his ass off while watching polar bears play in the snow. Now he was about to witness a ceremony where some sort of sacrifice was going to be made to Maya spirits who looked like tiny people. Didn't anybody else see this solution as a bit *loco*?

"Is Teodoro sure it's not a *uay*?" Juan asked.

Uay … what had Angélica told him that meant? Something about an evil sorcerer pretending to be an animal, wasn't it?

"He's not sure of anything at this point, Dad, but he says it feels more like the work of an offended *alux*."

Damn. Those Maya had a lot of time on their hands to think up all of these gods and tricksters.

"So, what's he going to sacrifice this time?" Juan asked Angélica. "Please tell me it's one of those rattlesnakes."

"The sacrifice does not require a life, just blood."

"What do you mean, 'just blood'?"

"Teodoro said he needs the blood of two crew members."

"That is different than any he's done before." Juan stroked his chin. "Any two in particular?"

"Well, yes." She grimaced at Quint. "Two scribes."

It took a couple of blinks for her words to reach the core of his brain. "He needs Maverick's and my blood?"

Juan slapped the table. "I get it."

"Get what?" Quint was still processing that it wasn't going to be a chicken or a snake or a javelina that was going on the chopping block, it was him.

"He's going to try to put an end to that curse."

"To the warning. It's not a curse." Angélica reached across the table and squeezed Quint's hand. Her palm was damp. "There's more. Maverick and you are the only two who will be drinking during the ritual."

This was beginning to sound like a fraternity initiation. What was next? Togas and beer pong? "So the rest of you sit around and watch Maverick and me drink Teodoro's special potion?"

"Something like that."

"And then what?"

"According to Teodoro, you'll have a vision."

Christ, what kind of hallucinogens was he going to mix into the drink? "Come on, Angélica. You of all people don't believe in any of this, do you?"

She hesitated. "Yes and no. I believe that Teodoro knows the Maya religion well, and I trust that he wouldn't do anything to hurt you two."

"That's not really an 'I'm a Believer' answer."

She let go of his hand and laced her fingers together. "I don't know what to think right now, Quint. But I do know that Teodoro is scared of what took down that jaguar. I can see it in his eyes."

"That's not good," Juan said.

"I also know that if I don't let him do what he feels necessary to protect us, he will take María and leave on that helicopter."

"We definitely don't want him to take María away," Juan said, butting in again. "We'll starve in no time. Angélica is a lousy cook."

"*If* Teodoro leaves," she continued after a quick frown at her father, "then I'm up shit creek. This place is too dangerous without his knowledge of botanical medicines and first-aid skills."

Ahhhh, everything clicked together for Quint—her fidgeting, lack of eye contact, hesitation. Her future at this site depended on Maverick and him agreeing to be Teodoro's guinea pigs. No wonder she'd been acting so antsy since joining him in the mess tent.

"You think Maverick will actually agree to this?" he asked.

"He already did. Teodoro talked to him about it on their way back to the tents after finding the jaguar's remains."

"What?"

"He thinks it's a good research opportunity for a future book."

Damned fiction authors! They were always game to try asinine shit for research.

"Which leaves you," Juan said, crossing his arms. "You have the ability to shut 'er down, son, and send us all home alive and breathing."

Angélica poked her dad in the shoulder and then implored Quint with a pleading look. "Or you could play along tonight and help us stay here a little longer so we can figure out what happened to the people who died at this site."

In other words, what happened to her mother.

If they stayed and anything happened to Angélica or anyone else, it was his fault.

If they left and Angélica didn't find the answers to her mother's death, it was his fault.

Fuck. Talk about a rock and hard place.

"So, if I agree to play along, Maverick and I donate blood and get drunk enough to have visions. Then what?"

"Teodoro says you'll receive instructions on what to do to protect us in your visions."

"What if nothing happens? What if I drink the Kool-Aid and instead of receiving visions I pass out stone-cold drunk?"

"That's a good question," Juan said. "What then, *gatita*? Do we evacuate?"

She shrugged, fidgeting again. "All I know is that I need to protect my crew, which includes keeping my shaman happy."

Quint covered her hands with one of his, stopping her fidgeting. "This isn't some diabolical plan of yours to pay me back for losing your number in the North Atlantic, is it?"

"No."

He leaned closer, whispering, "Are we talking about poking my unmentionables with a stingray spine?"

She turned her hands over, wrapping them around his. "As tempting as that sounded weeks ago, Parker, I don't want to harm your unmentionables. Teodoro said a drop of blood from your finger will do."

He blew out a breath. "That's a relief."

"But I reserve the right to change my mind about harming your unmentionables should you go incommunicado again in the future."

"Got it. What do you think?" he asked Juan.

"I think that my daughter has you by the balls right now."

"Dad!"

"What? The boy asked." He shook his head at Quint. "I understand your position, son. I was there a few times myself with her mother. But know that if anything happens to my daughter because of your decision, I may take aim at your unmentionables with Pedro's shotgun."

"Understood."

"And," Juan continued, "I think that if this secret potion is anything close to what Teodoro has had me swallow before, you'll get drunk, take off your clothes, think grand thoughts, and believe you've turned into an animal of some sort. By the time the drink wears off, you'll definitely have dreamed up something."

Quint frowned at Angélica. "Do I have to get naked?"

"Of course not, Parker."

"You don't have to," Juan butted in again, "but you might want to in order to achieve your true token-animal self. I've stripped down multiple times while under Teodoro's influence. Let's see," he said, holding up his fingers, ticking them off, one by one. "I've been a frog, a Quetzalcoatl, a chameleon, and what was I that time up by Uxmal? Oh yeah, a pink—"

"Dad." Angélica shot him a zip-it glare. "You're not helping." Turning back to Quint, she focused on him. "Quint, I need your help here. Will you allow Teodoro to work his magic tonight?"

He'd taken bullets for her last time.

Hell, what could a little bloodletting hurt?

Chapter Twenty-One

**Xtabay: Means "female ensnarer" in Mayan.
A beautiful Mesoamerican demon who snares and kills.**

White sandy beaches, ample supplies of alcohol, and indoor plumbing. What more could you want?" Quint asked Angélica that evening as they waited inside of their tent for a summons from Teodoro.

The scribe ceremony was supposedly under way, but the sounds of the jungle drowned out any chanting that might have been going on around the altar Teodoro and Fernando had constructed earlier. Quint lay in his hammock, his legs crossed at the ankles as Angélica leaned against the center pole, keeping him company. In the next tent over, Juan waited with Maverick for the same reason.

What were the chances of two writers visiting a site with an old prophecy that warned about two scribes inspiring the return of *Yum Cimil?*

"Apparently," Angélica said, "the idea of Maverick and you making blood offerings is more appealing than a weekend full of sunshine and debauchery."

Quint had expected everyone but Juan, Pedro, and maybe Fernando to jump on Angélica's offer for a break from the bugs and soupy humidity. Make that he'd hoped they would take her up on leaving the site, not relishing an audience for this show. But lo and behold, once Angélica explained the situation with the possible rogue cat and mentioned Teodoro would be performing a protection ceremony come evening, they all wanted to stick around and witness it. They'd paid money to come and bury themselves in Maya history. A ceremony involving bloodletting was a bonus.

He glanced over at her. The camp light left her half shadowed. "Did you and your dad make up?"

"For the most part. We agreed to focus on keeping everyone safe tonight during the ceremony."

They'd locked horns again about Angélica allowing the crew to stick around for the ceremony. Juan petitioned for a mandatory leave, but Angélica refused, based on the idea of safety in numbers. Everyone staying put meant having more bodies to help with guard duty during the night, especially if Quint and Maverick were out of commission after the ceremony. She was currently of the belief that they were dealing with a rogue cat making its rounds through the biosphere reserve, of course, since it was the most logical answer.

Quint fanned his shirt, wondering how much longer they'd have to wait here. He didn't think any good was going to come of this experiment, but if it would help Angélica calm Teodoro enough to stay, then he'd do his part.

"Are you nervous?" she asked.

"Wouldn't you be?" He preferred a position behind the camera lens, not in front of it.

She nodded. "It will only be a little prick."

"It's not really the bloodletting that has me sweating."

"What then? The drink?"

"No, it's the possibility of being incapacitated in the middle of the night, unable to help you if that thing decides it's hungry for something with more marbled meat."

"I won't let anything happen to you." She moved in the shadows, standing over him, running the back of her fingers along his jawline. "Trust me."

"I'm not worried about me, Angélica." He snagged her fingers. "If that thing can tear apart a jaguar, think of what it could do to you."

"I'll be fine. Remember my incredible set of guns?" She flexed her bicep.

"Bring those guns here." He tugged on her hand. "I've been curious if this hammock will fit two people."

She climbed in on top of him, almost tipping them twice in the process. When she stopped giggling, she stretched along his length, her soft curves pressing into him. "Thank you, Quint."

"For what? Sharing my hammock?"

"Agreeing to do this. You're coming to my rescue again."

"I'm not trying to play hero."

"Then why are you doing this?"

"Because I'm smitten."

She nuzzled his neck. "Smitten, huh?"

"One hundred percent."

She wiggled up the hammock until her mouth hovered over his. "Smitten with whom?"

"Your father. Those brown eyes of his are like warm chocolate."

She laughed. The deep, throaty sound was soothing.

Cupping her face, he kissed her until his anxiety was forgotten. She tasted sweet, like the *jamaica* drink she'd nursed during supper. It was too bad they couldn't shut out the world for a few hours and give the hammock a thorough test run.

"Promise me something," he whispered against her lips.

She pulled back, her eyes dark pools. "What?"

"If I do all of this ritual stuff and tomorrow morning we're still in the same boat, promise me you'll seriously consider walking away from this site and continue digging into your mom's death from the safety of your place in Cancun."

She was quiet for several heartbeats. "I promise."

He kissed her again, savoring this moment alone. His hands slid over her hips, pulling her closer. Hell, this hammock would work slicker than the cot. They just needed a few less clothes and no pending stingray spines.

She shifted against him, her curves enticing further exploration. "Quint." She pulled back again. "I want you to promise me something now." When he waited, she continued, "If you see some odd creature after you drink Teodoro's special brew, promise me you'll run away from it and not toward it."

What did that mean? "What am I going to see?"

"I don't know, a sexy *Xtabay* who will lure you to follow her into the forest and then wrap you in her demonic death embrace."

"And here I was worried about a silly rogue cat wanting to lick me to death."

"Stay away from the *Xtabay* and I'll lick you instead."

He grinned. "Oh, yeah?"

She kissed his chin, rubbing against him, making him sweat even more. "Oh, yeah."

"Where?"

Her hot breath in his ear gave him goose bumps. "All over."

He groaned. "You're torturing me, woman."

They needed to stop or he was going to have to make everyone wait while he tore her clothes off and finished what she was starting. He grasped her hips, stilling her, trying to think of something besides how soft and smooth her naked skin felt. "Have you ever wondered why the Maya were so morbidly superstitious?"

She licked the shell of his ear.

Squeezing his eyes shut, he tried to stay focused. "Why couldn't they have believed in less violent gods, like unicorns and cupids?"

She giggled. "Don't forget rainbows."

"Quint?" Pedro's voice cut through the waves of lust crashing down on him. "Are you ready?"

Angélica looked pointedly downward. "You feel ready to me," she whispered.

Siren, he mouthed. To Pedro, he called out, "Just about."

"Teodoro said it's time for you. Maverick is already there."

"I'll be right out." He looked at Angélica. "You ready to play monkey handler for me?"

"I just need to grab my leash." She rolled off of him, leaving him rocking in her wake.

He stood, adjusting things south of his belt buckle. "Thanks for the distraction."

Her gaze dipped low. "I'm not done with you, heartbreaker. Let's go get you poked."

He followed her out into the darkness. "For future reference, that's not something a guy likes to hear, especially when it involves a small crowd of onlookers."

Her laughter was swallowed up by the jungle's serenade as she led the way to the fire. The whole crew was sitting around the fire pit in a solemn circle when they arrived. He could feel their gazes as he joined the party. All they were missing were the hot dogs and s'more makings, maybe a guitar and some beer, too.

As Pedro had said, Maverick was already there, seated on a log across the fire pit from where Teodoro instructed Quint to sit. Maverick saluted Quint. "Howdy, scribe."

"I hope you take good research notes tonight," Quint replied, settling onto the piece of wood. Had Maverick been unwilling to play along, Quint wouldn't have needed to sweat about if he'd made the right decision to go along with tonight's jungle *fiesta*.

Juan stepped between them, nudging a piece of kindling deeper into the flames with his cane. "Teodoro has placed you at cardinal points. Your back is to the west and Maverick's is to the east."

"What's the significance of west and east?" Quint asked.

"The west is where the sun begins its trip down through the dark Underworld, and the east is where it pops up after its harrowing journey through the nine levels of Maya hell."

Quint wanted to ask a few more questions, but Angélica tapped his shoulder. "Teodoro says we need to get started before the moon rises."

Looking into the fire, he tried not to think about Juan's tales of clothing removal and animal-inspired dances. He'd have liked to take a moment to tighten his belt another notch, but a glance in Teodoro's direction told him it was too late.

The shaman was walking toward him with a small gourd bowl in his hands. He stood over Quint, chanting with his eyelids closed. Lorenzo stood next to him, holding a bowl full of smoldering incense, while Esteban waved a palm frond above him to spread the sweet-smelling smoke.

Angélica joined the trio, indicating for Quint to hold out his index finger. She took the bowl from Teodoro, centering it under Quint's finger. Her eyes held his while the shaman wielded a stingray spine wrapped in a narrow strip of leather. What looked like a long black claw stuck out the other end of the leather wrap.

The stab with the pointed spine was over in a blink. Teodoro squeezed several drops of Quint's blood into the bowl, continuing his chanting in a singsong voice.

The four of them moved across the fire to where Maverick sat. They performed the same steps, only with a different stingray spine. From what Quint could tell, it was also wrapped with a leather strip, but a feather stuck out the other end. Seconds later, Maverick's blood dripped into the same bowl.

Lorenzo and Esteban followed Teodoro over to the altar, while Angélica joined Pedro and her father in the circle of onlookers.

Setting the bowl with the blood offering down on the altar, Teodoro lifted two more gourd bowls, handing one to each boy.

While he continued chanting in Mayan, Lorenzo carried his bowl over to Maverick and stood next to him. Esteban brought the other one over to Quint, waiting.

At Teodoro's nod, the boys handed off the bowls, but remained in place.

Quint lifted the bowl and sniffed the contents, expecting the honey-sweet scent of *balche*. The light-colored liquid had a pungent odor, though, that made him wince. He tipped the bowl, grimacing at the syrupy consistency. What the hell was this, the Maya version of castor oil?

A cough from across the flames made him look up. Maverick was already pouring the thick drink down his throat, coughing and gagging in between swallows.

That was just fucking great. Once again, Quint cursed the damned author and his willingness to jump into the fire for the sake of research.

Raising the bowl to his lips, he stared over the rim at Angélica. The stubborn woman was worth this, right?

She nodded once, as if she'd heard his question.

Before he could change his mind, he tipped the bowl. The warm liquid coated his tongue. The intense bitterness made his eyes water. He squeezed them shut and swallowed, choking the horrible liquid down, fighting the urge to cough it all right back up. Fire raged in his throat, the burning sensation trickling down his esophagus. He swallowed again and again, tears streaming down from the corners of his eyes, gagging it all down as fast as he could.

When he finished, someone took the bowl from him. He leaned over, coughing and gasping, his throat blazing, his taste buds nuked to smithereens. He swiped the tears from his cheeks and then used his shirt to clean the bitter taste off his tongue.

Holy fuck! That crap had to have been shipped straight from the Maya Underworld.

He coughed again, the fresh air making his throat sting even worse. For several seconds, he felt the thick syrupy concoction coming back up his esophagus. Oh, hell no! He gulped several times, forcing it to stay down.

Finally, the tears and gagging subsided and he could breathe again without much pain, but the heat from the fire had him sweltering. Sweat poured down his face and back. He was too close, the flames were scorching his skin.

He opened his eyes, but everything was blurry, like staring through a layer of petroleum jelly. He tried to blink his vision clear, but it only smeared more. The world around him was a haze, glowing orange.

A sizzling sound filled his ears. Damn, he was so hot. He unbuttoned his shirt, trying to find relief from the intense heat. His fingers fumbled, his mind unable to make them work right. He gave up and tore at the cotton, needing to be free of the fabric, certain it was somehow trapping the heat inside. If he couldn't get free, he would surely burst into flames.

The odor of burning flesh made him struggle harder. Had the fire spread to his clothes? Was that why they were making him so hot? He tried to stand but his legs wouldn't move. The heat seared his skin, the stink of burned hair made him cough and gag again. He had to get free of the fire. If he could just get these damned clothes off. He tugged on his belt, growing manic from the pain.

"Stop!" A voice shouted in his ears.

Quint stilled, listening to the crackle of flames.

The burning in his throat ceased. The smell of charred flesh blew away in a fresh breeze that cooled his heated skin. He opened his eyes, his vision crystal clear. He blinked several times, testing the sudden clarity. With each blink, the flames before him shrank and flickered, allowing the night to creep closer and surround him.

Then the flames blew out. Cold blackness rippled over his face, filling his ears with cottony silence.

His heart thudded against his ribs.

Another cool breeze blew past him, making him shiver. In its wake he caught a whiff of something that made his heart thud faster. It was the same sulfur-soured odor he'd smelled back in the mine, only this was stronger, like two-day-old road kill on a hot summer day.

A twig snapped behind him.

"*Der Beschwörer*," a voice whispered past him on a breeze.

Dear what?

"Who's there?" he asked, his throat raspy.

"You shouldn't have come here," a woman's voice stated in the darkness.

Xtabay? Angélica's warning about the beautiful demon and her deadly embrace replayed in his head.

A deep guttural growl rumbled off to his left.

What in the fuck was that?

* * *

"I think he's convulsing," Pedro called out.

Across the crackling fire, he and Angélica's father stood over Maverick, who lay curled into a ball on the ground, his legs twitching. Pedro dropped to his knees, pulling his T-shirt off over his head. "Bernard, come here."

Angélica glanced down at Quint, who sat stiff as a rock, staring into the fire, barely blinking. The firelight reflected on his wet cheeks. She'd been keeping track of his vital signs ever since he'd stopped coughing and gagging while tearing at his shirt and went totally still. She didn't know which had her pulse racing more— Quint's sudden stillness or Maverick's violent thrashing.

With Teodoro also down for the count, they were all scrambling to figure out what went wrong and how to fix it. The shaman had collapsed behind the altar without warning. The bowl of *balche* he'd been offering to the *alux* had spilled all over his shirt. Fernando had rushed to his side, keeping an eye on the older man while Lorenzo and Esteban followed Angélica's orders and raced to the mess tent to get the first-aid kit, some potable water, and María.

"I need you over here, *Angel.*" Pedro rolled Maverick onto his side, instructing Bernard to cushion his head with Pedro's shirt. "He's struggling to breathe."

Angélica looked up at Daisy, who was hovering nearby. "Daisy, come here."

"What can I do?"

"Watch Quint, keep checking his pulse and listening for his breathing."

"He's so still," Daisy whispered, kneeling in front of Quint. "Like he's turned to marble."

But his skin was warm, which gave Angélica hope. "I'm afraid he might go into shock."

"What if he starts convulsing? What should I do?"

"I know what to do." Gertrude joined Daisy on the ground in front of Quint. "I used to be a lifeguard." She looked over at Angélica. "Go. Pedro needs you. I've got Quint."

Angélica frowned at the young girl. There was something about the way she'd swooped in and taken control that put Angélica on alert.

"*Angel*, now!" Pedro hollered, his voice tight with tension.

After one last wave in front of Quint's eyes to no avail, Angélica jogged over and joined Pedro.

Maverick's eyes were moving rapidly behind his closed lids, his breath coming in fast pants. His whole body trembled.

"I don't know what to do for him," Pedro said, dragging his fingers through his hair. He cursed in Spanish.

Jesus, what was going on? What had been in that damned secret brew Teodoro made? If it was something poisonous, they were screwed, because Fernando was having no luck rousing Teodoro. Her only hope was that María had witnessed something like this before and might have some answers for them.

Maverick began to thrash and kick, knocking his arm and leg into the log next to him.

"*¡Dios mío!*" Pedro grabbed the end of the log and heaved it out of the way. "We need to move him away from the fire."

Angélica and Bernard tried to grab Maverick in between the kicks and arm swings, but he was no lightweight, not to mention his strong arms and long legs. Fernando came to their rescue, along with Pedro. Between the four of them, they were able to move Maverick several feet away from the flames and popping embers. As soon as he was clear of the fire, he stilled, relaxing to his full length. His breathing slowed, growing regular, his pulse steady again.

Lorenzo came running into the firelight, a jug of water in one hand and the first-aid box in the other. Angélica directed him over to Teodoro first, since Quint and Maverick seemed to be stable for the moment.

"Where's Esteban?" she asked Lorenzo in Spanish as they kneeled next to Teodoro.

"He's bringing María and more water."

She had Lorenzo take off his T-shirt, adding it to Fernando's for more cushion under Teodoro's head. His skin felt warm, but not feverish. She opened his eyelids, checking his vitals with her flashlight, finding nothing visibly wrong. She sat back on her heels, staring up at the moon cresting the trees.

What in the hell should they do? A small colony of bats fluttered in front of the moon.

Wings!

She glanced at Pedro, who was directing Jane to dab Maverick's face with the water Lorenzo had brought. "Pedro, is the helicopter ready to fly?"

Looking up at her, he nodded, his face lined with concern.

"Lorenzo." She turned back to the young man next to her. "Grab Fernando and get the stretchers from the supply tent." When he frowned at her blankly, she clapped her hands in front of his face. *"¡Ándale!"*

Spurred into action, he leapt to his feet and raced over to Fernando, saying something as he passed him. Fernando jogged off after him.

"Dad, come here," she ordered, waving her father over. When he got close, she told him in a low voice, "We need to get these three to the hospital in Chetumal. Without Teodoro here to explain to us what's going on with Quint and Maverick, we're driving blind. They could be suffering from some sort of poisoning for all we know, and waiting could kill them."

"I agree, but we can only fit two stretchers into the helicopter at a time."

"I know. I'm thinking Teodoro and Maverick go first. Teodoro is older. I'm worried about a stroke."

"And Maverick is having the worst time of it," her dad finished for her.

"Exactly. I'm worried about Quint, too, but he's ..." she looked over to where she'd left him with Gertrude and Daisy and the words died on her tongue. The log was empty.

Her heart wrenched to a stop, her stomach bottoming out.

Where was he?

Her gaze darted around the fire, searching faces but not finding his.

"Dad." She gripped her father's arm, needing his sturdiness when her knees wobbled. "Where's Quint?"

"I don't see him." He took a step toward the empty log.

Angélica's focus locked onto Daisy. The woman was standing over Maverick, chewing on her knuckles. "Daisy," she called out. "Where's Quint?"

Daisy looked over at the empty log, her eyes widening. She raced over to Angélica and Juan. "I left him on the log with Gertrude. She told me to go help with Maverick, that she had Quint under control."

For a moment, Angélica thought her knees were going to give

way. Then she shook off the wave of weakness and took a steadying breath. "Dad, make sure Teodoro and Maverick get safely on the helicopter."

She strode over to her machete, gripping it in one hand and her flashlight in the other. She had to find him. She'd promised she wouldn't let anything happen to him while he was under and now he was missing.

"Angélica!" Her dad's tone stopped her as she turned to go in search of Quint. He limped over. "You're not going out in the dark alone."

"I'm not going to sit here and wait for a search party to arrive, Dad. Quint is God knows where and I'm going to find him."

"Maybe Gertrude took him to one of the tents for some reason."

Angélica bristled at the idea of Gertrude taking him anywhere out of her sight. "I need to know where he is."

"I understand, *gatita*, but if you go waltzing around in this jungle alone at night you are putting yourself in serious danger. Quint wouldn't want that and you know it."

She scrubbed her hand down her face, looking around in the thick shadows. "I have to find him, Dad. If something happens to him, it's my responsibility. I shouldn't have asked him to put his life at risk for this dig site's future."

"That's not the only reason you're willing to go slay dragons in the dark for him, *gatita*."

Her gaze whipped to his. "Am I that obvious?"

"Only to someone who knows the signs." He pulled her into a hug, kissing the top of her head. "I can't let you go out there alone, not even for Quint."

"I can go with her," a voice said from behind Juan. Daisy stepped forward, holding up a flashlight.

"That's a bad idea," Juan said, releasing Angélica.

No, it wasn't. Daisy was the best one of them at finding lost items. "I'll take you up on your offer, Daisy, but first go tell Pedro I need his handgun."

"Angélica, no," Juan started, but Daisy didn't wait around to hear his reasoning. "What are you thinking? Taking an inexperienced crew member out there with a rogue cat on the loose is too risky."

"Daisy has a knack for finding lost things, Dad."

"He's not lost. I'm telling you, Gertrude has him. She took him somewhere for his safety, that's all. You're overreacting."

I've got Quint, Gertrude had said before Angélica left his side to help with Maverick. Did that have a diabolical double meaning? Was that why Angélica's internal alarm had sounded? Where had she taken Quint, damn it?

Angélica unsheathed her machete. "Dad, we have a huge clusterfuck happening here. You need to get Teodoro and Maverick to the hospital, and I need to go find Quint. Daisy and I will be careful."

The older woman returned with Pedro's pistol, handing it to Angélica.

Shaking his head, Juan muttered a string of curses.

Daisy touched his arm. "Don't worry, Juan. I'll keep her tucked deep under my wing."

Juan stilled, his eyes widened. "What did you just say?"

"She said we'll be safe." Angélica went up on her toes and kissed her dad's cheek. "Don't let anything happen to the rest of the crew." A movement behind him drew her gaze. "You better go, Dad. María's here. Why in the hell did she bring Rover?" They didn't need to add any more acts to this circus.

Juan tweaked her chin. "Please be careful, *gatita.* If I lose you, I'll have nothing left." He touched his lips to her forehead and then left without looking back.

Angélica tucked the handgun into her back pocket. She took up her machete. "You ready, Daisy?"

"Lead the way."

First, she'd see if her dad was right about Gertrude having good intentions. If they weren't in any of the tents, she'd double back to the fire and start over, expanding outward via a search radius.

"Angélica," Daisy said after they'd left the ring of firelight and the commotion going on within it.

"What?" She searched the moon's silver-lit world with her flashlight. The bushes and trees at the edge of the main plaza trembled here and there, making her heart pound.

"Gertrude and Quint aren't in the tents."

Angélica had the same feeling, but she figured she'd better double-check all of the tents and the latrines before she dragged Daisy out into greater danger.

"What makes you say that?" she asked Daisy.

"Because I saw where Gertrude took him."

Chapter Twenty-Two

Náay: The Mayan word for "to dream."
**For the Maya, dreams offered windows of communication
between them and the supernatural world during which they
could contact companion spirits (aka *uays*) and speak with
ancestors and gods.**

Y ou shouldn't have come here.

Come where? Quint thought. The dig site? Mexico? The Land of Shadows?

A growl rumbled again, this time from behind him. It was quieter, but just as hair-raising as before.

He tried his wobbly legs once more, rising slowly from the log. Thank God his legs were back online, because his fight-or-flight instincts were itching to race fast and far. There was no way he could fight whatever was hunting him in the pitch black with nothing but his charm and quick wit.

"It is leaving for now," the voice said. "But it will find you again." The soft lilt in her tone reminded him of someone. "We must go. Follow me."

He tried to see who was there with him in the dark, but his eyes were useless. "Follow you where?"

"The time to change course has passed." Her smooth voice was moving away to his left. "Come now, before it is too late."

Too late for *what*? Change what course? Why were voices in the dark always so damned cryptic?

Then it hit Quint—this had to be the "think grand thoughts" part of the ritual Juan had warned him would occur. Quint had gotten drunk off the vile stuff in the gourd bowl, and then he'd tried to take off his clothes when he believed he was on fire. Now came the wild visions. Juan didn't mention anything about a disembodied voice, but to each his own style of hallucinations, he guessed. What else had Juan predicted? Something about imagining he was an animal, wasn't it? Did that come before or after Quint was supposed to dream up a solution to their problem?

"The solution will be unpleasant," the voice said, closer now. Of course she was reading his mind. This was all part of the fantasy.

The sulfur smell had been replaced by a sweet mix of lemons and … he sniffed … was that rosemary?

"Unpleasant, huh?" he said to the voice, his sarcasm thick. So far, this experiment of Teodoro's had been about as "pleasant" as snuggling into a sleeping bag full of snakes.

Whatever the hell he'd gagged down at the fire still tasted bitter on the back of his tongue. It was going to take gargling with whiskey for a week to burn the tang of that foul brew off his taste buds. On top of that, his finger now throbbed from that damned stingray spine. Teodoro better have sterilized the tip before poking him with it. Infections in the jungle often went south fast.

He sniffed again, lured by the citrusy sweetness along with her soft voice, allowing his nose and ears to lead him toward her. "Who are you?"

"You wouldn't believe me if I told you."

How did he know that voice? Was it someone from his past? Someone who his mind had conjured to join him on this head trip?

After several more steps, the veil of darkness surrounding him lifted. Quint looked up at the light shining down from above. The moon had crested the tree line. It was extra-large and bright tonight, a harvest moon minus the orange filter. The world around him began to take shape. That was more like it. His thoughts couldn't be very grand without a little light on the subject.

The ballcourt was to his right across the plaza. In front of him, the *Chakmo'ol* Temple loomed, reaching for the stars. From this viewpoint, he could see only the edge of the crumbling steps leading to the top. They were lined with thick shadows.

"They performed sacrifices at the top of the temple on moonlit nights like this," his companion said from behind him. "Especially after *Yum Cimil* returned. Not just a poke in the finger."

Quint stuffed his throbbing finger into his pocket.

"The blood ran down the steps as one victim after another was sacrificed to appease the god of death."

He could picture the scene with ease tonight. It had to be due to Teodoro's potent concoction spiking his imagination. "Who would they sacrifice?"

"At first, they offered children. Those with crossed eyes and flat foreheads were considered especially beautiful and pleasing to the gods. Young lambs, if you will, who were gentle and sweet."

"Christ, that's awful." Quint doubted he could stand by and watch a child be sacrificed.

"But that didn't satisfy the lord of death and the nightly terror continued. Next, the priests offered many of their mightiest warriors, but *Yum Cimil's* hunger continued to grow instead of wane. The blood spilled faster as more and more attempts were made to appease his appetite."

The temple loomed closer. He walked around to the western side, the steps now darkened in what looked like water. Or was it a stream of blood? He slowed, staring hard at the moonlit scene. In a blink, the steps returned to normal. Damn, the visual effects tonight were spellbinding.

"How did they satisfy him?" he asked, continuing along.

"They couldn't." Her voice was now in front of him. "The two scribes possessed the power only to lure *Yum Cimil* out of the Underworld, not stop him from killing. Once topside, his appetite was insatiable. As villagers fell victim night after night, the king began to worry. He didn't want his people to question his power, so he ordered the priests to move the sacrifices out of sight underground. The chamber beneath the *Chakmo'ol* Temple was left from a previous civilization's reign. The king had it excavated to use as a feeding tank."

And Quint had lowered Angélica down the chute into that feeding tank? Shit, that explained the piles of bones she'd seen amongst the snakes. This was turning into one hell of a nightmare. If Maverick was flying high on a similar mind trip, he now had the components to write a kickass horror story.

"But *Yum Cimil* is gone now," Quint said, thinking aloud. "So somebody figured out a way to get rid of him."

"The great white priest had a vision that told him to sacrifice the two scribes. He led them underground and performed the ritual, collecting their blood, leaving their bones for *Yum Cimil*. Once their summoning was no more, *Yum Cimil* returned to the Maya Underworld, not to be seen again. Finally, they were free of the lord of death's terror. The king had the remaining villagers build walls in the mine and in the feeding tank under the temple. The white priest sealed both walls with the scribes' blood in hopes of keeping the lord of death deep down in the earth for the rest of eternity."

That explained the flakes of blood in the grout that Juan had mentioned.

"Eternity is a long time, especially for a bloodthirsty god," Quint said. "He'll probably grow bored after a few eons. I imagine all of that soul torturing gets old after a while."

"A comedian," she said, her soft laughter familiar. "So different from the last one."

The last what?

"They posted warnings," she returned to her story, her voice off to his right. "Upon the king's orders, many stelae were placed around the site with glyphs and carvings. They told the grisly story of *Yum Cimil's* return to feast on the bones of the villagers, cautioning travelers and visitors to stay away from this blood-soaked land."

Many stelae with warnings? Angélica had been scouring the site for one stela in particular with a warning on it. The one her mom had written about in her notebook.

"The king then moved his people away to find a new home, leaving the warnings behind. But the stelae were ravaged by weather and time, their glyphs growing harder to read with each passing century. With the destruction of the Maya codices by the Spanish conquistadors and monks, the meaning of many of those glyphs was lost until the archaeologists came to this land and began piecing the puzzle back together."

Ah-ha! There was the tie-in to the cache of Spanish armor Fernando had found down by the *Baatz'* Temple.

They'd reached the base of the steps leading up the *Chakmo'ol* Temple. Quint stopped. What was next in this vision of his? If it included a slide down the chute into that feeding tank, he was going to have to take a rain check and return to the fireside ceremony sans a solution to their cat problem.

"Again and again, the train of history circles on the tracks of time," she spoke from beside him.

He looked over, half-expecting to see someone standing there, but he was still alone. "What do you mean?"

"In spite of the advances the Maya had made in the mathematical and scientific world, and their priests' wisdom about nature, the heavens, and the Underworld, the bloody events at this site were repeats of a previous incident. You see, if they'd only taken the time to learn about the civilization that had lived here centuries before, during the Formative Era, they might have been able to avoid so much loss of life. Instead of focusing their energy into building a lavish city surrounded by wide roads coated with the limestone they unearthed from deep within the mine, they could have put more brainpower into deciphering the clues their forefathers left behind. Clues that showed how the older Maya also had made large offerings and bloody sacrifices to the lord of death in an effort to appease him."

"So this had happened once before?"

"More than once. There are indications in the *Baatz'* Temple that the Olmecs also experienced a visit from their version of a death god. They were the first at this site to leave a physical record of his bloody deeds. Who knows how many groups came and bled to appease the god of death's hunger before them?"

Quint stared up at the *Chakmo'ol* Temple that was partially veiled by moon shadows rippling down the steps and along the crevices.

When he woke up, he was going to lay this whole story out for Angélica and Juan. He wondered what they'd think of his imagination's gruesome tale inspired by their teachings.

"This is not our destination," the voice told him. "Come."

"Where are we going?" he asked without moving.

"To the mine. That is where she has taken you."

She who? Never mind. This was as far as he was going to allow his mind to lead him. "I'm not going in that hole in the earth tonight. It's too much like a mausoleum for my peace and happiness."

"You must come with me if you want to stop *Yum Cimil* before he kills again."

"Again?"

"Tonight, I will not be able to distract him with a *uay*."

He tried to remember what a *uay* was. Was it sort of like an *alux*? "By *uay*, you mean an evil sorcerer who transforms into an animal, right?"

"You have learned well." Her voice sounded like she was standing in front of him. "However, evil was not my intention when sacrificing such a beautiful animal to *Yum Cimil's* hunger."

His gaze narrowed. "Are you talking about the jaguar that was torn in half?"

"She was such a spectacular mix of flowers and beast. So fast and strong. But he had to be diverted."

But she was not fast enough to outrun the hunter. Quint crossed his arms. "Who are you?" he asked again.

"You wouldn't believe me if I told you," she repeated. "We need to go now. Time moves differently on this plane."

That wasn't good enough. "If you want me to come with you to that mine, you have to show yourself to me."

"My identity is not important."

This was like playing chess with himself. "I order you to show yourself."

Several seconds passed with nothing more than the whisper of the breeze in the trees.

"If we do not go now," she spoke from behind him, "*Yum Cimil* will find her."

"Who?" he asked, turning around.

A woman stood before him bathed in moonlight. For a moment, he thought he was looking at Angélica.

"*Pik*," she answered. "He is on the hunt again, insatiable as always."

Pik was Angélica's childhood nickname. Quint stumbled backward, his mouth gaping. "Marianne?"

The pale light accentuated the lines of her face. Juan was right, Angélica's cheekbones were more pronounced. Her neck was not as long as her mother's, and her shoulders were broader—probably in part from all of that machete swinging. The pictures he'd seen of Marianne in the locket and at Angélica's house hadn't done her beauty justice, though. It was no wonder Juan had been so love-struck upon first sight.

"He found her scent in the feeding tank and then the mine," she continued. "Now he has set his sights on her. I can shield only one at a time from him."

Still dumbstruck, Quint didn't move.

Marianne cursed under her breath, sounding like her daughter. "I obeyed your command, Summoner," she said. "Now you must follow me. Once you are reconnected with your physical form you will be strong enough. Then I can leave you to protect my *pik*." She led the way toward the mine opening, moving unnaturally fast.

Protect Angélica from what? *Yum Cimil's* hunger? Damn, even in his visions he couldn't stop worrying about Angélica.

Shaking out of his daze, Quint followed with long strides, still comparing features. Marianne's body was more willowy than her daughter's, more lean. Her long hair was secured in a braid that swung like a pendulum at her back as she walked, hypnotizing Quint as he trailed her.

Of course! It made total sense that he'd conjured Marianne for his so-called grand thought. She was the perfect narrator of the past, since she was linked to this site's history. The recognition he kept feeling when it came to her voice had to be due to his closeness to Angélica. "How do you know so much about the events from this site's past?" he asked, jogging to catch up to her. And what did she mean about connecting with his physical form?

"I read about it in the glyphs," she said. "Trust me, I've had plenty of time to be thorough and figure out the details."

Angélica had told him that Marianne could read glyphs better than she could, even joking that her mom must have been a Maya in her past life. "So where is that stela that you came down here to read before the crash?" The stela that had birthed her daughter's mania.

They walked by the mound that Pedro had been excavating the day he'd found the mine. A trail led into the jungle, a route Quint didn't remember being there in real time. He slowed as the trees closed around him. The howls and caws and other nightly spine-chilling screeches were missing, with the crunching of deadfall under his feet and the breeze swishing through the canopy the only sounds.

"He took it," Marianne answered, continuing up the trail without him. Her light shirt grew dim in the thickening shadows.

Before she could disappear again, Quint closed the distance between them. "Who took it?"

"The other. The guard."

The *other* guard? He weaved along behind her, trying to make sense of what his imagination was telling him via Angélica's mom.

Marianne slowed as they approached the mine opening, her head cocked. "Do you hear that?" she whispered.

"I don't hear anything."

"Listen."

He stopped, focusing on the sounds around him.

The leaves rattled.

The breeze whistled slightly.

His heart thudded.

His ears rang.

Was that the beginning signs of tinnitus? His mom claimed to suffer from it so much some days that she said it was making her lose her marbles. His sister Violet was of the opinion that their mother's marbles had rolled away long before any ringing started in her ears.

"Watch, Quint," he thought he heard Angélica say. Her voice came from the deep shadows inside the mine.

"Angélica?" He took a step closer to the dark opening, resting his hand on the large strangler fig root they'd left for stability.

"She's here," Marianne was still whispering.

"Where?" He tried to see inside the mine, but it was too dark. He needed to conjure up a flashlight.

"In the mine."

"I'm afraid he might go into shock ... shock ... shock." Angélica's voice echoed out of the mine's mouth.

Who might go into shock? Quint looked around at Marianne. "Is she talking about me?"

"You need to enter the mine now, scribe. I must leave to protect her." Marianne swooped toward him, her eyes glowing orbs.

Stepping back, he bumped into the fig root. "You want me to go in the mine alone in the dark?" Her bright eyes were sort of freaking him out.

"You won't be alone." Marianne came closer.

He squinted in the light. "I won't?"

Who would be in there with him? Angélica?

"I've got Quint," someone said from behind him. It sounded like Gertrude's voice.

Something touched his shoulder. He looked down. A large hand gripped his shirt. He turned sideways to follow the arm up and see who had grabbed him. "Who—"

With one powerful tug, he was yanked into the darkness.

* * *

"You saw where Gertrude took Quint?" Angélica asked, shining her flashlight in Daisy's face.

Shielding her eyes, Daisy nodded. "We need to hurry. Time is short."

What did she mean? Not much time to find Quint? What did Gertrude have planned for him? "Why didn't you say something when I asked you about Quint back at the fire?"

"I was busy."

"Busy doing what?" Angélica's voice sharpened as her frustration rose.

"Being summoned."

Huh? Daisy wasn't making any sense. Was she in shock from the commotion at the ceremony? Had she snuck some of Teodoro's secret drink when nobody was looking?

"Enough questions." Daisy snatched Angélica's flashlight from her hand. "Come on." She turned and started striding away.

Angélica frowned after her, hesitating. Following Daisy away from the rest of the group screamed "Bad idea!" The woman could be leading Angélica into a trap. After all, her ability to find artifacts at this site spoke of someone who'd been there before. Could Daisy have had something to do with her mom's helicopter crash?

When Angélica didn't follow, Daisy stopped and marched back to her. "Did you hear me? There is no time to delay."

"You think I'm stupid enough to go with you alone in the dark now that you suddenly know where Gertrude took Quint? No way. I wasn't born yesterday."

"Gertrude led Quint to the mine," she blurted. "If you do not come with me to stop her, she is going to sacrifice him to *Yum Cimil.*"

Angélica squinted. "That's nuts."

"Gertrude believes it's the only way to save everyone."

"By feeding Quint to the rogue cat?"

"It is not a cat. The lord of death has returned."

The lord of … oh, hell! What kind of superstitious baloney had Gertrude been telling Daisy? Or was it the other way around? "Which one of you two is the ring leader here?"

"Neither. You have to trust me right now and come. I will explain later."

Angélica stole her flashlight back, aiming it at Daisy's face again. "Why should I trust you? I barely know you."

A pained expression passed over Daisy's features. "Angélica, you have known me a long time."

She had? "Were you in one of my classes back in college?"

Daisy shook her head. "You will not believe it if I explain."

"Try me."

"Not now. I have to get you to Quint. He is strong but confused. Gertrude will stop at nothing to save the rest of you from *Yum Cimil's* reign of terror." Daisy grasped Angélica's arm and tugged her several feet.

Angélica wasn't falling for Daisy's bullshit, though. She refused to end up like her mother, the victim of someone's twisted game. Digging her boot heels in, she pulled free of Daisy's grip. "Forget it. I'm not going with you." She was going back to the fire and getting Fernando to help her find Quint. She'd deal with Daisy and Gertrude when everyone was safe and sound.

"Damn it, *pik*!" Daisy whirled on her, her tone sharp and all too familiar. "Quit being stubborn like your mule-headed father and do as I say."

Angélica's mouth fell open. The blood rushed from her head so fast she stumbled backward. "Who are you?" she whispered, her throat tight.

"Search in here." Daisy tapped on Angélica's chest above her heart. "You know damned well who I am."

Angélica shook her head, taking another step back. This couldn't be real. Was this part of Teodoro's ceremony? Had María put something in the *jamaica* juice at supper?

"That's impossible," she said. "Both logically and physically, because you're dead."

"Yet here I stand."

"But you're not you." While it sounded like her mother, she was very much Daisy with her pixie haircut and blue eyes.

"Daisy is an open channel. An extremely rare gem. Through her, I can reach the living. I do not understand how this can be any more than you do."

"This is full-on straitjacket crazy. I must be dreaming."

"You are not dreaming." Daisy reached out and pinched

Angélica's arm.

"Ouch!" Angélica rubbed the sore spot. "How can this … oh, I know." She snapped her fingers. "It was the incense. Teodoro must have used some kind of potent herb that causes hallucinations."

Did that mean Quint was still sitting on the log and all of this about Gertrude was a figment of Angélica's drug-induced trance?

Daisy latched onto her arm again, pulling Angélica into motion. "You can analyze it on the way to the mine, *pik*. We have to get there before Gertrude eliminates the man your father has chosen to produce my grandchild."

Angélica allowed Daisy to tow her along, same as she had allowed her mother when Angélica was a child. Her head spun. The swirling chaos of memories drowned out the jungle's racket.

There was no way this was real. Her mother was long gone. Yet she could smell her mom's favorite perfume. The fresh scent of lemon and rosemary and a subtle blend of spices. She must be losing her … That was it. She'd finally cracked.

The pressures and stresses of proving her mother's theories, and the mad determination to find answers about her death, had finally broken Angélica's brain. She should have listened to her father about not working so hard and getting more sleep. He'd been right about letting go of the past. Oh, man. Living with him now would be impossible. She'd never hear the end of "I told you so."

Crap. This was going to ruin her career as soon as INAH learned of it. A nutty archaeologist hearing voices from the past would be an embarrassment to the Mexican government.

"Angélica," her mother said, waving her hand in front of her face. "Snap out of it."

She looked blankly at Daisy—or Marianne. They stood in front of the entrance to the mine, only something looked different.

"Who chopped off the fig root?" Angélica asked. "Dad said we needed to leave that one alone or risk the tree crashing down and blocking the entrance."

"It was not cut," Daisy said. "It was torn."

What could tear off a huge fig root like that?

"You need to go inside and help Quint understand his power before it's too late," her mother ordered. "But please be careful. The thing that ripped that strangler fig root is not of this plane."

She nodded, feeling like she'd stepped into a video game. This must be the part when Quint and Maverick were supposed to figure out a solution while under Teodoro's trance-induced state.

She looked at her mom. "Can I turn into a jaguar now?"

Marianne frowned. "What are you talking about?"

"Dad usually takes on the form of some kind of animal when he drinks Teodoro's potions. Remember that time he started flapping his wings and standing on one leg next to the fire, thinking he was a flamingo?"

Daisy's white teeth flashed in the semi-darkness. "He burnt his tail feathers that night. I had to rub some of Teodoro's special ointment on his backside for days." She sighed. "I miss your father, but now is not the time for memories. You must go."

Angélica started inside the mine, realizing she was alone. She turned back. "Aren't you coming with me?"

"I cannot put Daisy's life at risk."

But her mom wasn't real. None of this was. "Can't you just float along next to me?"

"It does not work like that, *pik*."

"Okay." She frowned, not wanting to leave her mom behind. "Will you be here when I come back out?"

"You won't be alone."

That wasn't really an answer, was it?

"Go, Angélica. Teodoro is waiting for you."

"Good. I have a bone to pick with him about dragging me into this mess. I wasn't supposed to get fucked up, only Quint and Maverick."

"You are not fucked up. And do not tell your father that I swore in front of you. He always gave me shit about cursing like a sailor while in your company."

Angélica laughed. "Please, I'm standing here having a conversation with my mom, who died years ago. If I'm not high, then I'm crazy. Between the two, I prefer being high. At least I'll recover from that and retain my job."

"I have been here all along, *pik*."

Did she mean here with Angélica or here at the site? It had to be the site, since this was the first time Angélica had conjured her mom up since saying good-bye to her. "Doing what? Waiting for Dad and me to show up so you could haunt us?"

"No. I ..." she shook her head. "That is not important right now. Just do me a favor."

"What?"

"Keep my locket with you wherever you go."

"Why?"

"Because I said." Marianne leaned forward and kissed her cheek.

Angélica's eyes burned, understanding why her mom wanted her to carry the locket with her. "You've been with me every day since I lost you, Mom. A locket won't make a difference."

"Trust me on this. You do not have to wear it, but please take it with you wherever you travel."

"Okay." She sniffed, shining her flashlight into the mouth of the mine, seeing only rock walls and roots dangling from the ceiling. "I'm going to go find Teodoro and ask him how bad my hangover is going to be tomorrow."

"Angélica, you must stop Gertrude. There may be another way to send *Yum Cimil* back into the Underworld. A way without so much bloodshed and sacrifice."

"Got it." She turned to blow her mom a kiss good-bye, but she—Daisy—was gone. "Good-bye, Mom," she whispered, her heart panging.

Shaking off her sadness, she tiptoed into the mine. She'd almost reached the broken wall when she heard whispers echoing off the walls. She rounded the final bend and relief warmed her limbs.

Teodoro was sitting on part of the remaining wall with his eyes closed, chanting away.

"Mom said you'd be here."

His eyes opened. "You took too long." He spoke in his native tongue. "We must hurry." Stepping over the wall, he waved at her to follow. "She has started the ceremony."

"Is there going to be popcorn at this show?" she joked.

"Why do you make fun?" he asked.

"Because I'm as high as a howler monkey at the top of a ceiba tree."

"That is not true. You are on the ground with both feet."

"Then how do you explain my mom inhabiting Daisy's body and you waiting here in the mine for me?"

"We were summoned."

"By *Yum Cimil?*"

"By the scribe." Teodoro caught her arm and pulled her past the altar stone. The little carved figurines lay scattered on the floor. "He is the one to be sacrificed in order to save us from the beast."

Chapter Twenty-Three

Der Beschwörer. **German for "The Summoner."**

Gertrude stood next to Quint in the shadow-edged catacomb, surrounded by the broken bones of the long dead. The flashlight she handed him after dragging his ass back into the mine did little to offset the chilling turn his dream had taken since leaving Marianne in the jungle.

The musty smell in the chamber was the same, but an underlying odor hovered over the bones now. When he'd asked Gertrude about it, she'd avoided his gaze, mumbling, "You'll see soon enough."

Her pacing and constant glances in the direction of the tunnel they'd crawled through to enter the catacomb were giving Quint indigestion. Or maybe the burning in his gut was caused by Teodoro's drink hitting rock bottom.

To add to his heart palpitations, there was something wrong with Gertrude's eyes. Her pupils were narrow black slits surrounded by glowing amber irises. Every time Quint looked at them, all he could think about were those dozens of rattlesnakes they had hooked and bagged. Sweat coated his skin at the memory.

What was with his brain screwing with her eyes like that? Was the drink starting to wear off and now it was time for creepy clowns and funhouse mirrors?

Gertrude kicked aside a partially crushed skull. Bone fragments scattered across the rock floor. "You should not have come here," she told him.

"That seems to be the theme of this dream." Quint pointed at a large hole in the wall. A hole he hadn't noticed the last time he was in the catacomb because it'd been hidden behind the big chunks of ceiling rock that Gertrude had apparently pushed aside on her own before bringing him there. His imagination had given her Amazonian strength to match her big hands and feet.

His flashlight beam showed the hole in the wall was more than a shallow cavity. "Where does that tunnel go?"

"That's not important."

"It will be if something with sharp claws and pointy canine teeth slinks out anytime soon." He walked over and squatted in front of the three-foot-high opening, shining his light into it. The tunnel ran long, the light losing the battle with the shadows about twenty feet back. It appeared wide enough for a man to crawl through on his hands and knees, but Quint would rather not find out for certain.

Another skull rolled across the floor. "For the record," Gertrude said, "I really don't want to do this, but you've left me no choice. You are *der Beschwörer*."

"*Dear* what?" That was the same garbled word he'd heard back at the fire.

"*Der Beschwörer*," she repeated, enunciating as if that would help.

He stood, avoiding her snake eyes. "What is that? German?"

"Do you not know your purpose?"

"I have a purpose?"

"Of course."

"You mean like a special purpose?"

"A life purpose."

He cocked his head to the side, pondering what he could do that would benefit him on a life level. Photojournalism was really only a way to make money when it came down to it. "I'm pretty good with an axe." He pretended to chop a tree. "I can split firewood with a single swing. My dad still says I should have been a logger."

She planted her hands on her hips. "Are you intoxicated?"

"I'm certainly not sober." Teodoro's drink had sent him on a wild roller-coaster ride tonight full of loop-the-loops and breath-stealing drops.

"You are *der Beschwörer*." When he continued to frown at her, she added, "The Summoner. That is your purpose."

"The Summoner?"

"That's what I said."

"Who am I supposed to summon?"

"Those who need to be executed."

His frown turned into a full-face grimace. "Am I supposed to execute them, too?"

"No. That's a job for *der Scharfrichter*."

"Dear shark-what?"

He nudged a skull onto its side with his toe, frowning at the fractured cranium. It had been crushed. Before or after death?

Gertrude grumbled in her native tongue, which sounded a little bit like she was gargling with marbles. "*Der Scharfrichter*. It means 'The Executioner' in your language."

Of course. The Executioner, as in one who executes. His subconscious was having way too much fun tonight.

"Executioner, huh?" He grinned. "Sounds like a shitty career. Does that job come with any benefits? I'd think vision coverage would be important to career longevity. I'd sure hate to have a near-sighted executioner show up for my final hurrah and squint down at me while trying to line up his blade."

"Executioners are always female." Gertrude's tone was terse.

"Always?"

"Yes. They use a combination of their seven senses to hunt down and kill their targets."

Seven senses? Where was his brain coming up with these wild ideas? He couldn't wait to hear about what Maverick had conjured while passed out from Teodoro's version of Maya moonshine. "And what do Summoners use to summon? Dog whistles?" He glanced up at her.

She didn't even crack a smile. One of the broken femurs on the floor must have been her funny bone. "How can you have lived this long, Summoner, and know so little?"

He shrugged off her insult. "I majored in Anvils and Dynamite at Acme's Cartoon College, with a minor in Wiliness."

"You have much to learn." She wrung her big hands. "Unfortunately, you will have to devote time to perfecting your craft in your next life, because sacrificing you is the only way to send the beast back to its regular hunting grounds."

The German woman's tension was becoming a real buzz-kill.

"Listen, Gertrude," Quint said as he leaned against the wall next to the hole, crossing his ankles. "It's been fun here tonight sharing shark-bite stories on this creaky boat in the Sea of Fiction, but I think you have the wrong guy. If you can just tell me what sort of animal I'm supposed to turn into so I can do a totem jig and then move on to experiencing a vision that will solve our cat problem, I'll be on my way back to the fire."

She moved closer, her snake eyes roving over his face. "You are *der Beschwörer*. I smelled it on you."

Okay, now he understood why Gertrude was in his dream. He was still trying to work out her eccentric sniffing behavior. But what was the deal with her eyes? Was he supposed to change into a snake? Were her eyes a clue?

"Summoners have a smell?" he asked, wondering if his eyes were already snake-like, too, and he didn't realize it.

"Of course. Same as a skunk and wolverine."

Whew! That bad, huh?

"So, how do we Summoners go about our summoning business? Do we use really big magnets to draw in our objectives? Or do we rely on our incredible charm to woo them closer?"

She glanced back at the tunnel leading in from the mine again, listening for a moment, and then turned back to him. "There is nothing charming about a Summoner, especially if an Executioner lies in wait. Your ability to beckon has more to do with your mental strength."

"Summoners are superintelligent, then?"

"Intelligence and mental strength are not the same."

He rubbed his jaw. "So how does one become a Summoner?"

"You tell me, *Beschwörer*."

"I won my mask and cape in a drunken card game. What's the usual route into the trade?"

"Your bloodline is the only way. That is why I asked you if you had relatives in the Black Forest region."

"I'm not following how the two are linked."

"Centuries ago, there were several of your kind in the Black Forest, along with as many Executioners." She grabbed his left hand and lifted it, palm up. Her fingers were icy cold as she traced the lines on his hand. The lines glowed for a moment before fading away.

He watched her trace his palm, mesmerized. "Why were there

so many Summoners and Executioners in one place?"

"A rebellion was on the rise. It was a caste war, actually, spurred by a handful of rogue demons and their guardians. The rebels had grown tired of hiding amongst the growing population of humans. They slaughtered thousands of people throughout the Black Forest region, aiming to rule the Earth again, but their time had not yet come. Executioners were hailed from all over, hired to eliminate the key troublemakers and suppress the rebellion. However, the rebels were not easy to find. They traversed between levels much easier than most of the Executioners. In order to lure the rebels from hiding, Summoners were called in to work with the Executioners. They were used as bait for the hunts."

He looked up into her snake eyes. "I changed my mind. Being a Summoner is far shittier than an Executioner."

Her smile was brief. "Tonight, you'll experience what your ancestors faced." Before he could ask what she meant, he felt a slice of pain in his palm.

"Ouch!" He tried to pull free, but her big hand was steely gripped. "What are you doing?"

"Hold still." She reached down to grab a skull from the floor. "You'll heal fast."

How did she know he healed quickly? His mother had always credited his ability to heal faster than normal to the herbal, meat-free diet she followed while pregnant with him, but Gertrude wouldn't know … oh yeah. This was all in his head.

The pain in his hand felt real enough.

She smashed the skull against the wall twice, breaking it in half. Holding the top of the cranium under his hand, she squeezed his blood into the makeshift bowl, just as Teodoro had back at the fire.

She released him and took the cranium bowl to the exit tunnel. Quint cupped his throbbing hand, watching as she used his blood to smear a symbol on the floor in front of the tunnel. She lifted the black obsidian statue off the shelf and set it in the center of the symbol she'd made.

"There," she said, tossing the bowl aside. "The beast will now know where to find you. After you are eliminated, your beacon will call to it no more, and the beast will return to its normal hunting grounds. The rest of us will be safe until the next Summoner arrives."

"Or," Quint said, "we could get the hell off this dig site, call 1-

800-Execute, and come back when we have a killer in our ranks."

That sounded like a fine solution to present to Teodoro when Quint awoke from this nightmare. They'd hire a hunter to take down the rogue cat.

When he headed for the tunnel, aiming to get the hell out of the catacomb, she blocked his path. He tried to nudge her aside, but she didn't budge, shoving back instead.

"There is no time for your plan. The beast is already hunting on this plane again. If you leave, it will follow you, killing many innocent humans."

"So then I lead it right to an Executioner."

She cocked her head to the side, listening through the tunnel. "I hear it coming."

Quint frowned down at the Maya glyph–like symbol she'd made with his blood. It sort of looked like the sun-skull tattoo on her neck. This whole scene wasn't really jiving with what Juan had predicted. Somewhere in the story, Quint's imagination had taken a wrong turn. "Aren't I supposed to morph into a totem animal now in my dream?" An eagle or monkey, maybe? Hell, even a serpent. Anything but some mythical Summoner to be used as bait.

"You are *der Beschwörer*. This is not a dream."

He checked his palm and did a double take. The bleeding had stopped, the cut in his hand appearing to mend before his eyes. "If this isn't a dream, how do you explain this?" He held his palm out for her.

"Injuries from non-humans heal quickly for a Summoner. It's one of your key defenses."

A shuffling sound in the tunnel behind them made them both turn.

"It's here," Gertrude whispered, hiding behind Quint. She clung to his arm as they backed up in tandem, bones crunching under their feet.

From out of the dark tunnel, a head appeared.

A machete slid out next.

Angélica frowned up at him. "You two play a hell of a game of hide-and-seek." She looked at the black statue in front of her. "Oh, that's definitely Olmec. They sure had a big crush on their were-jaguar god." Carefully, she moved it aside and frowned at the symbol Gertrude had made with his blood. "Is that the tattoo we saw on the scribe?" She stood, not waiting for an answer. Her machete was at the ready as she eyed Gertrude. "Are you okay, Parker?"

"At the moment." He pulled free of Gertrude's clutches and stepped away, needing to touch Angélica, craving the familiarity she offered. Her cheeks were warm as he cupped them, her lips soft under his quick kiss. She felt and tasted like the boss lady. His imagination had managed not to bugger up this part. "I've been having one hell of a bizarre vision so far, though."

Her forehead wrinkled. "What do you mean you've been having—"

"You shouldn't be here, Dr. García," Gertrude interrupted, shooting a worried glance at the tunnel Angélica had come through. "It's too dangerous."

Angélica stepped away from Quint, gripping her machete. "I won't let you sacrifice him, Gertrude. You need to shake off this absurd notion and return to the fire."

"There's no other way to stop the beast." The girl backed farther from the tunnel opening, stumbling on a pile of broken bones. "Besides, I've already made the offering."

"It's a rogue cat, Gertrude. That's all. You're overacting."

"No!"

"You probably caught a good whiff of Teodoro's incense," Angélica continued, slowly moving toward the girl. "I did, too, and it's twisting our sense of reality. Trust me, I understand what's going on. I've seen some pretty strange shit tonight since getting high on whatever weed he was burning. We just need to get you back to the others and try to calm you down."

"You are not high, Dr. García." She pointed at Quint. "And you are not hallucinating, *Beschwörer*."

"What did she call you?" Angélica asked Quint out of the side of her mouth, her focus still locked on Gertrude.

"It means 'Summoner' in German."

"Summoner? Sounds like I interrupted a game of Dungeons and Dragons."

Quint chuckled. "It's her game, I'm just making this madness up as I float along through my purple haze."

"What's with her eyes?"

"You see them, too?" How could she … oh, yeah. It was his dream. He was controlling what Angélica saw and said.

"You can't miss them. Were you trying to turn into a snake and screwed up your totem morphing process, looping Gertrude in somehow?"

"Dr. García, you must leave." Gertrude took a step toward them. "I was warned not to let anything happen to you after the incident with your mother."

The machete lowered slowly. "What do you know about my mother? Did you kill her? Sacrifice her like you're trying with Quint?"

"No. I was not here then." Gertrude paused, her eyes on the tunnel as she listened for a few seconds before continuing. "My predecessor became overzealous."

"Your *predecessor* killed her?" Angélica's tone was low, threatening.

Gertrude nodded frantically, licking her lips. "He felt it was necessary to keep this place secret. Much work had gone into sealing off the entrances to the other plane after the last attack. We could not risk your mother's knowledge leaving with her."

"Knowledge about what?" Quint asked. What could Marianne have found out that was worth being sentenced to death?

"The beast. Her ability to so quickly interpret the symbols and read the glyphs on the warning stela surprised the council. The decision was made to stop your mother uncovering long-buried secrets. My predecessor decided the only way to remove the danger of her knowledge spreading was to eliminate her. He devised a helicopter crash involving a renowned foreign scientist to embarrass the Mexican government. They would hesitate to send in others."

"Your predecessor killed her," Angélica repeated, the machete listing.

Quint stepped forward and took the blade from her, wrapping his arm around her shoulders.

"He was punished thoroughly for acting without the council's permission," Gertrude told Angélica. "Banished and forced to serve a long, pain-filled sentence."

"Good," Angélica said, sniffing. "In which Mexican prison can I find him holed up? I'd like to deliver a little pain myself." She took her machete back from Quint.

"Your mother was a brilliant puzzle solver, Dr. García," Gertrude said, holding out her hands as if to block potential blows. "You follow closely in her steps, discovering secrets in the ruins about forces that even the oldest on the council doesn't remember.

This is why I have been instructed to protect you at all costs."

"Protect me, but not Quint?"

"The Summoner was a surprise. They travel undetected until they exert their strength and summon an enemy. Trust me, sacrificing him to the beast is the only way to send it away again."

"Why not kill it?"

"There is no way, not without *der Scharfrichter*."

"Without what?" Angélica aimed her raised brow at Quint.

"An Executioner," Quint told her, grimacing. "My imagination tonight has gotten a little out of hand with this vision business. I blame all of those science fiction and fantasy novels I read growing up."

Her eyes narrowed, her expression more confused than suspicious. "But this isn't your vision, Parker. It's mine. I breathed in Teodoro's incense and then my mom's voice started coming out of Daisy's mouth."

"If it's your vision, did you see me with your mom at the *Chakmo'ol* Temple?"

"No."

"Marianne told me the story of what happened to those twin scribes in the past. Did she tell you about them?"

She slowly shook her head. "She didn't waste time with stories. She dragged me here and told me I had to save you from being sacrificed."

He smiled. "Your mom must like me."

"Quint, this doesn't make any—"

"Listen!" Gertrude interrupted.

Click-clack. Click-clack. Click-clack.

The sound came through the tunnel opening. It sounded far away, somewhere out in the mine's main adit.

"That's probably Teodoro," Angélica said. "I left him out by the cave drawings."

"It is not Teodoro," Gertrude said, plastering herself against the wall. "It's the beast."

"The rogue cat?" Angélica raised her machete.

"Gertrude is using my blood to summon it," Quint explained, grabbing Angélica to pull her away from the tunnel.

Angélica shook off Quint's grasp. "And once it has found Quint, then what?" she asked Gertrude.

"The beast apparently eats me," he answered.

Angélica looked up at Quint, her eyes wide. "And you're okay with this?"

"Hell, no. I offered another solution, but Gertrude is set on me being dinner. I'm just hoping I wake up before we reach the actual biting part of this vision."

"There's another solution," Angélica said, turning back to Gertrude. She held her hands out as if talking her down off a ledge. "We can catch the cat with a cage. That way nobody gets hurt."

The *click-clack click-clack* was growing louder, the sound of heavy breathing mixed in with it. Quint stared at the tunnel opening, half expecting a bulldog in tap shoes to appear at any moment. He tried to remember in which cartoon he'd seen a bulldog tap-dancing.

"I don't think you understand what you're dealing with here, Dr. García." Gertrude's voice was high pitched, fluttery. Her eyes darted around the chamber, panic clearly edging closer.

"It's probably just a big cat infected with rabies." Angélica's voice was level, her machete steady.

"I've only seen drawings," Gertrude continued. "Heard stories."

The odor of rotting flesh seeped into the room, making Quint's eyes water. He gagged, covering his mouth with the back of his hand.

"What in the hell ..." Angélica's voice trailed off.

A dark fur-covered arm reached out of the tunnel's black mouth. Long sharp claws extended from thick finger-like paws. One claw scratched across the blood smear on the floor. The arm disappeared back into the tunnel.

In the silence of their held breaths, Quint heard a sniffing sound. Jesus, was it smelling his blood?

A deep rumble filled the chamber.

Gertrude let out a squeak, covering her mouth too late.

A snout appeared out of the shadows, sniffing again.

The beast squeezed out of the narrow tunnel, its long muscled body stretching upright on its hind legs. Its spotted fur-covered head almost touched the ceiling. Sharp canine teeth reminded Quint of a saber-toothed tiger of old, but the cat-like resemblance ended at its head and claws. Its body had the physique of a hairy human, with a broad chest, narrow waist, and heavily muscled legs.

"What the fuck," Angélica whispered, her machete held out between her and the beast.

"That's no rogue cat," Quint told her, grabbing her by the shirt and shoving her behind him.

"It's a were-jaguar." She sounded awed by the beast about to eat him for dinner. "Now I know I'm high."

Drool hung in long strands from its canines. Its yellow eyes moved from Gertrude to Quint. There was a light of intelligence behind them that gave Quint a jolt. They weren't dealing with some mere rabid beast here. This thing was built to kill. Pitchforks and torches weren't going to cut it. Where in the hell had his imagination come up with this monster?

The beast sniffed in his direction, its yellow eyes narrowing in recognition.

"Shit," Quint said, finally understanding what this vision had been trying to show him all along since choking down Teodoro's drink. "I have an idea," he told Angélica and Gertrude.

The beast dropped onto all fours, preparing to pounce.

A roar filled the chamber, rattling Quint clear to his toes.

Chapter Twenty-Four

**Jaguar: One of the most feared beasts in Mesoamerica.
For many years, scholars believed the Olmec civilization had
only one major deity—the were-jaguar.**

"Whatever your idea is, Parker, you need to act fast." Angélica switched her machete to her left hand for a second to dry her sweaty right palm on her pants. Her eyes stayed locked on the were-jaguar. This was the last time she let Teodoro get her high. Why couldn't she be seeing dogs chasing butterflies instead of an Olmec god nightmare? Was this supposed to be some kind of test of her mental prowess?

"Gertrude is right," Quint said.

"Right about what?" Angélica gripped the machete, stepping out from behind Quint.

She sized up their adversary. Jaguars were cautious hunters, stalking their prey, analyzing the layout of the killing field, waiting for the right moment to pounce. If the three of them spread out and surrounded it, maybe they could confuse it. Then she could find an opportunity to slice the tendons on one of its legs and hobble it, giving them a chance to outrun it. But first, she needed to shift it away from the tunnel leading back into the mine.

"I need to be sacrificed," Quint told her.

"Wrong answer." Angélica inched away from him. She swung

the machete in front of her, drawing a figure eight in the air, seeing if she could attract the were-jaguar's attention.

Its golden eyes darted her way and then to Gertrude, who had picked up two broken femurs, holding the ragged ends out toward the beast.

"This is only a vision, Angélica. I have a gut feeling that once I get bit, it'll all be over, and I'll wake up with one hell of a hangover."

"What if it's not a vision?" She whispered the thought that had been scratching at her since leaving her mom at the mine's entrance.

"There's no way this shit can be real," Quint said, still standing next to the hole in the wall. "Just play along with me so I can finish my vision."

But it's *my* hallucination, Angélica thought.

"Gertrude," Quint said, "when the twin scribes were sacrificed by the great white priest, did he allow *Yum Cimil* to kill them? Or did the priest actually sacrifice them himself and leave their bodies in the feeding tank for the beast?"

Angélica frowned. Feeding tank? Great white priest? "What in God's name are you talking about, Quint?"

How was she supposed to play along with his vision when she was supposed to be hallucinating this story? Something wasn't making sense—besides her mom returning as a ghost and the were-jaguar snarling at them.

"Your mom told me a story about how they got rid of this nasty bastard when the two scribes were here last time."

"I ... I think," Gertrude found her voice finally, "the story goes that the priest drained their blood and then dumped their bodies into the feeding tank. The beast saw the bodies and returned to the other hunting plane, summoned no more."

"Why didn't you drain my blood like the white priest did the scribes?" he asked, sliding closer to the hole.

"I couldn't risk killing *der Beschwörer*." Gertrude looked from Angélica to Quint, taking a step toward the mine opening. "Not without the proper weapons and the council's approval. I did not want to end up like my predecessor." She took another step closer to the tunnel. "Or worse."

The were-jaguar turned toward the girl, its upper lip drawing away from its flesh-tearing canines. A deep snarl reverberated through the catacomb.

Taking advantage of the distraction, Angélica moved away from

Quint to form a three-pointed defense around the beast. Sweat coated her skin, her muscles trembling with unspent adrenaline.

"Angélica," Quint said. "Give me your machete."

"No. I'm going to take a stab at it, see if I can draw it back into the mine."

"And then what?"

"Lure it deeper into the earth so you two can get out of here." She'd find out for sure then if this was all a hallucination or not.

The were-jaguar looked her way, its head lowering. Angélica blinked, shaking her head. Her brain had to be playing tricks with her. Didn't it? Having fun turning what was probably a large rabid predator into a monster.

"Christ, do you hear yourself, woman? You're talking suicide. Give me the goddamned machete."

"I'm the captain of this ship, Parker. If I want to go down with it, that's my choice."

More curses came from Quint. "Listen, captain. It won't follow you now that it's found me." He held out his hand. "Now toss me your machete."

Angélica hesitated.

The were-jaguar sniffed in her direction, huffing several times. She took a step back and came down on a bone that rolled under her boot. She stumbled into the wall behind her, wincing when something hard poked into her hip. She reached behind her. A hard lump in her pocket made her gasp.

Pedro's gun!

She'd forgotten she had it. As much as she hated to harm her mom's favorite animal, if this sucker was even remotely real—she prayed not—it needed to be immobilized.

"How do we know it didn't follow me in here?" she asked.

"*Der Beschwörer* is right," Gertrude said. The sound of her voice attracted the were-jaguar's focus again, its growling growing louder. "The beast wants him. I lured it with his blood."

"Give me your machete," Quint ordered. "I know what I need to do."

"You're not going to sacrifice yourself."

"Trust me, Angélica."

Switching her machete to her left hand, she pulled the gun out of her pocket and pointed it toward the were-jaguar. "Let me take a shot at it first."

"Bullets won't stop it," Gertrude said.

She might not be able to stop it, but she could blind the creature. "Hey!" she called out to it, trying to make it turn back toward her.

The were-jaguar lowered its head and hunched its shoulders, prowling toward Gertrude.

"Whatever you're going to do," Gertrude's voice was high, her eyes wide, "do it fast."

The beast stalked closer.

"Angélica," Quint shouted. "The machete. Now!"

The were-jaguar closed in on Gertrude, pressing her into the wall. She waved her broken bones in front of the huge beast's bared teeth.

Jamming her blade into its leather sheath, she tossed the machete to Quint. He caught it and pulled the blade free.

The were-jaguar rose onto its hind legs, placing its huge finger-like paws on each side of Gertrude's head. It scratched one set of claws down the rock, the grating sound making the hairs rise on Angélica's arms.

Gertrude cried out, flinching.

Angélica edged toward the girl and the were-jaguar. "Stab it with the bones," she commanded, taking aim with the 9mm.

Why wasn't Gertrude defending herself? If she would just jam the damned broken femur into the beast's chest.

It rubbed its snout against Gertrude's temple. She closed her eyes and squeaked like a mouse caught in a trap.

Angélica heard the were-jaguar sniff. "Why is it smelling her?" she said.

"It's checking out her scent. Assessing its prey." Quint hurled a skull at the beast.

The skull thudded against the side of the were-jaguar's head. It grunted, its golden eyes turning to focus on Quint.

"Over here, you son of a bitch." Quint held out his left arm and sliced the machete blade over his skin.

Angélica winced. "What are you doing?"

"Giving it something else to sniff." He smeared his blood all over his arm with the flat side of the blade and then waved the knife in the air.

The were-jaguar lifted its nose, smelling.

"That's right." Quint backed toward the wall. "Come to papa."

Angélica looked at Gertrude. The girl's snake eyes bulged. Her chest heaved.

The were-jaguar sniffed the air again, licking its chops.

"It's dinner time, you bastard." Quint leaned against the wall, his hand gripping the edge of the hole. He shut off his flashlight and stuffed it into his side pocket.

Holding the gun steady on the were-jaguar, Angélica glanced between Quint and Gertrude. Neither of them moved as they waited to see if the beast would take the bait.

For a moment, logic clouded her thoughts. What was she doing here with this gun? This was all a dream. An incense-induced delusion. A figment of her ...

The were-jaguar spun back to Gertrude and snarled in her face, drool dripping.

The girl screamed. The piercing shrill blasted the remaining rationalizations from Angélica's head.

The beast swung with incredible speed, claws extended.

Then silence.

At first, Angélica thought Gertrude had ducked, avoiding the beast's sharp claws, but then her body folded, collapsing to the floor like a pair of loose coveralls. The flashlight she'd been holding rolled across the floor, lighting the corner next to the beast.

It took Angélica a moment to fully grasp the grisly scene.

The were-jaguar flicked its paw. Something clunked onto the floor, rolling into the spotlighted corner.

"Shit," Quint whispered.

Angélica couldn't pull her gaze from the sight of Gertrude's head, which was shriveling and turning brown before her eyes. The gun in Angélica's hand lowered along with her jaw.

"Oh my God!" she cried, the events of the last few seconds finally registering. "Quint."

"I know."

"She's dead."

"I know!"

"Why is her head shrink—"

"Get out of here!" he shouted.

The were-jaguar dropped onto all fours again and stalked toward him.

Quint wiped his bloody arm along the rim of the hole and then went down on one knee, backing into the shadows with his arm held out as bait.

When the were-jaguar hesitated, sniffing in Angélica's direction, Quint banged the machete on the floor. "Eyes on me!" he yelled.

Growling echoed throughout the catacomb. The beast crouched, locking Quint in its sights.

"Angélica, run!" He disappeared into the dark hole.

After one last check on Angélica, the were-jaguar lunged toward where Quint had been seconds before, slinking low to crawl inside.

Angélica pulled the trigger, aiming for its hindquarter.

The 9mm bucked in her hand, the bullet bouncing off the edge of the hole where the beast had been a split second before. It ricocheted into the ceiling and then veered into a pile of bones. Pieces of rock rained down around her. The ringing in her ears muffled the clatter of stones on the floor.

She shielded her head with her arm and squinted at the hole in the wall.

Quint and the were-jaguar were gone.

"No!" she cried, stumbling over bones, almost falling into the hole. She dropped onto her knees in front of it, aiming her flashlight inside, listening. Her still-muffled hearing made it hard to pick up any sounds. She pushed inside the hole, pausing again, holding her breath. Amidst the beast's grunts and snarls echoing along the rock walls, she thought she heard a rhythmic clanging.

She knew that sound. It was her machete hitting rock.

Stuffing the gun in her pocket, she followed the were-jaguar into the shadows.

* * *

Quint's arm throbbed along with his knees. He could hear the beast's snorts and huffs as it squeezed through the tunnel behind him. Its claws clicked on the rock floor, its snarls made his pulse pound. He didn't dare look back, afraid of what he'd see if he wasted a split second.

He moved in darkness, no time to pull out his flashlight and check his path. His knuckles and the heels of his palms burned from scraping along the rock in his blind haste. This damned dream-vision had morphed into one long nightmare with heart-stopping sound effects.

The rancid smell of the beast was thick in the enclosed space, making him cough and gag while he scrambled through the blackness. His eyes burned from sweat.

The tunnel spread wider the farther he crawled, his shoulders bouncing off the walls less and less. When he felt a breath of musty air on his face he scurried faster, figuring there had to be an opening up ahead.

He crawled on his hands and knees until the sounds of the tunnel changed, his ears picking up a difference in his surroundings. He stopped and reached upward for the ceiling. His hand touched only air. Had he reached another catacomb?

He kept his head lowered while rising to his feet. The smell in here wasn't much better than the tunnel, reminding him of the stench inside of the …

A rattle began in the darkness. Something bumped against the toe of his boot.

His breath caught.

The rattling sound doubled, and then tripled.

From the tunnel behind him, he could hear the clicking of claws on rock coming closer.

Fumbling with his pocket, he pulled out his flashlight and flicked it on.

Rattlesnakes!

He shone his light around, groaning.

Snakes dotted the floor and more slithered out of a foot-wide hole across the room. They slid between rocks that must have made up the wall that used to block the tunnel's access to the feeding tank. The same thing that had happened to the wall in the mine appeared to have happened here. Was this the were-jaguar's doing? Had it stopped by here earlier looking for dinner?

Stepping carefully away from the nearest forked-tongued rattler, he lifted the beam and directed the light around the walls of a familiar-looking stone room. On the opposite wall, a shoulder-wide hole was located ten to twelve feet above the floor. How he knew the place suddenly clicked in his head. Angélica had taken several pictures when she'd been dangling from that hole in the wall.

He was under the *Chakmo'ol* Temple.

This was the feeding tank Marianne had told him about earlier in his vision.

"Son of a fucking bitch," he whispered. He'd jumped out of the frying pan and into the snake-filled fire. This was the last damned time he agreed to participate in one of Teodoro's ceremonies.

He placed his flashlight on the floor to his right pointing toward the opposite wall, and then stepped around a small pile of bones over to the corner where only one snake hung out. He lined up the machete next to its coils like a golf putter and flung it across the room. It landed with a hiss and a rattle, which set off several other snakes.

Over the snake commotion, Quint heard several huffs.

The party-crasher had arrived.

The were-jaguar stuck its nose out from the shadows, its nostrils flaring. It crept out further, head lowered, upper lip wrinkled in a snarl.

Quint held still in the corner, the machete raised between him and the beast. Sweat trickled down his neck. Any time this nightmare wanted to hit the brakes would be good with him.

The were-jaguar eased from the hole. It swung its massive head in Quint's direction and bared its teeth even more.

"Fuck you and your big-ass teeth," Quint said, stepping away from the wall. There was no more running. Time to kill or be killed—preferably the former, but if he were a betting man ...

The thing rose up onto its back feet, towering over him by almost a foot. The snakes near it hissed and retreated without even bothering to shake their rattles. Even they knew better than to mess with this monster.

The yellow eyes narrowed. A glimpse of intelligence in their depths gave Quint pause. If this was his vision, couldn't he control what happened next?

"I summoned you," he told the beast.

It cocked its head, as if listening.

"*I* summoned *you*," he said again, with more confidence. "You are here because of me."

Could he un-summon it somehow? How did this fit in with the overall plan he was supposed to share with the crew when he woke up from this delirium?

The were-jaguar lifted its snout, its nostrils flaring again. A growl rumbled from its chest. It dropped to all fours and turned, hunching low while facing the hole it'd come through.

Angélica eased out of the shadows, Pedro's Glock 9mm pistol leading the way.

A cannon ball hit bottom in Quint's stomach. His nightmare

was pulse-pounding enough without having to watch the beast tear into her.

"What are you doing?" he said between gritted teeth. "I told you to run the other way, dammit."

"Have you forgotten who you're talking to, Parker?" she said with a calm, level voice. "I don't run from my problems." Using two hands, she held the short barrel steady on the beast. "If we both rush it, we might be able to disable it enough to allow us to make an escape."

The were-jaguar took a step away from Angélica, its back paw coming down on a rattlesnake. The serpent locked its jaws onto the beast's leg. With a kick of the were-jaguar's massive paw, the snake went flying, splatting against the wall.

"I'm going to shoot it in the eye," Angélica said, squeezing one eye closed as she centered her aim.

The beast's mouth opened wide, a deafening roar echoing throughout the room.

Quint inched toward Angélica, ready to dive in front of her if the were-jaguar lunged. "I don't think it liked that idea, sweetheart."

"I don't give a shit what it likes or not. It came looking for trouble at the wrong dig site. We need to end this shit here and now before anyone else gets hurt."

"What do you think I was trying to do by luring it in here? Tell it bedtime stories?"

"It sounded to me like you were sharing a heartwarming moment of self-awareness with it."

The were-jaguar's back haunches dropped. Was it readying to spring?

Quint reached for her. "You're real fun—"

The were-jaguar lunged.

Angélica got off two shots before she dove toward Quint, continuing to shoot toward the beast as she flew through the air. Explosions rang out in the rock-walled room, rattling Quint's back teeth.

He dropped the machete and tried to catch her, but he stumbled on some of the stone rubble that littered the floor. They crashed to the floor with him breaking her fall.

The were-jaguar disappeared into the hole.

Disoriented by the gun's deafening blast, Quint tried to sit upright, but Angélica's weight held him down. He felt as if he had

Pedro's helicopter headset on again, muffling all sounds. His shoulder and lower back ached from the stones he'd landed on when they'd fallen.

"Are you okay?" he shouted to Angélica.

She pushed up onto the heels of her palms, nodding down at him.

"Damn it, woman! You are going to be the death of ..." His voice trailed off.

The were-jaguar loomed over them, one eye bloodied. Its teeth were bared, its single yellow eye locked onto Angélica.

"Look out!" Quint yelled as it lunged again.

He managed to shove Angélica aside in time, but his raised forearm ended up in the beast's mouth. The were-jaguar bit down, sending a white-hot bolt of pain shooting up into his shoulder. Quint roared in pain, feeling its teeth puncture his skin as he struggled under the beast's weight.

A rebel yell filled the chamber. Over the beast's shoulder, Quint watched Angélica plunge the machete into its back.

The were-jaguar's bite loosened enough for Quint to pull free. He bucked and kicked at the beast, sending it rolling off of him.

It scrambled back onto all fours, snarling at Angélica. The dark hair that bristled on its neck made it look even more massive.

She glanced down as she stepped back, snagging a nearby rattlesnake by the tail. She whipped it at the beast.

The were-jaguar knocked the snake out of mid-air. With the machete still buried in its shoulder, the thing took a step toward her, licking its now-bloodied chops.

Quint clambered to his feet, holding his injured arm against his chest. He could barely feel the pain through the rush of adrenaline fueling him as he stumbled toward Angélica.

She grabbed another snake by the tail, throwing it at the were-jaguar's face.

The snake bounced off, slithering out of the way.

The beast rose onto its back feet, looming over her. Angélica shielded her head with her arm, her back against the wall.

A roar reverberated through the chamber. The beast shook its head, slobber flying.

Quint stumbled toward them.

It raised its paw, claws extending.

Quint slid in front of Angélica, blocking her from the beast's swing.

But the swing never came.

The were-jaguar staggered backward, clawing at its own throat. It crashed onto the floor, writhing on its back as it shredded at its own neck.

"What's wrong with it?" Angélica clutched his good arm.

"It looks like it's choking on something."

A wisp of smoke rose from its gaping jaws. More smoke escaped from its ears and eyes. Its fur began to ripple as it convulsed.

"What the hell?" Quint whispered, pulling Angélica toward the tunnel, back to the mine.

The beast let out a pain-filled, gargled yowl, its chest arching toward the ceiling. A flame shot out from its mouth, making them both flinch. More flames spread across its fur like wildfire. The room filled with intense heat and acrid smoke.

They both coughed, escaping into the tunnel. Neither spoke as they watched the thing burn from a distance.

When the smoke settled up near the ceiling, all that was left of the were-jaguar was an outline of black ashes. The snakes were mostly gone. The few that remained crowded the foot-wide hole in their haste to escape.

Quint stepped back into the room, offering his good hand to Angélica.

"I don't understand," she said, walking over to the ashes. "What made it combust like that?"

Quint joined her next to its ashes. "If I've learned anything about visions tonight, it's that there is no rational explanation for many of the events that occur while under the influence of Teodoro's Maya moonshine."

She shook her head. "Maybe when I shot it in the eye. No, it was fine until …" She looked at him. "Your arm."

Quint looked down at his forearm.

Angélica lifted his arm, her touch gentle as she inspected the bite marks. "It's healing already. How can that be?"

While the skin looked raw, the pain had dulled when the wounds had closed. Gertrude's words about a Summoner's ability to heal fast replayed in his thoughts.

Quint blew out a breath, pulling out of Angélica's grip. "This has been one hell of a fucked-up vision."

"I don't understand …" she trailed off, looking from his arm to the black ashes. She pinched herself.

"You don't need to understand," he told her. "It's my vision. You're just a visitor." Scooping up her machete from the ashes, Quint wiped the blade on his pants and handed it to her. "Next time I tell you to run, dream or not, you need to listen to me."

She guffawed. "It's *my* dig site, Parker. You don't get to give me orders, not even in your dreams. *And* especially not when it comes to keeping your ass alive."

"Bullshit. When you are in my head, I get to be in charge."

"I don't give a crap whose dream or vision this is. You shouldn't have left me back there in that catacomb."

"I was trying to protect you."

"We work as a team, damn it. There is no 'us' if you're dead." She walked over and picked up Pedro's Glock, pocketing it. "A team," she reiterated. "Even when we're both high from Teodoro's magic brew or happy weed."

When we're both high?

Quint cocked his head to the side, his mind grinding on her words. If Angélica thought she was high, and he thought he was having a vision, yet both of them were here together, did that mean …

"Hello?" Maverick's voice echoed through the room. A rope with a thick knot tied at the tail end slid down through the hole in the wall. "Anyone down there?"

Angélica weaved through the last three snakes left in the room, flicking them aside with her machete to clear a wider path. She tugged on the rope. "We're here, but Parker has a bum arm," she hollered up. "We're going to exit through the mine."

"No, you're not. The mine opening caved in from the weight of that huge strangler fig while you two were inside. This hole is the only exit unless you can wiggle your nose and blink your way out."

Quint scoffed. "Of course my only hope for escape is through yet another damned tunnel."

Angélica pushed the rope toward him. "You lead, Parker."

He shook his head. "Boss ladies first."

"But your arm."

He held it up and made a fist. "I'm fine, it's just a little tender yet." No lie there. The quickness with which his injuries healed was proof enough that this had to be a dream. "But hurry up before those damned snakes come back." Dream or not, he was done messing around with toothy bastards.

"Quint," she started to argue.

He grabbed her by the shirt and yanked her against him, kissing her hard on the mouth. "My dream. My rules." He took the machete from her. "Besides, it's going to take at least two of you to pull my sorry ass up through that damned hole."

She wrapped her legs around the rope, standing on the bottom knot. Quint reached above her head and tugged on the rope. "She's ready, Maverick."

"I'll be quick," she said, sliding up the wall.

"Good, because I'm getting the munchies. This is like college all over again." Well, except for the were-jaguar. And the rattlesnakes. And the ghost and the snake-eyed girl. Thinking of Gertrude made him grimace.

"If you don't follow me immediately," Angélica said as she scrambled into the hole, "I'm coming back down here and finishing what that were-jaguar started."

"I'll be right behind you, trust me." He'd scale that wall without a rope if those snakes came back.

He watched her crawl up through the hole until her boots disappeared, and then he turned back toward the pile of ashes. A rattlesnake slithered around them, its forked tongue sliding in and out.

What did it all mean tonight? Was this how Juan had felt during one of his demented head trips? Constantly questioning what was real and what wasn't? Or did he just go with the flow and enjoy Mr. Teodoro's Wild Ride?

Quint absently rubbed his arm, leaning against the wall as he waited for the rope to drop from the hole. He wiped away a trickle of sweat with his shoulder. Tomorrow, would he even remember everything that had happened since he'd swallowed that bitter-tasting concoction?

"The Summoner," he whispered in the shadowed room. He chuckled at his wild imagination.

What in the hell had Teodoro put in that damned drink?

Chapter Twenty-Five

Xtaabay (with two a's): Mayan word for "Demon."

D er Beschwörer!

Quint sprang from his hammock, bathed in sweat. Gertrude's words ping-ponged through his pounding skull.

Blinking the sleep from his eyes, he looked around at the empty tent. Angélica's cot was covered with books and wadded-up clothes. Nothing unusual there. Juan's sheet was folded neatly on top of his pillow, his red socks placed on his footlocker. Outside, the sun was busy baking the tent. The birds were chattering. The monkeys were howling. Normality had been returned to his world.

He'd made it. He was still alive and kicking after following the sun on a wild and freak-filled trek through the dark Underworld. He'd slipped through the fingers of *Yum Cimil* and his motley crew and returned topside. Thank the Maya gods for that.

Damn. Quint scrubbed his hands down his face.

The beige bandage taped on his left forearm made him pause. He carefully peeled back the sticky edge. Thick orange goop coated his skin, the cut underneath it barely visible. It smelled of herbs, probably one of Teodoro's homemade salves.

A fleeting memory of slicing his own arm with Angélica's blade flickered through his thoughts. Right. In his nightmare, he'd been trying to lure a were-jaguar away from Angélica and Gertrude. Shit, he must have really cut himself. Hadn't Angélica and Pedro told stories about Juan jumping into *cenotes* while intoxicated from

Teodoro's brews? What else had Quint done while he was under? He hoped like hell he'd kept his pants on in front of the crew.

Smoothing the bandage back in place, he grabbed his shaving kit and some clean clothes. First, a shower and shave. He needed to wash off the dirt and sweat from last night's temporary insanity. Second, food. Just one of María's breakfast burritos might not be enough this morning. He'd worked up a hell of an appetite during his head trip through the Underworld.

He pulled on a T-shirt and shorts. Unzipping the mesh flap, he stepped outside. The sunshine made him squint.

"*Buenos días*, sleeping beauty," Pedro said, striding toward him. "I was just coming to wake you with a big wet kiss."

"Save your spit swapping for the ladies, Prince Charming."

"Your loss." Pedro stopped in front of him, eyeing Quint up and down. "You look like the cat that swallowed the rooster."

"Canary," Quint corrected with a grin. "It's the cat that swallowed the canary."

Pedro shook his head. "There isn't anything cute and yellow about you in this light. I'm sticking with rooster."

Chuckling, Quint zipped the flap closed. "Where is everyone?" There was no din of conversation coming from the mess tent. Was the crew out in the field already?

"Here and there."

"How long was I out of it?"

Pedro fell into step beside Quint. "Long enough to miss out on most of the fun."

"What sort of fun? You and Juan didn't do anything to me last night, did you?"

"Besides point and laugh at you, we are innocent. Your *novia*, on the other hand, tucked you into your hammock. Only she knows her wicked deeds after she undressed you."

"Well, I hope she at least had her way with me."

Pedro laughed. "She has a few questions for you when you're done getting pretty."

They walked in silence for several seconds along the trail while the troupe of spider monkeys made a shrilling racket in the nearby trees.

"Did the rogue jaguar return?" Quint asked, his memory clouded with morning haze.

Pedro glanced over at him, his brow drawn. "You don't

remember?"

"What I remember from last night is too knotted up to untangle. Teodoro's concoction packed a killer punch." They were almost to the showers. "Did we come up with a solution for the cat problem?"

Pedro chewed on his lower lip. "*Sí.*"

"What was decided?"

Puffing his cheeks, Pedro stared toward the tree line. "Angélica should be the one to explain. When you're finished here, come to the mess tent. She's waiting for you."

Pedro headed back up the trail, leaving Quint trying to recall what had happened last night after he left the *Chakmo'ol* Temple. They'd returned to the fire, but it was only smoldering embers. The rest of the crew was absent. Then Angélica led him to their tent, helped him strip off his clothes, and pushed him into his hammock. He closed his eyes and that was all she wrote.

Shaking off the unease that Pedro's odd behavior had spurred, Quint stepped into the shower. He shaved and then stripped down, letting the warm water stream over his chest. When he reached for the soap, a faint scar on the underside of his forearm caught his eye. He turned his arm over slowly, rubbing his fingertips over the dark sprinkling of hair on his skin. Another scar lay hidden underneath. There was another scar further up, closer to his elbow. His heart skipped several beats.

He set the soap down and opened his palm, inspecting his skin. There it was. The mark was so faint it was almost indistinguishable from the intersecting lines that had been there since birth.

Blood rushed from his head. He gripped the shower partition. Leaning his forehead against the wall, he took several deep breaths, trying to block out the twister of flashbacks spinning through his mind, blowing around snippets of events from the mine and feeding tank.

What was real? He couldn't tell.

The scars were real.

Maybe they were self-inflicted like the cut on his arm.

But they were healed and the cut wasn't.

It didn't make any sense. How could …

Injuries from non-humans heal quickly, Gertrude had said. *It's one of your key defenses.*

It had been a vision, though. Not real. A side effect from the drink. There was no way …

"Quint."

Angélica's voice snapped him out of the spiral of confusion in which he'd been circling lower and lower.

"I'm almost done." He avoided her gaze as he wrestled with uncertainty. He turned away, rinsing off the last of the shaving gel, and shut off the water. "I thought you were going to wait for me at the mess tent."

"And miss seeing you in your birthday suit?"

When he glanced her way, she wiggled her eyebrows at him over the shower door. "Where's the fun in that?"

His hand trembled as he reached for the towel she held out for him. He grabbed it, hoping she wouldn't notice, but her quick frown told him the jig was up.

"Where is everyone?" he asked while drying off, trying to remember more details from last night. Everything was so warped. Trying to figure out what was real and what wasn't made his head pound harder.

She stepped back, looking up toward the mess tent. "Well, Pedro flew Bernard, Jane, Esteban, and Lorenzo to Chetumal last night. I gave them some time off after the excitement around the fire."

What excitement? What had he done? Quint dressed quickly, feeling naked in more ways than one this morning.

"Fernando?" he asked.

"He's over at the *Baatz'* Temple with Dad."

He packed away his razor and gel. "Teodoro and María?"

"Teodoro is resting and María is cleaning up after breakfast."

"Maverick?" Had the other so-called scribe undergone his own grand thoughts and transformation, including ending up with unexplainable scars, too?

She waited for him to step outside. "He's waiting in the mess tent for us."

What did that mean? Was he suffering from the same mental seasick sensation as Quint?

He sat down on the wooden bench seat next to the shower and took off his flip-flops, pulling on a sock and then a hiking boot.

"Daisy?" he asked, tying the laces.

"She's in the mess tent, too. Pedro is keeping them company until you're finished here."

He slid on the other sock and boot, tying quickly. "What about Gertrude?" He'd saved her for last, afraid of Angélica's answer. His flimsy grasp of sanity at the moment hinged on her whereabouts.

When Angélica didn't answer, he looked up at her. She was watching him, her face filled with too many lines for the news to be good.

"You might as well tell me the truth," he said.

"I don't know."

"You don't know if you should tell me the truth?"

She shook her head. "I don't know where she is."

Elbows on his thighs, he covered the upper half of his face with his hands. "She's in the catacomb."

"Quint," she started.

"Her body is, anyway," he muttered, his head spinning more than ever.

"We don't know that for certain."

He lowered his hands, peering up at her. "You were there."

She stared into the trees, the same way Pedro had earlier.

"You saw it all, too, didn't you?" he pressed.

"I don't know what I saw."

"Bullshit."

"Events happened last night that make no sense. Everything sort of blew up in our faces right after Maverick and you drank from the gourds."

He sighed. "I thought it was all part of the vision I was supposed to be experiencing."

"Maybe it was. Maybe Gertrude is just lost in the jungle somewhere."

"Have you sent out a search team for her?"

"Pedro and Fernando went out at dawn for a couple of hours. They couldn't find any signs of her."

Because she was in the mine. He grimaced, remembering the way her body had shriveled and turned brown.

"It's a big jungle. She could be anywhere out there."

Quint snorted. Of course Angélica's logical side didn't want to accept what had happened. "Did you send anyone down to look in the mine?"

"The entrance is caved in."

Oh, yeah. Quint remembered that detail now. Maverick had mentioned it after he'd sent the rope down to them in the feeding tank. "What about that tunnel leading to the catacomb from the *Chakmo'ol* Temple?"

"The snakes are back tenfold."

How would she know that, unless ... "You went down again?"

"Someone had to, and I have the gear." When Quint sputtered, she held out her hand. "Calm down. I waited until Pedro got back and took him to the temple with me. He made sure I was in and out of the chamber without a scratch."

"Did you tell him what you were looking for?"

"No. I told him I needed to see if the snakes had returned."

"Was the tunnel still open?"

She nodded.

"What about the ashes?"

"I couldn't see the floor through all of the snakes."

Quint cursed. "How did Maverick know we were in there?"

"He said that when he woke up, Daisy told him they needed to go to the temple with a rope."

"Daisy?"

"And," Angélica started, her voice husky. She cleared her throat. "And Daisy knew exactly where he needed to go, even though she hadn't been in that little burial chamber before."

How did Daisy know they'd be down in the feeding tank?

"When Dad tried to stop them from leaving the fire, she told him that Maverick had to go rescue us because the mine entrance was blocked."

"Daisy said all of this?" he asked again, scratching his jaw.

"Yep." She crossed her arms. "After you crashed in your hammock last night, Pedro pulled me aside. He badgered me until I told him I thought my mom had spoken to me through Daisy. He wasn't surprised."

"Why's that?"

"He believes she's carrying my mom's spirit."

"Does Pedro know about what we saw down in the mine last night? What we faced in the feeding tank?"

"No. I told him as little as I could for now. Just that the rogue jaguar had followed us in the mine and we had to put it down."

"You didn't tell him about Gertrude?"

"No." Her eyes held his. "I needed to talk to you first and find out what was real."

He scoffed. "I don't think I have any answers for you." He

held out his arm, opening his palm with the faint scar for her to see. "But I do have battle scars that might."

She took his arm, inspecting it and his palm. Then she pointed at his other arm. "Why didn't that cut heal like these?"

"Because I made that cut."

"So what?"

"Before you arrived in the catacomb, Gertrude told me that injuries from non-humans would heal very quickly."

She let go of his arm, frowning at him. "Non-humans?"

"It's a defense all Summoners have." He squeezed the back of his neck. "I guess it's what makes us so special."

That and the ability to call forth unnatural creatures from the depths of the Maya Underworld.

She sucked air through her teeth. "This is crazy, Quint."

"Welcome to my new altered reality." He stood, draping his damp towel over his arm, shaving kit in hand. "Shall we go play show-and-tell with the others?"

"Let's keep this between us." She turned and led the way.

"You mean the bit about Gertrude?"

"And your scars."

He matched his stride to hers. "What am I supposed to say if they ask me what I saw last night in my dreams?"

"Let me think about that. I'll run the show in there. You sit next to me and listen unless I specifically ask you to explain something."

"We can't hide the truth about Gertrude."

"We can until the *federales* come and take a look down in that catacomb."

"The *federales*? Have you contacted them already?"

"Not yet, but I will after we finish our little meeting in the mess tent. I'll have to let the crew in Chetumal know that I'm going to shut down the site early."

"I take it this dig's objectives are on hold for now?"

"Unfortunately. Dad and Fernando have been working on prepping the site for inactive status in case it came to that." She frowned at him. "After talking to you, it has."

"I'm sorry, Angélica."

"It's not your fault."

What if it was? What if that beast had come at his unintentional bidding?

"We need to be careful for now so that our stories match," she said more quietly as they neared the tents. "If Daisy or Maverick are interviewed by the *federales* and we all give conflicting stories, you and I could be even more on their radar as suspects tied to her disappearance."

"You mean her death."

She shushed him. "Trust me on this, Quint. I've dealt with the *federales* before. You don't want to end up in a Mexican prison for a crime you didn't commit."

She had a good point. Mexican prisons weren't known for their hospitality and soft beds. "My lips are sealed."

They stopped by their tent long enough for him to drop off his shower things.

"You ready?" she whispered outside of the mess tent.

Not even close. "Following your lead."

Maverick and Daisy looked up at him as he stepped inside.

Pedro was pouring coffee. "Hey, look who's showed up for the *fiesta*."

"Rip Van Winkle finally stirred," Daisy said, her smile warm.

Maverick searched Quint's face as he sat down at the table with them. "How are you feeling?" he asked.

"Hungover," Quint answered truthfully, thanking Pedro when he sat a cup of coffee and a plate with a breakfast burrito on it down in front of him. "How about you?"

His partner in the scribehood shook his head. "That was some messed-up, crazy-ass shit last night."

Quint grimaced. Maverick didn't know the half of it.

Or did he?

* * *

Angélica sat cross-legged on the ground next to Rover, who was busy snarfling the tortillas she'd brought him after supper. She stroked the javelina's bristly back, gazing out across the tree canopy at the rose-colored sky. The coo-cooing of mourning doves soothed her as much as the grunting troublemaker now sniffing around her hands for more treats.

Chuckling under her breath, she pulled another tortilla from her pocket, handing it over to the nosey javelina.

She'd escaped from the mess tent, needing a moment to breathe out in the open jungle, to soak up the smells of the grass and dirt, to feel the earth solid and sturdy beneath her … because her world was about to get really shaken up and messy.

A search team of Maya locals and nearby reserve federal agents would arrive tomorrow. Teodoro had used the satellite phone to contact the biosphere reserve next door, explaining that one of the dig site crew members had apparently wandered away during the night. The reserve agent he spoke to wasn't surprised at the news. He told Teodoro that many hikers tended to overestimate their ability to trek alone through the jungle, not taking into account that this forest teemed with many dangers from both plants and animals. He also mentioned the few but perilous, inescapable *cenote* holes hidden throughout the reserve by deadfall. They'd lost many hikers from either falling into a *cenote* and dying upon impact with the water far below or drowning when they couldn't climb back to the surface.

After hanging up, Teodoro and Angélica had agreed if Gertrude wasn't found after the search team spent a few days scouring the jungle and dig site, it would be time to call in the *federales*. They both knew the chances of Gertrude being alive and well somewhere were very slim, but there were processes to follow. Processes that didn't take into account that a supernatural Maya world could actually exist. That was an idea Angélica was still struggling to swallow herself.

In the meantime, Angélica planned on going through the paperwork Gertrude had submitted when she'd signed up with INAH to find out who the girl's emergency contact was. Until all parties were satisfied everything had been done to find Gertrude, Angélica would have to play along without giving away anything that had happened in that catacomb, because at this time—to her knowledge—none of the procedures about losing an employee detailed what to do if decapitation by an Olmec were-jaguar god was the method of death. Nor was there documentation that explained why a body would shrivel and turn brown immediately after decapitation. On both those fronts, Angélica was flying blind.

She scratched Rover under his collar—one of his favorite spots. He lowered to the ground and rolled toward her, giving her access to another favorite—his belly.

Learning that Quint shared the same memories about Gertrude and the were-jaguar had doubled Angélica's heartburn. Until she'd spoken with him at the showers this morning, she'd held onto the hope that she'd been delusional last night. That she'd been overtired, and after breathing in Teodoro's incense, she had made up the conversation with her mother along with everything after. That she'd be able to bring back the rest of the crew and finish as planned.

It was going to take some time for her to accept all of the events as real and make peace with it. Especially the story Quint had told her about the site's history. A story he swore Marianne told him before he'd joined Gertrude in the mine.

How was that even possible?

Even more impossible to believe was Quint and his bizarre ability to heal almost instantly. Her bruises from last night were still purplish blue and heading toward green, whereas the only evidence left of his bite wound were several small faded scars. Was there some truth to Gertrude's tall tale about who Quint really was? How could … why didn't … what the hell? Angélica shook her head, letting that one go for now.

Daisy and Maverick's accounts of last night's events hadn't helped make any more sense of the mayhem. This morning, after Quint had joined Angélica, Daisy, Maverick, and Pedro in the mess tent, she had asked Daisy to tell them what she remembered from the night prior.

Daisy had prefaced her reply with the declaration that her memory was sketchy from when Maverick had collapsed until she'd woken up in her cot this morning. Several times during the night, she claimed to have had blackout periods. When she'd wake up from one, she'd find herself either holding something she had no recollection of picking up or standing in a different location from her previous waking moment.

The instances when Angélica suspected Daisy wasn't really herself were these blackout periods. For example, Daisy had no memory of leading Angélica to the mine. Nor did she recall showing Maverick where to find Angélica and Quint in the *Chakmo'ol* Temple.

After asking Daisy a few more questions regarding what she knew about Gertrude's private life and family, Angélica had tried to smooth over the previous night by explaining that such chaotic and odd behavior was often experienced during Teodoro's ceremonies. Pedro helped her out, telling Daisy a couple of stories about Juan's wacky reactions to different drinks in the past. When he finished, Angélica had thanked Daisy and asked her to go pack up Jane's and Bernard's belongings.

That had left Maverick in the spotlight.

Quint stayed quiet while Angélica asked Maverick questions. He appeared to be focused on his breakfast burrito, but she caught him pausing mid-chew several times while Maverick spilled what he could recall after drinking from the gourd.

Maverick's tale had its own dark twist. He told them his vision had started with him running through the jungle while being chased by a huge jaguar. Then he stood at the base of the *Chakmo'ol* Temple's steps. His next memory was of being led up those steps while his wrists were tied with rope. He was laid out on an altar stone at the top and held in place by several men whose faces were painted to look like angry monkeys. A shaman or priest wearing the head and pelt of a jaguar then chanted strange words over him, lifted a sharp blade made of obsidian, and jammed it into Maverick's heart. Throughout the whole nightmare, he fought to escape, gasping for air, kicking and struggling. In the end, they cut out his heart as he watched, taking his final breaths in between screams of pain. After that, the world had gone dark.

Then he woke up next to the fire secured to the stretcher with Daisy leaning over him. That was when she'd freed him, saying they needed to take a rope to the *Chakmo'ol* Temple.

When Angélica asked Maverick if he was sure there wasn't more to tell, anything that might have happened after he was sacrificed, he shook his head slowly. "It was all pretty horrific from beginning to end."

The same could be said of Quint's night, which she'd found out later back in their tent. He'd filled her in on everything he could remember, starting with the part about her mom, adding in bits about Gertrude, and ending with what she already knew about the were-jaguar. Even though she'd witnessed the last part in person, his whole story was hard to swallow, especially the part about her mom. Could she really be here with them?

Quint's story explained why Angélica hadn't been able to find that damned stela with the warning glyphs her mom had written about in her notebook, solving that mystery finally. It also answered Angélica's questions about the site's multi-layered history as evident from the artifacts they'd found. But Angélica couldn't wrap her mind around the colorful idea of ghosts and supernatural beings existing. They didn't fit in her black and white world.

"Dr. García," Teodoro said, pulling her away from her

bewildering thoughts. He joined her and Rover in the grass and scratched the javelina behind the ear. "We'll need more supplies for the search team," he spoke in Spanish, their common ground.

After the mess tent meeting, Angélica had talked to Pedro about flying back to Chetumal in the morning to drop off Jane's and Bernard's things and pick up more food and gasoline. "Daisy said she'd like to stay and help María make tortillas and serve food to those who come to search."

Teodoro nodded. "María would be thankful for her help."

"Maverick is staying, too. He is going to join one of the search teams."

"He is a good tracker. I will keep him close to me to make sure he stays safe."

"*Gracias.*" She stared toward the eastern horizon, watching the rose-colored sky darken to violet. "Fernando and I will work on documenting the current status of the remaining dig site structures while Dad maps the buildings. We should be finished here in a week or so. When the search team wraps up, you and María can fly home."

He frowned. "What are you going to do about your *xtaabay?*"

Angélica did a double take. *Xtaabay?* That was the Mayan word for … "My demon?"

"*Sí, Señor* Parker. He is from *Xibalba.*"

"You think *Quint* is a demon from the Maya Underworld?"

Teodoro nodded. "Last night during the ceremony, he called my spirit to the limestone mine. I was given no choice. That is why I collapsed. It was not in my plans for how the ritual would end."

None of last night's events were part of *her* plans.

"He also called for the jaguar demon to come."

Summoner. She thought of the name Gertrude had used for Quint.

"He has more strength than he knows," Teodoro continued.

"A demon? From the Underworld?" she shook her head in disbelief. "Quint would never harm anyone on purpose." His penchant was more along the lines of covering mud puddles with his coat. "He's a protector."

Teodoro squeezed her shoulder. "There are many demons in *Xibalba.* Some are very bad. Others are good. The shaman at my childhood village would tell stories about bad demons. He said that when a bad demon escaped from *Xibalba* into the human world, a good demon would be sent by one of the death gods to capture or kill the tormentor. I believe *Señor* Parker comes from a long line of good demons who walk amongst us, sent to protect."

Angélica's jaw dropped. Teodoro could have reached out and pushed her over with a single finger. "A *good* demon?"

He squeezed her shoulder again. "Mating with him would be beneficial to the Maya people. His line needs to continue for our safety." After a final pat on Rover's head, Teodoro left her side.

A squawk burst from her chest. "Mating with a demon is a good thing now?" she asked Rover.

He rolled onto his belly, rested his snout on her knee, and sighed.

Criminy! This was too bizarre. Had her father put Teodoro up to this in his eternal quest for grandchildren? Her eyes narrowed. That was it. It made complete sense. Pedro was probably in on it. The two were always playing practical jokes.

But neither of them knew about the were-jaguar. She'd been careful to keep that between Teodoro and herself during the fallout from last night.

While the sky went from violet to midnight blue, Angélica sat with Rover, listening to the sounds of the jungle nightlife gearing up as she tried to make sense of what she'd experienced last night. In the light of day, she struggled with every part of what had happened, but as darkness fell, the area between logic and what she'd witnessed grew murky.

"*Gatita!*" her father called out in the twilight, bringing her out of her deliberation of reality versus temporary insanity.

She pushed Rover aside and stood, stretching. "Over here," she shouted. "I'm visiting Rover."

Her father's mumbles about "that dang boot-eating pig" traveled quicker than he and his cane did.

"You're going to hurt his feelings, you know," she told her dad, putting Rover back inside the safety pen Teodoro had constructed for him. "Can't you see he loves you so much he wants to eat your boot to get closer to you?"

Juan scoffed. "That's not love. It's an invitation to war."

"Whatever." She closed and latched the gate. "Did you put Teodoro up to trying to convince me to have kids with Quint?"

"No, but that's a great idea. We should form a pro-Quint team, hit you from multiple angles."

She crossed her arms. "You'd better not talk about this in front of Quint."

"How else is the boy supposed to know his role in life as I see it if I don't talk about it?"

She rolled her eyes. "There's a little more to having kids than the creation part, you know." Like taking into consideration that Teodoro believed Quint was some kind of emigrant from the Underworld, sent by the gods of death. Demon babies were notoriously difficult to raise. Things rarely ended well for the parents, let alone the rest of the world.

"I'm well aware of the heartache and stress children can cause, *gatita*," he said, chuckling as he put his arm around her shoulder. He let out an "Oof" when she playfully jabbed him in the ribs and released her. "Daisy says you're going to let her stay for a few more days."

"María can use her help when the search team gets here." Angélica winced, preparing for his argument against letting the outsider stay.

"I'm glad she's staying."

"You are?"

"I like Daisy. There's something about her that makes me smile."

Angélica glanced at him from under her lashes, remembering her mom's words about Daisy being an open channel. If there were such things as ghosts, and *if* the ghost of her mother was using Daisy as a megaphone, then it was no surprise Juan was drawn to the woman. Although to be fair, Daisy was warm and funny, and she loved all things Maya. Her father could be drawn to those elements of her personality alone.

For now, Angélica decided not to tell her dad about her experience with her mom's ghost. She couldn't think of any good that might come from that news.

She also wasn't going to bring up much of anything that happened last night to anyone other than Teodoro and Quint. She'd only told Pedro about hearing her mom's voice come from Daisy because he'd twisted her arm this morning—literally. The brat had noticed her tension when it came to talking about last night. He'd twisted her arm behind her back until she'd cried "Uncle" and tossed him a bone, telling him the bit about hearing from her mother. Being as superstitious as her father, Pedro wasn't surprised at her admission, especially because he'd already formed his theory about her mom haunting Daisy.

"Have you talked to your boss at INAH?" her father interrupted her thoughts.

"I left a message."

It had been a tough phone call to make, what with her career on the line due to Gertrude's disappearance. She'd told INAH the situation and recommended they shut down the site a bit earlier than planned. She hoped the artifacts they found and the information, pictures, and data gathered over the last month would be enough to satisfy INAH for now.

After the dust settled and she found out if she got to keep her job, she'd figure out if there would be a need to come back to this site before recommending another archaeological crew to continue the work. There was much to find and catalog, but that underground rattlesnake den would be a problem. The snakes would either need to be relocated, or the work restricted at that end of the site. The jungle was a fierce foe as well for an inexperienced team.

They approached their tent. It was dark inside.

"Where's Quint?" she asked.

"He went down to shower. He worked up quite a sweat over at the *Baatz'* Temple with Fernando and me this afternoon. We finished clearing that sub chamber of debris and made a few structural repairs that should keep the entrance from collapsing again. You wouldn't know by looking at Quint, but that boy has the strength and stamina of a Clydesdale, I swear."

Angélica smiled. "He works like a demon when put to task."

"Well, this old stallion is going to crash." Juan unzipped the tent and stepped inside. "After last night's fun and games and today's hard work, I'll sleep like a baby. What time is the search team arriving?"

She followed him inside and grabbed her towel and shower supplies. "Probably around the time Pedro and you return from Chetumal with more supplies."

"Good. I'd like to be here to help search. That poor girl has to be out there somewhere."

Or not.

Angélica hooked her machete onto her belt. "Don't forget to make sure Bernard and Jane get their tickets home. Don't worry about the costs. I have it covered. I have some leftover money in the budget that I was saving for an end-of-dig party back in Cancun."

"I won't."

"Oh, and I have envelopes for Esteban and Lorenzo. It's their payment for the job in full. Make sure they get their duffel bags and some bus tickets back to their villages." She stepped outside, zipping the mesh flap closed behind her.

"You don't want them to help with the search?"

She shook her head. "We'll have enough mouths to feed with the search team here. Besides, considering Esteban's clumsiness, we'd probably end up having to rescue him mid-search."

He frowned at her through the mesh. "Where are you going? I thought you showered after supper."

"Nope. I took Rover some tortillas and hung out with him while the sun set."

"You have an unnatural attachment to that pig."

"He's not a pig, Dad." She pointed toward his cot. "Go to bed. Pedro wants to fly out at dawn."

"How about I get you a real dog?" he called to her back as she walked away. "Would you get rid of the pig then?"

She laughed. "Rover stays. I'll buy you new boots back in Cancun."

The sound of him muttering followed her for several steps until the jungle's nighttime serenade blocked him out. She moved quickly in the moonlight down to the showers, scanning the tree line for glittery eyes. The were-jaguar might have been history, but there were still plenty of other predators hanging out in the trees.

Quint was in the midst of soaping up when she opened his stall door and walked inside.

He jerked back a step, his eyes wide. "Dammit, woman! You scared the hell out of me."

There was a joke in there regarding Teodoro's thoughts on Quint's lineage, but she wasn't in the mood to play jester.

He looked down at her ... all the way to her toes. "Are you naked?" he whispered.

She took the soap from him. "I don't know. You'll have to take a turn with the soap and find out. But first, it's my turn."

When she was done soaping him up and down, he certainly sounded like Teodoro's demon with all of his huffing and moaning.

"You're killing me, sweetheart." He stole the soap from her. "My turn."

"I have a better idea." She wrapped her arms around him and slid her chest over his. "We can share your soap."

He slid his hands over her ribs. "What if someone comes down here?"

"Nobody is going to come down here. We're the last to shower tonight." She went up on her toes and kissed him, running her tongue over his lower lip the way he liked.

He cupped her hips, feeling his way around her curves. "They might need to use the latrine."

"We'll be quiet." She pulled him toward her until her back was against the stall wall.

He pressed against her, getting her hot and soapy. "You're so slippery."

Lifting her leg, she took his hand and hooked it under her knee. "Hold this, Parker." She pulled his mouth back to hers.

"You're always bossing me around," he said in between her kisses, teasing her with his body until she tipped her head back and cursed his name.

"Tell me what you want," he ordered.

She looked up at him. Slivers of moonlight lit his mouth and neck, his eyes hidden in the dark. She didn't give a shit what he was—traveler, summoner, demon, whatever. He was Quint. Her heart ached at the thought of him leaving again.

She licked her lips. "I want you to stay with me."

The needy words were out before she could filter them.

He stared down at her. "Stay? Do you mean in Cancun?"

She nodded, not trusting her mouth. It might start begging if he resisted.

"Stay for a few weeks or stay for good in between jobs?"

Closing her eyes, she whispered, "For good."

"Angélica, look at me."

She opened one eye.

"Are you sure?"

She nodded, opening the other eye.

"Even after last night?"

"Even after last night, Quint." She gulped and took another risky step. "Without you, my life is black and white. I need your color. When you're done with a job, I want you to come home to me and my bed."

His teeth gleamed in the moonlight. "I got under your skin,

didn't I?"

His grin was infectious. "Like a chigger," she replied.

He chuckled, deep and sexy. "You're such an old romantic."

"Shut up, Parker, and finish what I started."

"Yes, boss lady."

And he did, kissing her senseless while he was at it.

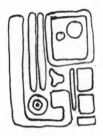

Chapter Twenty-Six

Siren (from Greek mythology): Dangerous female creatures who use their spellbinding voices and songs to lure gullible sailors to their rocky coast.

One week or so later ...

The moon was late to the beach party.

Quint tipped back his bottle of Corona. The beer was already lukewarm, thanks to the evening's sweltering humidity, but it was still refreshing.

Angélica was late, too. However, since she was packing for their trip, he'd give her a pass.

The breeze blowing in from the ocean outside of Angélica's bungalow did little to cool the warm night, but Quint wasn't complaining. The gentle crashing of the waves soothed away the tension from the last few sweat-filled days of working his ass off in the jungle amidst the bellowing monkeys and biting bugs.

They'd wrapped up what Angélica needed to accomplish at the site while the search team had scoured the jungle to no avail. Angélica and several of the skinnier team members had dropped smoke bombs into the feeding tank under the *Chakmo'ol* Temple, going down into the chamber as soon as the smoke had cleared out enough snakes to keep from getting bit. They'd tossed another smoke bomb into the snake hole and then sealed it off, trying to drive the rattlesnakes to the surface where Teodoro, Maverick, and a handful of volunteers hooked and bagged as many as they could catch.

Angélica had led the least superstitious of the crew into the catacomb, through the tunnel that connected it to the mine, and deeper into the earth as they searched for Gertrude. There were no signs of her, of course, except for her dried-up remains, which nobody but Angélica noticed thanks to all of the other bones and skulls distracting them.

They'd returned to the surface empty handed. Later, alone in their tent, Angélica had told Quint that the black ashes from the were-jaguar were spread out all over the floor thanks to the snakes, blending in with the dirt and snake droppings.

When the search was called off, a handful of *federales* came. They didn't ask many questions. As the federal agent at the biosphere reserve explained, there are many ways to die in the jungle, and even more for a body to disappear and never be seen again. After a few brief interviews, Gertrude was officially listed as missing.

To make matters more interesting, the names on her INAH paperwork were dead-ends. Calls to the phone numbers in her file were either wrong numbers or belonged to what the *federales* figured were burner cell phones no longer in service. Even more suspicious was the response from the university in Germany she'd supposedly been attending. According to their records, no such graduate student existed.

Before Angélica and her crew had taken down the tents at the site, the *federales* stopped by one last time to talk to her. They told her they suspected Gertrude had been acting as a "mule," sent to the site to steal artifacts for a seller on the archaeology black market. They believed she disappeared during the night with a few artifacts she might have found and hidden away in a cache in the jungle while working at the site.

Quint rested his elbows on his knees, staring up at the stars. Gertrude's tragic end still weighed on him. He should have tried harder to keep her from becoming a casualty, but he'd been so sure it was all a dream that he'd been caught off guard.

He'd thought about her words often over the last week, wondering how much was true. It was all so inexplicable that he had trouble accepting his title, yet the were-jaguar scars remained. If

Angélica hadn't been there with him, he might have checked himself into an asylum upon returning to civilization.

"Is this seat taken?" Angélica asked, standing over him.

The porch light backlit her curves, the fringe of the white crocheted swimsuit coverup contrasting sharply with her bare thighs. His blood heated at the thought of peeling that crocheted top off her later.

"It is now." He scooted over on his towel, making room for her. "The towel is damp."

"You went swimming without me?"

"Just a dip to cool off."

She settled onto the towel next to him, holding out a fresh beer. "Look, the moon is coming up." She pointed her Corona bottle at it.

"It was waiting for you. Did you finish packing?"

"Yep. Where are we going?"

He chuckled. "No questions asked," he reminded her, draining his warm beer and sticking the bottle in the sand next to the cold one.

She leaned her head on his bare shoulder. "Dad told me to tell you he's finished going through the article you two have been working on all week. He thinks it's ready to send."

Juan had been very generous with his time and knowledge about the Olmec civilization. Their article theorizing that the ancient civilization had migrated much farther south than previously accepted based on proof found at the dig site should inspire some interesting discussions in the Mesoamerican archaeology world.

"Great. I'll fire it off to the editor before we leave."

"He also thought you should let him know where we're going in case he needs to contact us." She switched her bottle of beer to her other hand and laced her cool fingers through his. "Where should I tell him he can reach us?"

"Good try, sweetheart, but he already knows." Quint had given Juan and Pedro both the details needed to get hold of them in case of an emergency.

"I could try to torture you sexually until you tell me."

"That sounds like a good idea. Let's get started right now. I hope you brought your whip?"

Her laughter was low and husky. It was nice to hear it again after a week of watching her shoulders bend under the stress at the dig site.

"Two weeks," she said, lifting his hand and dropping a kiss on the backside. "I can't remember the last time I've taken that much time off of work."

"We need to make it a habit, then. So, the head honchos at INAH aren't upset about how things ended at the dig site?"

"No. They're thrilled with the status report I turned in yesterday. Go figure." She took a drink of beer.

He pulled his hand free so he could run his knuckles up her thigh. "Good."

"When I get back to work, I'll choose the next site on their cleanup list and begin the prep work for a scouting trip via Pedro and his helicopter."

That reminded him. "Pedro asked me about your mom."

She pulled her knees up to her chest, resting her chin on them as she looked out toward the water. "What about her?"

With Angélica's approval, Quint had let Pedro know about Marianne's role in his vision that night.

"He wanted to know if she told me who killed her."

While the search through the pilot's logbook records had ended without success, Pedro's friend had managed to track down a couple of pictures of some of the previous crew, which Pedro had shown to Quint. The white-blond, pale-skinned crew member with the beefy arms reminded him of Gertrude. He would have been Quint's prime suspect.

"What did you say?"

"I told him she didn't know who her killer was." Quint had figured that might be true, since it was likely that Gertrude's predecessor had worked in secret. Marianne hadn't mentioned anything about who killed her during her history lesson on the site.

"Was he satisfied with that?"

"For now. But I expect he'll keep digging. He loved your mom a lot. I think he wants to make sure her killer pays for murdering her."

"According to Gertrude, he already is." She stretched her neck from side to side. "I hope he doesn't bring all of this up with Dad. It took him a long time to get over losing my mom. It's only been since Daisy's come along that he's started to show signs of interest in a companion again. I don't want to blow that with Pedro planting a seed about Mom's ghost channeling through Daisy."

Quint grimaced. "That's messy business." Especially since Daisy seemed to enjoy Juan's company.

"Exactly. It's better left alone for now."

"Did Maverick and Daisy make it to the airport okay?"

"Yep. Dad said he waited until they boarded the plane before coming back home."

"Are you going to invite them back?"

"I think so. I'm limited on crew numbers, though. It will depend on INAH and the budget they give me for the next site. I may need to accept extra paying guests in order to hire more crew."

They sat in silence for several beats, drinking, staring out at the ocean.

"Did Maverick ever mention anything else about what he experienced in his vision?" Quint asked her.

"No. Teodoro thinks it's haunting him, though. He said Maverick's shadow has changed."

"His shadow?"

"Yeah. I don't question the shaman on these things. If he says Maverick's shadow is now blue, I nod and ask if we need to have a ceremony about it."

"Smart of you." Quint grinned. "Teodoro is a wise man. Although I'm not volunteering to be his guinea pig for any more rituals."

"That's probably a good idea. He told me on the phone earlier today that Rover misses you."

"Please. Rover misses the tortillas I kept sneaking him when nobody was looking this last week."

After Teodoro had shared with Quint his belief that Rover's arrival at the ceremony that night had been part of the reason Quint's spirit had made it back from his tour through the nine levels of the Maya Underworld in one piece, Quint had decided daily rewards were in order for the javelina.

She giggled. "Dad offered to get me a puppy."

"Really?"

"I told him one dog is enough for me."

Chuckling, he ran his hand down her curved back. The crocheted coverup got in the way of feeling her smooth skin under his palm.

"I have something for you." He pulled out a heart-shaped, wooden box he'd hidden beneath the corner of his towel, holding it out to her.

She lifted her chin from her knees. "What's this?"

He shrugged. "Open it and see."

Taking the gift, she held it up in the light. "Mexico," she read aloud the word written on the top.

"There wasn't time to have one custom made with your name on it." He leaned back on the heels of his palms, watching as she figured out how to open the box.

"Tricky," she said, pushing on the heart-shaped locking piece on the side.

"The lid slides off," he told her when she tried to pull it off without luck.

She slid the top off and lifted another wooden lid inside that covered a felt-lined compartment. She took out the silver necklace chain, letting it hang from her finger. "You bought me a necklace?" she asked, holding it up in the glow from the porch light. "What's this?" She cupped the charm made of glass and silver that he'd strung on the chain.

"It's a protection charm."

"Protection?" She looked at him, her forehead drawn. "Protection from what?"

Honestly, he didn't know. His aunt had given him the charm strung on a strip of leather when he stopped back home before returning to Mexico. Aunt Zoe had been giving him "special" wristwatch bands and leather necklaces with charms on them since he was a kid. When she'd given him this latest piece, she'd made him promise he'd wear it for protection while on his travels. Unfortunately, he'd forgotten about it in his duffel bag until he arrived in Cancun and unpacked. After what had happened at the dig site with that were-jaguar's bite, he figured Angélica needed it more than he did.

"Protection from troublemakers," he said. "My aunt Zoe made it. She's a glass artist who dabbles with metals, too."

"Really?"

He nodded. "She has a workshop with a kiln behind her house." Maybe he'd take Angélica to Deadwood sometime to meet Aunt Zoe, but he didn't want to rush her. Wanting him to move in had been a big trusting step for Angélica.

She secured the necklace around her neck. "It's beautiful."

The porch light shut off.

"Lights out?"

"Dad's going to bed." She rose to her knees and moved closer, straddling him. Moonlight bathed her face in a luminous glow. "Now how can I thank you?"

He looked south of her chin, admiring the way her coverup accentuated her curves. "I can think of one or two ways."

She reached inside the crocheted shirt and slid one arm out of her tankini top. "For example?"

He raised one eyebrow. "You want me to show you out here or in your bedroom?"

"*Our* bedroom," she corrected, slipping off the other strap.

"Our bedroom," he said. "But if we're sharing, we need to talk about those flower pictures on the walls."

"You don't like the flowers? They are from a local artist." She reached inside the coverup and somehow slipped the swimsuit top out through the deep neckline and over her head, tossing it aside.

He sucked air through his teeth at the thought of her half naked under those gaping threads. "Flowers aren't very manly."

"Would you rather I put up the pictures of my parents that used to hang there?"

He laughed up at the stars. "Please, no." The last thing he needed was Marianne's ghost haunting him while he was in her daughter's bed. Correction, make that in *their* bed.

Angélica hauled him up, pulling him close. She smelled like beer and limes, a combination of flavors that made him want to lick her all over.

Her lips traveled along his jawline. "What then? Sylvester the pussycat?"

"You're getting warmer." He slid his hands under the fringe, feeling his way up her smooth skin.

"*Au contraire*, heartbreaker. I'm getting hot."

"I've always had a fondness for that famous Raquel Welch movie poster where she's wearing a Tarzan-like leather bikini," he joked.

She bit his ear, making him laugh again. "Strike one, smartass."

"How about the Maya equivalent of Kama Sutra poses?"

She reached down and pinched his stomach. "I'll give you one more try. Otherwise, the flowers stay."

"I know." He sobered, his thumbs stroking over her breasts, making her arch and moan. If she kept moving her hips like that, they weren't going to make it to their bedroom.

"What?" she gasped more than asked when he leaned down and licked her where she was sticking out through the threads.

"Dogs playing poker."

Her husky giggle was sexy as hell. "No, Parker. The flowers stay for now."

"Fine." He flipped her onto her back on the other half of the towel, done talking about pictures. "But these go." He tugged her swim shorts off. His followed.

She smiled up at him, her eyes and teeth shining in the moonlight. "I'll make a deal with you. If you will tell me where we're going tomorrow, I'll reconsider the dogs picture."

Sliding the fringe up over her bare hips, he shook his head. "No deal, boss lady. Now wrap your arms around me and tell me how mad you are for me."

She tugged him down on top of her. "I could tell you, but I'd rather show you."

He groaned and kissed her. He was a grade-A sucker for her and her sweet mouth. "You're such a siren," he whispered above her soft lips.

"I haven't even started singing yet, sailor."

El Fin ... for now

Sneak Peek!

Nearly Departed in Deadwood
(Book 1 of the Deadwood Mystery Series)

If you haven't read Ann's Deadwood Mystery Series starring Violet Parker (Quint's sister), here is a sneak peek from the first book in the USA Today bestselling, award-winning series.

Chapter One

Deadwood, South Dakota
Monday, July 9ᵗʰ

The first time I came to Deadwood, I got shot in the ass. Now, twenty-five years later, as I stared into the double barrels of Old Man Harvey's shotgun, irony was having a fiesta and I was the piñata.

I tried to produce a polite smile, but my cheeks had petrified along with my heart. "You wouldn't shoot a girl, would you?"

Old Man Harvey snorted, his whole face contorting with the effort. "Lady, I'd blow the damned Easter bunny's head off if he was tryin' to take what's mine."

He cocked his shotgun—his version of an exclamation mark.

"Whoa!" I would have gulped had there been any spit left in my mouth. "I'm not here to take anything."

He replied by aiming those two barrels at my chest instead of my face.

"I'm with Calamity Jane Realty, I swear! I came to …"

With Harvey threatening to fill my lungs with peepholes, I had trouble remembering why I'd driven out to this corner of the boonies. Oh, yeah. Lowering one of my hands, I held out my crushed business card. "I want to help you sell your ranch."

The double barrels clinked against one of the buttons on my Rebecca Taylor-knockoff jacket as Harvey grabbed my card. I swallowed a squawk of panic and willed the soles of my boots to unglue from the floorboards of Harvey's front porch and retreat.

Unfortunately, my brain's direct line to my feet was experiencing technical difficulties.

Harvey's squint relaxed. "Violet Parker, huh?"

"That's me." My voice sounded pip-squeaky in my own ears. I couldn't help it. Guns made my thighs wobbly and my bladder heavy. Had I not made a pit stop at Girdy's Grill for a buffalo burger and paid a visit to the little *Hens* room, I'd have a puddle in the bottom of my favorite cowboy boots by now.

"Your boots match your name. What's a 'Broker Associate'?"

"It's someone who is going to lose her job if she doesn't sell a house in the next three weeks." I lowered my other hand.

I'd been with Calamity Jane Realty for a little over two months and had yet to make a single sale. So much for my radical, life-changing leap into a new career. If I didn't make a sale before my probation was up, I'd have to drag my kids back down to the prairie and bunk with my parents ... again.

"You're a lot *purtier* in this here picture with your hair down."

"So I've been told." Old Man Harvey seemed to be channeling my nine-year-old daughter today. Lucky me.

"Makes you look younger, like a fine heifer."

I cocked my head to the side, unsure if I'd just been tossed a compliment or slapped with an insult.

The shotgun dipped to my belly button as he held the card out for me to take back.

"Keep it. I have plenty." A whole box full. They helped fill the lone drawer in my desk back at Calamity Jane's.

"So that asshole from the bank didn't send you?"

"No." An asshole from my office had, and the bastard would be extracting his balls from his esophagus for this so-called *generous referral*—if I made it back to Calamity Jane's without looking like a human sieve.

"Then how'd you know about my gambling problem?"

"What gambling problem?"

Old Man Harvey's eyes narrowed again. He whipped the double barrels back up to my kisser. "The only way you'd know I'm thinking about selling is if you heard about my gambling debt."

"Oh, you mean *that* gambling problem."

"What'd you think I meant?"

Bluffing was easier when I wasn't chatting up a shotgun. "I

thought you were referring to the ... um ..." A tidbit of a phone conversation I'd overheard earlier this morning came to mind. "To the problem you had at the Prairie Dog Palace."

Harvey's jaw jutted. "Mud wrestling has no age limit."

"You're right. They need to be less age-biased. Maybe even have an *AARP Night* every Wednesday."

"Nobody told me about the bikini bit 'til it was too late."

I winced. I couldn't help it.

"So, what're you gonna charge me to sell my place?"

"What would you like me to charge you?" I was all about pleasing the customer this afternoon.

He leaned the gun on his shoulder, double barrels pointed at the porch ceiling. "The usual, I guess."

No longer on the verge of extinction, I used the porch rail to keep from keeling over. Maybe I just wasn't cut out for the realty business. Did they still sell encyclopedias door-to-door?

"This ranch belonged to my pappy, and his pappy before him." Harvey's lips thinned as he stared over my shoulder.

"It must hold a big place in your heart." I tried to sound sincere as I inched along the railing toward the steps. My red Bronco glinted and beckoned under the July sun.

"Hell, no. I can't wait to shuck this shithole."

"What?" I'd made it as far as the first step.

"I'm sick and tired of fixin' rusted fences, chasing four-wheeling fools through my pastures, sniffing out lost cows in every damned gulch and gully." His blue eyes snapped back to mine. "And I keep hearing funny noises at night coming from out behind my ol' barn."

I followed the nudge of his bearded chin. Weathered and white-washed by Mother Nature, the sprawling building's roof seemed to sag in the afternoon heat. The doors were chained shut, one of the haymow windows broken. "Funny how?"

"Like grab-your-shotgun funny."

Normally, this might give me pause, but after the greeting I'd received today from the old codger's double barrels, I had a feeling that Harvey wore his shotgun around the house like a pair of holey underwear. I'd bet my measly savings he even slept with it. "Maybe it's just a mountain lion," I suggested. "The paper said there's been a surge of sightings lately."

"Maybe. Maybe not," Harvey shrugged. "I don't care. I want to move to town. It gets awful lonely out here come wintertime. Start thinking about things that just ain't right. I almost married a girl from Taiwan last January. Turned out 'she' was really a 'he' from Nigeria."

"Wow."

"Damned Internet." Harvey's gaze washed over me. "What about you, Violet Parker?"

"What about me?"

"There's no ring on your finger. You got a boyfriend?"

"Uh, no."

I didn't want one, either. Men had a history of fouling up my life, from burning down my house to leaving me knocked up with twins. These days, I liked my relationships how I liked my eggs: over-easy.

Harvey's two gold teeth twinkled at me through his whiskers. "Then how about a drink? Scotch or gin?"

I chewed on my lip, considering my options. I could climb into my Bronco and watch this opportunity and the crazy old bastard with the trigger-happy finger disappear in my rearview mirror; or I could blow off common sense and follow Harvey in for some hard liquor and maybe a signed contract.

Like I really had a choice. "Do you have any tonic?"

More Books by Ann
Books in the Deadwood Mystery Series

WINNER of the 2010 Daphne du Maurier Award for Excellence in Mystery/Suspense

WINNER of the 2011 Romance Writers of America® Golden Heart Award for Best Novel with Strong Romantic Elements

Welcome to Deadwood—the Ann Charles version. The world I have created is a blend of present day and past, of fiction and non-fiction. What's real and what isn't is for you to determine as the series develops, the characters evolve, and I write the stories line by line. I will tell you one thing about the series—it's going to run on for quite a while, and Violet Parker will have to hang on and persevere through the crazy adventures I have planned for her. Poor, poor Violet. It's a good thing she has a lot of gumption to keep her going!

Short Stories from Ann's
Deadwood Mystery Series

The Deadwood Shorts collection includes short stories featuring the characters of the Deadwood Mystery series. Each tale not only explains more of Violet's history, but also gives a little history of the other characters you know and love from the series. Rather than filling the main novels in the series with these short side stories, I've put them into a growing Deadwood Shorts collection for more reading fun.

The Jackrabbit Junction Mystery Series

Bestseller in Women Sleuth Mystery and Romantic Suspense

Welcome to the Dancing Winnebagos RV Park. Down here in Jackrabbit Junction, Arizona, Claire Morgan and her rabble-rousing sisters are really good at getting into trouble—BIG trouble (the land your butt in jail kind of trouble). This rowdy, laugh-aloud mystery series is packed with action, suspense, adventure, and relationship snafus. Full of colorful characters and twisted up plots, the stories of the Morgan sisters will keep you wondering what kind of a screwball mess they are going to land in next.

Connect with Me Online

Facebook (Personal Page):
http://www.facebook.com/ann.charles.author

Facebook (Author Page):
http://www.facebook.com/pages/Ann-Charles/37302789804?ref=share

Twitter (as Ann W. Charles):
http://twitter.com/AnnWCharles

Ann Charles Website: http://www.anncharles.com

About the Author

Ann Charles is a *USA Today* Bestselling Author who writes award-winning mysteries that are splashed with humor, paranormal, suspense, romance and whatever else she feels like throwing into the mix. When she is not dabbling in fiction, arm-wrestling with her children, attempting to seduce her husband, or arguing with her sassy cat, she is daydreaming of lounging poolside at a fancy resort with a blended margarita in one hand and a great book in the other.